The Lady *A*

Part Two of Above All Others: The Lady Anne

By G. Lawrence

For Dan and Gema,
For becoming a part of my family,
and for giving me more family to love

And for Derek,
Because, as you always said, life is for living
and taking a chance when you want something.

Whoso list to hunt, I know where is an hind,
But for me, helas, I may no more.
The vain travail hath wearied me so sore,
I am of them that farthest cometh behind.
Yet may I by no means my wearied mind
Draw from the deer, but as she fleeth afore
Fainting I follow. I leave off therefore,
Sithens in a net I seek to hold the wind.
Who list her to hunt, I put him out of doubt,
As well as I may spend his time in vain.
And graven with diamonds in letters plain
There is written, her fair neck round about:
Noli me tangere, for Caesar's I am,
And wild for to hold, though I seem tame.

Thomas Wyatt

We are the music-makers,
And we are the dreamers of dreams,
Wandering by lone sea-breakers,
And sitting by desolate streams.
World-losers and world-forsakers,
On whom the pale moon gleams:
Yet we are the movers and shakers
Of the world for ever, it seems.

With wonderful deathless ditties,
We build up the world's great cities,
And out of a fabulous story
We fashion an empire's glory:
One man with a dream, at pleasure,
Shall go forth and conquer a crown;
And three with a song's measure
Can trample an empire down.

We, in the ages lying
In the buried past of the earth,
Built Nineveh with our sighing,
And Babel itself with our mirth;
And o'erthrew them with prophesying
To the old of the new world's worth;
For each age is a dream that is dying,
Or one that is coming to birth.

Ode, Arthur O'Shaughnessy

Prologue

The Tower of London
The early hours of the 18th May, 1536

The darkness folds in around me. Only the light of a small candle is left to me now, flickering in the light breeze which ripples through my prison. The women sent to watch me slumber on, unaware of the quiet, dark world in which I sit thinking on the past.

Outside the window the stars glisten in the heavens. I feel as though I could touch them if I reach out my pale hand to the velvet skies, and yet I know that they are far away. They light the entrance to Heaven, where soon enough I believe I shall be. I am sure that one of those lights is my brother's soul, looking down on me, whispering to me that all this shall be at an end soon enough. I hope I will see the light of his soul once more when I am come to the Kingdom of G od.

There has been no word from court, no word from Henry's men, or from my husband himself. The promises carried by the lips of my friend Cranmer are likely to be as I suspected them; false hope offered to me in order to extract a last soothing balm for Henry's conscience.

I have agreed now that I was never his wife, and that I was never his queen, and yet still he will take my life. I know it. I know it with the kind of awful certainty that comes from knowing the man I married so well. He will not allow me to still draw breath in this world, not now… not when he wishes to remove me from his life and his memories. In order to do such, he must destroy me.

Will they come for me tomorrow? Take me to face Death at last? I know not. I hope that I will be given some warning before the time comes that I will face my death. I hope that I will be given a few hours, perhaps, to gather myself. That I will not face the arms of Death opening for me without having a little time to gather the last bare threads of my courage to me. But I know not how many mercies are left to me in this life. Henry's patience with the lady he once so longed for has all but run out....

I want to touch the stars with my fingertips. I want to reach out to them and stroke the source of their light and power. They rest so majestic in the skies, so peaceful... higher than us all; they are secure in their position as I was perhaps never secure in mine. They have looked down on a thousand lives of men, seen their births and their deaths, and they will go on after we all have died... after me... after George... after Mary... my father, my mother, and even Henry himself. They know eternity, the stars, and that is what gives them beauty and peace. Perhaps they saw the very start of the world as God crafted man and beast with His own wondrous hand; and perhaps they will see the end, when Jesus comes once more to this earth to take the righteous into his Kingdom.

When one knows the end and the beginning of all things, one understands peace in the moments of the present.

Perhaps that was why I was never a creature made for peace. I knew where I had come from, but in all things, I never knew how high I could climb, or how low I could fall. The path of life is a strange one for many people, and none more so than for me. You read of stories like mine in the pages of chivalric romances, and yet I *lived* such a love, I *had* such a love... once. But this ending I have come to is not the happy one of the fairy stories... My end will be different. There is no prince to save me; there is only one who will murder me.

But there was a time... Yes, there was a time, when my heart was graced with a love like no other. My heart called for his long before he ever really saw me... as a child I thought him handsome and powerful... but there came a time when his eyes finally fell on me, and two souls who were so alike in all things, came to burn for each other in truth.

I thought our love was as eternal as the stars, and perhaps so did he, at first…

Chapter One

The Road to Hever
January 1522

I came out onto the ship's slippery deck as we sighted the shore of England and stared out despondently at the mist-swathed, hazy coastline, shuddering as I saw the great white cliffs poking out from what seemed like an endless bank of fog and drizzle. Rain fell; a light yet relentless descent of moisture which soaked through my clothing even as I pulled my heavy cloak about me to protect my fine French gown of luscious green velvet. Mist seemed to seep from every part of the land looming ahead of me, and the little lights of fires within the squat houses further up the shore seemed dismal and bereft of hope, desperately flicking against the gloom of England.

Storms raging across the oceans had meant that I had spent Christmas at the port of Calais, amongst friends of my father. I was not given the choice of spending that festive time of celebration in the birth of our Lord with my family, or within the familiar halls of the French Court. Many a time, when I sat within my chambers at Calais, I had looked out over the seas and berated Fate for having sent me from the comforts of my home, in France, back to a life I barely remembered in England. As the waves arched themselves, like a cat's back as she stretches, extending their white, frothy claws up over the shore, I thought dismally of all I had lost upon leaving France; friends, companions, excitement and danger... All these things were part of the life I had once had at court and now had no longer. I was being brought back to England, for a marriage chosen for me by my father. I was being ripped from all I had loved and held dear in this life.

What a blank and terrible homecoming this was, I thought miserably. The whole land was covered in a fog that obscured the earth and met the skies. Gulls flew overhead in great wending clouds, marking my own sorrows with their mournful shrieks. Was there no sun in England? Was there no horizon? My temper that day was such that I believe even if the sun had dappled softly on the lush green fields and splendid forests of England I would have thought it too hot and too shiny to be borne.

I was desolate to leave France, to leave the court and my friends behind. And I was afraid, though I should never have admitted it to anyone... I was afraid that I would not fit in, in England. I had been so long in the courts and countries of other lands that I knew not what the country of my birth was like. Fears plagued my soul: that I might not have such friends as I had enjoyed in France; that there might be none of the dancing and entertainments I had loved so; that there might be none who shared my views on philosophy or religion; that there might be no one who knew or understood the passions of my heart; that I might be soon married off to a man of whom I knew nothing. England seemed, and looked, like a miserable back-water to me on that day. Even though the English had done many brilliant things I had seen with my own eyes, this island that I hardly knew seemed provincial, dull and crude; an outpost teetering on the edge of civilisation... and the weather was helping my temper nothing at all.

Where was I to find a place to be myself? Who was this man my father wanted to marry me off to? Where would I live? Would he be a man of the court, or a country lord? I had been told nothing of this man I was to marry. I was trained and polished for a life at court; for the glitter and pomp of living close to the seat of royalty and power. I was not meant to be a country wife. Would I have to stay on the estates of this husband that my father had found for me and wile away my life in seclusion and loneliness? Thoughts such as these plagued me as my ship arrived at Dover. I was miserable and bad tempered. My guards were careful in their attentions to me, but I snapped and snarled at them for the slightest offence. I saw them lift their eyebrows at each other when they thought I could not see them, and that only increased my feelings of loneliness and self-pity.

I missed Marguerite, I missed Françoise, I missed my gentle mistress Queen Claude and the wry, dark eyes of King François lighting upon me at court. I wished with all my heart that I was back in France, waking to help Claude in her apartments at Bloise or planning entertainments with the beautiful and wise Princess Marguerite. I wished I was back in Mechelen; attending to the whims and wants of the Archduchess Margaret… Truly, I would have wished myself anywhere but where I was, as we alighted onto the damp, sodden shores of misty England.

But wishing will not bring one what is wanted or yearned for. As I came from the ship, the men showed me to a party of horses and carts for my belongings. I climbed into the slippery saddle and pulled my heavy cape over my head, cursing England for having caught me in her hands and stolen me from all that I loved and understood.

We were to travel up-country, to Hever, through the soggy countryside escorted by the men that my father had engaged in Calais, by letter, to see me and my baggage back home from France. There was also a young maid waiting at the harbour, sent from my mother to help me. I was to grow fond of Bess. She watched me with round-eyed amazement when she saw me alight from the boat, her round, pretty face wondering at my clothes and bold manner as I ordered the men sharply to have a care with my trunks. Her pale, fair hair stuck to her cheeks in the damp air, and she nodded to each of my commands and demands, looking at me with wide, wild eyes. She seemed to me so young, being perhaps thirteen years of age, but then, I reminded myself that I had been younger than she when I set out for the Court of Burgundy.

There was mist everywhere, it seemed, and as we started to ride out from the port, I felt as though I should never see a horizon again. This was all this country was, I thought; misty and damp and horrible with nothing to look forward to. The people looked ugly, rough and uncultured. The port was wet, muddy, dull and common. The roads were slathered in sludge and flowing with little streams of running brown water, tumbling over small banks of pebbles and stones. There was nothing to recommend England to me. I shivered in the wind as I pulled my cloak tighter about me.

We rode through that wet day, growing steadily more sodden. That night we stopped overnight at an inn on the road, to rest and to eat what seemed to me the paltriest pottage of watery grains, followed by dry meats, insipid herbs, sour, cold wine and inferior bread that I suspected had been made with broad peas. I ate little of what was offered, so unhappy and homesick for France was I.

The inn was near to other small alehouses of the village where women made pots of crude ale for purchase by the poorer folk of the small village. Coarse sounds of laughter and ribald jests were clearly audible late into the night when the ale had flowed for long enough. I pretended not to hear, wrapping my thick woollen blanket around me on my bed of prickly hay. The English tongue sounded so abrasive and crude to me that I felt I could hardly bear it. My English was accented with a French lilt now after so many years speaking French as my primary language. I was indeed more of a French-woman than I was English; I felt like a foreigner, a stranger… an outsider.

More and more that feeling haunted me as we rode out the next morning. More and more I felt isolated. More and more I longed only to return to France. The air blew fierce and cold against my cheeks as though it too wished to push me back to France. I wished, then, that I could have obeyed it.

Eventually, we neared the lands surrounding Hever in Kent. It was a wild, late afternoon in January. Darkness was falling fast upon us and the winds started to blow so powerfully that I thought we should be caught up in them and thrown all the way back to the seas. The mist was still hovering, being tossed backwards and forwards in swirling blankets so that one could hardly see the road ahead. The horses bowed their heads against the wind and oncoming rain, snorting to show that their dissatisfaction was as deep as my own. Bess whimpered in her seat at my back, and I reached around to take her cold hand and squeeze it. The poor child was soaked through, and was as miserable as I was, so I felt as though I had a companion in my sorrow at least.

"We should cut across country," shouted the leader of the riding party, drawing his horse level with mine. His face was dripping with rain and he glowered darkly at the road ahead. "We can send the carts on by road, but if we take the paths through the forest, I am told we can have you back to Hever faster, Mistress Boleyn."

"I will take any road that will take me from this hideous tempest faster," I cried against the wind and the rain. "Take us on the path you recommend, Master Cooper, and I will follow you eagerly if it means I am taken to a warm fire and a good bed sooner."

The man nodded and went to order his men on the carts to continue on the road as we took to the paths through the forests. As we steered our shivering horses into the cover of the trees I breathed a slight sigh of relief; for within the dark shade of the forest, there was at least a little respite from the chilling winds.

The bags and chests were better protected than the riders.on the mounts, they at least were covered in leather and nailed shut. Even if they took the longer road, my fine gowns and precious books would likely know a happier time of this journey than I.

We rode on through the forest; watching the skies with wary eyes as the darkness drew around us. By the time we got within some miles of my family's home, we riders and our horses were drenched. The men were sure that we were close to the lands of the Boleyns, they told me, but within the forest, the winds and the rain were replaced by the cursed fog once more. It seemed to settle about us, taunting us with its swirling tendrils. We stopped before a fork in the track, and Master Cooper admitted to me that he knew not where to head; the horses were struggling in the mud and we were all exhausted and sodden. Night was coming and we could not find our way.

"We cannot stay in the forest!" I cried, laughing, although the situation hardly deserved such mirth. "We have neither tents nor food, nor means to make a fire. Everything here is soaking, and soon it will be very cold. Come, we must press on or we shall freeze to death out here. Like as not we shall find somewhere to shelter. Hever cannot be far now."

Master Cooper agreed, although his flat face held little hope to stir my spirits. My horse protested and shuddered as I pushed him further on along the path. I thought, then, that there was indeed a possibility that we might die in the countryside; there seemed to be no end to the pain that England wanted to cause to me.

We pressed on through the freezing mists until, suddenly, one of the men gave a shout. In the wilderness, lights dancing through the mist, we saw the outline of a small country hunting lodge nestled deep in the forest. Candle light shone from its windows against the quickening darkness, struggling against the haze of the mist and the storm. It was a sudden ray of hope, and some small cheers rang out amongst the men.

"Come, Masters!" I encouraged the men and poor Bess. "Let us get there and petition them for shelter before we are all lost forever in this foul fog."

We got to the door of the little lodge and heard the sounds of music within; a lute was being played by skilled fingers. It was a sound of civilisation amongst the wilds of the forest; a sound which made my heart ache for France. Master Cooper knocked at the door loudly, and, after a surprised, sudden end to the tune, a voice came to the door.

"Who goes there?" The question rang out in a strong, masculine voice.

"We are a party escorting a noble lady to her home," Master Cooper bellowed against the noise of the storm. "We are lost in the woods and would seek shelter at this place."

The door was unlocked and a dark face, obscured in shadow with the light of the chamber behind, peered out into the darkness. "Lost in the storm with a lady?" the voice asked curiously.

"Yes!" I cried out impatiently. "Soon to be a lady, *late of this life*, should you delay in opening that door any longer!"

There was a deep, warm laugh and the door was flung fully open. "Never let it be said that a gentleman should fail to aid a lady in distress," said the amused voice. "There is stabling around the back of the lodge for your horses. My man will show you where." From behind him came a servant, who stepped out into the winds with a sour expression, pointing and gesturing to Master Cooper where to take the horses. I dismounted and helped Bess from the saddle behind me. She was soaking wet and shivering violently. I pulled her under my cloak and turned to look at the man standing in the doorway.

He was tall, with a short, brown beard and dark hair. His amused voice was cultured, his clothing was fine, and although in shirt and hose, with only an overcoat, hardly dressed for company, he was clearly a man of good breeding. I felt somewhat reassured that we would be safe in this place until the storm passed. The man seemed like a gentleman at least, and I had many guards with me. My men took the horses around the back to the stables with the servants, while Bess and I entered the lodge. Master Cooper and another of his men stayed with us. There was no sense in abandoning all security, after all, we did not yet know who this man was.

As we entered the lodge, my poor maid was taken with weeping. I pulled her to me, under the heavy cloak. "Hush, child, there is no need for such… We are safe now."

Bess nodded and managed to stop her tears. A woman in the garb of a kitchen maid took her off to a back room to dry her. I breathed a long sigh and walked to the fire at the centre of the large room, trying to warm myself. I held out my hands to the welcome, flickering flames of the fire, and looked about me.

The owner of the lodge was watching me with some interest as I stood for a moment trying to collect myself before the dancing flames. I looked up, and, over the fireplace, I saw the crest of the Wyatt family, a crest I remembered well from my childhood. I looked around the room quickly, blinking with amazement as my eyes seemed to view the place anew. It slowly dawned on me that I recognised where I was. Looking around in delighted astonishment, I realised that this was one of the small hunting lodges of the Wyatt family; the noble neighbours of my own family. My brother George and little Thomas Wyatt had played at being knights of Bosworth Field here in the forest when we were children so long ago. We were not as far from Hever as I had thought. As I recognised the place, and the crest, I understood something else… Surely the man standing in the room before me must be a Wyatt himself? My family's nearest noble neighbours. I was safe, for I was within the house of a family friend. And, as my quick mind raced through such thoughts, I realised that there was really only one Wyatt the man before me could be; there were no other male children of this age, I was sure.

The handsome, grown man before me had to be little Tom Wyatt… the boy who had given roses to my sister Mary in the games of our childhood.

Suddenly I looked at him and laughed gaily; the memories of our childhood games prancing in my mind along with the strangeness of this reunion. He looked taken aback, as well he might, when a strange lady comes from nowhere out of a storm, stands dripping in his house and then laughs at him. His expression made me want to laugh again; I restrained myself but continued to smile warmly at him as I pulled my deep riding hood back a little.

"It is *you*, isn't it?" I asked, pausing and holding the deep cowl of my riding cloak over my head. I felt a little mischievous suddenly. This day had been so tiring and so wearisome that my heart seemed to sing for a little entertainment. This was almost like a masque at court; for at the moment I wore a mask of unfamiliarity that obscured my true identity from the man before me.

"You are little Tom Wyatt, the brave knight of Mary Boleyn; giver of roses and winner of battles. I am right, am I not? It is *you*!"

He started at my words, stared hard at me, and looked me over, puzzled, but with some light of recognition dawning in his mind.

"Come, Tom," I laughed merrily, much to the surprise of Master Cooper who was looking nervously about him still, worried about bringing a lady under his protection into a strange house.

"Come, Tom… do you really not know me?" I turned to face him and pushed back my hood so that it fell about my neck. I untied the heavy cloak and pulled it from my shoulders revealing my fine gown. Throwing the wet cloak over a chair by the fire, I turned on him with a grin. "I'll wager I have changed since you and my brother played at Bosworth Field and you claimed my beautiful sister as your prize..." I sighed in mock anguish, putting my hand to my heart. "I was never the one picked to play queen to such brave knights as you and my brother George."

And now he laughed too, his face looking on in amazement at me.

"It is *you*? Little Mistress *Anna Boleyn*?" He walked towards me, taking my hands and stretching them before me so that he could look me over. My clothing was wet, but it was still fine and sophisticated. My hair had been protected on the journey by my hood, and it flowed, long, thick and dark, down my back. A black riding-hood decorated with pearls crowned my head. I could feel my large, black eyes sparkling at him with enjoyment.

Tom Wyatt shook his head. "*This* is Anne Boleyn?" he asked wonderingly. "*This…* the tiny sister of George Boleyn? It is not possible! The tiny sister of George is but a little girl, and you are a fine court lady." Tom laughed again as he bowed to me with a playful smirk. "Albeit, a rather *damp*, fine lady!"

I laughed with joy. What a fine way to end such an awful day! It was such a pleasure to find this old friend just as I had thought we were lost from all civilisation and safety. "I have been long away from England, Master Wyatt," I said merrily, bobbing a curtsey to him. "You, too, are not the boy I remember."

And he was not, for this man was tall and strong. Gone were the spindly limbs of childhood, the plump cheeks of infancy… and here was the virility and strength of a grown man. His short, dark beard covered his lower face, accentuating a fine jaw and well-formed, stalwart mouth. Tom had dark brown hair and warm hazel eyes; his look was bold and intelligent, his manner polished and bubbling with good humour.

He was a fine and handsome man now; I took to him immediately. I could not see how any woman would not…

Chapter Two

The Hunting Lodge, Kent
January 1522

Although both Tom and I were much surprised and pleased to be reunited in such an unexpected way, he bade me to go and get dry before we spent time in company with each other. It was sensible advice, for I and my party were soaking wet. Tom offered me his own chamber for the night, in which a goodly fire was burning bright, dispelling the chill and damp of the winter night. My clothes were with the carts which no doubt still trundled along on the dark roads, lit by torch light, to Hever, but the maid who tended the kitchen found me a dry kirtle from an old chest of clothes left by the Wyatt family here, and although it was nothing to the finery of my own clothes, it was at least warm and dry. With a new kirtle upon my body, and my own gown drying before the fires of the chamber, I felt much happier. When my gown had dried a little, I put it on over the rough, borrowed kirtle. Bess, too, had been found a smock, and now that she was warm and dry she was looking ready to fall asleep standing up. I would have left my poor maid to sleep, but I needed her at my side if I was to converse with Tom without scandal, and I was eager to speak with him. This strange, chance meeting had enlivened my spirits and brought heart to me. I had been feeling so very low that I wished now to continue talking to the man who had managed to vanquish the power of my despondency with his appearance.

When I had changed my clothing, we returned to the main chamber of the lodge, where Tom's few servants had prepared us some food and were warming spiced wine to drink. The scent of the wine was something quite remarkable after a day spent with only the smell of the mud and the rain whipping about my face and body, and I took a cup with a thankful heart which felt a thousand times lighter than when we had set out that morning.

The hunting lodge was not a large place; one large chamber and a small kitchen below, and three petite rooms above. Tom had been using it merely to stay in during the nights as he hunted through the lands of his family estate. Many noble families had such buildings on their lands; little spaces where the men of the household could remove themselves for a length of time, to spend time in the wilderness with noble companions, or with just a spare few servants, as Tom did now.

I could not but help be grateful that he had decided to stay here this night. It seemed as though Fate herself had reached out a hand to help me find shelter with the company of an old friend. Perhaps she had felt my misery and taken pity on me. For a while I had feared we might have had to make camp in the storm with nothing but our cloaks. It was so heartening, after our journey through the tempests, to taste sweet spiced wine, and to eat the tangy dried rings of pippin apples and little cold pies of venison, pork and ginger which were hastily produced from the kitchens for us. With a full belly, a goblet of wine cupped in my hands and a dry place to sit at the warm fireside, I felt suddenly so content in England that I knew not how I had thought so ill of it.

Tom and I talked of my time at the French Court and his time at the Court of England. I told him of my travels, from Hever to Mechelen, and from Burgundy to France, and he was full of admiration to hear of the circles of people I had met and made friends with. He told me of his youth, firstly as a young student at St John's College in Cambridge University, then in the service of noble families, and how he was now in service to King Henry at court as a clerk of the jewel house, although his father, Sir Henry Wyatt, hoped for much more advancement yet to come for his son. Tom told me briefly of his marriage to a lady named Elizabeth Brooke, the daughter of Thomas Brooke, Lord Cobham, also of Kent. Although it was an advantageous marriage, which had placed Tom well at court, I gleaned from his sparse words and heavy glances that it was not a happy one. He had one child of the marriage, however; a son, he told me, so at least there was one thing to give comfort to him in this unwanted match.

"How came you to be here, with so little company?" I asked, sipping the sweet, spiced wine as we sat late by the fire. Bess was nodding, half-asleep, her head almost upon her breast at my side, and my guards talked softly and wagered with dice on the stone floor near to the windows. The night had grown old, and the storm still raged outside; rain battered at the window shutters as though enraged that we travellers had escaped its icy fingers and misty arms.

I did not feel tired at all, despite the rigours of the day. I was excited to meet Tom again, and to know him now that we were both grown. I knew that he felt the same, and perhaps, more; there was a speculative manner in the way he glanced at me. I knew what he was thinking; it was a natural way for men to think about women, after all. His eyes glowed with the warmth of the flames, and lighted upon me with the growing embers of another kind of fire. His expression told me all that I needed to know, and I was flattered to feel his interest in me... and a little wary.

"I like to escape the court, from time to time," Tom said, frowning at the fire for a moment as though it vexed him, and then glancing up into my eyes with a quick, wry smile. "Although my duties, and some entertainments and company may be found at court, which bring satisfaction to me, I feel as though the court wears heavy on my soul after some time. I need solitude to recover my good humour. After a while at court, I feel as though the very walls are watching me, and the furniture is listening to all I say. There comes a time when I must ask my father and the King to excuse me, as I seek a peace in my own company." He smiled. "And, after all, how often does a gentleman get the chance to rescue a fair maiden in distress from a winter storm? Such things are not possible, within the confines of the court, within the palaces and the gardens of the King."

I laughed. "Well, then I am glad that the court's watchful walls and much-observant tables drove you here to save me. It was already a strange trip back to a land I barely knew. I was feeling miserable even before we were lost in the storm. And then, suddenly, in the midst of a great enveloping tempest, I found there was an old friend opening a door to me." I smiled at Tom and raised my glass to him. "This was a good welcome home, my old friend."

Tom stared at me with a gaze that was half-amused and half-suspicious. I could see that he knew not where my mocking ended and my real thoughts began. But there was truth within my mocking. This *was* a good end to a bad day.

There was a moment's silence between us as he gazed at me, and in the warm flickering lights of the fire, I could see something within his eyes, something of that first interest in me which was already growing; embers growing to flame... I was suddenly most aware of the lateness of the hour, and of the inattention of my sleeping maid at my side. Abruptly I rose.

"I should be abed," I said softly, and nodded to Tom. "You have been most gracious to me this night, Master Wyatt, and your kindness will not be forgotten. On the morrow, I must set out early for my family's home at Hever; no doubt my family will fear that I am lost or have been set upon and murdered. I do not wish to keep them lingering in their fears for longer than I have done already."

Tom blinked at me for my sudden movement from easy conversation to swift departure. His gaze was warm with friendship and with wine, but there was, too, a curious and captivated sense in the look he gave me. He stood, looked at me and smiled teasingly. "It is the custom, in England, for women to kiss on the lips when one meets or parts from a friend, Mistress Boleyn," he said, lifting one eyebrow in a rather naughty expression which made him look like a charming boy, caught trying to steal sweetmeats from the kitchens.

I smiled at him. I could not help it. The look on his face was so impish that it forced the ends of my mouth upwards. But I was not some country maid to be lured into such games as men would play. In a warm, yet steady, voice I replied, "But I have tarried so long in the Court of France, Master Wyatt, that I am more French than English. In France, ladies are kissed on the hand when they depart noble company and friends."

I offered my pale, slim hand out to him and he laughed good-humouredly. He looked genuinely amused at my lofty demeanour and took my hand gently, kissing my fingers with soft lips. His beard tickled my skin, and I felt an unexpected rush of pleasure flow over me. Tom looked up at me, his lips still lingering over the top of my hand; his eyes were warm and misted with the fog of desire. I felt a light blush creep over my cheeks as I was held in his gaze.

He lowered my hand from his lips, and yet still held it in his as he softly said, "Goodnight, Mistress Boleyn; and may God grant you sweet dreams."

His voice was slightly gruff and his gaze soft and somewhat pleading. I knew what he wanted of me. But he was not about to get what he pleaded for… I was no easy prey, to welcome a man to my bed when I barely knew him.

"Goodnight, Master Wyatt," I said firmly, taking my hand from his. I roused Bess who stumbled to my side, trying to hide her yawns and pretend that she had not been deep within the arms of sleep as I talked to this handsome courtier through the night. As we reached the door leading to the upstairs chambers, I turned back to see Tom standing by the fire where I had left him, staring at my retreating back. Our eyes met, but neither of us smiled at the other. We held each other's gaze as a recognition of mutual attraction seemed to be made between us, and then I turned, and made quickly for the short flight of stairs to the chamber I had been promised for the night.

Bess was quickly asleep, falling onto the little pallet bed on the floor stuffed with hay. She was asleep before she had even pulled the woollen blanket over herself. As I covered her over, and removed my own gown myself, I thought of the soft, warm eyes of Tom Wyatt, and the manner in which he had looked at me as we said goodnight. Had he hoped for an invitation to my bed this night? I believed so. And perhaps, had I been made of another mettle, I might have offered such to him. Tom Wyatt was a most attractive man. He had a warm, wry humour, and was a cultured and cultivated creature with good looks and fine legs. I had enjoyed finding such a man just as I was despairing of the bestial nature of this country I had been brought home to. But I was not about to abandon all my principles on the warmth of one handsome man's eyes! If Tom wished for a woman to warm his bed, then he would have to look to his own kitchen maid, which, I was sure he was no doubt already doing…

My thoughts tumbled over themselves as I climbed into the bed and pulled the curtains about me. The night air was cold, despite the heat of the fire, and I pulled the covers over me, feeling each muscle in my legs and back let out pleasurable groans for finally finding rest. And yet my mind was still busy with its thoughts; thoughts and images of Tom… of his eyes and his mouth, of the way that he smiled and the flickering lights of interest in his gaze… oh yes, he was indeed a temptation.

Outside, the rain pelted against the walls of the lodge, and the winds pulled and battered at its windows. The noise of the wailing wind was such that even as I started to drift into sleep, I was pulled from its depths again and again with each new onslaught of the storm. From far below, I could hear the noise of a lute playing softly, its lilting strings doing battle against the noise of the storm. My mind tried to follow it, to imagine the fingers which lifted and plucked at its strings, and as I listened to the lute, I heard the storm less and less. It was soothing, to hear the noise of music against the wild, irrational noise of the tempests outside. Memories started to dance in my mind… of France, of Burgundy… of Mary and George dancing as children in the long gallery at Hever… of my mother running through her gardens of roses… and soon, I was in a place not of sleep, nor of thought, but somewhere in-between, where memory meets the dreaming mind, and takes her to dance upon half-made thoughts.

It was as I drifted in this restless slumber that I became aware of a noise at the door. The lute had ceased, and footsteps had made their way along the corridor. Outside my room they paused, and I seemed to stumble from my half-dreams with a start, waking to draw back the curtains of the bed a little, and stare at the closed door. Then, the steps resumed, walking on to another room at the back of the lodge, where Tom was taking the bed of his steward, after giving his own chamber to me.

As his footsteps resumed along the corridor, I found I had been holding my breath, and I let it out in a great sigh. My heart, which seemed to have all but stopped when Tom paused at my door, resumed beating with strong and booming force within me. I dropped the curtain, and lay down, staring at the hangings of the bed. It was a long time before I found sleep again that night, but whether that was due to fear or excitement, I could not seem to decide.

Chapter Three

The Road to Hever
January 1522

The next morning I awoke to find the storm had passed. The air was fresh and cold. I walked to the window, gasping in the cold, and wiped the mist from its panes. I looked out onto a forest where every twig, branch, shrub and blade of grass was covered in tiny glittering crystals of ice, like diamonds. The world around me shone silver in the dawn's light, brilliant against a frost-blue sky.

The sun was bright and yet pale, stroking the battered lands with her gentle hands and making my eyes blink to look on her. There was beauty here, I thought, in these wild places of England. I watched the stillness of the forest at dawn for some time before the cold took hold of me once more. Eventually, with a chill in my bones, I started to shiver and hurried back into the warm bed, pulling the covers about me as poor Bess quivered with cold, trying to coax the embers of the fire back to life with new shards of wood. Even though her little hands shook with the cold, she made good with the fire, and took my gown and kirtle to warm in front of it. I praised her, and she looked at me with pleased eyes, blushing lightly and returning to her tasks to warm my clothes.

A knock at the door saw rolls of fine, new-baked bread and small ale brought up to us, sent by Tom from the kitchens as though we were invalids who needed feeding when first we woke. At court, we did not eat until ten of the clock, unless one was ill, or aged. I smiled at the extra attention, but had to admit that I was famished. Our long journey in the cold and rain of the night had worn heavy on me. Bess and I shared the bread at the fireside, ripping the little rolls apart eagerly to feast on the fluffy freshness of their innards. We sipped the ice-cold ale before the now-roaring flames of the fire Bess had brought back to life. Although I had stayed talking with Tom late into the night, and had not slept well, I did not feel tired. I had that sense of glassy wakefulness that comes from a night spent in excitement rather than repose. I climbed into my warmed kirtle and gown, feeling their goodly layers of velvet and wool cloak my body from the chill of the air, and as Bess brushed and dressed my hair, I closed my eyes feeling quite at ease with the world.

England may not, after all, be such a crude and backward land, I thought with a smile, since it contained men fashioned in the mettle of Tom Wyatt.

But once my morning preparations were done with, anxious concern for my family came to intrude upon my thoughts. They had been expecting my party to arrive the night before, and would be concerned for my safety. Leaving the chambers with Bess, and bidding a hearty good-morning to Tom in the lower chambers, I asked that one of the men be sent ahead to inform my family that I would be arriving soon.

"It has already been done, Mistress Boleyn, with the coming of the first light," Tom smiled at my troubled face. "And we will be ready to ride out whenever you will it. The horses are already prepared."

I glanced at him and arched one eyebrow. "We?" I asked.

Tom laughed a little. "I cannot possibly allow you to return to Hever without my escort," he said. "Such a story as ours cannot end with my merely waving you a good-bye from the doorway… No… Surely the chivalric knight must see the lady Anne home to the bosom of her family… and be rewarded with a kiss?"

I smiled at him, a little ruefully. It seemed that no matter what, Tom Wyatt was determined to gain a kiss from me.

"It will be good to have some company on the road to Hever, Tom," I nodded.

We set out almost immediately. The hunting lodge was, it turned out, barely eight miles from my family's lands. In the dark and confusion of the storm we had wandered slightly into the Wyatt's lands, but what a fortunate accident to find old friends in the midst of such misery! Tom was right; it was a good story to be told. I should enjoy relating it to my family, although perhaps excluding the part where the handsome Wyatt had paused at my chamber door in the night…

We mounted horse, and started at a rather languid pace through the forests. Tom and I talked of books and ideas we had both come into contact with. As I spoke of France, and of Marguerite, I felt my heart and stomach ache with the pangs of homesickness. It is strange to think that even as I rode for home that I should be thinking still of another place *really* being my home. I had made France my home, and the court my family in my years there. To own the truth, I was almost nervous to see my own kin once more. Perhaps they would not like me if they came to know me for a longer time than we had spent together either at court, or at *The Field of the Cloth of Gold*… my fears of the last few days came back to me, gnawing at my sides even as I conversed with Tom. It was only finding true interest in him and his exploits that saved me from dissolving once more into a sunken pool of my own misery and fear about England.

Tom recited some of the poetry he had written for court entertainments, and told me of games he and the other gallants often devised to lighten the time spent at court. I was impressed; I had to admit it… I found myself liking Tom more and more as we talked, and a slight edge of regret entered my heart upon thinking that he was a married man. Since I was apparently soon to enter into that same state, with a man I knew nothing of, I found myself wishing suddenly that such a man as Tom was not married… A good match could have been made between a son of the Wyatts and a daughter of the

Boleyns. But I dashed such foolish thoughts from my head even as I thought them. Had I not wished for a higher match than a man of merely my own station? Had I not thought that my training and polishing at the courts of France and Burgundy could lead to a marriage with a lord of higher status than my own? To think such thoughts of Tom, merely for enjoying his easy ways and friendly openness was foolish. Marriage, as all knew, was made for wealth and standing, and all else that might come of friendship or love would grow later as the couple came to know each other. But there was, too, a part of my heart that whispered other thoughts to me… that I would so much like to marry a man who would satisfy the wishes of my heart *and* of my head… a man who could bring me great standing, and still encourage the fluttering of love within my breast. A man who could match my spirit's strength, and bring further glory to my family. A man who could be a friend, a husband and a lover to me. Would there be such a man for me? Was it too much to hope, in a world such as ours, to wish to find true love with the one I was chosen to marry? Was this man I was affianced to, this man whose name I did not even know, such a man?

I knew not. But many thoughts flashed through my mind as I talked with Tom on that crisp morning. And not all of them were as honourable or as dutiful as I would admit to.

We approached Hever and my heart leapt a little within me as I saw the fair stones of the castle, gleaming with still-clinging frost and shining in the sunlight. I pulled my horse up as the castle came within sight; as a thousand memories of home, childhood and family came pouring back to me. I could see in my mind's eye three small children playing at hide and seek through the gardens with our mother. I could see George and Mary as we rode on our small ponies through the marshlands, dogs running at our sides as we honed our hunting skills. I could hear the light steps of our feet practising dances over and over again in the long gallery. I could almost smell the foods which had graced the tables of Hever in the long days of our childhood and see the gleaming eyes of our mother as she told us stories of the past, of the court, of kings and queens and knights. I felt a rushing sense of excitement; a joy that was almost painful to my heart, to think of coming home, after all this time. And in that moment, Hever was indeed *home*. Perhaps I had forgotten its magic and it beauty. Perhaps I had forgotten the memories which bound me to it, and to my family. But now I remembered. And each of those memories brought a sharp strike to my heart; both of happiness and of sadness combined. Memories are such, at times. They come to us with loss and sorrow, and with happiness and joy, mingled together and inseparable from one another.

Tom looked at me and smiled, pulling his horse close to mine. He watched my eyes sparkle as I looked on the memories of my childhood home. "It is good to be back in merry England then, my fine lady of the French Court?" he asked in a jesting tone.

I smiled and nodded. "I had forgotten just how beautiful Hever was," I said in almost a whisper. "I have forgotten much, of England, or so it seems to me now."

Tom laughed. "But all that has been forgotten can once more be remembered," he grinned at me.

I inclined my head. "I believe, Master Wyatt, that this may well be the truth."

"Let us not keep your family waiting, Anna," he nodded to the castle. "Your mother will be anxious to see your face once more."

Although I knew that he was right, I insisted that we stop briefly at the church upon our Boleyn lands, so that I might give thanks to God for delivering our party from such troubles as had been ours on the previous night. It was also a chance for me to gather my errant thoughts to me, for my heart had become so awash with senses of joy and sorrow with the return of my memories, that I felt a little overcome. I wanted to face my family with a triumphant return to our seat at Hever. I was reluctant to return to them overawed with emotion, especially if my father was likely to be there. He, after all, had little patience with such.

Our small party rode up to the front of the castle and dismounted, walking into the cobbled courtyard with a great clatter. Servants in my family's livery came rushing from all sides to take our horses, and all about us there was shouting. Relieved voices, crying out to others to run and tell the mistress that her daughter was home safe, bounced from the walls and seemed to fill the air. The singing of the birds in the skies could not be heard over the noise of the household pouring from the castle. Maids came forwards to take my riding cowl from my head, and I looked around me, trying to see where my family was in all the clamour of our arrival. It was then that I saw my mother, emerging from the house and hurrying through the crowd. There were tears in her golden-brown eyes as she strode towards me, her hands and arms outstretched. She took me in her arms and pulled me to her. As we folded our arms about each other I smelt sweet musk and rose-water on her skin; a scent which brought more memories flooding through my mind. I felt as though I were a woman no longer, but a child once more, wrapped in the loving arms of my beloved mother.

She took hold of my slim waist and hugged me, kissed me and laughed. I was overcome with joy.

"Oh, what fears I had for you the last night!" she cried as she pulled my arms out to look me over. "I was so worried for you! Your carts and belongings arrived late in the evening, and we thought that you were with them… when I saw you were not! Ah, Anne, you do not know what terrors went through my head! I did not sleep at all last night thinking that you had been set upon by villains, or that you were lost somewhere in the rain and the mist! And then this morning your man arrived to say that you had found shelter with our neighbours and I have never felt more relieved!"

My mother shook her head, as though she could stop the tirade of her thoughts with such a light motion, and then smiled broadly at me. I had been about to start apologising for giving her such fears, even though there was little I could have done to allay them in the night, but then I understood that she was not wishing for me to offer apologies or a solution to the fears which had so beset her. She merely wanted to air her tortured thoughts aloud, and allow them to escape her heart at last, in the manner that many women seem to have; just to allow their thoughts to be spoken, and to feel the better for having them released.

She turned to Tom, speaking words of gratitude for having rescued her daughter from such danger. And then, to my utmost surprise, she kissed him full on the lips! Leaving me staring at Tom, my mother turned and called us to come into the house where there was a warm fire, and people waiting to see me.

As my mother bustled off to the doorway, Tom leaned over to me and whispered in my ear. "You see, Mistress Boleyn? It *is* the style in England to kiss friends on the lips when one meets or parts. I was not telling an untruth last night."

I looked around at him and smiled, flushing slightly at his words. I was not going to deny that I thought he had only said such in order to steal a kiss from me. But I was not going to admit to such thoughts either. To cover my embarrassment, I merely nodded at Tom, and walked into the house, following my mother. As I left, I could feel his impish enjoyment at my discomfort radiating like the sun on my back. He knew well enough that he had caught me out. I bristled at his mischief, even as I found myself wanting to laugh for it. In truth I was more embarrassed than amused; Tom Wyatt was a slippery creature at times, I thought.

In the hall, I found George and Mary walking towards me, with great grins gracing their faces at having caught me by surprise. They had come to Hever to meet my arrival. I let out a short cry of happiness, and ran to embrace first my brother, and then my sister. I had thought that their duties at court would not allow them to see me come home. But yet here they were. Our father was not at Hever, they told me; he was not even in England, but in the Low Countries on a diplomatic mission. The letter he had sent to me in France had come from there, but he had not thought to tell me that. They assured me that he would be home in a matter of months, once his duties with the Archduchess Margaret and her nephew, the Emperor Charles V, with whom Henry of England was trying to make an alliance, were done with. There was a sense of relief for me as I heard that; my welcome home was so… *welcoming*… If our father had been here, perhaps it would not feel as warm here in the midst of my family.

They took me to the fireside and our mother called for spiced ale and wine to be brought out to us. She sat beaming at me, reaching over to touch my hand as I told her of the storms that had delayed us, and of my strange meeting with Tom in the wilderness. As my family chatted lightly around me, and their faces smiled on me, I felt indeed as though I had come home. I still had fears in my heart about England; the court I was to go to, the future husband I was to meet… but despite the rain and the mist, it seemed there were good things to be found on these sodden shores too. Perhaps it would not be as bad as I had imagined. Perhaps this man I was promised to might turn out to be acceptable. Perhaps the English Court would be a good place, not as cultured as the French Court, or as beautiful as the Court of Burgundy, of course… no other place could match my two first loves, but perhaps it would not be as bad as I had thought… And perhaps I would indeed find friends here, and would not find myself alone and isolated in this land that was, at once, both new and at the same time, familiar, to me. My brother, my sister, my mother, and Tom… they were here. Perhaps, just perhaps, this England would not be the place of my nightmares.

"Your gown is much different to the ones we wear at court, Anne." Mary regarded me with her soft brown eyes, narrowing them slightly. "It is most elegant, but you will not fit in with the styles of court if you wear such there. We shall have to look over your wardrobe and see what we can make of it." She smiled happily. "It will be like old times, in France!"

A little cloud darkened our mother's face at Mary's words, but I smiled at her. "If my gowns were good enough for the French Court, Mary," I laughed, "then I believe they will do for the English, too."

"You would want to fit in with the present style, though?"

"If all at court took to wearing leather aprons and metal helmets, would you do the same?" I asked. "My gowns are the height of sophistication in France, I doubt not that they will be viewed the same in England. I am told the English ape the French in all they do… so perhaps my gowns will not offend."

Mary looked a little bemused by my confident manner, but she smiled and nodded. "We can still go through all your things together," she said happily. "It will be good to talk about France, and I have much to tell you of what has been occurring here, too."

I nodded. I was sure she had plenty to tell me. No doubt her career in the bed of the King was progressing well; otherwise I was sure that she would seem less merry and content than she did now.

Tom and George were in deep conversation with each other. I gathered that they were still great friends. I looked on them with a little impatience. I had so little seen my brother in all the years of my absence that really, I did feel as though he should have been talking to me, rather than to his friend! Perhaps they felt my scowling heart, for Tom looked up and smiled at me, and said he would take his leave of us.

"You have much to talk of to each other, and I can come to call on another day that is not the first day of Mistress Boleyn's homecoming." He smiled. "I have taken her from you for long enough, even if it was not my will to do so."

"Do come to visit soon, Tom," I said, feeling a little sorry suddenly that I had thought ill of him for taking my brother's attention from me for a while. "Come to Hever, and I shall play for you the new songs that we were dancing to at the French Court. I have books of music, and of poetry too, that I brought from Mechelen and from France… even some of my own poor scribbles, which I should like you to have a look at, if you were willing?"

"I would be honoured, Mistress Boleyn," he said in a jesting tone, and bowed deeply to me. He bowed to my mother and kissed her again, and did the same to my sister. With a bow to George, Tom started to make for the door, calling for his riding cloak as he did. Impulsively, I rose from my chair, asking my family to excuse me for a moment, and walked towards Tom.

"Master Wyatt?" I called, and he turned to me. I leant forward and kissed him lightly on his lips. His hard beard brushed against my soft lips and set them tingling. As I drew back he looked both surprised and pleased. Then a naughty smile started to dance around his lips. He raised an eyebrow at me questioningly and I smiled back.

"Since to kiss on the lips is the present style in England, I would not wish to be thought behind the times now, would I?" I asked mischievously.

Tom shook his head and laughed. "Not you, Mistress Boleyn," he said. "I don't think there is a man or woman in the world who could accuse you of being without style." He placed his cap upon his head, and nodded to me, his eyes warm. "I shall see you soon, and often, I hope." He turned for the door, which was opened by our servants, and walked out to his horse. I watched him go with a merry and lightened heart. I had at least one friend in England, I thought, and a handsome one too…

But for now handsome men could wait their turn. There was family waiting for me at the fireside, and I went back to them with a fine skip in my step.

Chapter Four

Hever Castle
January 1522

We talked for most of the day on what my family had been doing, on their duties at court and on the events of our lives. I told them of France, and admitted that I had been full of sorrow to leave, but told them, too, of my joy to return to them, which pleased my mother in particular. George and Mary informed me that our father had secured a place for me in the household of Queen Katherine, alongside Mary, as one of the Queen's maids of honour. A maid of honour was a lesser post than a lady-In-waiting. My duties would be largely decorative: to play music, sing and entertain the Queen and any visiting her chambers; to help her to dress; to run errands and take messages, but I would also have a post in the Royal Wardrobe, keeping stock of and caring for the Queen's many gowns, hoods and fabrics, which excited me greatly. In a month, perhaps, I would be making my entrance into the third court I had served in. I was both excited and a little worried at this news. I hoped that my accomplishments would stand up well to those of the other ladies of Henry's Court, but I knew nothing of this court really. Although on the journey to Hever from France I had spent quite some time mentally discrediting the English Court as a provincial back-water full of fools, I really did know nothing of it. It could easily be filled with ladies that were far above my own talents and accomplishments. I did not like to think that I might be out-matched by other women. My fears returned, nibbling at my belly, making me wish I was back in France once more.

George, perhaps sensing these unspoken worries, reassured me that none at this court were as elegant as I. "You hold yourself like a queen!" he said laughing, when I danced for my family later that evening in the great hall. I performed a *basse danse*, one of the more difficult dances I knew. As I reached the end of my performance, holding my last pose with a delicate yet strong poise, I realised I had impressed Mary, George and my mother. The looks on their faces assured me that my time in Mechelen and France had taught me much that would allow me to shine over the English-taught ladies whom I was about to meet. I was different, and I would do well. The thought reassured my jangled nerves, and pleased me.

Later, when our mother had taken to her bed, Mary, George and I remained by the fire, immersed in the happy world of our conversation. Mary told me of her successes in and out of the King's bed. From a light fancy, she had managed, discreetly and subtly, to obtain a long-term arrangement in the King's good graces. She pleased Henry, she told me, because she was undemanding and because she knew how to make him feel like a man. She flattered him, and blushed prettily at his stories of valour. She was willing and buxom in bed. She asked for nothing and so he rewarded her with much. Our father had done well for his own skills, but also because the King had taken note of his eldest daughter, and George was Henry's constant companion, although that was due as much to his own talents, wit and character as to the nightly adventures of his older sister.

"He is a fine knight and a great king in any case," Mary said, "so my flattery is honest in truth, even if my maidenly blushes at his stories are not." She grinned at George and me, and my brother lifted an eyebrow dryly, making me snort with laughter.

"It has been a goodly while since any would accuse *you* of being a maiden, Mary," George said, earning himself a playful cuff from her, even as she smiled at him. She did not seem to mind being teased.

"What of the Queen?" I asked. "Does she know that one of her ladies beds her own husband each night?"

Mary shrugged, as though this was a foolish, unimportant question to ask. "Queen Katherine knows, I am sure, that I am the mistress of her husband," she replied. "But the King wishes that I keep my place within her household, and so I do. Henry's will is the only one that matters at court. Well… his will and the will of the Cardinal Wolsey, the Lord Chancellor, who does all things for the King. But I do not flaunt myself before the Queen. I am humble before her, and discreet in my affair with the King. Katherine would much prefer that if her husband must take a mistress, as all men do, then it should be one like me, who does not cause further hurt by flaunting herself about the court. That is the way to be a mistress to the King of England, sister. Henry likes to think that he is an honourable knight, without flaw or fault, and my subterfuge allows that belief to continue unchallenged. I am a good mistress to the King, and a good servant to his Queen. And, since I please Henry and keep him occupied, the great Cardinal does not interfere. He likes the King to be amused and happy, which is the office I perform."

I nodded thoughtfully at this. So Mary was doing well at court. She spoke little of her husband, William Carey, but when she did speak of him her voice was happy enough. William was at court now, and, like our father and brother, he was prospering, and not only because of Mary's position with the King. Carey was a Gentleman of the King's Privy Chamber, an Esquire of the Body to the King… a personal servant. Carey held one of the most coveted positions at court, and was a great friend and companion to the King, being skilled at, and enjoying, many of the things which Henry enjoyed also; hunting, jousting, playing tennis and discussing the literature of the day. Apparently, Carey did not mind that his wife was also one of the King's intimate companions. Although this suited Mary well, I wondered how I would feel about a partner in life who would be happy to share his wife with another man. The thought did not sit easy with me.

But my sister's career in the King's bed had also benefited her own husband and our family, and I could not think ill of her for that. Mary held favour with the King of England, and he had granted many more offices and appointments to our family since the beginning of Mary's relationship with him. Our mother was also in attendance upon the Queen on occasion, and appeared, despite her daughter's antics, to be genuinely popular with Katherine, who appreciated her quiet decorum and efficient service. George was in service to Henry as a page of the Royal Chamber. Henry liked to be surrounded by young men of talent, vigour and wit, such as my brother. Our father carried favour with King Henry also; being sent on a diplomatic mission to the Hapsburgs demonstrated the King's high trust in him. There was much scope at the English Court for a man of our father's many and varied talents. I had returned to the seat of a popular family which was rising at the Court of England, and my prospects were good.

I was most anxious, however, to hear details of the match that was intended for me, for which I had been brought home from my beloved France. I questioned Mary and George on the matter and was given some information, perhaps more than I would have liked, in truth.

"His name is James Butler, Anne." Mary looked sideways at George with a little frown and a worried brow; evidently they had not been looking forward to giving me such information.

"I have heard that name before, I think," I mused, trying to think where I had heard it.

"You have." George shook himself slightly and waggled his head at Mary. I got the impression that Mary wished to try to change the subject, whereas my brother, who always seemed to understand me so well, knew that I would not allow it to drop from the conversation. "James Butler is one of the Butler clan of Ireland, Anne…" George continued. "If you remember the dispute about the title of the Earl of Ormond…?"

With that little nudge, I did remember. The Butlers were a noble family of Ireland; their blood was that of the English nobility mingled with the blood of ancient Irish chieftains… or barbarians, depending on how one viewed them. I had heard of the Butlers before, as they were involved in a hereditary dispute with my own family over the title of the Earl of Ormond. Butler's family thought they owned it; during the confusion of the civil war between the houses of York and Lancaster, the natural heirs of the title had been much removed from their estates in Ireland as they engaged in war, and their cousin, one of the Butler family, had managed their estates. So long had this Butler cousin stewarded the estates that he came to view them as his own and when Thomas Butler, the seventh Earl of Ormond died, the dispute over the inheritance of estates and titles of Ormond intensified. Thomas Butler was my father's maternal grandfather, so we Boleyns had a claim to the title.

We Boleyns believed the title belonged to us, while the Butlers, our distant cousins, believed it was theirs. Sir Piers Butler, the father of this James Butler I was apparently destined to wed, had a claim to the title in that he was cousin to the late Earl, and was the nearest male heir. But the Earldom was entailed to heirs *general*, not to the nearest *male* heir. Those who could claim descent from a female of the Butler bloodline could also inherit. Therefore, in law, our father actually had the better claim; he was a more direct descendant than Sir Piers, since his mother was the elder daughter of the last Earl.

No one had the title officially at this time, but it was a rich one to have as it came with many lands and offices. The King had once granted the livery of the Earldom to my father, and Piers Butler had disputed it, seizing the lands of the Ormond estates, and swearing that he would not give up the title. Piers Butler was popular amongst the Irish lords and their people, and he had a lot of support for his claim. The King had no wish to offend Sir Piers, who was useful in controlling the often unruly lands of Ireland, nor our father, who was a useful and loyal member of his court and whose daughter was, after all, in the King's bed. Our father desired that the title, and all the wealth that came with it, should come to our family. I understood the logic of the match, but I had no desire to enter into it… to marry a son of an Irish lord? Would I be expected then to live *in* Ireland? It was a wild place, full of disorder and vying clans… I had been fashioned for a life at court, surely! What was I to do in Ireland? I felt my heart drop lower and lower as my brother explained the proposed match to me. Had I been brought from France to go to Ireland then? This was worse than simply being exiled to England! Why had I spent so much time polishing my skills for a life at the glittering courts of Europe, only to be brought home and sent away again, to the bogs of Ireland?

"The suggestion to unite our families came from our mother's brother," said George as I stared into the fire trying to gather my thoughts on the matter. I looked up at him and he must have read the disquiet in my soul, for he shrugged as though to show it was not *his* idea. "Uncle Thomas, the Earl of Surrey, was stationed in Ireland some time ago as Lord Lieutenant," George continued. "He had many dealings with Sir Piers and became his friend. Uncle Thomas suggested that with a union between the Butlers and the Boleyns, the Earldom of Ormond would go to Piers Butler now, and his son, James, would inherit the title after his death… as would the children born of the proposed marriage. Such an arrangement would allow both parties to be satisfied, since the title would remain within the blood line of both families, united as one."

I grimaced at George and he smiled at me; it was a smile of support. Mary looked more and more worried. She did not like that the conversation had turned from merry to ill in such a short space of time. My gentle sister was good at reading people, and she could sense the fear and dissatisfaction of my heart with ease.

"He seems a pleasant type of gentleman, Anne," she consoled, "from what I have seen of him about court."

I nodded to her, and tried to smile, but I felt as though my heart had dropped into my fine shoes of Spanish leather. All my previous happiness about returning home seemed to have fled; after all, I was about to be sent from this home, to another… to Ireland!

"Cardinal Wolsey looks on the plan with favour," said George, leaning forward to allow a servant to re-fill his goblet of ale. "And the King sees there is worth in it too. Both of them are trying to convince our father… But to our father, it is not such a good match."

"Why so?" I asked. "It seems all the world believes that I should marry with this Butler boy and live out my days in the swamp!"

George laughed. "Our father wants the title of Ormond, *now*, and for himself, Anne," he said. "This plan might well be tempting for Sir Piers, but not so for our father." George grinned and shook his head. "And without our father's consent to the match…" he spread his hands.

I took his meaning and took some comfort from it. At least if my father was not keen on the match then there was a chance that I might not have to undertake it. I understood all the reasoning of course. It was not an uncommon idea, to unite two houses for the sake of better title and wealth for their heirs, but I was appalled at the thought; not so much of marriage, for I knew that was to be my destiny eventually, but of living so far from court and my family. In Ireland! It was an untamed and distant place filled with unruly, battling clans by all accounts… I was not suited to be a country wife! Why had I been sent to polish my achievements abroad, to learn all that I knew now, if my family intended to marry me off to an Irish lord who would keep me in a remote castle in the middle of nowhere?

George told me that James Butler was already at court, and was in his early twenties, much of an age with me. He had fought alongside King Henry's forces at Therouanne, and had thereafter spent much of his youth in Ireland, with his father. He had been recently brought to the English Court, and into Cardinal Wolsey's household, some suspected as a sort of hostage to secure his father's loyalty for King Henry. And there James Butler waited… for me.

Mary turned the conversation away from the subject, but I went to bed that night with a more troubled heart than I had had when I arrived at Hever. To be taken to live in Ireland! To be snatched away from all that I had just found pleasing to my heart in England! Oh, how I wished I was back in France then! How I longed for the merry eyes of Marguerite and the soft consolation of Claude! My friends in France would have been appalled as I was, to think of me being taken to a wilderness such as Ireland! Unhappy thoughts of bogs and savage people filled my mind as I tried to sleep that night. I tossed and turned, thinking of ways to extract myself from such a match. Being fair to the country of Ireland and its people, I knew nothing of it; but it seemed to me a foreign and uncouth place… and I had no wish to marry into a family whose seat was within its lands.

I awoke with a sore head and a heart full of fears. I questioned my mother on the match in the morning, and she looked at me rather sadly. I gathered that she was not enamoured of the idea either. George saw my troubled visage and furrowed brow as we walked out to ride through the lands of Hever that morning, and tried to reassure me, musing aloud that it was an unlikely match.

"I think our father is most unwilling for the match to actually go ahead, Anne," George comforted. "After all, our father knows that the Earldom of Ormond is *ours* by rights and should not have to be secured on his heirs by marriage. And he would much rather have the title conferred on him, *now*, rather than on the children of a match between the Butler lad and you. However, it is often politic to enter into these kinds of talks and see where they lead. He could not disobey the King or Wolsey in bringing you home to meet with James Butler, but I doubt it will go any further." He looked over my pale and worried face and smiled, reaching out to take my hand. "Fear not, sister," he said gently. "I doubt our father is likely to waste his one unwed daughter in marriage to this Butler; with your talents and our rising fortunes, we may be able to secure a greater marriage for you… one that will keep you near us and the court, where you belong."

I nodded to him and smiled, but I continued to worry. It was not the state of marriage that I feared; part of me *wanted* to marry. Mary was married, and there was a bride for George emerging on the horizon in the person of Mistress Jane Parker, so I had heard. One day I wanted to have sons and daughters of my own. I was of an age to marry… but I did not want to be wedded and then taken to Ireland, even if we would occasionally visit the court and my family here. I had just been wrenched from France, from a life and from people that I loved. To arrive back and to find friends and family so warming and sweet to my heart had been a great pleasure, but then to find that I might soon be taken from all this too? Was I to be tossed from one place to another like a piece of seaweed caught in the tide? And to go to Ireland? It was a lawless and dangerous place. Rebellion lifted its ugly head time and time again against the Crown. The lords who governed there, placed in Ireland by the English King were, by necessity, hard men, taught to rule and quash the population with a mighty fist. How was that a place for me? A life where I should be kept alone much of the time, having baby after baby in solitude and never seeing the court again? That was not a life for me, surely.

Over and over I wished myself back in France. Over and over I wondered on the uselessness of my education abroad. If all I was destined for was a life as a country lady, kept within a castle in the wilds of Ireland, then I might as well have passed my youth at Hever. Perhaps then, I would not have the imagination to think so long and hard on my present fate…

During that time at home, I worried greatly about my proposed marriage. But fortunately, not all the time. Distractions from my worries came with the joy of rediscovering my family, and Tom Wyatt kept his promise to visit, and visit often. Tom came riding over to Hever almost every day after George and Mary had left for the court, and as I missed them, I filled the hole they left in my heart with Tom's conversation and companionship. Sometimes he brought his sister, Margaret, to visit with us, and I was delighted to find that the wry humour of the Wyatt's bred as true in her blood as in Tom's.

We would walk together through the physic gardens where my mother grew medicinal and sweet tasting herbs for the table or for the still-room, through her rose gardens which were stark and fragile in the winter's light. We rode out through the silver-frosted forests, racing each other through the land on our horses, or played at cards and dice when the rains kept us indoors. Tom seemed to have taken a long leave of absence from court, which somehow coincided with my arrival at his door on that rainy night of our first meeting. Although he said nothing of his diligent and attentive appearances at my side, I believed that he had become a little infatuated with me. And perhaps I had come to see him in a similar light. It was a heady experience to have such a man court me. But I would only be his mistress in the games of courtly love, I told myself sternly. Tom was married, and however much he was a pleasure to me, he could be nothing more.

I believe I could have lost my heart to Tom Wyatt, if I had let myself. He excited me; he was a fine man, cultured and witty, full of humour and jest, but also strong and robust. He loved games and riddles, and we spent much time devising such diversions for each other that winter. He had an impish quality about him, and loved mischief, but there were deep feelings hidden under the glare he put forth to disguise such. I found him quite intriguing. He was the type of man that any woman would find hard to resist. And from what I gathered from my sister, who always knew more about these things than I, he had quite a reputation with the ladies of the court.

"No lady can resist Master Wyatt when he turns his fine charm upon them." Mary told me with a smile on one of her short visits to Hever. She and the King used nearby Penshurst Place as a rendezvous for their private meetings at times, and she would sometimes take a few days to come and see me as well. I lifted my eyebrows at Mary's words and shook my head resolutely. *I* would prove to be the exception to this rule that no lady could resist the allure of young Master Wyatt.

But even if it could be nothing other than friendship, or the office of a courtly admirer, it was exciting to have Tom around. It was also flattering and reassuring that I had an admirer already in this new land where I was still trying to find my feet. I knew well enough that if someone had proposed a match of marriage between Tom Wyatt and myself, and had he been free to marry, I should have been most happy to consider it. We would have made a good match in terms of our characters. But such dreams were not reality. Tom was taken. He was married, and I would be no man's mistress, even one such as Tom, for whom I had such admiration and affection. Yes, I could have loved him, but I would not let myself. My heart would remain enclosed from harm, from falling for him, by the warnings of my mind. I was no foolish girl likely to break her heart for a man who could never be hers in truth. Tom and I were good friends, I told myself, and I was fortunate to have such a friend.

Perhaps you will think me cruel, for at the time I thought not of the other heart in this matter. But it is not the place of any one person to be the master of the feelings of another. I could speak only for my own heart, and it could not be allowed to break itself for a love that could never be.

Margaret Wyatt and I grew close quickly too; she told me of the household of the Queen, and of what my duties would entail. Margaret was an attractive woman with pale skin, soft brown hair and a small, pointed nose, but it was her humour which drew me to her, much like her brother's. She was quite open in her admiration for me; seeming to think that I was far more sophisticated than any other she had ever met, which pleased me. When she returned to court, a little before I was due to leave, I missed her company, but looked forward to seeing her once more at court. It was nice to think there would be a friendly face there.

Soon enough those languid, pleasurable days wintering at Hever were called to an end as our father wrote to command me to court. After a month or so in the country, I was more than ready to go once more to the life and vitality of a royal court. I was eager to see the English Court, and perhaps learn more of this match, and how I was to stop myself from being caught in it.

My father wrote from Mechelen, ordering me to the English Court at Greenwich. It was like the summons of a general, calling his soldiers to war.

Chapter Five

Greenwich Palace
1522

In late February, I entered the court that I was to call home for the rest of my life. The storms of winter had died down a little, but the air was damper and felt much colder in England than in France. I had to line my clothing with furs and layers of good English wool to ward off the cold.

My father released money for new garments, and I was given family jewels to enhance my already sophisticated appearance. New furs and thick velvet cloth graced my chests of new clothes, but I took with me also most of the gowns, sleeves, kirtles and hoods I had made myself in France. My sister had warned me that the styles of the England were different to those of France and that I should look out of place in my own gowns, styled to suit my form and shape. I cared little for her opinion on this matter, though; I knew what suited me best and I should not wear the dull garments that my sister flung on herself rather than the beautiful, elegant gowns that I was known for in France. I was going to make an impression here, just as I had everywhere else I went, and no one was going to tell me how to do that. As Marguerite had once said to me, sometimes it is better to keep one's own counsel and to trust one's own instincts.

I had been chosen to enter the Queen's service as a maid of honour and also as a servant of the Royal Wardrobe. It was a high honour, and one which brought much pleasure to me, for the Royal Wardrobe was full of the most gorgeous and expensive materials. I would be helping with the upkeep and cleaning of fabulously glorious materials, gowns, dresses, kirtles, stays… and I would hopefully be called on to counsel the Queen in what items to wear. I longed to see its riches and its splendour; fabric and dress being ever a grand passion of mine. I was not disappointed when I looked on the Royal Wardrobe; it was magnificent.

The court was at Greenwich Palace when I joined it. It was often situated here, when near London, as Greenwich was the King's favourite palace of residence. It was also large enough to contain not only most of the legitimate courtiers and statesmen, but also all the hangers-on; people who had no real reason to be at court, but were there anyway. These people were often a nuisance, and a drain on the King's finances, but there was little that could be done about them. Cardinal Wolsey had tried many and varied ways to reduce the numbers at court in order to preserve more money for the King's coffers. But even if sent away once, these unofficial courtiers always found ways back in. The court was so large that it was like some mythical beast, a many-headed hydra, made of many different parts of different animals. It was hard to tell who belonged and who did not.

We came up to London along the river, and then took to horseback on the banks of the Thames just outside of the city. I wanted to see the city. Riding into London for the first time, as an adult, was quite an experience. Although I had seen cities in France and Burgundy, London had an identity all its own. And I smelt it long before I saw it.

We rode through the outer-lying areas where rickety huts and basic villages sprawled into and up against the walls of the city. Riding into London with George and my family's servants, there was a smell that was like no other: excrement and piss; baking meat pies and dirty, sweaty pigs; jasmine, lavender, rose and musk perfume; frying spices and human perspiration filled the air. I knew not whether to feel repulsed, rejuvenated or possibly, hungry. But I tell you, it was a heady feeling. The city was marked by its great monuments. Goldsmiths shops lined the street named the Strand to the great Cathedral of St Paul's. Westminster Abbey stood tall and magnificent, its great towers stretching out above the skyline like fingers reaching up to God. London Bridge was hectic with masses of people and with shops all piled on top of one another in what looked to me to be less architecture and more grand lunacy. The Tower of London, with its great White Tower at the centre of the palace confines shone brilliant white against the light falling rain and grey skies. Around the edge of the Tower of London were the many smaller towers that lined its huge walls; they seemed to stare down on the crowded masses of people thronging through and about the great structure, watching the everyday comings and goings of the streets of London.

Paris was bigger, but London was *saturated* with people; it felt as though every person in the realm of England was in those streets. Merchant's stalls crowded the markets, selling hot meats and cold ale; ample, plump livestock jostled and brayed as they were herded through the streets; bake-houses puffed steam and wood smoke from their chimneys, crafting breads and pies for the houses nearby. There were novice lawyers in dark clothing wandering past and talking earnestly of that day's lessons; pages running errands for their masters and maids out collecting or delivering laundry, their hands caught up in bundles and baskets of overflowing cloth. Ravens and jackdaws picked at scraps on the streets, flying off, squawking with annoyance when they were shooed away. Banners hung low and long over the streets in front of each shop, each seeking to be more prominent than the other, their bright pennants moved softly in the winds that blew through the streets. Flocks of hundreds of wintering swans flowed along the edges of the Thames like a fine trim of ermine on a cuff. And the noise! Everywhere, it seemed, people were talking, laughing, shouting and whispering as we bright and stylish young nobles rode past them. They scattered before us as we came, our horses and servants cutting swathes through the crowds.

George had been sent to escort me through London to Greenwich. He rode beside me, an expensive pomander of orange oil, frangipani and lavender in his hand that matched my own made of lemon, cloves, sage and spices. It was necessary to move through many of the streets holding something to your nose; otherwise you would be overcome by the variety of smells battering your senses. Sweat and mud and blood and piss; bread and meat, baking pies and perfume. It was an exciting place to be taken within; a hungry, active, assault on the senses.

As we rode, George pointed out sights to me. I was glad to have a guide to my own country, for it was all so strange to me… and yet it was not so different from France.

"There," he said as we rode near to London Bridge. "Look on the mark of a noble."

I looked to see what he meant and saw the place where they exhibited the heads of traitors, executed on the orders of the King. Some heads were rotting still upon their spikes, rooks and magpies picking at dark, pink threads of flesh waving gently in the wind. Some were just bare bones; skulls grinning widely in death, their eyes blank hollows. I shuddered and looked away, feeling suddenly cold despite the warm layers of wool under my fine gown of crimson.

"It is said that the mark of a true noble is to have at least one relative up there on a spike…" George turned and grinned at me, and then, noting my reaction, he added with a more gentle tone. "And there is ours."

"Who?" I asked, looking back at the repulsive heads on their spikes; a futile gesture. There was no way I could have told you whose head was whose even if I had known them in life, from the motley collection of bones and flesh residing there.

"Why… the Duke of Buckingham is right there." George said, pointing at a skull which gaped at me. "He has been granted prime position! His daughter, Elizabeth, is married to our Howard uncle, Thomas. So, you see, we have our claim to true nobility right there on that spike… A duke, no less!"

"Speak no more of such things, George," I shivered. "It is a foul thing to look upon. There are other ways a family may count themselves as noble, without noting the traitors amongst their past."

"True enough, sister," said George. "The King must take swift action in all cases of treason, just as he is a clement master to all those who are loyal to his name." My brother spoke loudly enough for the servants to hear, as well as any about us, and then smiled sardonically at me, as though apologising for having to make a point of the righteousness of the sentence of death for treason. There were ears in all places, it seemed, and it was better to always be seen to support the King than to question. I nodded to George, understanding him well.

"Come, he said, turning his horse from the spectacle of death. "Let us speak of brighter things."

We reached Greenwich later that day, and I was allowed a change of gown and a little time to brush and dress my hair before I was called to an audience with the Queen. She preferred to meet her new ladies swiftly, I was told, so that she could ensure that their behaviour was in correlation with her expectations.

Katherine was seated amongst her ladies in her privy chambers when I was brought to her. The chambers were quite dull to my eyes and dusty to my nose. Katherine's ladies were used to the gloom. Remaining ensconced in poorly lit chambers helped to preserve their white faces and keep them warm in the chill airs of England. I liked more air and freshness around me. It seemed I would not get that in the service of Katherine. I walked softly into the chamber, my eyes downcast, and made a curtsey, awaiting notice by the Queen.

One of the ladies was reading aloud in Latin from a book of devotions and the rest were sewing. Katherine had perhaps six or seven ladies of the noble families of England around her and as I entered, they all looked at me. Margaret Wyatt's eyes were warm and welcoming, but the others looked on me speculatively. I was struck with the resemblance to my first entry to the court of Mechelen, but Katherine, Queen of England was no Margaret of Austria. She looked at me gently and bade me to rise from my humble pose before her. I looked up at her face where I saw a quiet, yet proud reserve, and a steady, thoughtful gaze. She had a somewhat serene sense about her, but Queen Katherine had none of the beauty or understated brilliance of Margaret of Austria. Her clothes were of the finest materials, and her jewels sparkled amongst the gloom of the chamber, but Katherine looked tired, where Margaret had seemed brilliant in her effortless beauty.

Katherine seemed old beyond her thirty-seven years; weariness and unhappiness lined her face. Once she had been a pretty girl, I knew from portraits I had seen, and from my memories of her as the new bride of the King on the day we had seen their coronation procession. But that was long ago. Her figure was ruined by constant and unsuccessful child bearing, her waist was thick, and her lemon-shaped face, with its wide top and little chin, was fattened, but, somehow drawn at the same time. Katherine's once-auburn hair was now streaked here and there with little strands of grey. Her skin was still fair and clear, but thick circles of darkness lay under her eyes and an intrusive smell came wafting from her body that was not pleasant. I was fastidious in cleansing my body with herbs and sweet rose-waters, taking lozenges of mint and lemon balm to sweeten my breath and changing my undergarments regularly, as benefited a lady of my standing. I also used perfumes and sprinkled rose-water to infuse scent into my linen underclothes; I liked to have sweet smells around me. I had difficulties not wrinkling my nose at the Queen as the sour smell, not quite hidden by the heavy musk of rose perfume that she wore, crept up my nose and stuck at the back of my throat. But I had been trained well to mask my true feelings behind a courtly demeanour, and I gave no sign that the smell of my Queen and new mistress offended me.

I was told later, by Jane Parker, my brother's future bride, who was also in Katherine's service, that the smell came about because Katherine wore a hair shirt at certain times as a mark of her piety under her fine clothes. It was something that monks and nuns often wore to suffer for the glory of God, but many people of religious piety wore them too. The coarse shirt rubbed against her skin, causing irritation and sweating. Often this assault on the flesh also caused ruptured skin and pustules to develop. Nobles washed their hands and faces with regularity, and changed undergarments daily to prevent unpleasant odours that could lead to sickness, but full bathing was infrequent, especially in the months of winter, due to the risks of illness it could bring. The hair shirts Katherine wore therefore constantly rubbed corrupted cloth against her body. This caused her to smell, even though she used perfumed oils liberally in an effort to mask the scent of corrupted flesh which drifted about her. It was something the King abhorred, Mary told me later, and whenever Katherine took to a period of wearing one of these shirts, Henry would not deign to visit her bed. I could understand why.

Katherine greeted me with a small nod of her head. She welcomed me to court and enquired as to the health of my mother.

"My mother is in excellent health, Your Majesty," I replied, with another small bow. "And she sends her love and best wishes to you. She is most grateful, as am I, that you, in your graciousness, have offered me a place within your household. I hope that I can meet both your expectations of me, and hers, whilst in Your Majesty's service."

The Queen nodded at me with gentle approval. At her side she kept a little beast; a tiny ape, with a jewelled collar of diamonds and rubies bound around its neck. At first it seemed fine to me that such an exotic creature, brought from the new lands being discovered so far away, should rest quietly by her side, but as I watched it, the creature began to rock gently backwards and forwards, pulling at the patchy hair on its scaly arms. Its eyes were both flat and wild, seeming to hold something akin to madness under the dull sheen of its gaze. It plucked at its own hair, ripping it from its skin as it rocked.

Katherine noticed me looking at her pet and smiled. "He is a *capuchin*," she said to me in her heavily accented voice, "named for an order of monks of Italy; they say that when he moves in this way, he is seeking to pray as the monks do. He is a holy creature, given to the mortification of the flesh, just as the monks are…. Although animals do not have souls as we children of God do, still we see within beasts such as this the wonder and glory of the hand of God. He reaches even to these beasts, and makes them copy the movements of the holy men. I keep him at my side, to remind me of the ever-reaching power of our Lord. He touches even the barren minds of such creatures as these, and so His power is as wondrous as it is unlimited."

"Yes, Your Majesty," I said, agreeing with my new mistress, as I must. But in the ape's dark eyes I saw no holiness. I saw dead desperation. I saw the places where the heavy jewelled collar had rubbed and stripped the wretched creature's hair and skin, leaving scabby, flaking flesh. Like its mistress, its flesh was tortured and like its mistress, the creature smelt. I discovered later that the ape had a habit of rubbing its own piss on its body. Katherine fed it sugared treats which made its waste sticky. Its hair often stood up in little spiky tufts. All it seemed to do was glare balefully at the world around it and rock. It was often a duty of the Queen's maids to watch over the creature, but I would not touch it unless Katherine handed it directly to me. I thought it was a foul little beast, but more than anything else, the creature made me sad. I preferred the company of my dogs and hawks; at least they could join me in the freedom of the open air.

Katherine went over my duties with me, and admonished me to be ever humble and chaste in my behaviour at court. Having been a servant to two great queens already, I knew well the sermon given to new ladies at court. The Queen wanted her women to be virtuous, graceful and interesting, since their reputations reflected on hers. I agreed with all that was said to me; assuring the Queen that I was, by nature, a good servant and a lady of virtue. There was no sign on her face that she did not believe me, but I was sure that she was wondering on the truth of my words, given the reputation of my sister, and that of my brother, at court. Although he was young, George was a favourite with the ladies at court, and had already made a name for himself. It might have seemed impossible, to a woman as obsessed with virtue as Katherine, that the third sibling of the somewhat notorious Boleyn family could possibly hold her virtue in high enough regard as to be yet still a virgin, as I was.

Katherine's dark eyes were kind, but she had a distant and slightly irritating air about her; that of someone who has known great sadness and wishes all about her to know that too. She was kind, softly spoken and would be a gentle mistress to me, but I found her self-pity cloying even then. Katherine had suffered, it was true; she had brought many children into the world, and lost all of them but one; her daughter, the Princess Mary. Such suffering is to be lamented, but people who wear their suffering outwardly as though it were a cloak are often tiring to deal with. There are many who know suffering in this life and yet manage to wake each day with a sense of merriment in their souls. There are those who become wise for the trials they have known. And then there are those who have known sadness and wish everyone to pity them for it. Even in this brief meeting with Katherine, I understood that she was one of those. I also understood quite clearly why the King should wish to tarry well and often with my sweet and merry sister. Coming from Katherine's chambers to the arms of my happy and ever-positive sister must have been like walking from a charnel house into the fresh air of spring. No wonder then that Mary had done so well as the King's mistress; she was a balm of happiness to Katherine's cloying self-pity.

Katherine was regal, yet polite to me. She loved my mother well, she told me, and my sister was a good maid to her also. I tried not to smile at the irony of hearing my sister described as a *maid* as Katherine continued with her speech of welcome.

I agreed to be a true and honest servant, to be virtuous in my manner and apparel; to be loyal to God, the King and my new mistress. I was sworn into her service, and then I left her presence when bidden.

I had entered the service of the Queen Katherine of England. I was now a part of the English Court.

Chapter Six

Greenwich Palace
1522

After I had been at the English Court for a few weeks, it was announced that the Cardinal Wolsey was to put on a diversion to welcome Spain's ambassadors to court. The Queen herself recommended me for a place in the entertainment, which must have meant that I had made an impression over the short time I had been in her service. I was a good maid of honour. I had served three queens now and I knew how to act; humble and modest and useful, talented, efficient and interesting, graceful and helpful. I was amongst the best of her servants and she knew it well.

But it was primarily for my dancing skills that I was chosen for this entertainment. Katherine was most often given to passing the time with her ladies in her chambers by reading from the Bible in Latin, or embroidering cloths for altars as she sewed shirts for her husband. Still, there were times when we ladies would dance with each other in the Queen's chambers. Katherine was not opposed to the dance, although she tended to prefer to dance with her ladies in private rather than before the court; even then, she was a little portly to be too energetic in the dance. Katherine had admired my talents in the dance, and had complimented me on my fine form and grace.

"You hold yourself like a fine swan gliding on water, Mistress Boleyn," she had complimented me after one such dance in her chambers. I smiled and curtseyed to her, accepting the rather lovely accolade with happiness.

Since the Cardinal's entertainment was to end with a dance, it would do honour to Katherine's name to have her best dancers shown before the court, and so I was picked.

The entertainment was to be a pageant about the cruelty of love. Ladies, such as me, were to play the roles of feminine virtues. My sister was to be *Kindness*. *Beauty* was to be played by my old mistress Mary Tudor, Dowager Queen of France and now Duchess of Suffolk. I was chosen to take the role of *Perseverance*. There were others; Jane Parker for instance was to play the role of *Constancy* and the Countess of Devonshire was *Honour*. In all, there were eight virtues, each played by a lady of the court. We were to be guarded in a wonderful construction, a wooden castle, by the vices of femininity; by *Strangeness*, *Unkindness*, *Scorn*, *Danger*, *Disdain*, *Jealousy*, *Gossip* and *Sharp-Tongue* all of whom were to be played by boys from the Chapel Royal, dressed up as women. Armed with weapons of petals and sugared plums, the vices were to keep us virtues prisoners in their castle.

We were to be rescued by the *Knights of Love* who would command the vices to release us virtues, and vanquish the unkind aspects of the feminine with their masculine ardour. When they had defeated the vices, the knights would escape with the virtues as the prizes of true love. Then there would be a performance of dancing for the ambassadors, which would lead on to an evening of dancing for the whole court. It was a simple idea really, and not a new one. I had appeared in such entertainments as these in France, and had seen the same ideas performed in Burgundy many years ago. But I was learning that the English Court sought to ape its cousins across the waters… England was a few years behind them in thought and ideas. But even though it was not an entirely original idea, it was still a courtly entertainment, and a chance to engage in dancing, which I had missed. Dancing with other women in the chambers of the Queen was well enough, but there are dances that require the strength of a man to lift and skip his partner through some of the more complicated steps. This would also be a chance to demonstrate my talents to the court, and to be noticed within the constant clamour of anonymous courtiers. If I was to advance at court I needed to be noticed.

Ambassadors of the Emperor Charles V of Spain had come to make a new alliance with England. Their talks, many also whispered, would include the betrothal of the King's daughter, Princess Mary, to the Emperor. The Spanish and the English were to be united against France now. The dealings of kings and countries were as changeable as the English weather, I thought dryly.

This alliance against France was not to my liking. I considered myself as French as I was English, but it would not do to say things like that here. I must bite my tongue and laugh at jests about the French. They were no longer my countrymen; I was English now and must remember that. It made me sad, but I could not show my true feelings. Katherine was overjoyed about the new alliance, or as overjoyed as she could show outwardly. She was not a woman much given to spontaneous outbursts of happiness, preferring to set an example to her ladies and maintain a demeanour of quiet calm. But all about court knew that she was happy to find her husband's interests once more aligned with her nephew, Charles of Spain, and I think the idea of marrying her precious daughter back into the house of her birth was also a great pleasure to her.

The Princess Mary was six years old when I joined the English Court, but her household was usually kept at royal residences such as Eltham Palace, away from the main body of the court. This was in part to protect the King's only heir from the ill airs of London, but also from the court itself. She was a precocious child, so I heard, having delighted French ambassadors when she was four with a spectacular performance on the virginals, and already learning with great fluency French, Spanish, Latin and even some Greek. Although she was not the son for whom our sovereign longed, her father the King loved her greatly, saying that "this girl never cries," for whenever she was brought to him she was ever a merry little girl, which pleased him greatly. The Princess was a pretty child, and she was a great prize in the games of marriage in the courts of Europe. As it stood then, as she was Henry's only legitimate heir, it was supposed that if Katherine bore no son, that whomsoever came to be Mary's husband would also one day become the King of England.

This was something that concerned many people greatly, not least the King himself. However proud he was of his little daughter, he wanted a son to follow him on the throne of England. But, as yet, a male heir had been denied to Henry and Katherine. They had once had a son, the little Prince who had died in his golden cradle when I was just a girl. Then, the royal couple only seemed to be granted babes brought dead from Katherine's womb until the Princess was born. All of England had rejoiced at her birth, but even so, she was a girl and not the longed-for boy. Since Mary's birth, there had been a few more pregnancies, but all had ended in miscarriage or stillbirth. It was generally believed that it would take the direct intervention of God to bring a living child from Katherine's worn womb. People feared that should no living son come to the royal couple, that England would be ruled by a woman in the future; this would not do, since women were held to be weaker and less able than men. The other possibility was that the Princess' eventual husband would become King. If that happened, then England could come to be ruled by a King of another land… something that brought great fear to the proud hearts of the people of England. The succession was a trouble to the minds of many, not the least of them the King himself. All watched Katherine and hoped that God would yet perform a miracle for England. But God, it seemed, was not inclined to act for the royal couple on the English throne.

But such thoughts were only on the horizon of my world then. These matters were weighty indeed, but I believed I should have little to do with them. How little one ever knows of the path of one's life… Who knew that the first strides upon the path I would one day walk were already in place, even then?

I was starting to enjoy the English Court. There were still many things that pained me about England; the weather was still atrocious and the freezing winds that crept through the palaces were like ghosts that snuck upon you, reminding you of the chill of death as they swept through clothes and up undergarments. There had been little of the outside entertainments of hunting or hawking that I enjoyed, mainly because I had been busy with the Queen and her pleasures were more cerebral than physical, but also, because the accursed mists of the winter would not abate long enough, it seemed, to *see* a beast to hunt in the parks used by the court.

But I had a few friends now at court, and the worries that had beset me about not finding friends I could love, or company I could endure, were abating. I mostly kept the company of Margaret Wyatt, and a lady named Bridget Wingfield, another neighbour of my family, originally of Stone Castle in Kent, and now married to Sir Richard Wingfield. Both were ladies in the Queen's household, and so we saw each other often. Bridget was a few years older than me, and had been another of the young nobles that Mary and George and I had been introduced to as children. We spent much time reminiscing on those days! Bridget had been married for some years, and had given birth to many children; almost one a year since her marriage. Although she had a full and bonny figure, as befits a mother of seven, her continual childbearing did not seem to tire her or fade her good looks. She loved her many children and spent much time flitting backwards and forwards from her family estates to court in order to spend time with them. Although she was in truth only a few years older than me, perhaps in being a mother, she seemed to adopt her friends as her own children as well. She was, I have to admit, the best peacemaker in our group. Whenever there was a problem, sending merry Bridget into the fray would always ensure that each combatant was admonished as though they were chicks to her mother-hen. But despite all this motherliness, she was also still a most attractive, and pleasant companion with a beautiful voice.

Margaret was quick and clever, with a humour much like her brother's. She wrote poetry, like him, and loved him a great deal. She, too, had a fine voice, and we often wiled away time together by singing, or arranging the poetry of Tom or George to song. When Bridget joined us, we three could sing together well in harmony, and I started to think on times when we might convince the Queen to allow us to perform for the court. I was sure that we would make a fine impression on the ears of those about us.

I was pleased to have found such friends as Bridget and Margaret. Although they were not the same as my friends in France, I had a sense of familiarity with them quickly, and it made me feel less alone. Courting the company of clever, cultivated women, as I had done in France, made me feel better about England. There *were* friends here for me and they were quick witted and good company. The English Court was not as sophisticated as that of Burgundy or France, but it was not an unpleasant place to be. Especially since another old friend had appeared… strangely, at the same time I did…

Tom had returned to court when I had entered service with Katherine. Tom, George, and Mary were also my constant companions when we were not in service to the King or the Queen. George's future bride, Jane Parker, had too returned to court from a spell at her family home in Essex, and she was pleasant enough to me, at least on the surface. Jane was of rich descent and good birth. She was the daughter of Henry Parker, the tenth Baron Morley. Morley had been brought up within the household of the King's grandmother, Lady Margaret Beaufort, and had been a cupbearer at the coronation of Henry VIII. Morley was a learned man, much in favour, who often worked making translations of valued works by Plutarch, Cicero and Seneca, amongst others, for the King. Jane's family were also devoted to the Church which made them good friends and favourites with the Queen. Jane would bring great wealth to our family with the dowry our father was bargaining for, and she was extremely attractive with fair golden hair, a petite face and large green eyes. I found her quite arresting to look on, and felt a stab of jealousy when I did look on her; Jane was far more beautiful than I would ever be.

George seemed happy enough to have her name put forward as a wife for him, but curiously he did not seem overly interested in the lady herself. I believed that George, with his already exciting reputation amongst the women of the court, enjoyed a challenge and a chase when it came to his conquests. Men such as George tire of easy capture, and what prey is easier to capture in the end, than a wife who is bound by law and by God to obey her husband? Perhaps because he saw no challenge in the prospect of a wife, he was less interested in Jane than he might have been had he tried to attract her as a mistress in the games of courtly love. Jane was certainly beautiful enough to have caught his attentions otherwise. I felt rather sorry for her in this matter, and when I thought of George's indifference to his bride, I thought of the Jane I had first seen at the funeral of the tiny Prince Henry… A little girl who received a hard slap about the face, merely for playing with a black ribbon on her dress.

Since she was likely to become our sister, Mary and I had started to try and tarry with Jane. She was a strange creature. There was never anything in the way she behaved that was reproachable. She was the perfect courtier, but that meant that she was amply able to hide her true feelings. She had been largely brought up within the court, coming to serve in noble households here from the age of twelve, and now in the service of the Queen. In many ways, her career had mirrored that of my sister Mary, aside from my sister's habit of attracting the notice of Kings… Jane was hard to read, which made me wary of her, but in time I came to understand her better.

Sometimes I caught her eyes looking searchingly at me, but when I looked up, that expression would vanish, to be replaced by a courtly smile. I fancied that she viewed me as a rival for the attentions of the gallants of court, although I had no proof of this. If so, she was correct, for I *was* a potential rival. I was not as beautiful as she was, but my French-style manners, my slight accent which always lilted on English words, and my fine clothing made me stand out. My gowns were already being aped by the other ladies of the court. I was quite different to all of these English born and bred ladies. I also had a confidence drawn from relying on myself during my travels. I had seen and experienced far more of the world than these pretty English does knew existed. I was different. I was already starting to stand out from the crowds, and was therefore swiftly finding myself at the centre of a most sophisticated group of women and men at court. My old mistress, Mary Tudor, had seemed pleased to find me in the service of her beloved sister-in-law, Katherine, and was already seeking me out as she said she enjoyed talking with one who had loved the diversions of the French Court as she had.

So yes, I could understand why Jane might have viewed me with resentment. She had been long at the English Court, and yet I had made more of an impression in the short time I had been here. I was hardly modest about my accomplishments, but I have ever viewed false modesty as a pretentious affectation; people only say they are not good at something to gain a compliment. I was aware of my talents and I made sure others were too. Perhaps that does not paint me in a humble light, but at least it was honest.

Jane may have viewed me with umbrage too because I was also a rival for the attentions of my brother. George and I had quickly grown close again, as we had been when we were children. He was becoming a great friend as well as a brother, and we were often found writing, reading or walking together. As his prospective bride, Jane may have found this annoying; no doubt she thought he should pay all his attentions to her instead. But George seemed to have little interest in her besides being charmingly polite and attentive when at entertainments or feasts. George did not seem to warm to her conversation or company any more than he warmed to those of any other women in particular. But Jane had hot eyes for George; she was always watching him. She would be a wild cat in the bedchamber if he liked, I could see that in her... She burned for him. She would be his whenever he wished... And

George, the hunter of court ladies, saw that in her, and was less attracted to her because of it. That which can be had easily is never as attractive as that which is hard to attain…

This proposed marriage then, like so many others around us, was unlikely to be a success. But there were many matches made on less fertile ground than this which still turned out to be manageable in the end. I hoped for Jane's sake that George would prove to be a satisfactory husband. Mary and I continued to seek the company of Jane Parker, and slowly she seemed to warm to us a little. It was to her benefit to be within the company of those favoured by the King or Queen, and to be friends with the King's mistress was an advantage. As we spent time rehearsing for the pageant of the *Chateau Vert*, as Wolsey's entertainment was named, I did find myself liking her a little more than when we first met, but I still found her steady eyes watching me when my back was turned. At times I found such jealousy satisfying… It is always somewhat gratifying to know that you are envied, however unattractive that admission may be. At other times I felt more uneasy of her watchful eyes. But at the time, I thought little of the jealousy of Jane Parker.

Chapter Seven

York Palace
March, 1522

My sister was much astonished to suddenly find that she would have to ape her younger sister in apparel if she was to be thought stylish at court. She had thought that *I* would have to change my style to fit in, but instead, all over court there were versions of my elegant long-hanging sleeves and French-style hoods popping up. Mary Tudor, Duchess of Suffolk, had made the French hood popular when she returned from France, but with the changing ways of the court, the unflattering yet modest gable hood had made a resurgence in more recent years. But with my arrival, it seemed that all ladies about the court were now wearing the flattering French-style head-dress, which sat further back on the head, allowing a slight amount of the wearer's hair to be shown. Since my long, dark hair was one of my best features, I had no desire to hide it under the ungainly English gable hood. Even if we were not at peace with France, I would still not garb myself in such inelegant clothing.

Mary shook her head at me in wonder at the growing popularity of my manner of dress, and I showed her how to set her gown, how to sew sleeves so that they accentuated the waist with their long, swooping lengths. I designed some clothes for Mary, too, that I thought suited her fuller figure better, and she was pleased with them. When I had first started to sketch and design gowns, I could only make them for my own form, but it seemed that my closeness to my sister allowed me to think on her form well enough to know what would suit her. We chose new materials in rich blues and bright crimsons to accentuate her fair colouring, and I was pleased with my successes in designing for a body not my own.

The rehearsals for the coming entertainment of the *Chateau Vert* were progressing well. We had all been learning the steps; both with some of the men chosen for the entertainment, and with each other when the Queen gave her ladies time to practise together. We were given dresses for the entertainment; the virtues were to wear long shimmering gowns of white satin which sparkled in the light when we moved and hung on our young bodies like another, more perfect, flawless skin. Golden ribbons hung here and there on our costumes, glowing in the light of the torches.

On the night of the entertainment, we washed our skin in water infused with petals of roses and wild lilies, and anointed our hair and necks with Italian perfume: hard blocks of ambergris and musk with heavy scent that clung to our bodies like the silks we wore. This heady perfume ignited the senses. On our heads were cauls of Venetian gold topped with Milan bonnets in white silks and velvets. They were expensive costumes and made to impress the servants of the Emperor.

The vices were dressed in a similar style, but they were in the darkest black silk decorated with silver ribbons. Across our dresses, the names of the characters that we represented were picked out in delicate embroidery. Such beautiful stitching was not done by our own hands; for this occasion we were given the best work of the finest seamstresses and tailors of England and Milan. The King and Queen wanted to ensure that we stunned the Spanish ambassadors, both in our clothing and our talents.

The entertainment took place at York Palace, the London stronghold of Cardinal Wolsey, the King's Chancellor and Bishop of York. Wolsey was the King's most trusted, treasured servant, and the Cardinal did everything for the King. Some might have said that Wolsey was the one, in fact, who ruled England, for he had a large finger in every event that went on. He was the King's own hand… and one of the richest men in England. I had seen Wolsey before, of course, at the *Field of the Cloth of Gold*, but I was amazed at how the years had caused him to expand... in riches *and* in girth. Constantly swathed in the richest red robes, he rode a humble mule and yet glittered with gold. He owned vast tracts of land, and his coffers overflowed with coin. Wolsey seemed a great deal more interested in the affairs of the realm, and in the constant accumulation of wealth, than he did in the offices of a Cardinal and spiritual leader of the people. To me, the Cardinal was all that was wrong with the Church; a shining example of all that required reform.

I could not, of course, say something like this aloud. Wolsey was the most powerful man in England, next to the King, and he had the ear and the heart of the English King as his own.

The entertainment started early that night. There was first a sumptuous feast, the like of which I had not seen since leaving France: pottage of butter-soft mutton in white broth; stewed ribs of venison with parsley, sage and hot black pepper; frumenty with saffron and cinnamon; chicken *mortis* made with almonds and rose water. Then came capons, roasted boars' heads, whole sides of venison, and cranes, herons and plovers roasted with their heads and beaks still upon their bodies. Herbed, open pies of pork and pheasants cooked in melted butter stood next to leeks and sops bobbing in fine sauces rich with wine. French-style balls of meat in cubeb berry sauce were sopped up with fine white manchet bread, and warm sallats of white and purple boiled carrots and fine-sliced onions made the trestle tables on which we ate colourful and gay. The meal was finished with sweet tarts of cheese, golden with browned sugar; imported oranges made into fine marmalade; dried rings of pippin apples which swam merry and bobbing in cinnamon-spiced pools of sweet sauce, and tarts wobbling with thick custard, which were so large that they made the tables groan as they were placed upon them.

The ambassadors of Spain were further entranced as Wolsey called for the last course of delicious and strange subtleties of sugar to be brought out, for then huge works of sugar moulded into the crests of the Kings of Spain and England were placed before them. Wolsey received the admiring cheers of the company and the beaming smiles of the ambassadors with obvious glee. At his side, King Henry clapped his servant hard upon the back to see his own crest set next to the King of Spain's. Wolsey understood how to make a show.

I could eat little during the feast, due to excitement, but I took a small sample from the dishes before me and engaged in slightly distracted conversation with those at my side as I ate delicately. Then, as the feast ended, we players subtly disappeared as the company thronged around the hall and the tables were folded up and removed. The entertainment was a secret to most, thought up by Wolsey and created by William Cornish, the King's Master of the Choristers. It was to be a secret until unveiled by Wolsey himself for the greater glory of the King… And perhaps also, many whispered, for the greater glory of Wolsey.

We crept, sixteen of us, into a side chamber, restraining our giggles of excitement as we changed into our beautiful costumes and took our places on the battlements of the great wooden castle. This wasn't a creation as notable as the castle at the *Field of the Cloth of Gold* had been, but it was still impressive. Great turrets stretched up high into the rafters with clever, hidden stairs for us to reach our places behind the painted battlements. The vices in their brilliant black gowns took up their places in the front line of defence, and we awaited the entrance of the company. Some ladies, my sister amongst them, were so overcome by anticipation that they could not quite stifle their giggles as we waited.

I cast my sister a look that she told me later was reminiscent of our father. It was enough to stop her from disgracing our family. Mary of Suffolk was, too, looking a little scathingly at my sister, although this probably had more to do with my sister's affair with the King. The Duchess loved her sister-in-law, Katherine, and disapproved of my sister's relationship with the King; the Tudors could be a prudish family with all other affairs but their own. Mary of Suffolk had, after all, caused a great scandal herself by marrying where she wished rather than obeying her brother's commands. The Dowager Queen of France could hardly turn her perfect little nose up at my sister for wanton behaviour.

We waited by candle light in that great chamber; my heart pounded with exhilaration. This was what I had been waiting for since I left France; a great way to show all that I had learned there and all that I was now… a skilled court lady.

The company were led into the great adjoining hall; their feet crunched over the fresh rushes and herbs strewn over the floors. Wolsey was not one to do things by halves; the fresh rushes were infused with costly scents and sprinkled with newly-picked herbs from his gardens at York Palace. Scents of the coming spring seemed to follow the steps of the company as they entered this hall lighted with great wax candles and hung with tapestry and cloth of gold and silver.

When they glimpsed the great castle, a hearty applause, heavy with surprised laughter, burst forth from the company and there was much clapping and cheering. As with all our entertainments at court, it was for the audience to guess what the story was. That was part of the diversion, but we aided them by calling phrases down to them as they took their places to watch the unfolding story.

Lady *Sharp-tongue* cried out first, "No knight shall come to vanquish my resistance," he called to the company, the high voice of the boy residing in the costume of a woman squeaking out. "Not if he would keep his honour unscathed by my tongue!" This caused some ribald laughter, and more than a few jests whispered at the back of the company.

My sister, *Kindness*, called out that she would mend that hurt with *her* tongue, which caused even more laughter and a few raised eyebrows from some of the ladies. I blushed slightly. Mary had altered her phrase a little, much to my embarrassment. She was supposed to say that she would mend such hurt with her *words*… but had obviously decided it would be merrier this way. Mary of Suffolk lifted an eyebrow to me which arched over the top of her mask, and then turned to the company. Despite the mask she wore, all knew this was the sister of the King, and fell silent to hear her, in respect for her position.

"*Beauty* is held captive by the whims of feminine cruelty," she cried in her strong voice. And then she sighed. "How long shall *Beauty* have to wait, to shine her light upon the heart of a true knight?"

I called out my own phrase which was to be the signal for the entrance of the *Knights of Love* from the back of the hall. "*Perseverance* shall wait forever if need be… for a great knight offering his true heart would be worth all the time in the heavens and earth to a maiden such as I."

How those words have echoed down the years to me!

At the sound of my words there came a great banging at the doors of the hall and without any man moving to open those doors they were flung open. In charged the *Knights of Love* with a great shout and a great yell. The company scattered backwards from the charge of the knights, laughing and pointing at their fine forms and magnificent costumes. Their caps and coats were made of gold and blue velvet; cloaks of deepest azure with gold tinsel adorning them swept over their broad shoulders. Across their chests were scrolls of yellow damask upon which was written their names, values of masculine ardour and virtue. They were *Amourness, Nobleness, Youth, Attendance, Loyalty, Pleasure, Gentleness* and *Liberty*. We all knew that the man standing at the head of them all was King Henry himself, playing *Amourness*.

The knights charged in to the loud cheering of the crowd and we could see the Emperor's ambassadors laughing delightedly and asking Wolsey questions; they were anxious to know which knight the King was. Wolsey's face was alive with joy seeing his great entertainment unfold. He shook his head at the ambassadors and wagged a finger playfully at them; they would have to discern who the King was themselves.

The vices jeered the knights as they marched to the foot of the battlements: "Knights? I see none!" *Sharp-Tongue* shouted over the cheers of the crowd. "Where are these knights of whom you speak?" He made a great show of looking over the knights' heads. The crowd booed him but laughed, too, to see the knights heckled so. All the vices appeared to be having the greatest of times insulting the knights. The knights called back to them, demonstrating their virtues by the phrases they cried out.

Loyalty called out above the roars of the crowd, "I would never abandon a lady, even one as ugly as Lady *Gossip*!" to which the crowd bellowed with laughter. Lady *Gossip* jeered back to him, "I would never wish for such a knight as you, if what has been whispered in mine ear of your *prowess* is true!"

The spokesman of the knights, William Cornish, dressed as *Ardent Desire* brought forth *Youth* and *Desire* to the head of the party of knights to beg the virtues to come forth from the castle and escape with them. *Beauty* called out to them, "We are prisoners here, good sirs, held at the will of the vices that hold us. Only knights of *true* love could rescue us from the battlements of this lonely castle."

There was a great roar, and the *Knights of Love* charged the castle pelting the vices with dates and oranges. The vices threw armfuls of rose petals and sugared plums back at them. It got slippery and sticky on the castle walls rapidly and I could not help but burst out with laughter as I ducked to narrowly avoid a date covered in honey that flew like a missile and bounced from the castle walls. Mary, too, was rolling with laughter as she ducked rather ineffectively and stood covered with the juices of oranges, with petals of white and red roses stuck to her cheeks and her gown. She looked beautiful, even in such a strange garb as this, as she always did when she was happy.

The crowds were screaming with laughter, egging on the knights and booing the vices as they kept up their defence of the castle. I was already weak with laughter myself, although I joined with the others to encourage the knights.

Eventually the knights won their way to the battlements and under the torrent of oranges and dried fruits the vices fled from a side door of the mock castle, screaming insults to the knights as they ran. The gates of the castle were thrown open and suddenly, to the crowd's surprise, hidden musicians inside the castle began to play, striking up a lively tune. There was another great cheer as indeed it seemed as though the music came from nowhere and everywhere at once, like magic. To the sounds of that beautiful music we ladies took to our heels and fled from the castle. Mary ran straight into the arms of *Amourness*, as I am sure was intended. The King grasped her laughing in his arms. For a *virtue*, my sister had little resistance to his great arms as they engulfed her, claiming her as his prize.

I ran out, and, whilst looking where my sister had run to, ran straight into another knight dressed as *Liberty*. Flung into his arms by the force of my racing feet, I almost lost my footing in my surprise. He turned quickly, and in a graceful and elegant move, twirled me in his arms so that I was caught and suspended backwards, lying across his arms. I laughed merrily; my black eyes sparkled at him. He had saved me from a fall with his clever move and strong arms. I looked up into blue flashing eyes and for a second I thought it was the King I was looking up at, but it was Edward Neville, a man who looked so like the King himself that some thought them to be brothers.

I laughed again, thanking him as he lifted me to my feet; he swept a graceful bow to me, and held out his hand, claiming me now as his prize. I gave him an elegant curtsey and my hand. As he led me to the centre of the room for the main dance, I suddenly caught sight of the King leading Mary to the floor; he was looking our way with an expression of slight displeasure. Although his hand was holding Mary's gently, he appeared to be looking only at myself and Neville with irritation. I was confused, wondering if my accidental trip into Neville's arms and his subsequent move to stop me from falling to the floor had been too inelegant and had displeased the King. I blushed and was led to the floor by my partner, trying to not look at the King. I could not believe that my exit from the castle would have been *so* inelegant as to cause such a look of displeasure.

But during the dance that followed between the virtues of femininity and the knights of love, there seemed to be nothing amiss. The King, dancing with my sister, looked merry and happy. The ambassadors were eager to praise the wealth and intelligence of England, impressed by our little scene. I thought perhaps I had imagined the dark look from the King, and strove to think no more on the matter, but to give my attention to the challenging dance we performed for the crowd. After the formal dance was ended we were unmasked by the King to great applause, and then the courtiers in the hall came forward for the next dance. As the floor filled anew, we virtues, and the knights, escaped to change our clothing and to return in our best apparel for the rest of the night's entertainments.

As Neville released me to go and change, he kissed my hand. "I believe I was the most fortunate of knights to dance with the most beautiful woman in the castle."

I laughed merrily. "And yet, my lord, I was not chosen to play *Beauty*," I said. "I believe that others with more measured vision chose the roles well."

Neville shook his head and was about to say more when the King called to him to attend on him and help him change. Neville bowed and swept away from me. I went to change my sticky dress, its beautiful silks entirely ruined from the night's entertainment. A true show of wealth, when one can buy the most expensive fabrics and cast them into ruin for a night's pleasure!

When we returned to the hall, I partnered Tom in the dance; he was as swift of foot as he was of tongue and it was a joy to dance with him. Although I was trying to be a little aloof with him, given my sneaking suspicions that he was infatuated with me, I could not help but feel my heart skip in excitement when I saw him. We were much of an age and rank and he was clever, handsome and witty. But he was also married, and those pleading eyes could offer me nothing I could accept.

"What did you think of the entertainment, Mistress Boleyn?" Tom asked as we danced together.

"I thought that perhaps the vices were the wiser creatures," I said laughing. "For they saw truth through disguise and fled from capture, as I would do in reality."

"Shall none capture you then?" he asked with his eyes sparkling and his hand clutching mine as he turned me.

"None, but they whom I will to," I said warningly. "And that shall be the greatest prize I offer to the man I will call husband."

"No one chooses who they marry, Anne," he said with a sigh. "And love cannot happen just because one has vowed to marry someone; most people find love outside their marriage bed."

I sniffed and bowed the last of the dance to him. As I rose to standing I leaned forward and whispered in his ear, "I am not most people, Tom." I took the hand of Henry Norris, a Gentleman of the Bedchamber, to partner me in the next dance.

I was not trying to be cruel to Tom, although it must have seemed that way to him. But I could not allow my defences to lower around him; he was a danger to me because, in truth, I desired him as he desired me. The only difference between us was that he would not suffer if we acted on that desire, and I would. And who was to say that his desire would not be over as soon as I had succumbed? Men were fickle in their desires, this I knew from my experience within the Court of France. For a moment of pleasure that would not last, should I be expected to lose all the virtue and honour I had sought so hard to retain all these years? I thought not.

Chapter Eight

Greenwich Palace
May 1522

Easter came, and I was astonished to find that the great offerings of fish at court were more fabulous than I could have imagined before coming to England. Meat was not allowed during this holy time, but the fresh waters, streams, pools and seas of England, it seemed, were more than able to keep us stocked with good fish during this time.

The court feasted on roasted pike, sallats of Alexander buds with whelks, boiled shrimp and mussels in leek and onion broth, dressed crab, sturgeon in aysell vinegar, baked oysters, fried whiting, and trout pate pies. There were tarts and stews, roasted fish, fried fish and fish stew. Lamprey, herring and even porpoise and seal were added to our platters. I had thought the French understood fish and seafood better than any other country, but when I tasted of the fish dishes of England, I understood better. Perhaps it was only to be expected really; England was an island. It stood to reason that they would understand the offerings of their many shores and streams perhaps better than nations not wholly surrounded by water.

As the bright celandines appeared, yellow and golden, shining through the dull mud, they heralded the coming of the sun once more to this wind-swept and rain-splattered isle. The celandines glinted like little suns themselves in the spring sunshine. The common people called these flowers 'the Spring Messengers' and welcomed their appearance, for then all knew that life was returning to the land. Youthful shoots of grain crops started to appear upon the fields and the singing of field-workers was heard in the distance in the parks when we rode out. Hoglets of wild boar began to appear, their striped and spotted brown bodies rustling through the undergrowth as they raced after their gigantic mothers. All about us were the cries of young rooks as they nested in the giant rookeries in the grounds of the palaces, their loud squawks for food being answered by the deeper, throaty calls of their parents.

It was as though life was truly returning to these lands. I felt it more keenly than I had ever felt such a thing in France or Burgundy. Each day, as I rose to see whether ill storms or bright sunshine covered England, I would feel a little skip of excitement within me. England's weather was so variable, and changeable, that it was almost a constant adventure to see what might happen in the skies each day. I had come to hold some admiration for the bold storms of winter, but looked towards the coming of summer with relief, like the rest of the country, and in hopes for clement skies and the warmth of the sun returning.

In May, as the woodlands and forests burst forth with bluebells and white-purple wood anemones, coppicing began and charcoal burning erupted through the forests, bringing the rich scent of burning hazel and willow floating through the trees. And as we lifted our noses to sniff for the coming of summer, there came a most important visitor to our shores; Charles, Duke of Burgundy, Holy Roman Emperor and King of Spain.

Although other rulers of other lands would never care to admit it, Charles was the most powerful ruler in Europe. He inherited the Low Countries and Burgundy through his grandfather Maximilian I, and held the elected title of Holy Roman Emperor which came from the Prince-electors and was secured by a crown from the Pope. He also inherited the crowns of Aragon and Castile through his mother, the mad Queen Juana, and from the Hapsburgs he inherited Austria and other lands through Europe. Charles' empire was vast, and also included lands extending into southern Italy, and far across the oceans, the lands of the New World. Since he was the first King to take both the crowns of Aragon and Castile as his own, he was coming to be referred to as the first true King of Spain.

I had seen Charles at the court of the Archduchess Margaret in Burgundy, when he was a young man, but since then, he had come into lands and fortunes that could hardly be imagined. He was a cultured and educated prince, who spoke many languages, and once said, "I speak Spanish to God, Italian to women, French to men, and German to my horse," which was something much quoted of him.

Charles came to England to form an alliance with his uncle-by-marriage, King Henry, against France. He wanted Henry of England to become a part of his military aspirations to take Italy as part of his empire. Later stages of this plan also included the invasion of France, and the quiet betrothal of Henry of England's only daughter, Princess Mary, to the Emperor. The King of England and his ally may have thought this betrothal was a secret, but all at court knew of it through rumour and gossip. It was controversial, as in marrying his only heir to the Emperor, Henry was effectively making Charles the future King of England… something which could cause great fear and unrest amongst his people.

At the time, Charles was threatened by a rebellion in Castile and was bringing 4,000 troops from the Low Countries and Germany to subdue the revolt against his power. He could hardly bring these troops to England whilst on a diplomatic mission, and so he left them in the Low Countries, with my old mistress and his aunt, the Archduchess Margaret, for the six weeks he visited England. It was a testament to how highly the King of England valued this visit that Henry offered to pay for the costs of Charles' stay in his lands.

At first, it was reported that Charles intended to bring over two thousand people to attend him on his visit, but later this number was reduced, much to Henry's relief, to just under four hundred men of rank and about the same number of servants. The others were to wait for him in Zeeland and join Charles at

Southampton when he sailed. Leading nobles, men of the Church and administrators were brought from Spain and the Low Countries, with the Duke of Alba leading the Spanish nobility, and the Prince of Orange leading the Dutch delegation. Not only the palaces of England, but the homes of all nobles were to be opened to these visitors during their stay, for there was no place large enough to house all of them, as well as the court, in one place.

The French were most put out by this extraordinary show of friendship between their two rivals, and several arrests of English merchants in Bordeaux were attributed to this bile. Wolsey summoned the French ambassador to court, and shouted at the man as though he were a child, demanding to know what the promises of the French King were worth, if he went against the terms of the Treaty of London which was still held between France and England. The ambassador was reduced almost to house arrest, and the Lord Mayor of London was given leave to imprison French men in the capital and sequester their goods. Henry even sent the English navy into the Channel to attack French ships... but he had not declared outright war on France yet; the English King wanted to see what might come of this visit from his nephew first.

Wolsey went with a great entourage to Dover, where he met and entertained Charles in magnificent style, and the King went to meet them there. He proudly showed his nephew his great ship, the *Henry Grace a Dieu*, the flagship of the huge English fleet. Charles was most impressed, not only by the naval fleet, but also by the artillery, of which, he claimed, he had never seen the like before. The party rode on through Canterbury and Sittingbourne where they were entertained by Bishop John Fisher, and on to Gravesend where thirty barges waited to carry them to Greenwich Palace and to the heart of the court.

We waited for the arrival of this great Emperor at the waterfront at Greenwich. I stood to one side of Katherine, with Bridget and Margaret, and watched as my mistress tried to contain the excitement she felt at seeing her nephew. Although she was usually a master at such control, I looked down at her feet, noting that she was bobbing a little up and down on her toes, like a child, as we watched the barges approach. She saw me looking at her, and met my eyes with a smile.

"You see all with those great black eyes, Mistress Boleyn," she whispered to me, bringing her heels down on the wet ground once more.

"I am sorry, Your Majesty…" I cast my eyes downwards, trying not to smile. Katherine grinned at me and reached out to lift my chin. At her side, Lady Margaret Pole looked on her friend and mistress' excitement with pleasure.

"Yes, you see I am excited," she said. "I try to maintain my dignity of course, but I cannot hide it as well as I would wish. This young man, my own beloved sister's boy… He is now a great king, and an emperor! I have so longed to see him; blood of my blood, flesh of my flesh… and now I am to see him, and he is in alliance with my beloved husband…" She smiled and let out a contented sigh. Then a shadow seemed to fall over her face, and she shook her head. "I had a son once, Mistress Boleyn, did you know that?" I looked up at her and nodded shortly.

"A great and goodly prince he would have been, Majesty," I said softly, "had God not seen fit to call him from us."

She nodded. "He was the sweetest babe I ever looked upon," she said with a catch in her throat. "Although I cannot speak against the will of God, I admit that I miss him. I mourn for his loss each and every day. I would have liked, above all things, to see him grow, to see him become a man, a king, as great as his father." Her face creased with sorrow. "But it was God's will that my son be called from this life and into the Kingdom of Heaven," she continued. "In some ways… seeing the son of my dearest sister… it is as though I am shown what my own boy might have become. As though Charles is not only my sister's son, my nephew, but as though he is as my *own* son… Does that make sense, Mistress Boleyn?"

I nodded to her. "Of course, Your Majesty," I said.

She nodded happily and shook herself. "My mind wanders in my excitement," she laughed and touched the hand of Lady Margaret Pole, turning her eyes and attention from me as the barges carrying the Emperor and his retinue docked at the waterfront.

The arrival of Charles was greeted by fanfares of trumpets and great cheering. Henry, who had ridden ahead to greet the Emperor rushed forward to take his hand and help him to the shore in a great show of friendship. As Charles came to the waterfront, he bowed to his aunt, asking for her blessing.

"I give it to you with great joy, my beloved nephew," she said, stepping forward so that he could kiss her. Behind her, Lady Margaret Pole brought forth the little Princess Mary, who tottered forwards with wide eyes to meet the man she may well marry when she was old enough. The Princess greeted Charles with great dignity, for a six year old, and he was polite and charming to her in return, giving her a little jewel as a present which she kept forever after in a pouch worn on her side. It was a momentous occasion for all in England, as we were all quite possibly looking on the face, and much over-long chin, of our future King. It had been four years since Katherine last conceived a child, and if no more heirs were to come of this royal marriage, then Charles could inherit the Kingdom of England to add to his other lands if he married with our princess.

Even though we were not supposed to know of it… it was a thought that caused some rumblings of fear about the court and country even amongst the celebration and entertainments. Would England become but a small part of such a large empire? Would her glory be forgot? Her men become but servants to a vaster empire?

Henry was keen to keep such fears hidden. He little wanted the Emperor to see anything but the glory of England on that visit. Endless rounds of entertainments were given; jousts, feasts, banquets, masques, hunting trips… The days were filled as were the nights!

During a joust at Greenwich, Henry was arming himself for a match against the Duke of Suffolk, when a messenger from the French ambassador arrived. Henry invited the Emperor to read the missive with him, and together, they announced to the court that Henry had sent a messenger in his stead to François at Lyons, listing many grievances Henry had against the French King. He had also declared that Henry considered François his enemy. Nobles cheered the news about the jousting ring, calling for war. The match went ahead with the Emperor Charles smirking greatly. His purpose in coming to England had been achieved; we were now to war with France.

I heard the news with dismay, even though I had known that war between England and France was certainly on the horizon. I had hoped that it might not occur, but this was foolish. Within weeks our uncle, Sir Thomas Howard, was sent with the naval fleet to patrol the coast, and as the two kings went on with their merry dance of friendship through the country, England prepared herself for war.

Chapter Nine

Windsor Castle
June 1522

Along with the arrival of the Emperor's party, came our father, returning from Burgundy to give his reports to the King in person on the alliance he had helped to negotiate with the Emperor and the Archduchess Margaret. He was often busy, and was due to go to Spain before the winter that year, to complete many more tasks for the King, but he found time all the same to bring me to him, and assess my person and my talents as he had done periodically when he visited me when I was young, in Burgundy and France. He spent some time catching up with Mary, George and our mother, and seemed satisfied that in his absence, his family had not disgraced him. I wanted to talk with him on the matter of my marriage, or proposed marriage, from which I desperately wished to be free, but he was distracted by his work, and, at least at first, did not seem to pay much heed to my worries. Perhaps he thought them unimportant.

Despite such concerns, the court was interesting to me and I felt increasingly comfortable there. I still did feel like a foreigner at times; my accent was hinted with French, my clothes and my manners were French and yet my blood was that of an English woman. You might have thought that my French ways would have made me unpopular at court, seeing as we were to war with them, but it was strangely not so. I was accepted as an English woman, and my French ways were simply something which made me slightly different to the rest of the women at court. My duties to Queen Katherine were not demanding. In all there were about thirty women serving the Queen at different times. Katherine usually had perhaps eight or ten women about her; the Lady Margaret Pole, and Maria de Salinas, the Baroness Willoughby de Eresby, Katherine's closest friends, were with her the most, and Katherine had more ladies who could be called on to replace her standard flock if any were taken sick, had to attend on duties to their families or if there was a public ceremony of some kind. Most of our duties were menial, decorative or ceremonial and I had learnt my lessons well in France in attendance to Claude. I was efficient and discreet in my ways around the Queen's chambers and that pleased her, but I was not one of her confidantes or close friends. Even with my duties to Katherine, I had some time in which to pursue pastimes with friends and admirers, which were growing in number around the court.

The court moved much in general, but especially so during the visit of the Emperor. We had spent time that year already at Greenwich, Richmond, Wolsey's great houses of York Palace and Hampton Court, and then moved on to Windsor Castle where the two kings spent time hunting, and we nobles of the court were allowed to do the same. I spent much time with my own circle of friends when not with the Queen. Mary was often away from the chambers granted to her husband, occupying the bed of the King, although less so during the Emperor's visit, as Henry hardly wanted his nephew to witness the existence of a mistress, and take offence on behalf of his aunt.

My sister's ongoing relationship with the King was something, for which I must admit, I still felt a jealous pang. It had been long since I was that child who looked with hot eyes on the King of England, but he was a man to be much admired. Knowing that my sister was allowed to enjoy a relationship with such a man with our father's blessing irked me, for I would never be allowed to occupy, say, the bed of Tom Wyatt under the same blessing. I had still not entirely reconciled my feelings of jealousy for my sister's relationship with a man such as Henry of England. I told myself that such thoughts were foolish; but the heart does not care what is foolish and what is wise. It knows only what it feels and nothing more. There had been times, especially when I first heard of Mary's affair with Henry, when I had envied her most heartily. He was a fine and noble man, aside from being a great knight and powerful king. When I remembered the feelings that had stirred within me when I saw him as a girl in the Court of Burgundy, I knew, most keenly, why a part of me envied my sister her position. But with the duality common to many such thoughts, I knew too that I desired to be a wife, not a mistress as my sister was.

Still, I was growing contented with life at court; friends who loved poetry and writing, like Tom, Bridget and Margaret gravitated to me. The Gentlemen of the Royal Bedchamber were always dancing attendance on we ladies of the Queen's chamber; Will Compton, handsome Henry Norris and Edward Poyntz were the most attentive. There were many jousts and entertainments to enjoy during Charles' visit and I lapped up the pleasure of all of them. We young creatures of court gathered in groups to walk in the gardens during times when we were free of our duties, and to talk on books and music. George and Tom recited their poetry, and Margaret and I would set it to music. We were a merry band who would take to the archery butts in the parks on Sundays, and practise our skill with the bow. We took hawks out into the parks to hunt wild birds, and rode out on swift horses through the countryside. We wagered on tennis matches, usually being played by our rakish cousin Francis Bryan and the King.

England was not France, but I was coming to believe that I could make a semblance of the cultured life I had enjoyed there, here. With the help of Tom we started to draw out ideas for entertainments that we would show to the King's close friends. Some were traditional in theme, but all came to have our clever little slants on their production. We also played games in and about the court; many were made up by Tom and George and sometimes involved childish-seeming games, such as hide and seek, but put together with riddles. One such game involved the ladies in Katherine's household searching the court for Tom's *heart*… which turned out to be a little inflated balloon made of stretched pig-skin, shaped like a heart and painted red. The riddle he gave to Katherine's ladies read thus:

Help me to seek for I lost it there,
And if that ye have found it, ye that be here,
And seek to convey it secretly
Or else it will plain and then appair
But rather restore it mannerly
Since that I do ask it thus honestly
For to lose it it sitteth me too near
Help me to seek.

Alas, and is there no remedy
But I have thus lost it wilfully?
Iwis it was a thing all too dear
To be bestowed and wist not where:
It was mine heart! I pray you heartily,
Help me to seek.

The game caused quite a stir about court as people searched here and there, trying to find it. The idea was to ascertain who had the heart, and gain it from them. The heart could be either stolen by force, or won by a verse. The one who claimed the heart would then take it back to Tom, avoiding all others who might try to take it.

It may not surprise you that the little balloon was in my keeping. I gave it to Mary for a pretty verse of poetry; she guessed that I would have Tom's heart in my keeping almost on the instance that the riddle was given out. George stole it from her, then Francis Bryan stole it from George. Jane Parker managed to trick the heart from Bryan, and returned it to Tom as fast as her feet could carry her… And then it was her turn to hide the heart with another, and the games began all over again. It was not hard to guess that it was George she gave her heart to, and so the games went on.

It sounds like a childish game for fools, perhaps, but if so, then, we were happy fools. It was a merry game, and went on for many rounds before anyone tired of it. And then we would think of another, and another, and all the court came to play our games and watch our entertainments.

I felt stretched mentally for the first time since leaving Marguerite's side in France, and I smiled to think what she would make of our little writings next to her own works. The King's sister, Mary, was pleased to be a part of such groups, and we often took our little entertainments to be approved by her, knowing that in turn they would be approved by the King. I was working my way into the centre of a new era at the English Court, one where I could use all that I had learnt in France and Burgundy, to make this court shine as they did.

I ceased to feel so homesick for France, although I worried still about the coming war; instead my heart was filled with England. The weather was getting better; through May and June the sun was starting to appear… What wonder the sun can be to the spirits! Our rides into the forest started to include meals in the cover of the woods, a diversion which Mary of Suffolk seemed to have made popular in England, enjoying the fresh air and sunshine after months of being cooped up in dusty palace rooms. Fresh strawberries appeared in pies on our tables at court, and beef calves mewed in the fields. The skies around us seemed suddenly filled with bristling bees and floating butterflies and in the woodlands and marshes, the sound of the cuckoo rang out softly. It was a time both of gentleness and activity, where all of England seemed to have woken to beauty. I must admit that in the parks and woodlands I felt myself more at home than I would have thought possible.

There was one thing that spoiled this happiness, however, and that was the appearance at court of the man proposed to be my husband. It was not that he was bad of looks or seemed evil of temperament, but I still could not believe that I should be sent away to live in the wilds of Ireland. Especially at a time when I was just starting to truly love England. My father introduced us at a courtly disguising in the Great Hall at Windsor Castle, and sent us off to talk to each other. Since his arrival back in England, I had had but little time to talk with my father, and to allow him to understand my opposition to the match. And now, here I was, already being shunted away, being asked to converse with the man who in my eyes, would steal me away from a life I was just starting to enjoy.

James Butler was young, with thick red hair and a fine build. He had rosy cheeks which were often given to a faint blush and a broad but pleasant face. He had good wide shoulders and a muscular quality to him which I did not find displeasing. He walked with a limp, from an old wound taken at Therouanne, which caused some in Ireland to give him the name, in the Irish tongue, *Bocach*, or *the lame* in English. He had been at court for some time, but seemed somehow newer than I. He was constantly delighted with everything, and, from the sizzling looks he gave me from under the cover of his eyes, he was not averse to becoming my husband. He told me that I should grow to like Ireland and that there were many entertainments there that should satisfy my love for courtly pleasures.

"But there is no court," I said quite flatly.

He laughed. "Not such as there is here, no, but it is not quite the country of giants and rogues that you obviously imagine it to be." He laughed again at the expression on my face. "You shall grow to love it! I hear that you love to hunt; you will love Ireland and her game. And after we have started a family, there will be much to occupy you. I may be away a lot and therefore you will have the privilege of running my estates, raising my children and holding my lands for me when I am away."

I stood up, my heart pounding with anger. "You go too fast, Master Butler," I snapped, feeling panic rise within me. "There are but *talks* of our engagement, and yet you converse already of our children? We are not engaged and yet you talk idly of giving your Irish estates to me to defend from attack? Do I look to you like a warrior or general? I am none such. Do not rush ahead with all the details of our life, when nothing has been secured in truth!"

I was furious and spoke harshly to him. There were few men that would have taken my words as calmly as he did, for he took my hand and pleaded with me to sit. "There is fire in you, Anna Boleyn," he said and there was a sparkle in his eye and a roaming look to his gaze on my body that I understood well enough. I was sure he was already imagining the wedding night when I would have no choice but to subject myself to him in the debt of marriage. I am sure he thought he would tame my spirits, and well he might, if they were quashed in the wilds of Ireland. "The fire will serve you well in Ireland. Your pride does not displease me. I will be a good husband to you, I promise."

"*I* will need more time to consider such a match, Master Butler," I said stiffly. I caught my father's watchful eye on us, and steered the conversation to lighter matters; the weather and the roads… the dance… such subjects of conversation that would not endanger my hands to slap this man about the face for his presumption, and enrage my father with my behaviour.

When James left me, with a kiss to my hand since I would not offer my lips, my father came to me to ask my opinion of this potential husband.

"Does my opinion matter, my lord father?" my voice was measured and that of a smooth courtier even though my temper was ragged and frayed. "It is my family's choice that matters; I am but a humble daughter and will do as directed by those who know better than I."

I drank deeply from my cup of bright ale; its sweet crispness was comforting and as the liquid swept down my throat I looked up on to the beauty of the tapestries that decorated this great chamber in which we mingled, watching the others dance with happy faces by the light of the great torches. I swallowed the lump in my throat, which rose, threatening to choke me. I did not wish to leave England. It had just started to become my home.

My father looked at me. "They taught you that evasiveness in France, did they?" he asked with a wry smile. Not looking for an answer, he continued, speaking softly, for James Butler was not far away. "Then I shall tell you what you really think… as every father should be able to of his children. You think that Ireland is a rough place and no home for you," he said. "You think this Butler is a country-born clod and no man for you. You think that sending you to France and to Burgundy was a waste of time had you been destined for the fate of marrying an Irish lord to make Irish brats and live in the Irish bog."

I looked at him for although his face smiled and his voice was smooth as a serpent, I was suspicious; my father had shown me in the past that he could hold furious anger well. I did not wish to be flung against a fireplace as he had done to Mary all those years ago in France. "Bogs are not overly appealing to anyone, I believe, father" I said smoothly. "Unless they be toads."

There was a twitch around my father's mouth that looked for a moment as though he might laugh, but then it was gone. "The lands and titles of the Earls of Ormond are *ours* by right and by law, daughter. The marriage proposed between you and the Butler boy is a diplomatic way to solve the problem. It has allowed discussion of these titles to open with the King and Cardinal Wolsey, and that is to our advantage. But marrying you off to the Butlers is not the route that I shall be taking unless there is no other option. This talk of marriage is but a mask; in time, we will have what is truly ours by natural right, and I will not sacrifice the hand of my one unmarried daughter to gain it."

I looked at him sharply; there was hope in my heart suddenly. "We are rising well at court," my father continued. "Your sister is pleasing to the King, your brother is a growing friend to him too, and you have made a goodly impression on the court these few months that you have been here. Already you have been chosen above others for entertainments and, I see, all the women here are now dressed like you! There is not a gown that has not your sleeves, nor a headdress that does not look like you designed it. Everywhere I turn I see women aping you. That shows promise, child, even if these are just women's matters. And that shows that I was right to choose you for education abroad. You have done well with it. Your marriage will be greater even than Mary's, I am determined of that, and between you, George and Mary, greater wealth and prestige will come to our family. If I thought that the only way to gain the Ormond title was through your marriage to the Butler boy, then I would do so; but our star is rising here at court and we need not waste you on this marriage when we can amass that title by other means."

"You play chess with your children, father," I mused lightly. "I hope to be more useful than a mere pawn."

"And hence the delay in packing you off to Ireland," he ignored my last comment. "Besides," he said with a slightly puzzled look, "the King does not seem as enthusiastic now as he was for the match at first. It is strange, for I have said nothing to overly deter him and I know Wolsey has not either. Usually he listens to the Cardinal in all things... But now, His Majesty seems less interested in the idea, and without the support of the King..." He lifted his eyes to heaven. "Without the support of the King, a *loyal subject* such as I could not continue in good conscience with talks of such a match."

He smiled at me and his eyes seemed soft for once. "Worry not, daughter, we shall not waste you in the quagmire of Ireland... There will be better moves we can make with you."

I felt my heart race in pleasure. I nodded my head to him, but could not help but smile widely. I turned the smile to James Butler and waved a little at him, causing my father to grin, making him look like a lion who has just devoured its prey.

The treaty between England and Spain was agreed upon at Windsor. Henry agreed support for Charles in the war against France, stating that the French King had made it impossible for his nation to join with England; that François had gone against the old Treaty of London, and would not stand with Spain against the incoming threat of the barbaric Turks and their empire, which was already straining at Charles' outer empire. Henry of England and Charles of Spain agreed that they should stand united against this threat, and were honour-bound to defend the Church. If François refused to make peace, then war would be declared on France, until both parties had seized the territories to which they had ancient right. For Charles, there would be the old duchy of Burgundy and Italy, and for Henry, the lands of Gascony and Normandy, although all knew that Henry was hoping for the whole of France to be his, so that he could take the ancient right of the King of England, to be known also as the King of France.

Henry and Charles were to invade French lands; Henry's forces were to march from Calais towards Paris, and Charles' armies would invade from Spain. When France fell, it would be torn up and divided between the two Kings, like two dogs tearing at a deer carcass.

A second, more secret treaty was made, although all knew about it at court; that the Emperor would marry the Princess Mary in eight years' time. They tried to keep it a secret because of the political repercussions of the match; it meant that Henry of England was accepting he would have no son, and that Charles would one day become the King of England… But also, the Princess was at that time betrothed to the French Dauphin, something that might cause complications along the way. Charles promised himself to the little Princess, swearing to take her as a wife when she reached a marriageable age. The incongruous couple would require a dispensation from the Pope, seeing as they were related with a second degree of affinity, being cousins, but this would be petitioned for later, when the marriage became public knowledge. For his support for the match, and help with the negotiations, Charles promised Cardinal Wolsey something that meant more to the greedy Cardinal than anything else in the world; support in the next papal elections. Wolsey wanted to become the most powerful man in the Church, and possibly in the world... He wanted to become the Pope.

Henry invested Charles with the highest knightly honour in England, the Order of the Garter, in a grand ceremony in St George's Palace in Windsor. That evening, there was one of the greatest feasts we had ever known at court, and a few days later, Wolsey assembled a legatine court; acting as the papal legate, the Cardinal received the declarations of the Emperor and the King as though he were the Pope himself. If either of them broke from the terms of the treaty now, then it was understood they would be subject to the terrible possibility of excommunication from the Church. They were bound by God, by the laws of man, and by promise to each other, to go to war with France.

Chapter Ten

Windsor Castle
1522

It was at another entertainment, put on for the King of Spain in June, when I finally came to be presented personally to the King himself. Henry was the head of the court and of the country. He was constantly surrounded by people of his own choosing, and one did not approach the King uninvited. I had seen him often enough when he came to visit with the Queen, but his time then was taken up by with dining with her, talking with her, or on the rare times when he came in his night-shirt, escorted by his servants, by sleeping in her bed. When he came to the chambers of the Queen, she had eyes for him alone. The way in which she looked on her handsome husband was almost embarrassing; for the gentle calm of her face would give way to a kind of desperate hunger. We all knew that she hoped above all things to once more become with child by him, and this seemed to be the source of her desperate appetite for him. I found it a little distasteful; her want for Henry was so keen and clear that it was like a banner writ in blood and held over her tired, fattened body. Katherine loved him, of that I was sure, but it seemed that her desire for a child, a son, was her most keen and poignant wish.

The candles had been lit and the light of the approaching summer's sky had not yet fully retreated. Every night and day when Charles of Spain was here in England we had entertainments; jousting had gone on during the day, with Henry breaking the spears of all whom rode against him, and in the night, tumblers performed during the meal as we ate. Music was to be performed afterwards, as well as dancing. The tables of court were always heavy with food, as Henry liked to show his wealth at all times. We took from the shared platters of braised beef with *poudre fort*, tasted young rabbit cooked in a sauce that was both sweet with sugar and sour with wine vinegar. We spooned out portions of stewed mutton, spinach fritters, and roasted salmon. There was fine, fluffy white bread to soak up the sauce of venison pottage, flavoured with sage, hyssop and parsley. There was bright, expensive ale and there were good, rich wines with which to wash the courses down. After, there were fried fig pastries, peach marmalade, and huge fruit pies, dusted with sugar and decorated with the Tudor rose, the three-towered castle of Castile, and the Queen's own pomegranate badge. There were decorated salt cellars of silver, moulded into shapes of hunting dogs and royal lions, from which to dip salt onto one's plate, and fine linen cloth to use as napkins over one's left shoulder.

It was easy to over-eat here, to give in to the sin of gluttony, but I was a spare and sparse eater, and had been tutored well in Burgundy and France. Even if it had not been considered impolite and un-Christian to eat all the food before me, I still would not have done so. I had learned that too much food made the senses dull and too much wine led to danger, such as I had faced in France on that night when a man had tried to take me by force. But a little wine to loosen the senses and some foods to fire the body were enough for me. My waist was a thin as a whip, but my body was strong as a horse. Hours of dancing and hunting made my figure beautiful and lithe, and although I did not meet the English round-cheeked standard of beauty, my fine figure and small but raised breasts were far more attractive than their soft and lumpy bodies... So I thought, at least. It was generally considered to be a sign of nobility, to be a little rounded in the belly and the form, but in being slim and slight, I stood out more from the other women... and standing out was what mattered if one was to be noticed at court.

After the feast there came dancing and music; the trestle tables that we had dined upon were taken away, and the uneaten foods were taken as alms to the palace gates to feed the poor. I gathered myself and went to talk to the musicians, as I was to play and sing this evening along with other women of the court for the entertainment of the Emperor and our own King.

As I was readying myself, my father made his way to me and took me by the hand. "The King wishes to be introduced to you, daughter," he said, and there was an inference of something else in his eyes. Perhaps he hoped to have *two* daughters to grace the King's bedchamber… perhaps doubling the generosity of the sovereign to our family? I flushed at the thought, which my father took as feminine modesty upon being favoured by the King.

"That is good," my father nodded approvingly at my flushed cheeks. "The King likes to see that he creates a humbling impression on his subjects."

I flushed deeper, as though on command, and was led over to the great and imposing figure of Henry, King of England, who sat next to his queen and the Emperor at the head of the hall. Although I had seen him often enough around the court, and fleetingly as he had visited Katherine's chambers, I was taken aback by the brilliance that hit my eyes as I looked at him; dressed in rich red and cloth of gold, his hands covered in rings and diamonds winking from his coat, he was a dazzling figure.

Although he was older now than that young king I had spied on in Burgundy, he was no less handsome and his golden-red hair was bright and thick. He was a large man, so broad in the chest that I could think of no equal to him. And he was tall, standing head and shoulders over many other men. His legs, which I had heard he was proud of, were fine and strong and covered in close-fitting silk of deep, crisp white. Upon his head was a handsome cap decorated with feathers and jewels. His blue eyes sparkled as he watched my approach, and he looked at me with narrowed and interested eyes. I was dressed in a fine gown of rich greens; my hair was covered by the French-style hood that I always wore, but there was enough of it uncovered that anyone could see its fine sparkle and body. My skin was fresh and clear and I had youth in my blood.

I was but twenty-one years old when I was presented to the man who would later become my husband and my heart's true love… and eventually, my murderer.

My father brought me before this great King and my heart raced in my breast. Suddenly, all those thoughts and feelings that I had felt for him from afar, as a young girl, came flooding back. I curtseyed and looked up into his striking face; those blue eyes, bright as the sea on a clear summer's day, looked down into my black eyes and I saw his breath quicken as he took in my form and face. His eyes smouldered upon me as I stood before his awesome figure. He liked well what he saw before him; that was obvious from the first.

I looked up into the figure of the most glorious prince who had ever ruled our lands and I felt the power and charisma that extended from him; there was never another man to match him. Other rulers may have more lands, more wealth and more power, but none had the magnetism of Henry of England, nor his strikingly handsome face.

My mouth parted as though to speak, but my breath was stolen from my body by the look he gave me. There was a sense between us of attraction, so profound, so powerful… it called to him from me. I wanted him then as I had never known desire or want before. There was an aching feeling of want between my thighs and from my chest which seemed to speak to him. I was soft and ready for him at that moment and overwhelmed by my sudden lack of control. Had he taken my hand and led me to a chamber then and there, I should have been as eager for him as a starving man for meat. My mouth went dry and my heart pounded on the bars of my chest. I was overcome. He could see that, and it pleased him.

And all this occurred just an instant before I remembered that this man was my sister's lover, and the husband of my mistress! He was the King of my country. I swept to the floor in another curtsey to cover my embarrassment at being aroused. I felt like that girl at the balcony in Burgundy once more, caught in her first flush of attraction.

He smiled at me and spoke. The whole court was looking at him; he was always the focus of attention and would have been even if he were not the King, I think. "You are recently come to my court from France, so your father and my wife tell me, Mistress Boleyn," he said in a clear and strong voice, patting the arm of Katherine who sat beside him, smiling gently at me. She was dressed in a shade of surprisingly unbecoming purple, which made her skin look almost yellow. As a member of the royal wardrobe, I cared for Katherine's gowns, but a servant can never tell their master if something looks unbecoming on them. Katherine so often chose to wear regal colours, as was her station, but they were more often than not unbecoming to her, in truth.

On the other side of the King, sat Charles; his robes were of cloth of gold and royal purple. He looked magnificent, but even the fine cloth he wore could not detract from the length of his chin. He always seemed to try and duck his head slightly, as though trying to cover the pointing chin which protruded before him. Although he was younger than Henry, he was no match for him in looks, nor in bearing. The court had much whispered with amusement on the fact that Charles ate like a hog at feasts; lifting his fine pewter or silver plate right to his face, and shovelling food into his mouth as though he were a starving peasant. There, too, was something cold about Charles, just as there was something warm to the energy of Henry. Strange, is it not, that two Kings, both with great power, can seem so very different in the flesh. The young Emperor nodded to me, in greeting, as I looked to the blue eyes of Henry, feeling my heart race within me.

"Yes, Your Majesty," I swept my gown to the floor in another curtsey, this time directed at the Queen. "Her Majesty the Queen has allowed me a placement in her household, for which I am most honoured, for she is the best of women, and the kindest of mistresses."

The King smiled at Katherine and patted her hand once more. The Queen's gentle smile rained down on me; she was pleased with the manner of my expression, as was her nephew, who looked at her with eyes sparkling with happiness to see her honoured.

He looked at my father and beckoned him forward, which my father did with a bow. "One might call this treason, Thomas," King Henry declared with a deeply ominous tone that made my father look slightly panicked for a moment. "To keep such a beautiful English girl away from my court and give her to France instead!" Henry laughed, his face breaking from ominous darkness to light jesting in a moment. The court laughed with the King and my father looked relieved. Henry was obviously a changeable man. Even my father, who was so good at reading people, had been unsure that the King's talk of treason was a jest when he first spoke it.

"We are glad to see you home, Mistress Boleyn," Henry continued. "And home to stay I think, eh, Thomas?" The royal eye flashed a wink towards my father, which I presumed had something to do with the Butler match and the King's present lack of enthusiasm for it.

"It pleases us to see you home, Mistress Boleyn," Henry turned his smile on me. "I am happy to have such an ornament with which to grace my court. Your father tells me that you are a good musician, with a sweet voice, and this pleases me, as I love music and song. You will play for us, and for my nephew, this evening?"

I was already due to play for the court, and sing, and so I nodded to the King, and then added, "Of course, if Your

Majesty wishes." I smiled up at him. "But it must be on one condition."

The King looked a little taken aback; he was not used to conditions, only obedience. My father, too, looked shocked, and his hand came out slightly, touching my arm, as though to draw me back from the Henry's presence before I could say aught else to shame our family. But I knew well enough that kings are men, like all others, and I curtseyed before him again. "No true knight would refuse the request of a lady." My voice was sure, steady and lightly teasing, yet my face was all innocence and purity.

Henry laughed suddenly, gazing down on me with more interest even than before. "What is this condition of yours, Mistress Boleyn?" he asked. "For it is correct that as a true knight, I must listen to the requests of fair maidens when set before me." His eyebrows were raised and there was a playful look of delight on his face; he loved to play the knight, as though he were King Arthur of old, and I were Guinevere.

"Then I request the condition that you, too, play this night for the court, sire," I said. "I heard stories of your great talent at the Court of France, and I was honoured to play a song of your own composition, at the *Field of the Cloth of Gold,* when I served Queen Claude there. It would be a great pleasure to hear that of which I have heard so much, and yet have never experienced."

With my teasing jests, I felt more in control of my emotions than when I had first come to stand before this king. And I felt more in control of him, in some ways. I had gambled with my bold talk, yet I felt as though my wager had been a safe one, for it seemed that I understood his mettle well. From the way he was smiling at me, I knew that there was no danger that my father would be displeased in me. That thought, along with Henry's dancing bright eyes, made me feel even bolder. The King smiled and his blue eyes softened as he looked on me; there was something there between us, I could feel it. I felt as though I understood his boyish heart, and I knew that I had pleased him through flattery and mischief. It is not often that kings find surprise in the world any more; I think he found me refreshing.

Henry laughed heartily, and even the dour Charles smiled. I could almost hear my father's inward sigh of relief that I had not disgraced our family with my boldness. "You heard of my playing in France?" Henry asked, shaking his head. "Then perhaps the French do listen to something other than the *amours* of the heart after all, eh?" He looked about him and the Queen smiled softly at her husband. "I *shall* play then this evening, Mistress Boleyn, to please you."

The court cheered, sycophantically, Henry moved his hand to hush them. "After all," he said looking deep in my eyes. "I would not deny any pleasure to you… that I was able to give."

I felt a little flush reach over my cheeks, and for a moment, Katherine's face seemed to freeze. I saw her jaw twitch slightly, and then she resumed the gentle smile that she wore for the eyes of the court. I lowered my head and curtseyed again. "Thank you, Your Majesty," I murmured.

Chapter Eleven

Windsor Castle
1522

My father led me back to the musicians and gave me a single nod, denoting that I had done well, and then a slight shake of the head, indicating that I had perhaps also almost given him a fit of apoplexy. He walked off, leaving me to allow a little smile to dance about my lips as I watched his back retreat through the crowds. It was rather satisfying to catch my wily father off-guard.

As I readied myself for the performance, my heart was racing and my fingers felt like sticks of wood. I breathed in and out deeply, steadying my nerves with the well-practised methods I had used over and over in the years I had performed at court functions. I took up the lute in my hands and readied myself. I had danced for this court, and now they would hear my voice. It was a beautiful one, and I was most proud of it. Years of training in Burgundy and France had allowed my once-raw talent to be shaped and moulded into a high, sweet and true voice that flew along the edges of notes with clarity and timbre.

I finished the first measure of *The Agincourt Carol*, accompanied only by the lute I held in my arms, and then as I took up the next chorus, the other two female voices, those of Margaret and Bridget, came in with mine and male voices, George amongst them, took up the bass line. It was an old song, and a haunting one, of the great victory of the English over the French during the reign of Henry V. I knew that the song would appeal to Henry's taste for war, and to the general court sentiment of anti-French feeling as the negotiations between the Spanish and the English progressed. This was why George and I had chosen it. It was a clever move. The song needed little accompaniment. I sang the main verse, and the others joined me upon the chorus giving praise to God. It went thusly:

Our King went forth to Normandy,
With grace and might of chivalry
There God for him wrought marvellously
Wherefore England may call and cry:

Deo gratias:
Deo gratias Anglia redde pro Victoria!

He set a siege, the truth to say
To Harfleur town with royal array
That town he won, and made a fray
That France shall rue 'till Doomesday

Deo gratias:
Deo gratias Anglia redde pro Victoria!

Then went our King with all his host,
Through France, for all the Frenchmen's boast;
He spared no dread of least or most
'Till he came to Agincourt coast.

Deo gratias:
Deo gratias Anglia redde pro Victoria!

Then, forsooth, that knight comely,
In Agincourt field he fought manly;
Through grace of God most mightily
He had both field and victory.

Deo gratias:
Deo gratias Anglia redde pro Victoria!

There duke and earl, lord and baron
Were taken and slain, and that well soon,
And some were led into London

With joy and mirth and great renown.

Deo gratias:
Deo gratias Anglia redde pro Victoria!

May gracious God He keep our King
His people that are well willing
And give him grace without ending
Then we may call and safely sing:

Deo gratias:
Deo gratias Anglia redde pro Victoria!

Poignant, politically safe and polished, we came to the counterbalanced end that hung on the last lingering note. As we finished, the people of the court stood silent for a moment, and then broke into loud applause. I smiled at George; we had much amazed them, and so our plans had worked. I looked up and saw that Henry, too, was clapping his hands with great enthusiasm. He turned to Charles, saying something I could not hear, and the young Emperor smiled, clapping his hands in a slightly more measured way than our own King. Henry's eyes sparkled with pleasure and his eyes were fixed on my face. Henry was deeply moved by music, and I knew that we had chosen a good song which had pleased him. We rose and bowed and returned to our places.

I was flushed with pleasure and success. As I joined the throng, Tom Wyatt slid in beside me. "It would seem," he said in a low voice as he handed me a pewter goblet of wine, "that your shameless flattery of the King may have added a royal admirer to your growing crowd!"

I went to cuff him, but he danced free of my ready hand, laughing. "Just forget not those who have long admired you and will always do so," he said softly as he came back to my side.

"I will never forget my *friends*, Tom." I looked into his handsome fine-boned face, feeling a little regret not for the first time that he could only ever be my courtly admirer. "And it was but one line of flattery I offered. You should know how little store I set by such."

"Ah, but the King *does*, you see..." Tom grinned at me, whispering. "He believes himself great in many ways and the flattery of the court is but truth to his ears." Tom inhaled deeply as Henry took up the central platform to perform amid the shouts and cheers of the court. "Although," Tom said grudgingly, "I will say this honestly; that the King is a fine musician and there are few that can match him."

"Indeed?" I asked, interested, for what I had said before the King was just court flattery.

"Oh yes," Tom looked over as Henry readied himself to play. "He has a great talent for music, although I would add, and add quietly to only you, that his playing is better than his poetry." I stifled a giggle; were we to be overheard by unfriendly ear, such words could get us in a lot of trouble. Tom smirked at me, even as his sister Margaret opened her eyes wide and shook her head in warning at him.

Henry began his song; his fingers, large and broad though they were, flew like the most delicate and quick of birds over the notes of his song. His voice was rich and deep, it was true to each note, and his range was broad. His light touch upon the nine-stringed lute was matched by the masculine depth of his voice. There was passion in his voice as he sung a song of love and knighthood. It was not a song I had heard, but evidently all at court had, as some were tapping feet and murmuring along with the song as he sang it. The rest of the hall was silent and all eyes and attention were for Henry only. I looked about the hall and saw that people were captivated by him; this king who looked so like a warrior and yet sung like the very poet of love. It was beautiful, it was good, and with a slightly rueful heart I knew it was better than that which I had sung before.

As Henry finished, the court burst into applause, and as I joined in, I glimpsed Queen Katherine on her dais. Her hand was poised on the arm of her chair, and she seemed not to notice the words of flattery her nephew was whispering to her. Her face was so alive suddenly, applauding her husband; this golden sun-king who contrasted so sharply with her wasted appearance. It was as though Henry had taken all the life of the two, and she was left with all the semblance of decay. But now, watching him, it was as though light and love had come into her again, like the rays of the first dawn creeping into a darkened room. She truly loves him, I thought, it could be no clearer to me than it was now. She drew life from him; he was the source of her happiness, such as it was… With her husband, she still knows joy in this life. The thought made me sad, slightly. Perhaps it was a sense of pity for her. For however much Katherine might adore her handsome, younger husband, it was clear that her feelings were not reciprocated in kind. Respect her, he may well do… need her, in this coming treaty, he did… but love? I wondered. Perhaps it had once been there between them, but after all the years they had been married, I wondered if he still loved her as he was supposed to have done when they were first wed. He, certainly, did not look at her with the same eyes that she had for him. He looked on her kindly… calmly… She looked on him with fire and love.

Poor Katherine, I thought then… for it is poor to be the one who loves more than the other will give. There is poverty in such love; she must beg love of him. They were not equals, however much they might look the part on their dais, for he did not love her as she loved him. What sadness there was to be found in marriage… even when one finds love… if it is not returned in kind, I thought.

I shook myself of such ponderous and sad thoughts. At the end of the hall I saw the swift movement of court servants, who had tarried at the doors to hear their King's singing; they disappeared quickly in case anyone should see them at rest from their work. I saw the lightened look on the faces of the people around him. Henry was loved, greatly, by his people, and this was something that despite everything that happened in later times, he would never lose. He always had that ability to make those around him care for him, adore him.

After Henry had returned to his chair and the cheering had subsided, a group of singers came on to sing the country song *Bring us in Good Ale* which was received well. A rougher song; it was far less elegant than those tunes that had gone before, but the men loved to hear it, as it was a song that they could sing along to without needing to be able to sing well. Charles Brandon, Duke of Suffolk, sang boisterously along with the others, banging his pewter goblet on his hand. His wife, Mary Tudor, looked on this behaviour with a little frown. I wondered if at times she found him as crass as I did.

I was still captivated by the echoes of Henry's song in my heart. Tom's words had been true; there were no princes I had heard sing that could match him, not even the cultured François. There were few men I had ever heard who were the match of him. I loved music, and song; they were a part of my spirit as were the beats of my heart and the flowing of my blood. I admired Henry greatly for his talents and for his voice. A feeling of warmth opened in my heart, knowing that we shared a passion. Now he sat, flushed with pleasure at his queen's side and still I felt that feeling, that compelling feeling, drawing me to him. Quite simply, Henry, King of England, was the most attractive man I had ever met, not only in his looks, but in his talents. I once again flared with jealousy towards my sister who shared his bed. I wondered what they talked of in private. Did they talk of songs and music? Did he play for her? Had that song of love been for her? I believe I liked him even more, to find that we enjoyed something in common, and that thought made my heart throb with the pangs of envy for my sister.

I shook myself slightly; these were fool's thoughts and I was no fool. It mattered little that I desired him; most women in the world must desire him after all. He could not be mine. He already had a wife and a mistress... what could I be to him? Another mistress? That was not what I wanted. I sighed a little inwardly. Tom... The King... both were attractive to me, and both were entirely distant from my grasp. Was I only to meet and be attracted to men that I could not have as my own? And when I was presented with a possible husband, such as James Butler... was I only to be presented with situations in life I wanted not? My sister had a husband she liked, a lover she enjoyed, *and* she had a place at court, where I wished to stay! Although I did not want to be a mistress, I found jealousy's sharp little teeth tearing into my flesh. My sister had two good men, and I had none. Where was the man to whom I could be free to release my heart? Perhaps he did not exist. Perhaps my expectations were too high. I looked at Katherine again. Would I too, some day, look on my own husband with such eyes of desperate adoration? Should I not be happy to take what my father and family decided for me, and hope for the best, as so many had done?

But there was yet something within me that seemed to whisper comfort to me. It told me that there would come a time when I would love, and not fear to give my heart to one who deserved it. There would be a man with whom I would not have to compromise either my own wishes, or my virtues to have... one day, there would be a man for me.

I must marry; it was the way of things. If I did not find myself a suitable husband, then one would be found by my father, and I could not predict where *his* ambitions might send me... No, *I* must find a man whom I could truly love, and marry with... a match that would keep me here in England, and a match that my father would allow me to take.

I danced with Tom that evening in a pre-occupied way that I believe he noticed, although he paid no comment to it. After the dance he asked me to walk with him in the private gardens. I hesitated. Warning memories of France, and the monster who tried to take what I would not give freely, sounded in my mind like cannon fire. But I consented to walk with him near to the parties of people in the centre of the gardens who were playing music and singing still. My brother was close by, and although I trusted Tom, I was more careful now than I had ever been when I was a young girl. Close to the others we should stay.

Tom took my hand in his as we walked out through the scented knot gardens of Windsor; the gardens were designed for pleasure, modelled on the French gardens at Bloise. I allowed my hand to remain in his; it was warm and had comfort to it.

"Anne, do you believe that love exists between men and women despite the restraints of society and rank?" he asked softly as we wandered.

"Yes," I sighed a little, "although even if it exists it is not always possible."

Tom looked out over the garden. The light of the moon was not full, but nearly so; it made his handsome face silver in its light, like a statue of old. "And for you and me?" He turned his eyes from mine, even as he asked, because he already knew my answer.

"No," I said softly. "Not because it is not possible, but because you could never be mine in truth."

Tom turned to me and grabbed me suddenly, with force, and turned my lips to his. Although my feet prepared for flight at his sudden movement, the gentleness with which he held me, as his lips sought the feeling of mine, caused me to stay. Tom did not hold aggression towards me, I could feel that... Love, passion, urgency, yes... But there was nothing in him that screamed fear and flight to me. He wanted me, yes... But he wanted me to want him in return. He would not force himself on me. He loved me; I knew that then, perhaps for the first time, in truth… beyond his impish ways, and the games of the court. But he respected me too much to try and steal from me what he could not win. He was a different type of man from the beast that had sought to ruin me in the gardens of France.

Tom's kiss was lingering and sudden. I found my hands reaching behind his head and running through his fine thick hair as he kissed me. His hands remained; one at my waist and one that ran through my hair under my hood. But his hands did not threaten to move elsewhere upon my body. As his mouth and beard stroked my lips, I felt a tingle of excitement leap through me and for a moment, I pressed closer to him, willing on the feeling of exhilaration and abandon which rose within me. But as I felt his body stiffen in response to my movement, and felt the pressure of his hands grow on my flesh, I released myself from him and stepped resolutely back from his arms. I could not continue the kiss, it was unfair. I was shaking a little, partly I think with desire, but partly also with some fear. My experience in France had made me wary, and caused me to fear such a close encounter with a man. Tom was breathing hard, too, and staring at me with a pleading look. He went to step forward, but I held up my hands before me.

"It is not possible, Tom… What you want from me can never be," I shook my head. "You are married, you have a son, and all I could be is your mistress… That is not enough for me."

He sighed and sat down heavily on a bench. "What would you have me do Anna?" he asked wearily. "I am separated from my wife; she dallies with all kinds of men. I am a common man and cannot do more than leave her. I cannot divorce her, even if I had proof of her adultery, for her family have such a powerful hold over me. Few men can leave their wives at all. She was chosen for me by my family. I did not choose her, my heart did not choose her… My heart has chosen *you*!" He sighed again and ran his fingers through his hair. "For God's sake, Anna… I have never felt like *this* about any person before. I doubt if there are more than a few living who have ever felt this way about another person. I cannot think of anything but you. You are in my dreams as you are in my heart. I love you. It is torture to know that you do not feel the same way that I do."

I shook my head and sat beside him. "I *cannot* feel the same way, Tom, because if I allowed myself to love you, it would lead to naught but my own ruin. My reputation, my honour, my chances at marriage… they would be destroyed. Yours would not, for it seems that morality and virtue are only issues when they rest on the shoulders of women. I will lose *myself* in gaining your love. I cannot love you, and give up myself. Can you not see that?" I sighed. I could explain nothing clearly, it seemed, to Tom.

"For a woman of much wit and intelligence, that was the most convoluted nonsense I have ever heard," he mumbled. I looked at him and there was a half-smile on his face, which was just about covering the bitter twist of his mouth as I refused him and his love.

"Do you understand what I mean though, Tom?" I asked. "All I could be to you would be your mistress, and I will not be that. You can offer me nothing more, and that is the way of things. If I were to give in to you, and become your mistress in truth, then I would be untrue to myself, and that is not love. Love cannot ask a heart to be untrue to its own self. Do you not see? I cannot love a man and leave all that is *me* behind in loving him; there must be some Anne Boleyn left in any love I have, or it is not love, it is only possession. I cannot be other than what I am, and to love without my own honour is something I could never do. You are my friend, Tom. And that is how it will stay. We are not meant for each other."

He nodded. "And if my wife went to a nunnery? Or died?"

A chill fell over me and I looked sharply at him. There was nothing in that charming face that made me suspect him capable of what his words seemed to suggest. People often died before their natural course of life was through, and yet... did Tom mean something else with that question? Would he be willing to remove his wife, by some means? I thought not, surely, but in the moonlight, there fell a wolfish expression onto his fine angular face and I drew back from him.

He noticed and raised his eyebrows. "You would think me a murderer now?" he asked lightly. I shook my head, although I was still not certain.

"I have not the slip of the soul required for cold-blooded killing, Anna," he said ruefully, his tone returning to jest. "Although, give me a few years of being under your heel, and I might consider it, just to release myself of my present pain."

I laughed a little, even though, in truth, I had little heart for it. Tom reached towards me and took hold of the jewelled tablet I wore at my waist on a ribbon. It was a pretty thing, made of gold and pearls with our family's crest on it. My mother had loaned it to me when I was a child, to wear to the coronation of the King and I had begged her to allow it to remain with me, because I admired it so much. I had kept it with me all these long years, and worn it often. It was precious to me. "Give me this," he pleaded softly. "So that I may remember well this night, when you all but said you would love me, were it not for the rest of the world getting in our way."

I unclasped the pendant and gave it to him. Although it meant a great deal to me, he looked wounded, and I wanted to ease his pain. Thomas put the tablet in his pocket and took my hand again. We were silent as we walked back to the others in the garden. George, Henry Norris and Francis Bryan were singing a soft, sad song by the moon's light as ladies of the court looked on, and, as we reached them, Thomas and I both joined in; the sorrow of the song reflecting the sadness in our hearts for something lost that had never been allowed to begin.

I had many courtly admirers in my time, but Thomas Wyatt loved me as true as any man loved a woman. I knew the difference between false flattery and honest devotion. But I could not love him as he loved me. All he could offer me was the place of a mistress, and I did not want that, no matter what my heart whispered to me in the darkness as I fell into the arms of sleep. I had feelings for Tom, yes... and I struggled with them then... But they were not like the feelings which came to me later... with the man who would finally claim my heart and make me believe that anything in this world can be overcome, with the might of true love. That knowledge, that awareness, came to me later in my tale...

In early July, the Emperor Charles left England for Spain from the docks of Southampton. A fleet of one hundred and eighty ships carried him and his entourage, and it took two days of near-chaos to arrange their departure. The Bay of Biscay was calm, for once, and Charles arrived in Spain happy to have a new ally in his war against France. For Henry, there was the possibility that he would one day wear the mantle of the King of France, and for Wolsey, there was the possibility that he would one day rule over the Church as Pope.

But the future power each man would hold had come at a price... and all at court secretly knew that we had just said a farewell to the man who may well, one day, become the King of England.

Chapter Twelve

Richmond Palace
1522

Months passed and, much to my relief, nothing further had been said on the matter of the proposed union with James Butler. This silence on the matter seemed, however, to distress the young man himself. James still seemed eager for the match, and kept his attentions to me alive at court; often asking me to partner him at dances and trying to walk with me to talk. But there was a distinct lack of anything approaching effort on my father's side towards completing the match, which really should have been sign enough to everyone who knew him that he favoured it not. It seemed also that the King was not in the mood to discuss the matter further, and Wolsey seemed, too, to have cooled on his enthusiasm for the match. My father believed that Henry was considering granting on him the title of Earl of Ormond, and all that title's holdings, *without* the match; but we waited daily for some news to come either from Mary, or from our father. We waited in vain.

I was, however, overjoyed to find that support for a marriage between James Butler and I had cooled. In my relief at not having to face a life in far-off Ireland, I felt a carefree and somewhat wild exhilaration come upon me. This was somewhat tempered by sorrow for Tom. I could not reciprocate his feelings of love for me, and although I had made this clear, his attentions continued. I offered him my friendship, and position as a courtly admirer, which was all I was willing to give, but he would always want more of me. This was perhaps the first man I knew who had truly loved me. All other admirers had been just that; admirers. They admired me and courted me, but it was just part of the game to them. Tom was the first man who I think loved me for who I was… But I could not give my heart to him. He wrote poetry for me, including a riddle that he gave to others at court and challenged them to find the answer:

What word is that which changeth not,
Though it be turned and made in twain?
It is mine answer, God it wot,
And eke the causer of my pain.
It love rewardeth with disdain:
Yes is it loved. What would ye more?
It is my health eke and my sore.

Tom was a clever poet, and the riddle caused a stir at court as all were trying to work it out. Although it accused me of disdain in the face of love, I liked the poem and laughed when I worked out the answer was *Anna*. I complimented Tom on his work, and yet remained aloof from his continued protestations of love for me. I had given my answer and could offer him no more.

Despite such complications as a jilted would-be lover and a jilted would-be husband, life at court was increasingly sweet to me. The spring cold had dissipated and the true summer had arrived, bringing with her fine long days and warmer nights. Wheat and barley grew golden in the fields and the songs of the field-workers tarried late into the evenings. Harvest time was coming close, bringing hard work and good toil for the common man. Soft cheeses became a part of almost every meal at court, and we waited for the tang of the cheeses still ripening in their moulds to come to our lips. The court's council broke for summer, and hunting of grouse started in the moorland amongst the purple flowering heathers.

The festivities at court ran on late into the evenings and when one arose for Mass in the mornings there was sunshine in the Churches, replacing the chill gloom and mist of the months in which I had first arrived. I read from my own book of devotions, feeling the warmth of God as I read. Many people brought their own devotional books to Mass, for often the priests rambled on in unintelligible and inarticulate Latin, but I had to hide the words of some of my books, for they included such works as *De Maria Magdalena et triduo Christi disceptatio*, by Jacques Lefevre; a work, amongst others I owned, which was deeply controversial. It had been condemned by many leaders in the Church, including John Fisher, once the chaplain of Margaret Beaufort, the King's grandmother. Fisher was Bishop of Rochester, and had once been a tutor of theology to the King. Such men were not to be made enemies of in the court.

I could have simply listened to the droning of the priests at court, but I chose to read of other things and encounter other thoughts. My time with Marguerite had taught me not to close my mind to new thoughts, and even though I was removed from her circle, which I still missed, I would not abandon her teachings. I spoke Latin, yet what some of the priests spoke sounded to me more like nonsense. If I could barely understand them, and I understood the language, then what hope did the common people have of understanding the word of God through the priests of this land? My own French works of theology, even the more moderate ones that I did not hide, were looked on as a little scandalous; most people read their religious texts in Latin. I was no heretic, but I understood the sense, as Marguerite had in France, of the word of God being available to people in their own language. It was not an idea the Church was happy with at all, but it made sense to me, and to many others. If the priests could not be trusted to transfer the word of God to His people in an understandable way, then the people of God should be given the chance to understand it by themselves. The Church called this heresy, but I thought it was just good sense.

The Church feared, I knew, that if the common man were able to read and interpret the word of God for himself, then there would be less use for priests and bishops, for cardinals and popes. This frightened the men of the Church who drew power from control, but it also limited their understanding of the amazing good that might come if the whole world were able to truly understand the word of God. They were blinded to goodness, I thought, for fear of losing their power. But such power was not granted to them to keep all other children of God in the darkness. If they had a real care for the people, then they would have supported the notion of translating the Bible and other works into the vernacular.

I did not often voice my opinions on this subject aloud. It was dangerous to do so, as hostile eyes may turn on one who is outspoken in the defence of practises thought by the Church to be heretical. But in my private circles, especially with George, who was of the same mind as me, I did raise opinion on the matter.

How can one call something heresy, if it can bring a person closer to understanding God? I also believed that the Church needed to make certain reforms. The scandal of selling indulgences, and the many worldly vices of many priests, monks and nuns required attention. In order for the Church to hold itself as holy, and close to God, it must be without stain of sin, which it was not at this moment. The wealth of the Church should be used to ease the suffering and to educate scholars, whereas now it was hoarded in the coffers of cardinals and bishops. New ideas should be listened to, and some embraced, such as offering the word of God to His people in their own language. Trust must be set between the word of God and His own people.

When I sat in church each morning and afternoon, and said my prayers in the evenings, I prayed to God that the Pope and his cardinals would come to embrace the thoughts of His people having a closer union with Him, and in so doing, allow a greater light to enter their lives through His Grace. The Bible was the source of all true authority in my eyes, and I understood those thinkers who believed that redemption from sin was achievable through the loyalty of faith, and the grace of God alone. I saw the sense in putting faith ahead of ritual, as many Lutherans wrote of, for in truth, the Church had become awash with false ritual, for reasons of profit. But whilst I saw and understood all of these things, I did not consider myself to be a Lutheran. The Church required reform; it had done so in the past, and may do again in the future. It was up to us, as the children of God, to work towards a time when the new ideas of faith could be united with the old, and each benefit from such a marriage of minds.

My father had many men, such as Master Reyner Wolf and others, on the continent who sought out new books by learned thinkers on such subjects as these, and he shared them with George and me. We kept these books secret, just as I had done in France, for to be caught with any of them was to enter into a great deal of trouble. Many of the volumes my father procured for us to read had been banned by the Church, and so George and I, with others of the court who held the same views, met in secret to discuss them. We kept our books well-hidden when they were not on our person. My mistress, Katherine, would have dismissed me from her service in as much time as it takes a colt to leap, had she found me with works she considered heretical and against the laws of God.

But court life was not all shadow and secret. Soon enough, there was a lighter time for me. It came with a new face at court. His name was Henry Percy, the young heir to the Earldom of Northumberland. He was new at court, I knew, for I would have quickly noticed such a handsome, and yet innocent, face as his. He had been sent to serve in the household of Cardinal Wolsey. He had the air of a boy about him and this I found most appealing. I was so used to cultured gallants of the court who flattered and danced their way into the hearts of maidens and matrons. But Percy was different. He had an air of truthfulness about him which many would have called naïve, and perhaps he was; but he was refreshing to me. He was tall and broad of shoulder… and almost from the first day of his arrival I noticed that he could not take his eyes away from me.

Think not that this is reckless flattery of myself; by this time I was enveloped in the centre of an exciting group of people at court. Tom and my brother George were great wits and their merry ways attracted people to them like wasps to fresh-baked fruit tarts. Margaret, Bridget and I were at the centre of many court entertainments and I was often chosen to sing, dance or perform in pageants alongside my sister and Jane Parker. We were amongst the best dancers and often came up with new and witty entertainments. The King chose more and more often to be present in our lively throng with his sister whenever she was at court rather than at her family seat at Suffolk Palace, or Westhorpe. Mary of Suffolk had lost her eldest son, Henry, earlier that year, at the age of only five, and his loss weighed heavy on her, even though she never failed in her duties to her brother during the visit of the Emperor. When she was at court, however, she tried to cast off her sorrows and make light of life. It must have been hard, but she knew her brother's spirit well; he did not like to be surrounded by sadness. Henry loved to be in the most interesting place at court, but it also gave him every excuse to be near to my beautiful sister with little observed scandal.

I was a new and rising star in this band of poets, wits and dancers and I found myself happy and content. I thought of France now and then with a pang of homesickness, but my present life was so filled I had little time to remember my old life with sorrow. Our father was satisfied with our progress and situation at court, and was pleased to see that his children were making such an impression on the King. I was free of the yoke of marriage to Butler, even if James knew it not, and I had admirers courting me. I was flushed with happiness and my eyes sparkled to think of the day ahead as I rose each morning. This was the Anne Boleyn that Henry Percy first saw when he came to court; this wild and happy girl, free from care and rising in the estimations of the court, her family and the King. It was an exhilarating mixture… that I see now, looking back. There is no treatment more conducive to true beauty, than knowing the joy of a happy soul. When Percy first saw me, he saw the lady Anne who shone like a star at the centre of the court, and when I first saw him, I was indeed drawn to his innocence, and the truthful nature of his boyish heart.

Henry Percy was heir to one of the greatest seats in the country; when his father died he would be the Earl of Northumberland, an ancient and great title. The house of Northumberland had been the wardens of the north for as long as any could remember, but their influence had waned slightly after the civil wars between the houses of York and Lancaster. The Earl of Northumberland had tried to return his house to a position of prominence, but his efforts had made the King somewhat distrustful of him. Percy was brought to court perhaps in the same way as my erstwhile suitor, James Butler, had been; to secure the Earl of Northumberland's loyalty through the King's possession of his son at court. But even with these issues surrounding them, the Percy family were still most important, and potentially, very powerful if they could secure the love of the King upon them. I had lived all my life within the bounds of courtly life; the attraction of such power was not lost on me. Although my sister may profess that she chose to take the King's bed for the man himself, I was more pragmatic. After all, part of the man *was* his position; part of the man *was* the sphere in which he moved, the influence he wielded. It was not wrong to desire a man's power, as it was not wrong to desire a man for his good looks. They were all part of the things that made him as a person. When Henry Percy of Northumberland cast his boyish and open face in my direction then, I will admit that it was not only the handsome man I saw, but an interesting opportunity for a good and safe future. Was I wrong to think thus? To consider that such a match might bring power and influence to me also? Women are used as bargaining tools in the world of men often enough. Should I not think on a future I could devise for myself in the same manner?

Percy was slow in becoming a part of our throng. He tarried on the edges of our group at dances and when we walked out through the gardens. But eventually he dared to come forward at an evening's dance. Percy stepped into conversation with George, whom I gathered he knew fairly well since the households of the King and the Cardinal were often together. Percy then conversed with Tom and Henry Norris, and finally came towards me. His eyes had been glancing at me the whole time and everyone noticed it, and they were laughing at him, thinking that perhaps the sharp-tongued Mistress Anne would slice poor Percy into marmalade. Tom was concealing a smile behind his laced sleeve and Mary was agog with the future giggles she should have to share with me. I smiled politely at the approach of the young nobleman, excusing myself from speaking with Bridget, who was once more heavy with child. Although Percy was of an age with me, he seemed so much younger. His eyes were hazel and the beard on his face was short. His clothes were of the finest, as one would expect from an Earl's son, and he wore them with the carelessness of one who has always had the best of everything, and may always expect to. He was broad and quite tall and looked strong. He was attractive, yes, and I was pulled to his boy-like manners and the blush upon his cheeks as he stepped forward to me.

"I would ask for your hand to dance, Mistress *Boulain*," he said, saying my name the way that Margaret of Austria had done when she named me *La Petite Boulain*. It made me warm to him.

"You shall require more than my hand of me, should you wish to dance, my lord," I said smiling. Bridget snorted a giggle, and the others around us laughed merrily as Percy blushed deeper. But he looked into my eyes again with a good-natured smile on his lips; other men might have resented such a jest, but not he.

"Then, may I be so bold as to request the whole of you, Mistress Sharp-tongue?" he asked.

"*Even* the sharp tongue?" I smiled at him, rather liking the flush on his cheeks. It made his eyes bright and warm.

"I would not do without it," he said, reaching out to take my hand.

"I'd take the tongue too!" a voice yelled from the back of the crowd and the people around me burst into roars of laughter at the jest. No one took such things too seriously; although the rules of the game of courtly love dictated respect, the rules of the court did not and most jests were bawdy. We all thought little of it then, but there would come a time when all men would learn to guard their tongues.

Percy took my hand and led me out for the next dance. It was a French *pavanne*; slow and sonorous. My hanging sleeves always made my figure look its best when I danced such dances. My waist was thin and each slow turn of my body and clap of my hands called attention to the finery and distinction of my clothes. My toes tapped across the floor with the grace of one who has been dancing all her life. Around my neck there hung a new adornment that I had designed and my father had had made for me: golden letters in the shape of my initials *AB* which hung from a long double string of tiny pearls. Pearls were my favourite jewel as they complimented my skin and dark hair.

Thus I was when first I danced with Henry Percy. He was a fine dancer, better than I had expected from the manner of his bearing. He was elegant despite his tall stature and light of foot despite his broad shoulders. I was impressed, and I was a harsh critic of the skills of others in the dance. As the dance ended he led me back to my friends and released me. "I hope to claim the whole of you once again, Mistress *Boulain*," he said, softly kissing my hand. "For the whole of you is more enticing than even I had imagined."

I blushed, feeling suddenly like a child in my happiness. "I hope you shall claim both me and my hand once more, my lord," I felt my heart race a little faster. "My tongue I shall speak to on your behalf and I will remind it that as you are now our friend, it needs must be gentle with you."

His eyes widened and he bowed looking very pleased. I was amazed at how easily he allowed his emotions to ride over his face. There was no guile in this young man at all. It was uplifting. And I realised that I liked him even more for it. Tom slid over to me once Percy had wandered back to his crowd. "It is *nice* of you indeed, Mistress Boleyn," he said, with a sly note in his voice.

I sighed; I had been enjoying the aftermath of pleasure that Percy's words and dance had offered me. It was an invigorating and pleasing sense of happiness without court games or guile, which had put a feeling almost akin to homesickness in my heart and belly. This feeling was reminiscent of childhood, a *longing* for the innocence that had once been ours. That was the feeling that Percy had granted me, and I liked it. But now, Tom was here and I could smell the jealousy on his breath as he spoke to me. I sighed because I knew that he was going to try to spoil the lovely feeling I had from Percy. Tom was jealous; he wanted me to be his. I found his jealousy of Percy to be rather unattractive, and wished he was away from me. It was the first time, perhaps, that I had come to think ill of Tom.

"What is nice of me, Master Wyatt?" I asked curtly.

"Nice of you to rock the cradle of a youngling just come to court," he said with a smile dancing on his lips. "Will you soon to be showing the whelp how to button his shirts also?"

The throng around us burst into laughter at Percy's expense. Margaret shook her head at her brother, even though she tittered. I smiled too; the mischief in Tom's eyes was infectious, but I was not going to allow him to get away with insulting a man I admired so easily. As the laughter drew to a close I spoke. "Perhaps he is young in his ways," I mused as though perturbed by a thought. I held my hand to my lips and tapped a finger on them. "But of course, Tom," I continued, catching his arm and drawing him towards me, "the advantages of youth are that a man is able and willing to hear what a woman may say. But in age…" I patted his arm like he was a feeble old dotard and raised my voice to his ear, speaking loudly. "In great age, Master Tom Wyatt, a man may not be able to hear a woman through the thick growth of hair in his ears!"

The crowd roared and the rest of the room looked our way. I stood in the middle with a quip on my lips and felt the interest of the court upon me. Both the King and the Queen were looking over from their position on the platform at the end of the room to see what the source of the amusement was. I felt the eyes of the court and the royal couple turn on me and I basked in it. I loved to be the centre of attention. Of course I did… I was young and proud.

"And therein, you see, Master Wyatt," I said, smiling still at Tom, who although laughing with the rest, did look rather disgruntled, "that therein lies *some* of the attraction of youth for a lady." I laughed merrily and nodded to the others in the group. "In youth there may be truth," I quipped, and grinned. "Whereas age may become a cage… Do you not think?" We carried on in our merry ways, and I went to bed that night exhausted and invigorated by the night. For the moment, I thought little of the young Henry Percy asking to dance with me. But it was in truth the start of something momentous.

Chapter Thirteen

Richmond Palace
1522

The King and his men would come to the Queen's quarters from time to time to visit formally and to allow Henry and Katherine to spend time with each other. Percy was now one of the Cardinal's men, a page in his household, and, since the Cardinal was often with the King, Percy was at times present in the Queen's chambers too. The young man would seek me out when possible, and we would spend time playing at cards, or he would listen to me sing for the company and compliment the sweetness of my voice. When attending on Henry, my father noticed this, and at one such meeting in the Queen's chamber came over to talk to me about this new development in my life.

"You must excuse me, my lord," my father bowed to Percy who was laughing heartily at a pun I had just made. "I must claim my right as a father to steal my daughter from you for a moment."

Percy bowed to my father and to me, and withdrew. My father looked at my cheeks, flushed with pleasure from Percy's attentions, and I ruefully blushed further; feeling excited at the attentions of a man in front of my father was embarrassing. I tried to cover my discomfiture by playing with the strings of my lute, but my father was not a man to be fooled. "The young heir to Northumberland, it would appear, finds you most interesting, daughter," he said softly with a musing expression on his face. "Henry Percy is engaged, I hear, to Shrewsbury's daughter, Mary Talbot."

The colour and pleasure drained from my face. As I looked at him, I thought I caught a momentary flash of pleasure in the ability to steal my pleasure from me run over my father's face. It was another type of power, after all, and my father liked power.

"Is he so?" I asked carefully and with a measured voice that showed no care behind it.

"Engaged is not *quite* the same as married, daughter." My father cast a sideways glance at Percy who was now chatting to Norris and Will Carey on the other side of the room, near to where some of Katherine's ladies were playing at cards with other gentlemen. I looked at my father questioningly and he smiled at me. "He seems most taken with you. I have seen the glances he casts your way." He scratched at his short beard a little and then continued thoughtfully. "Looks like that may lead a man many places… And a woman, also."

I arched one eyebrow and my father shook his head. "I mean not *that*," he said. "But I would not object to seeing the Boleyn name aligned to the house of Northumberland honourably. It would be an advantageous step for our family and one that is not out of our reach, even though they better us in blood and titles. I believe that a match to align our families may be within the bounds of possibility. Would this one be more to your tastes than Butler of the Bogs?"

"Most things are preferable to bogs, father," I said. "Consider the laundry that would have to be done; it would take all week to cleanse my gowns."

My father ignored my jest, and went on. "Then consider his advances and your responses well and play this game to your advantage… I am soon to leave England for Spain to resume my post as negotiator for the King, but in my absence, I would like to see you make the most of what this situation may bring to you." He smiled and nodded a greeting across the room at one of Henry's entourage; ever keeping up with the business of advancement, even whilst talking with his daughter on her marriage prospects. "Take the blessing of your father to do *whatever it may take* to capture that rather charmingly innocent heir to such a large fortune."

He looked directly at me. "Whatever it may take, Anne, I think should be sufficient." And with that, my father moved away, leaving me to stare at his back. At first I did not know what to think; had my own father just insinuated that I *whore* myself to gain a Northumberland as a husband? I was not fool enough to believe that I had misunderstood him. I understood my father well, but I was still not willing to forgo that which I held most dear about myself in order to succeed in life at court.

Still, the more I thought on it, the more the idea of being Percy's wife did genuinely appeal to me; he was young and handsome, he was tall and broad. He was heir to a great title and fortune. He was bright and he was indeed innocent. It was the boyish turn of his innocence that appealed to me most of all. Much as I loved life at court, its snap and its fire, it is a place often of illusion where all talk of love is but games, and little is real between men and women. Yet in his attentions there was something so genuine and open that I believed it to be true affection and admiration for me. Perhaps, in becoming his wife, I could have a husband who would really love and adore me. Perhaps I could have what so many around me did not have; a marriage to someone that they loved. It was what I had always wanted; what I had dreamed of when I had been in France. That I could have love, and marriage, as one... And now I had my father's approval for the match also. A thing of wonder, indeed!

I could not help but feel excited. I was given approval to follow my heart... I was equally sure that if Percy had shown me attention and I had *not* reciprocated affection, that my father would have ordered me to attract him despite my feelings. But as it was, I knew that I liked Percy, that I was attracted to him. My feelings for him were simple and almost strange to me. I felt like a child when I was near him. I felt... almost unlike myself... as though I had found a simpler version of myself hidden in all the court gowns and concealed under the fine

French headdresses. Percy brought something out of me which no other man did; a sense of my own innocence. At times, I almost felt shy to think about him.

Percy saw my father move away and as he returned to my side, the King rose and hastily called an end to the meeting in Katherine's chambers, asking the Cardinal to bring his men and follow him. Percy cast a rueful look to me and kissed my hand, moving to follow the Cardinal as was his duty. As Percy left the chambers, Henry turned, and in the light cast by the candles in the hallway, I saw an expression on his face that I had seen before… when I had danced at the *Chateau Vert* pageant. Henry, King of England, cast a look towards me of displeasure and… anger. I shivered to see it, but it was gone in a flash of gold as the King turned and left. I sat, wondering what it was that I had done this time to so displease the King's grace. Once more I wondered if I had imagined it, but I did not think that I had.

My father left for Spain that October, and was to remain in those lands until May of the year following. As he left, I increasingly thought on his orders to secure a match with young Percy, and although I thought on them with a little discomfiture, I also found more and more that I liked the idea. To marry with a man I found engaging… to become a countess! If I could indeed *secure* Percy, as my father had put it, then I would marry far above my own station. It would be a good match, and as time went on, I found my affection for Percy growing ever more. Tom was almost green with jealousy, and spent much time making jests at the expense of my would-be suitor, but in some ways, this only made me warm to Percy further… and recoil from Tom more. Tom made jests on Percy's youth and inexperience, but I *liked* his boyishness, and his sense of innocence.

"He is a dullard," said Tom as I watched Percy leave by boat for York Palace, the residence of Cardinal Wolsey.

"He is a lord," I warned Tom, meaning that Tom should be careful in his speech on those of higher rank than him.

"As you wish," Tom continued. "My *lord*, is a dullard."

I laughed, but then I turned to him in seriousness. "I like him, Tom." I said softly. "And I am truly sorry if that admission gives you pain, for that is something I would never like to cause. But in this, it seems I have no choice. For my liking Henry Percy will give you pain. But it is done, and I have no choice."

Tom looked away from me, staring out of the window. I moved to touch his arm and he moved away from me. "Will you not take friendship at my hands, Tom?" I asked gently.

"I have taken many things at your hands, Mistress Boleyn," he said waspishly.

"I have always been honest about my feelings and intentions towards you, Tom. You cannot accuse me of deceit."

"I think I may have preferred deceit," he murmured. "It might have had less sting to its tail."

"Tom..." I went to say more, but he stopped me. Standing away from me and bowing to me, he drew away.

"I am, as ever, your servant, madam." He bowed to me, his dark eyes seeming to have lost that sparkle I had ever loved to see in them.

"I would have you as my friend, rather than my servant, Tom."

He nodded. I saw the pain in his eyes and I flinched from it. I felt guilt for causing it. But I did not love Tom. I knew that now. Could I help it if he loved me? What could I do? There is nothing to be done in such situations.

"I would read you George's latest verse," I said softly to him. "I think it is his best work."

Tom nodded again, and tried to smile. "Later, perhaps, my lady," he shrugged and nodded at the palace to our side. "I have matters to attend to. I will wait on you anon."

I nodded my head, but before my chin dropped back into place, Tom was gone. I felt as though my heart might break, and not for me, but for him. Truly, I had no wish to cause him pain, and now I regretted somewhat that I had been so enthused for his company, and eager for his time. Tom had been the first thing, the first person who had made me feel at home in England, and I had long known about his feelings for me. But I had never deceived him. I had been truthful, and told him that I did not, and could not, love him.

I looked over the river, feeling sad. But even as I looked, I could see the boat that carried Percy, and felt as though that brought me strength, and courage. I believed that I loved Percy. The manner in which he approached me was respectful, sweet and charming. To a woman who has seen the darker side of men, and who has lived her whole life surrounded by false flattery, he was revitalizing. When I saw him it was like feeling the first breath of spring wind through the dull gloom of winter. Here was a man that I could love, that I could grant my heart to, and I believed that if I did so, then my heart would be safe in his gentle keeping.

In my father's absence, I took it upon myself to charm Percy all I could, knowing that if I could indeed secure such a match, then I would do so with the blessing of my family, *and*, the blessing of my own heart.

Chapter Fourteen

Greenwich Palace
1523

The winter swept through England with driving storms of snow and freezing rain which lingered well into the spring. We celebrated Christmas at court, and then came the New Year with presents exchanged between courtiers, and between masters and fortunate servants. Throughout the winter, whenever we were able, Percy and I would meet, to talk or play at dice together, and our attraction seemed to deepen within each of our hearts. He looked for me at every entertainment, and my eyes sought him out too. I felt as though something sacred and sweet had touched my heart, and went about the court with a flush of happiness within my blood. The freezing airs of the winter could not touch me; I felt warmed by the growing love between this innocent young man and me. Tom was not happy with me, but that, too, I seemed to be able to cast off just as I shrugged off the cold of the winter. I walked through the spring snowdrops and daffodils feeling as though my heart was as merry as those bright little flowers.

Many verses came from Tom that winter about the hardness of a mistress who could discard the feelings of another so cruelly. But I did not mean to be cruel. I had explained my feelings to Tom. I had tried to be kind to him, but I could not spend my life waiting for a love that could never be. And despite my attraction to Tom, I had come to realise that if one is able to shut one's heart to love, then it is not love. I was able to shut my heart to Tom, and so I knew that I did not love him, not truly. But my feelings for young Percy crept into my heart bit by bit, until I found there was little of my heart left without his touch.

"My brother is much sorrowed these days," Margaret said to me one stormy afternoon as we walked in the long galleries at court. I sighed, and gave her a half-smile.

"And I am sorry for it, Margaret," I replied, "but your brother has a wife already… I can be nothing more to him than a friend, and that is what I have offered him."

She nodded. I believe she understood, but she was still worried for her brother. They were close, as siblings and as friends, much as I was with my own brother and sister. "I will talk to him on the matter," she assured me, pressing her pale hand to my sleeve.

"I would be grateful," I said. "I mean to cause him no harm. He is very dear to me… But I cannot help what he feels for me… you know that well enough. I would that he would accept me as his friend alone, but I wonder if he ever will." She tucked my arm through mine and gave me a little smile; we continued to walk, talking of lighter matters.

In May, our father returned from Spain, happy with his efforts there to negotiate on behalf of the King. He brought back many gifts for his family, including a work that he had had smuggled into Spain, which George and I discussed avidly; a French translation of the New Testament by Lefevre. The notes on the text suggested a belief that the Holy Scripture was the only true rule of doctrine, and that redemption from sin was based on faith alone, rather than through penance, or pardon as the Church taught. Later that year, Lefevre would publish translations of the Gospels and Epistles, which we also gained copies of, and talked on at great length. In that same year, Martin Luther would publish a German translation of the New Testament, with much the same philosophy held within its pages. It was wondrous to me that two such thinkers, whom many considered heretical, could come to such revelations in theology at the same time. Surely, I thought, it must be the hand of God, touching on the minds of such men, and bringing forth such ideas. Lefevre was much attacked by leaders of the Church in France, but Marguerite had him under her protection. Her obvious love and support for the man only increased the value that his work held for me.

Our father brought word that François intended to invade Italy, pursuing a claim to the lands of that country and taking action against the Emperor Charles. The Emperor and Henry were increasingly determined now to unite against him, and take Italy, and even France, from François. The treaty that united England with Spain was now secure, and Henry was eager and willing to join with Charles on this military venture. I found the idea distressing. Perhaps in knowing François personally, and in having great love for his sister Marguerite, and for Claude, his queen, I would that my country was allied with France. It was a glorious country, sophisticated, filled with poetry, wit... a country that offered protection to philosophers and theologians... But my personal feelings were of course of little importance to men like my father, who were sent to do the King's will, and strove to gain the King's love through such efforts.

One day, as the warmth of the summer began to return to England, I was in the gardens at Greenwich. Every day at court, provided that the weather allowed it, I would walk accompanied by my sister or Margaret and Bridget. We walked along the knot gardens and physic patches, crushing the leaves and stems of herbs in our fingertips and relishing the smell of rosemary, sage and thyme. I loved the fresh and scented airs as the summer blooms burst forth. I had been at court for over a year now, and there were many aspects of England's palaces that I had come to love greatly. The Queen too, liked to wander the gardens, but not as much as her ladies did. Katherine's chambers were kept hot and often gloomy in the chill of winter, and even into the spring, for fear that the cold airs might bring illness. But as the warmth returned to England, Katherine's ladies escaped the dreariness of the Queen's chambers to tarry in the gardens with pleasure.

More and more, Katherine would commit herself to prayer in the afternoons, as well as in the mornings and in the evenings, hearing at least three or four Masses each day and locking herself away in the gloom of her chambers and Chapel to pray when she was not at Mass. Her charitable acts increased three-fold that year, as though she were petitioning God for clemency. We all knew what it was that she prayed for so long each day. There were rumours growing, whispered in the stone halls of the great palaces and repeated behind closed doors all over the land; that the Queen was now barren and could not produce children. She would never give Henry a son.

The Princess Mary was the only child of their marriage to survive infancy, and although she was adored by her mother, and loved by her father, a male heir was needed to follow Henry on the throne. We knew it was not the King who was at fault, for he had a few bastards from his past mistresses; good proof of his fertility. One of these, and the only bastard the King acknowledged, was a boy; Henry Fitzroy, the little son of Bessie Blount, my sister's predecessor in the King's bed. All knew that Henry was capable of getting male children. The fault must lie therefore with the Queen.

Katherine was growing desperate, and in her need she turned increasingly to God, in whom she placed all her trust. The secret plan to marry the Emperor Charles to the Princess Mary was well-known about court. But we also knew that this was not the ideal path for England… England needed an English King, not a foreign Emperor who watched over such vast lands and territories as those under Charles' control. There was, too, a sense of pride in the hearts of the English; they wanted to be ruled by the blood of their blood, by the English heart which beat through the lands. Henry had laid a plan to provide a successor should he and Katherine fail ever to have a male heir… but we all knew that he desired a son above all other things.

Perhaps it sounds cold, but many of us who served the Queen came to the gardens with relief at having a few hours away from her quiet but relentless desperation. The endless praying and good works, the continuous noise of her lips murmuring to God, praying for a miracle child to grace her womb; all these things weighed down the spirit and the soul after some time. We needed to escape from the sense of overwhelming sadness that Katherine exuded.

If you think me flighty, remember that I was young, and forgive me for having the faults of the young. We are none of us perfect beings.

Whilst we walked in those glorious gardens we would talk of court affairs, of the admirers that the ladies had amongst the court gallants, of the latest entertainments and of poetry and humanist thought. Many days, such gallants would spy us out walking and would come to join us. It was a merry time in my life. There was flirting and singing and laughing in this happy throng, and Percy came to my side whenever he was able. I looked for his face in the crowds at court and was always disappointed if I could not see him that day. At each meeting my affection for him grew. Since my father's talk with me, I had grown used to the idea that Percy was a match of which my family would approve and a match that I wanted also. And he wanted me. There was no doubt, for I read it in his open face as easily as one could read a book. Had I asked him, I believed in those days, Henry Percy would have done anything for me. As it turned out, I was mistaken… but that was later.

That day he spied a book that hung from my waist, decorated with jewels and covered in fine leather and gold; he asked if he could read over it himself. "I would deny you nothing," I said with a mischievous look that made him almost shiver. "But I swore, when my friend gave this book to me, that it would not leave my sight, and to this I hold. But you may read it when I am here."

"It was a friend… dear to you, then?" he asked. The look of fear in his face, that this friend might be a man, was almost comical.

"Yes, *she* is," I replied most deliberately. The look disappeared and he was happy again. "Marguerite, sister to the King François gave me this," I opened the soft pages of the *Miror de l'ame pecheresse* and looked lovingly at them. "It is her own work and it is precious to me."

"Sister to the King?" Percy lifted his brows. "You rose high in France."

I nodded. "I served the Queen Claude, and was in the King's sister's circle of intimates," I said, thinking of France with a pang of homesickness.

A look of concentration came over Percy and he stared away into the gardens. "Anna, there is something I would say to you," he said. "But I know not if I have the right or the courage."

I put my hand on his arm. "We are good friends, are we not? What may not be spoken between friends?"

"That is what I wish to talk to you of," he sighed. "You know, I suppose, that I am engaged to be married to the Lady Mary Talbot, daughter of the Earl of Shrewsbury?"

I flushed with sadness. It was not contrived; the thought of Percy leaving my side brought great unhappiness and tears flooded to my surprised eyes. I had not realised the full depth of my feeling for him, even now. His gentle hands reached to my face and drew my eyes up to his. There was gentleness and concern in his eyes and also surprise. "Is it so, then, Anne?" he whispered to me. "Do you feel the same as I? It is so hard to tell what you think beyond those black eyes of yours. Other ladies are so easy to read, they give away all, but your eyes betray nothing and I know not if you love me or if you are simply kind to me as you are to all who adore you."

I shook my head, but tears stifled my response; still he held my chin in his hands and looked at me. He took my hand and led me to an alcove in the walls of the palace, leading to stairs which went to the chambers of servants below. The others in the group had wandered away and there was no one about, it seemed, but us. He pulled me into the alcove and then into his arms. I reached out suddenly, impulsively, and threw my arms over his shoulders, drawing his lips down to mine. I felt him gasp as he drew me close. There was fire in his lips as he kissed me. He pushed me up against the cold stone wall, his hands stroked my body… and I let them I wanted him to touch me. I wanted him to have me, to hold me… I wanted to be his.

"Then it is done," he whispered, breaking from the kiss, smiling down at me and moving me closer to him as he spoke. "I am engaged… if you will have me."

I gasped, for I had not quite expected that to come from his mouth. "To me, you mean?" I asked, stupid for once in his arms.

"I would have no other." He lowered his lips to mine once more. I felt the hardness of him through his clothing, the sinewy muscle of his chest and the rock hard aspect of his manhood against my hip. I heard him groan a little, through a mist of pleasure, and then he pulled back and tugged me from the alcove. "Here, Anna," he said, moving me to an arbour where there was a seat. "We need to talk."

I sat down, re-arranged my clothing and put my hands to my flushed face. So pale was I normally that colour in my face made me seem unearthly in appearance. Percy stroked my face and tucked my hair back in my hood.

"I am engaged, it is true, but it is an old engagement and can be broken," Percy said earnestly. "Our families put forward the idea long ago… talks have gone on for more than eight years. But she has no love for me, and I none for her. We have met on several occasions, and I find her utterly repellent. I am of an age now where I can choose my own match, my own bride, and that is what I intend to do. The minute I saw you, I knew I could not rest unless I was by your side and now I cannot rest unless you are by mine for the rest of our lives. I want to marry you, Anne, and I *will* marry you." He frowned. "My family may have some objection, your blood is not as noble as ours, but your family is in high favour at court… And you…" he paused, smiling at me. "I see not how they could not fall for your charms as easily as I have done, once they meet you."

"My family will have no objections," I said breathlessly. Our moment of passion had opened my mind to all I had not realised about the way it could be between a man and a woman. I felt a little dazed; passions that I had never known flowed through my veins. "There can be no objections," I said firmly. "We *must* marry and then we shall be the happiest in the world, for there are few who find love in their marriage bed."

"You and I will have great sons, Anne," he said. "I see them now. We will have a fine life together."

I laughed. I was happy. I was abandoned in happiness; it seemed as though there could be nothing in our way and there could be no objection that would make sense against our marriage. I was to have everything I had ever wanted; marriage and love together in one, a place at court and an adoring husband who loved me for who I was. I reached out and kissed him again fiercely, but he was respectful of me in his love, and would not take the matter further between us until he had talked to his master, Wolsey, and to his own family.

I was elated and I burned for him. That night I dreamed of his hands pulling at my dress and forcing their way down and over my breasts. I dreamt of his fingers and lips at my nipples, of the hardness of his manhood pressing into my heated and reckless body. I dreamt of passion I had never known. I felt his hands sliding up my thighs, I felt him pushing against me and finally, entering me, as soft and wet as my mouth as it sucked the fingers he put through my lips. I groaned in my sleep as I felt him deep inside me and awoke suddenly, cheated of the final moment of pleasure as the bells for Mass pealed through my chamber. I awoke hot and desperate for Henry Percy. I had only ever felt such a passion once before; when I was young, and my feminine ardour had been first awakened at the sight of Henry, King of England. But this was no remote passion now, and I no young girl with no understanding of her feelings. This was the passion of love, I thought, and it had stolen my senses.

I sat through Mass trying to get my thoughts concentrated on God, where they should have been. But I could not draw them from thoughts of Percy's body conjured by my dreams. I was fidgeting and restless. I could not concentrate on anything I was doing; all my thoughts were of him. My sister noticed this change in me and was speculative, watching me with some small measure of amusement. I had after all, always been the sister in charge of her emotions and now, it seemed, I was not.

"*Are you in love*?" Mary whispered to me as she helped me clear a dish that I had dropped in Katherine's chambers. Fortunately the Queen herself was not there, but at her second Mass of the day, held privately in her chapel. Otherwise, I should have been in trouble for breaking the dish. I flushed at my sister and nodded, smiling. I could not contain my excitement and it seemed that this was the time to tell her. I felt as though I had to tell someone. I was bursting at the seams of my fine crimson gown to talk of my love.

"Yes," I whispered. "And I am *engaged*."

Mary gasped with excitement. "To whom?" she shrieked, and I sought to quieten her, shushing her and waving my hands. "Wait, I know!" she cried in triumph. "To Thomas Wyatt!"

"What?" I laughed. "You think me engaged to a man already married?" I giggled again at the sudden, crestfallen look on her pretty face. "No, Mary… I am engaged to Henry Percy."

"Heir to the Earl of Northumberland?" she gasped again, looking at me with wide eyes. "There is a fine match for you! Do you love him? Yes, I see the look in those great eyes of yours. You are in love, Anne! Oh, I am so happy for you!" She clasped my hands and went to jump up and down like a child and then, suddenly, the happiness fell from her face and she gaped at me like a fish on a chopping block. "What will our father say?" Mary looked pale and concerned. She was right, after all; it was not as though our family was of noble enough blood to ordinarily consider a match with such an old and noble family. Had I not had our father's permission to advance, I could have been in a great deal of trouble from it. Mary was afraid for her younger sister. I felt a little flush of affection and love for my older sister.

"Our father *encouraged* me to it," I assured her. "Fear not, father knows… He *told* me to persuade Percy to enter into an engagement." I raised my eyebrows and flashed my black eyes at her. "Father said to me that *by any means necessary* should be sufficient."

Mary looked at me and smiled a somewhat sad smile, although not so much for my news. She, too, understood the nature of our father. "That is what he said to me when the King first became interested in me," she said. "It was not what he said when François was interested though… Do you remember?" Her eyes trailed away, seeing the past, just as I did… Seeing her fly across that room and hit the fireplace… Seeing the look of disgust in our father's eyes as he looked down on us both, calling his daughters whores and liars.

"He is a courtier," I shook my head, seeing the look on Mary's face. "He does what he does to advance his family, as do we."

"Sometimes I should like to do some things that are just for myself and my own pleasure," she said ruefully.

"Your place in the King's bed is not unpleasant?" I asked. "Surely not?"

She sighed. "No, he is a kind and generous lover and I get pleasure from him... I do not find it unpleasant, no." She paused. "But I am less a lover to the King as I am... a convenience. He is a complicated man and he enjoys many things; I am one of those things. I know well how to please men and I know how to last long in the King's bed. I know how to be everything he wants me to be and nothing more. I will be the whore he wants when he comes home restless from hunting, and I will be the romantic lady he needs when he wishes to write poetry. I am soft and gentle and demand nothing. I am his perfect lady, because I do nothing to upset him or unnerve him. I agree with all he says and does. That is my place, as his mistress."

She looked at me and shook her head. "But I feel that I am less and less in this affair. I am there physically, but I am not there in truth. I am not *whole* when I am with him. I am not me. I am only what he wants of me. I derive pleasure from our encounters and I feel desire for him, yes Anne, but he does not in truth want *me*, only the convenience of this illusion I have designed for him. It is a winning mixture and it will keep me in his bed for longer than most, I think," she looked at me. "But it is not *love,* Anne. That I know, and that is where I envy you and the look you have on your face. For I, who have known many men, have not known love. Not even for my husband, although he is a good man and I respect him. For love to happen, they would have to want me as I am, not only the parts of me they wish to see. And I feel that you, who know nothing of men in one way, have found a way to that which I desire most." She shook herself and smiled sadly at me. In her own way Mary was as much a consummate courtier as George, my father or I. She wore a mask, and played a role, as we all did. I wondered on her words for a moment. So often had I felt jealousy for Mary that I could barely conceive she might feel the same for me. Perhaps it is the same for all sisters, or all people; that we always want that which we do not have.

 "Come," she said, taking my hands and shaking them as she smiled at me. "This is no way to behave! My sister is to be the Countess of Northumberland! This is a time for celebration!" She released me and poured a measure of wine into a goblet, handing it to me. "To the Lady Anne of Northumberland!" she whispered with glee. "May you find all the happiness you desire with your new noble station, and stallion!"

And with a flushed face and her words ringing in my ears, I drank to the marriage that, in a very short time, was to be no more.

Chapter Fifteen

Greenwich Palace
1523

One afternoon, perhaps a month later, Percy found me in the gardens with a group of courtiers including Tom and my brother and sister. It had been many days since I had seen him, and I was beginning to wonder what duties in the Cardinals' household at York Palace were keeping him from court.

It was a glorious afternoon and the gardens were filled with the scent of rosemary and lavender. At the sides of the ponds, and near to the river, willow trees hung over the waters, their silver-green long pointed leaves dancing in the wind. A light, balmy breeze was blowing, and we sat in the welcome shade of some trees, reading over poetry that George and Tom had composed and rolling in our hands the lemon-scented wood sorrel that grew in little clumps in the shade. The summer roses had started to show their heads in delicate blooms of red, pink, and white, and as they danced in the little breeze, I thought of my mother. The sight of roses always reminded me of her. She was not at court much that year as a bout of ill health had caused her to return to Hever to take the healthier air of the countryside and recover in peace away from court. It was always when I could not see her face that I longed the most for her presence. When she was by my side I could barely see her through the throng and noise of the court, but when she was not there I could clearly see and feel the gap left by her presence. It is often the way, that when we love someone we feel their absence more keenly than we ever recognise our need for them when they are at our side.

When Percy came towards us, I was pleased and rose to meet him. Tom glowered, as he always did these days when

Percy was near. Tom was bitter to see my affections for another man increase. Perhaps he wanted me to remain perpetually alone, because I could not be with him. Or perhaps he could see that my love for Percy was indeed real. For whichever reason, Tom was given to a dark face of jealousy when Percy came near. Tom often used his young rival as a subject for jests, which I liked not, and his spiteful japes hardly made me think better of him.

But then, that is often the way with the human creature, is it not? We become so blinded by jealousy that when it takes hold of us we cannot see that it is removing us still further from our goals with its malicious fingers. Had Tom been willing to put his feelings aside, had he been happy to see me make a good match for myself, then I might have thought him a greater man, I might have thought more of him. As it was, I by no means disliked Tom, but knowing that I could not give my heart or body to him, I could not allow myself to love him. But until he could stop loving me, there would always be a somewhat strained friendship between us. We had managed thus far by not returning to talk of it, but it was always there, unspoken, between us.

When Percy neared me, I could see that something was wrong. Across his handsome, boyish face there was a pale concern and there were lines of worry that should not have been there when a man meets his love.

"What is it?" I whispered, drawing him away from the throng. "What has happened?"

He looked up, as though to seek guidance from God for what he was going to say. "I… I sought the Cardinal's help in asking for my father's permission to marry you… as we talked of. I told him that you and I were engaged." He coughed and looked about himself nervously, his eyes only daring to dart to my face. "I told Wolsey that we intended to marry as soon as we were able." His voice wavered slightly as though he were terribly afraid.

The insecurity in his voice was unsettling; it made me afraid, and impatient in my fear. I wanted him to say something that would stay the growing fears of my heart. I sought to look into his eyes, but he kept moving them from mine. I stamped my little foot with sudden anger at him. "And what?" I cried loudly. "What happened?"

He looked at me now with concern and worry. He feared my anger and frustration. This made me angrier still, frustrated at this weakness I had never truly noted in him before. I grabbed his hands; they were cold to the touch. "*What happened*?" I shouted, almost shaking him.

At that, both Mary and George were suddenly at my side with Tom in tow. I could see Margaret and Bridget looking on from where they still sat in the shade of the trees with worried faces. Percy looked intimidated. I stared at him, wondering on the foolish look on his face. Until that moment I had never realised how much of a boy he really was, and right now, it did not seem as attractive as it had done before. The tone of Percy's voice was causing fear to pump like blood through my heart. What was going on? Why was he so afraid?

"The Cardinal went silent," Percy said, "and he sent me from his chambers. He called for me the next day… and in front of many other servants, he began to admonish me for my words. He said that there could be no such marriage between myself and the younger daughter of the Boleyns, as I was already engaged and that engagement was approved by the King. He told me, or reminded me, that nobility does not have the luxury to marry where it wishes, that marriage for love is a fool's wish, and that I and my father are vassals to the King and must do his will, not my own."

He paused, swallowing hard at the furious look on my face. "I protested. I said that I was of an age to choose a bride myself, and spoke of your many virtues and your family's standing within the court. I told the Cardinal of your descent from the

Dukedom of Norfolk and the Earls of Ormond. I protested that the King honoured your family... But then, the Cardinal shouted at me. He shouted that you were nothing but a *silly girl*... that you were an unworthy match for a Percy. He said that he already knew of our plans... that the *King* knew of our plans to marry and was most displeased that I should think to go against his will. Wolsey said you were foolish and wanton to so over-reach your station and rank in life by seeking to marry me." Percy's voice was less hesitant now, but it was as weak as a dying lamb. "Wolsey told me that I should be ashamed of stooping so low as to seek to marry you. The Cardinal shouted that I *would* marry Lady Mary Talbot and be grateful that I still had a head on my shoulders after so displeasing the King."

Percy looked at me. His face was almost grey and his hands shook. "Anne, it is over. I tried and I tried to placate the Cardinal, I told him that our promise to marry was known to many witnesses, that we had made promises to each other and the matter had gone so far as to be irremovable... but he only became more furious. Wolsey has sent for my father and he is come to court. I am ordered go and face him. I have only a moment spare to come and tell you this for I am called to my father's apartments even now. No doubt the Cardinal has told him everything. Wolsey said to me that my father would order the match with Mary Talbot to go ahead, and that I would marry her, or face being disinherited and cast off. The King disapproves of our match and is most displeased that we attempted to become married without his approval or consent. I am to be banished from court. The Cardinal ordered me to send you to him, and your father wishes to see you afterwards."

He swallowed. His hands were shaking. "It is over, Anne," he said again and my heart dropped even as my eyes filled with tears.

"No!" I shouted, making him start and stare at me in horror. "No, it is not so! Come... We will go away, you and me... We will find a willing priest and we will be married now, this day, and none can tear us apart then! Come, fly with me and we shall be man and wife as we were meant to be. Hang the kings and cardinals of this world! What are they to us?"

"*Anne!*" exclaimed my brother, sister and Percy all at the same time. They all looked about them as though they feared my words would bring the great rage of the King down upon our heads. But I cared not. I was staring at Percy with desperation in my eyes. Tom was the only one who seemed unafraid. He looked as though he thought my idea was the right one.

"If it were me, Percy," Tom said slowly, with pain in his eyes. "I would follow the lady."

I looked at Tom with wild and grateful eyes full of tears as I held on to Percy's hand, pleading with him to run with me. Percy swallowed on a dry throat, ignoring Tom; he looked at the floor near my feet. He could not even look me in the eyes. "No. You do not know what you are saying, Anne. We cannot, there would be nothing for us anywhere. The King would have us thrown in the Tower, or worse. My father would disinherit me... We would have nothing."

"We would be man and wife... as we were meant to be!" I wept, half mad with grief and half with frustration. "That cannot be *nothing* to you?" I hesitated and looked into his face, searching for answers and with a dreadful fear in my heart. "You do not..." I stuttered as I thought I saw a doubt in his face as he looked on me. "You do not believe what the Cardinal has spoken about me? That I am not *worthy* of you?"

He did not answer the question, but said instead, "it may be that I can persuade my father to relent and he can talk to the King. The only objection can be that we planned in secret to marry, and that can be apologised for... and then perhaps we can be together..." He smiled, weakly, and I did not believe him. "We shall be together anon," he said. I knew in that moment that he was lying. I knew in that moment that he was trying to placate me, trying to run from this situation. He was a *coward*. He would not fight for me, or for love. He would hide in the bushes like an infant doe shivering for fear of the hunter.

I released his hands; mine dropped to my side and watched him walk away from me, hurrying towards his father's chambers. I felt Mary's hand upon my shoulder and I turned towards her with a heavy heart. "Wait, Anne," Mary consoled gently. "It may still turn out well."

But I watched Percy trotting like a lamb towards his father's rooms and I knew then with perfect clarity that even if he was given the chance, he would not fight for me. He was too scared; too scared of his father, too scared of the Cardinal, of the King… of losing his inheritance. He was not strong enough to face their displeasure. Indeed, who was?

"No," I whispered slowly, the tears drying on my cheeks as I felt an icy coldness spread from the hole Percy had left in my heart. "No, it is over. He will not fight for me."

I turned from them and walked as though in a dream towards the Cardinal's apartments to face my own fate. Behind me, I could hear Tom and George talking quietly to Bridget and Margaret, no doubt telling them what had happened. I felt as though my heart had become a block of stone. Mary scuttled to my side, taking her hand in mine. I could barely feel its warmth beneath the coldness that had washed over me.

Chapter Sixteen

Greenwich Palace
1523

I stood outside the Cardinal's apartments with Mary for a long time. The Cardinal sought to make me realise how unimportant I was by making me wait upon him. Finally, I was called in. Wolsey sat behind a great desk, surrounded as always by the affairs of state on papers that covered his desk. As Mary and I entered, he raised his head and motioned to her as though swatting at a fly, rather than speaking to the King's mistress. "*You* were not called, Mistress Carey," he said. "If I were you I would not seek to be aligned with one who has incurred the King's displeasure in such a fashion."

Mary looked helplessly at me and then curtseyed to the Cardinal, turned and left. I stood alone, apart from the Cardinal's servants, who stood near the walls wearing grave expressions like their master. In that moment, I hated them all. Hated their long faces and their disapproving eyes. But most of all, I hated the Cardinal who sat before me, exuding an air of superiority and virtue. Who was this man to look so upon me? A man of the Church who had a mistress and at least one bastard son? This man was to be the judge of my morals and virtue?

"The plans that you have made to marry the heir of Northumberland were arrogant, immoral and presumptuous, Mistress Boleyn," he said slowly, not looking at me; continuing instead to read the papers before him as though I was of little importance. "You are banished from the court by the King's order and are not to return unless summoned. You have acted wantonly, immodestly and rashly. The King does not welcome women such as *you* into his court. Your family is too low-born to be considered a match for the Percys and you have shamed both yourself and the Boleyn name in attempting to seduce and cajole a foolish young man into such a disadvantageous match for him."

He looked up, his fat face stern and unmoving, but under the mask he wore I got the impression he was enjoying this. "You are nothing but a low-born slattern in truth; a silly, devious girl who sought to entrap a noble heir with wanton tricks and wicked ways." He smiled, but there was no humour in it. "But of course," he mused slowly, "your family must be so proud… to see you following in the steps of your sister. And I have heard tales of your mother too, when she was a young woman at court. Bad blood breeds true enough, so they say."

I swallowed, my face flaming and my temper barely under control. "I am no whore, my Lord Chancellor," I said calmly, though my heart was pounding with rage. My anger pressed my lips to speak on, without thinking. "And my blood is more noble than you can claim."

"How dare you speak so to me?" he shouted, rising from his chair and flinging the papers from his desk into disarray all over the floor. "You are banished from court, you are not to return. You have incurred both *my* displeasure and that of the King. That Percy dotard you have tried to trap will marry where he is told to, to a lady worthy of his title and his blood. Get out of my sight, and think yourself fortunate that the King has not thrown the both of you in the Tower for your treason and arrogance!"

I bowed stiffly to the Cardinal, and left, my face flaming and everything in my blood crying for retribution. I had never felt anger as I did that day. The Cardinal had taken my family, my future, my past, my reputation and wiped his filthy feet all over them. I was banished from court, my reputation was stained and the love-match and happiness I thought to be mine was ruined.

As anger flooded through me, taking the place of my sorrow, I swore I would have revenge on the Cardinal for his words to me and for his insults against my family. How dare he insult my family, my... *mother,* so? I was so angry that I marched straight past Mary who was still waiting in the antechamber outside, and almost flew to our father's chambers, half-wondering if I was to receive another barrage against my virtues and honour. But when I came to him, I found him in a surprisingly understanding mood.

"What went wrong?" our father asked of me when I entered. I shrugged my shoulders despondently and sat down without asking. Father was not angry at me, I could already tell, and I felt tired and old suddenly. I relayed all that Percy had said to me, and all the Cardinal had said also, feeling as though I were a soldier giving a report from the field of battle. My anger was subsiding, and in its place came a blankness of disappointment and shock. I almost wished I *was* angry again, for that would have been better than the emptiness I felt now.

"The Cardinal and the King knew of our engagement before Percy could ask his father's permission... before Percy went to Wolsey even," I continued with a sigh. "I know not why, exactly, but all were heartily against it. The Cardinal shouted at me, called me a commoner... and a *whore*. Percy has been scared into submission; he has the displeasure of the Cardinal and the King and his father to deal with. And you may incur some of that wrath also, father," I looked over at him. "I swear, father, that I thought this was a deal done. I thought that it would not be hard to gain permission to marry, and that I should be joined happily and quickly to Percy, as you instructed me to try to do. I never thought that the King and Cardinal should get so involved in such a matter."

"Yes," my father mused, looking concerned. "It is strange that they should involve themselves so much in this matter. Less fitting marriages have been made before. But the Cardinal has no love for our family; he has in the past managed to remove honours and titles from me, and he took your brother from the

King's chambers once before, too… although it did the fat bat little good, for George is well-loved by the King and was brought back in time. He is suspicious of our leanings towards reform I believe, and that makes him afraid, as it does for many of the clergy who fear their power taken from them. He fears also that we are rising in the King's estimations… Wolsey does not like others to threaten his influence."

My father sighed, and looked at the fireplace, musing on his thoughts. "Northumberland holds power still in the north of England, in the very seat of Wolsey's own archbishopric. Perhaps he saw the union of two houses he has cause to fear as something that could be dangerous to his position. The King is easily moved to anger when he believes his power is being undermined… I doubt not that Wolsey saw fit to paint this in the worst manner possible in order to rile Henry's anger." He sighed again. "I should have foreseen a danger such as this… I was foolish to not think on it when I gave you your instructions. From what I hear, the King heard of this first, and took the matter to Wolsey. Had we approached Henry first, then we might have won his support for a tale of two young people much in love, who wished to marry. The King is, after all, a sentimental man at times… but Wolsey… Wolsey will always think of Wolsey first, and he must have convinced the King this match was an affront to his dignity, enough so to cause furious anger. The King is not to be approached at the moment."

My father stood up and walked to me, putting a hand on my shoulder. It was the closest thing to a gesture of comfort I had ever had from him. I looked at him in surprise, for I had expected anger at my failure to secure the match he wanted for me.

"No matter now what should have been seen and done, Anne, we must seek to limit the damage from this disastrous end. You are to be banished from court, the King orders it. You shall return to Hever until this matter cools. You will keep your mother company and we will weather this until it is forgotten and then I shall send for you to return. The Cardinal is our enemy in any case, daughter; he would never have been kind to you. His insults against you are insults against us, and will not be forgotten. That cow-herder's son thinks that our lineage is not good enough! Hah!" He scowled. "There will come a day when he will regret all he has done against us. But in the meantime, you must disappear… We must not let this damage your sister's relationship with the King."

"No, father," I sighed and rose to leave.

"How did the Cardinal and King find out?" my father asked as I turned to leave the room. "You said that they both knew of the match, even before Percy had spoken to him of it."

I hesitated. "I know not, father," I said. He grunted and I left the room.

But I did know, or at least I thought I knew… After all, I had only told two people besides our father of my engagement, and only one of them had the ear and other parts of the King to herself. But Mary could not have known that this would cause such trouble. Perhaps she thought she was laying the ground for my marriage to Percy, by telling Henry. But in actual fact, she had destroyed it.

I saw Mary before I left and she confessed that she had told the King.

"I thought as much," I said dully.

"Anne!" she exclaimed. "I feel terrible! I have ruined everything for you!"

"Hush… You could not have known it would do this," I assured her. I shivered a little. There was a still, ominous air all around the court, as though a storm were about to erupt. It was Henry's great, foul temper. All who could were avoiding him, for his rage was such that it could alter the air of an entire building. Percy was gone already and I was banished. The word was all over court. People whispered of it everywhere. The Queen had sent a messenger to release me from my duties; she did not want to see me in my disgrace. But none knew why the King was *so* furious. Yes, we had presumed to talk of marriage, but it had gone no further... Henry seemed angrier about the matter than he should have been. Wolsey must have done his work well to make it seem as though Percy and I had challenged Henry's power, in seeking to marry for love.

"The King is furious," Mary said, her eyes wide and still surprised. "He will not see anyone."

"Why should he be so?" I asked, puzzled. "I don't understand... Why should he be *so* angry? We did but fall in love, and seek to marry.... But, Mary, listen to me, you must forget that I am your sister for a while and pretend that I don't exist. Mention nothing of me, wear nothing like my clothing and be the opposite in all ways that you can think of; if he is displeased with Percy and me this much, then you must distance yourself from me as much as possible and hold on to your position. Do nothing and say nothing that might remind him that I am your sister. I do not want the King equating the two of us together and finding fault with you for it... Our father will be far angrier with me if you should fall from favour as a result of my disgrace."

She nodded. "I am sorry for you, Anne. But I will do as you say."

I shook my head and tears leapt back into my eyes. She reached out and held me. I cried into her velvet puffed shoulders, suddenly reminded of all that I had just lost and of the knowledge of the one truth that hurt the most.

"He wouldn't fight for me," I cried to her. "He wouldn't fight for me, Mary. He believed, in truth, that I was *not* good enough for him." I cried bitter tears into her fine gown. I knew that Percy had never truly loved me, for in love, one could never believe that the other was not worthy.

Chapter Seventeen

Hever Castle
1523

I returned to Hever, and to the arms of my mother. Hever was always at its most beautiful in the late summer, when the roses and the gillyflowers were in bloom. The parks and fields were lush and ready for riders and hunters to take enjoyment from them. But I must do so alone.

I was in disgrace; banished from court for daring to try to make my own marriage, for being too bold and too forward, as did not become a woman; for seeking to over-reach my station in life, and challenging the authority of the King himself. Percy languished on his lands as I did on mine; too weak to fight for me, to cowardly to stand up to those men around him who controlled his money and his titles. My friends at court wrote to me, counselling me to be patient and to wait out this period of banishment. I was pleased to have their letters, for those pages made me feel a little less alone.

I walked with my mother in her rose gardens when she was strong enough. The illness she had contracted over the last winter had taken a great deal from her, but not her beauty. Although now she was as thin and fragile as a sheet of glass, she was still as lovely as ever before. But her beauty seemed strained and stretched. She was tired often and had to rest through long hours of the day. Our father visited home but rarely and saw her infrequently. I knew not why. Once I had thought that the love between my parents was strong and sure. Now I felt as though both my mother and I were somehow recovering from lost affairs of love together, in secluded Hever, amongst the gardens of roses and the long grassed fields of home.

She asked nothing of me until I was willing to tell her. Her soft ways were so opposite to mine that I wondered sometimes that I *was* her daughter. She waited where I would have demanded, and listened where I would have questioned. But she knew what I needed, and she was sensitive to all my changes in mood and feeling. My mother could have been the greatest statesman alive, had she been born a man rather than a woman.

"He just seemed so different to everyone else," I said to her as we sat in the gardens.

"How so?" she asked softly.

"He was innocent and boyish," I smiled sadly. "He hardly understood all the bawdy jests and mischief… he just seemed so…" I trailed off looking for an ending. "*Different.*" I said again, for once lost for words.

My mother played with the white rose bud in her hand; her newest creation. The beautiful white petals smelt so sweet and their innards were blushed with the faintest pink. My mother had started to breed her roses together, hoping one day to create a Tudor rose to present as a present to the King and Queen. It seemed for all her efforts that it was a thing impossible, although she spent much time trying.

"Was I a fool?" I asked.

"To hope that a man may be *different* to all the rest?" she laughed and shook her head. "That is what all women hope for, despite the lack of evidence."

She seemed sad. Sad for me, and for herself, and still too ill to return to the court and the side of her husband. "I shall give you some advice, Anne," she said, still looking at her flower. "The promises that a man or a woman give may be false or they may be true. None can ever know which until it is too late. There are ways that you may protect yourself from people but those methods and means will close your heart to love and that would be a great and terrible shame to your life. You must sometimes be made to feel a fool; you must be prepared to take a fall. But let not the risks deter you from the game itself. If you choose to close your heart and only work for that which may avail you of position and power, you will be a weaker person for it. It is the risks we take with our hearts and the risks we take with other people that make us stronger. A life with no risk taken, especially for love, is a life that is not worth living."

She turned and smiled at me. "You were not a fool to take a risk, not if you believed in the love you felt. You would have been more fool to not try." She scowled. "*He* is a fool for not fighting for your hand as a real man should have done."

I laughed a short and bitter laugh. "I think that the boyishness I loved him for was perhaps too strong."

My mother nodded. "Next time, Anne, be sure to risk your heart on a *man,* not a boy. Choose next time a true man, a man with courage, to risk your heart on, and I shall wish you all the joy that marriage is able to bring you." She smiled; it was twisted. There was in that smile such remembrance of happiness and such bitterness of unhappiness that the smile knew not which way to turn. I almost burst into tears to see it upon my mother's face.

"Mother," I leaned forwards, clutching her sleeve. "Are you…" But she stood and gathered me up before I could say more.

"Come," she said, all business now, like my father. The twisted look of sorrow was gone from her face, but I began to wonder. Had my father dallied with another woman? My mother seemed so sad… Was that the reason? Had she uncovered some infidelity?

"We must go and rally the kitchens or there will be nothing for dinner this evening." She looked around and sniffed the fresh, clean air. "Perhaps tomorrow you should hunt," she said. "Take the falcons out into the fields. It would be good to have some fresh meat on the table when your father and brother arrive tomorrow."

"Father and George are coming?" I asked as we walked into the cobbled courtyard.

"Yes, they will be home for a few days in passing. The King's progress route is to take him near to here and not all the court can fit in the small manors along the way."

We said nothing more of the conversation and the next day when George and my father arrived, they brought news. Percy had been promised firmly to Mary Talbot, and they were to be married come the winter, once negotiations on the match were finalised. My father's face was as stone with the disappointment that one of his daughters could have married into the grand family of the north and had failed to. I left my face clear and impassive. But inside me, a once bright and excited girl flung herself to the floor of my heart and died there. On my face, as I ate delicately, there was nothing to show that I had thought anything more of Percy than my father. I would reveal my pain to my mother, but I did not want to do the same for my father. He would have no patience with such emotions. My mother glanced at me with concern; she knew I was hiding my true feelings, and it troubled her, although I do not doubt she understood why.

"Next time, Anne, it will turn out better," my father counselled. "And I do not blame you for this result. I realise that you did all you could to succeed and yet did nothing that should disgrace your family name or personal honour. This matter will be forgotten in time. The Cardinal sought to insult me, through you, and I listen to nothing that great ugly bat has to say. Your reputation at court will be restored. You did all you could, in line with my instructions, and when you return we shall continue on another path."

"Yes, father," I said with my eyes cast on my plate of stewed capon with plums. I had eaten little since I had come to Hever. All was as ash in my mouth.

It took a while for food to taste better. It took a while to stop dreaming of the life I would have had. It took a while for me to take an interest in the things that had fascinated me so before. But when I did heal, I took my mother's advice to my heart and mingled it with the wise counsel that Marguerite had offered me so long ago. When I returned to court I should do so with my head held high. I was still Anne Boleyn. I still had pride in myself, despite the damage this affair had done to my heart, or the wounds it had inflicted on my faith in love.

Chapter Eighteen

Hever Castle
1523

Mary occasionally visited mother and me. She and Henry had often used near-by Penshurst Place as a meeting spot; away from the court, it was a goodly place for two lovers to meet. But with my disgrace, our father did not want the King coming too near our estates, where there was always a chance he might see me and grow angry at our family once more. So Mary came when Henry was away. She tried to coincide these trips with the King's hunting visits to far-away parks or stated to him that she was visiting her sick mother. My name was still enough, apparently, to make him angry. Since Henry was on progress during the summer, visiting honoured courtiers, this light deception was easier.

On one of these visits, as the autumn came bringing golden days and chilly nights, my sister and I were sat together, sewing an altar cloth in the great hall near to the fire, when Mary whispered to me that she had a secret.

"Are you about to tell me then?" I asked waspishly. My time in the country was starting to tire me and my temper was often sharp these days.

"Only if you cease barking at me, Anne," she said calmly with her eyes on her work. The altar cloth was complicated and I had been embroidering it for weeks as something to keep myself occupied. I sewed and rode and read here at Hever, but I had no one to talk with aside from my mother about the books I read, no one to share the joy of the hunt or ride with, no one to dance with me as we did in the Queen's chambers or at court entertainments. Now that I had that company I had so longed for, I was being rude. Mary deserved better.

"I am sorry, sister," I said with a sigh. "I was not made to be a country woman and it tires me, all this… doing nothing all day. Please tell me the secret you are hiding."

"I shall not be able to hide it for much longer," she giggled, one of her hands reached to stroke her belly in the protective gesture that is so easily recognised by women.

"It is the King's?" I asked with my eyes as large as pewter serving plates. It should not have been a huge surprise that she should conceive, but it had been a long time that she had shared his bed without becoming with child. Mary had once told me that she understood the application of various herbs and plants to keep a babe from growing in a woman's womb. I had wondered if she had continued using them in her affair with the King, perhaps not wanting to have a bastard child to foster on her husband. But if she had been using such, they had evidently failed. Mary did not look unhappy about it though; her face was flushed with pleasure to tell me.

Mary shrugged and blushed. "In truth," she muttered, "I am unsure."

"Unsure you are with child, or unsure who the father is?"

She laughed and blushed deeper. "I *am* with child," she assured me. "But the King is not the only man I share a bed with." I looked aghast and she hurried on. "I am married, Anne!" she laughed. "Or had you entirely forgotten my husband?!"

My eyes were larger now. "It is Carey's?" I asked.

Mary shrugged again. "I know not… It could be either in truth." She sighed. "I am *wedded* to Will, Anne, I promised on our wedding day to be bonny and buxom in bed and I have never refused him entry there unless I was visiting with the King that night. The King has been my lover for some years now, and at our father's command I have *never* refused him. Now I am with child and I know not whether it be the King's or my husband's... But legally it will be Carey's child." She made a face. "It is a strange thing when a woman must justify sharing a bed with her own husband," she said. I could not have agreed more.

"Do the King and Carey know?" I asked.

"Neither, as yet," she said. "But they will soon."

I looked at her carefully. I should have been able to tell the moment she walked in, but I had been too busy in my own thoughts of frustration and annoyance. There was a shine to her face but also pallor in her usually rosy cheeks. There was a sweat on her brow, delicate and almost unnoticeable and there was a slight tightening of her gown around her belly. Yes, I should have seen it before she told me. After all, I had waited on Claude of France who had been pregnant almost perpetually through the time I had known her. I had never missed the signals with my mistress, or with my friend Bridget, who also seemed to be continually carrying a babe within her... but I had with my own sister. I had been dwelling too deep in my own troubles to think on her. I felt a little ashamed suddenly, and moved to embrace her, as I could tell she was not displeased by this turn of events. "Mary," I asked slowly. "What if the child is a boy and Henry was to acknowledge it as his own? Bessie Blount's son Fitzroy lives now as a little prince; why should your babe not be the same?"

Mary shook her head a little. "No, I think not, Anne," she said. "Bessie Blount was unmarried when she became great with the King's child. He acknowledged Henry Fitzroy because there was no one else to take responsibility for the child. Although he loves the boy, and has heaped favours on him, the child is still a bastard and the King rarely acknowledges his sins so publicly. In my case, there is Carey, and he is the man whom the King and his Cardinal chose long ago to take responsibility for any children of this affair. Since I have a living husband, Henry's sins are not made flesh for the world to see. They can make Will take responsibility as the father." She stopped sewing and shook her head. "But, if the child turns out to be a boy, there is a chance that Wolsey and the King might think to alter their plan."

She looked around her and ushered me in closer to her. "The Queen has finished her courses entirely," she whispered. "There has been no blood now for almost a year, and although she prays each hour on her knees for the blood to return, it does not. There are other signs too: she cannot keep cool; she tries constantly to control her moods; she cannot sleep at night and has a racing heart even when she is resting. I think that she has passed from the time when she can naturally give a son to the King and is going through the change that all women must face when they cease to breed. And she is afraid, so very afraid that the King will find out and cease to come to her bed entirely." Mary sat back, her face in a grimace. "And soon I shall be in front of her with a great belly," she shook her head. "I do not feel good about that idea."

I sighed. "If Katherine has ceased to be capable of breeding, it is not your fault." I took her hand. "Think not on Katherine now," I whispered. "Think on your child. Were it a boy he might rise as high as Fitzroy in the favour of the King."

"Perhaps, but I think not," Mary said. "The King can be no more sure than I of whether the child is his or not, and he is not one to be cuckolded with another man's child." She shook herself. "But I care not," she smiled. "I shall tell the King it *is* his and Will that it *may* be his. Will is a practical man; he will be happy to have an heir, and pleased that the child might be honoured by the King. And I shall have a baby finally, after all this time, and it will be *my* baby. Both are fine men; I am not ashamed to call either the King or Carey my babe's father."

She paused and a worried look again crossed her face. "But I do wish I could keep it concealed from the Queen," she said. "She is so desperate for a child, so sad... and now I am to parade a great belly before her in this time of her sorrow." Mary shook her head and returned thoughtfully to her sewing.

Our mother was happy to feel Mary's belly and to immediately order cloth with which to make baby clothes. I groaned inwardly at the thought of more months of sewing, even if it was for the arrival of my new nephew or niece. I was tired of the country and of my solitude. I missed my friends. I longed to dance and to play and to sing; to see the fine clothing, new styles, and walk the rushed halls of court. I longed both to gossip and to talk of serious matters; I longed for the flash and the bustle of moving from palace to palace and I longed most of all to have the court turn to hear me sing or quip or play as it had done before I had fallen for that oaf of a boy, Henry Percy.

I could not think of him now without disgust. How could I have loved such a weakling so? And my love for him had caused me to become estranged from the court, from the place where I was supposed to be! I could not see what on earth had possessed me to fall in love with such a whinging, weak, spineless fool! I had given up the court for him? I would have run away with him? Oh, I was a fool to have thought that such a cowardly witless worm could have been my husband! My mother was right; I needed to find a husband who was worthy of me. Should I find a husband, then this time, I swore that he should be a *man* in all he did. Or else I should never marry and content myself with Mary's children or the rooms of a nunnery. I should take no more worms disguised as men into my confidence or arms; from now on I should look for strength in a husband. I would look for a man who had the courage to love the woman he chose, and to face all odds with valour to gain her.

Chapter Nineteen

Oxenheath
1523

During my time of disgrace, as I still languished, an exile, in the country, a messenger came to Hever to tell our mother of a dangerous illness that had befallen my aunt, Jocasta Howard, the wife of our mother's brother, Edmund.

Jocasta had been brought to bed with her tenth child, but had fallen gravely ill with childbed fever and our uncle had sent word to our mother, as a near-by relative, to ask for help with the household. But mother was too weak at this time to attend to her brother's needs and so I, with a volley of servants, rode out for Oxenheath where the aunt I had never met lay apparently close to death.

I arrived at the house late, and was shown in to see my uncle Edmund in the hall. He sat near to the fire with a large cup of wine. He looked up at me with hollow eyes and rose unsteadily to echo my bow to him. His mouth grimaced at me in a strange smile; the innards of his mouth looked entirely black, either stained by wine or due to rampant decay, I knew not which. Either way, the rank smell that came from his fetid mouth was deeply unpleasant. I had to muster all my self control to keep from recoiling from him as he greeted me.

"So, you are Elizabeth's youngest?" he asked after a few moments, staring at me. "You must have been quite a child the last time I saw you."

"I am her youngest daughter, uncle. My brother George is the youngest in the family."

He snorted. "Only three children living!" His gaping grin showed blackened stumps of rotting teeth. "Your family is fortunate in that."

I was silent for a moment; I knew not quite what to say to this extraordinary statement. "My mother regrets the death of her other children... She has loved all her children, uncle."

"Then she is a fool!" my uncle shouted and then laughed. He was clearly very drunk. He fell back into his chair and gulped more wine from the cup in his hands. "I have more children than I know what to do with or how to feed," he spat bitterly. "Each one comes, and is only another mouth to feed, another body to clothe, and with what? I have nothing. I am reduced to the state of a pauper, but must still present myself to the King as a great lord when he calls on me. There is no fuel for the fires of this household, no relief from the incessant bills or taxes; no honour for a knight who fought for his King amongst his brothers and father at Flodden... No! I am undone and unable to do a thing to help myself. What am I to do, Elizabeth's girl? Tell me. I cannot work for my bread like a poor man, and I cannot gain my coin from inheritance as my great brother Thomas has all of that. I am in debt everywhere, and all men refuse to offer me more credit... And I am a gentleman! My wife is dying and the child that has killed her cries in those chambers all day and all night. I have nothing to offer it, just like the others." He took another deep swig of wine, spilling it down his already stained doublet as he guzzled.

"Is there no one that can take the child?" I asked gently.

"My step-mother, your step-grandmother, Agnes Tilney, Dowager of Norfolk will have to take her, and the others." He muttered, his head was getting closer and closer to his cup, his words slurred and then, promptly and clumsily, he fell from his stool to the floor. His head bounced off the dirty rushes and his wine slopped all over his face and neck. It did not wake him. I looked at the pile of flesh and dirty clothing that was my uncle as he started to snore loudly on the cold floor. Then I sighed and rose.

"Take Sir Edmund to his chambers," I said coolly to the servants standing nearby, one looking horrified and the other clearly trying to contain his laughter. "He will need tending during his time of grief," I stared hard at the giggler, who looked immediately chagrined.

"Of course, Mistress," they said and rushed to do my bidding. It took several more of the household servants to carry the dead weight of my uncle to his bed. It took more still to clean up the piles of vomit he left trickling down the stone stairs. I watched him taken away with a heavy heart, and then was brought to the pitiful form of my aunt in her bed. There were two women tending her, but no doctors. Perhaps my uncle could not afford them. I gave them coin, and bade them to send for a doctor from town in the morning light. Through the night I sat with my aunt, trying to keep the fever of her body contained. We washed her with water heated over the fire, and tried to get her to drink something. She muttered feebly in her sleep, a grey sheen of sweat over her skin. I feared greatly that we would lose her in the night, but she was still living when the dawn came. In the morning, a doctor arrived at the house, and was brought to me.

"I have seen worse," he nodded grimly, putting a hand to her forehead, "but not many." He looked up at me. "You did well to keep her cool, Mistress Boleyn. I shall see what can be done for her."

"Please do all that you can, and I shall see you are paid well for your efforts," I replied, and went with a sigh down the stairs to see if my uncle had risen. He had not.

Edmund appeared in the later afternoon looking pale and ill, shaking with the left-over illness caused by his indulgence in wine. I showed him the arrangements that I had made with the servants for his wife's care, and told him that a doctor was now attending on her and I would ensure he was paid. Edmund looked at me with a glance that was at once hopeful and desperate. I asked to see the new child, and he merely indicated up to the chamber and called a maid over to guide me, as he called for a pot of ale to settle his stomach.

In the nursery there were several children, all my cousins, I thought, as I took in their ragged garb with dismay and disapproval. Their clothes were passable from a distance, but close up I could see how old they truly were. My trained eyes could see where sleeves and hems had been let out, where clothes on one back had been made for another, where thread had grown dull. I could see places, carefully concealed by their maid's work, where stitching was loose and tears had appeared, all hidden under cloaks and under arms where only a careful observer would note them. Despite the rather desperate appearance of my noble cousins, they were sweet children. They bowed to me in the manner of gentle-born children and took me to see the baby, Catherine.

"Our mother wished her named for the Queen," the eldest, Henry, told me. The baby was plump and hale; my aunt had given her good health, it seemed. Catherine was sleeping, and certainly not crying constantly as my uncle had said. I sighed. I was becoming increasingly attracted to the idea of having children. Bridget had a full flock of children. Mary was also now having one, and watching her belly swell made me envious of my sister. I would not have minded holding a babe of my own in my arms, although my prospects of making a marriage that I wanted were looking slim these days. All my ventures into the state of love seemed doomed. The men I had thought to marry were either too cowardly, or already attached, or undesirably placed, in the case of James Butler. When was I to find happiness, to find a suitable match... to find a man whose spirit could equal my own?

"Our mother is dying," Henry said, springing me from my thoughts, and the faces of the other children puckered as they looked at me.

"And our father is not well," said Margaret.

"I have seen your father this day and he is well enough," I said. "Who has told you he is unwell?"

"May we beg forgiveness, Mistress," a maid rushed in, with a cautious look on her face. "Their father is not well enough… to see them *today*."

I looked at her expression and sighed a little, understanding. The maids did not want the children to see their father in a state of intoxication. This Howard uncle, it seemed, wanted nothing more than to drown in self-pity and wine whilst his children ran around in rags and his wife lay close to death. I nodded to the maid and she looked relived I had understood her.

"Never mind your father for now," I said. "I am sure that when he is well enough he shall come to you. And your mother has a doctor with her even now. Although we must trust in God, we can trust too in the knowledge of such men. If he can make your mother well, then he will."

They all nodded at me.

"And you will all pray for her, and all be good children?"

They all nodded at me again and I smiled. "Then you are good children and your mother will be proud of you. Now, your father tells me that you are to be placed in the households of relatives to learn to be gentlemen and ladies. One day, you will all grace the court of the King and serve your family well."

They all looked at me expectantly. Despite their fears about their parents, I believe the opportunity to go somewhere other than here was still interesting. "I know not which houses each of you will go to, but you must make the most of all opportunities that are given to you. You must make your father and mother proud. Your father is my uncle, you know, and he is a great war hero; he defended this country against the Scots. You must strive to make him proud of you."

They all nodded at me. I was beginning to think that they must all think as one to have their heads nod in such unison. I left the nursery and turned to the maid who had spoken to me. I put a bag of coins in her hand and spoke through gritted teeth. "Buy those children some clothes. They are the grandchildren of the Duke of Norfolk. They should not be left so, to roam in rags about this place. I shall check to see that those coins have been spent on them and not on anything else."

I was suspicious that the servants might be stealing from Lord Edmund, which was why I included the warning at the end, but she dropped to her knees and held on to my rich skirt. "Thank you, Mistress Boleyn," the maid said in a rough voice, gruff with emotion. She looked up at me with tears in her eyes and I was quite moved to see how much she appreciated this small gift to the children in her care. "It's been so hard to try and keep them going with what little we had," she said, starting to cry.

I put my hands down to her and picked her up, regretting my dark suspicions. "Your loyalty to my family does not go un-noticed," I reassured her. "Look after my cousins and I will see what I can do with my family to send help. This situation cannot go on. These children are *Howards*; we shall get them into better situations than this." I looked at her and nodded. "Remain as loyal as you are and God will reward you for it," I said, "as will I."

The maid nodded and went to show the children the money I had left them. I blinked away tears, both of sympathy and frustration. I went to the doctor, who seemed more hopeful than I had thought about Jocasta's recovery. I stayed for another few days, until the lady herself was well enough to sit up in bed and take some broth. Then, leaving what I could for her care, and asking the doctor who still attended her to send his bills to my father, I rode back to Hever to see what help there was for my uncle Edmund and his children.

"Mother, it was a *disgrace!*" I stormed around her room as she sat calmly on the floor near to the fire on a cushion. "Those children are of noble blood, *Howard* blood, and they look like paupers; thank God and *Jesu* that the servants are loyal or they would be starved and naked running around the place like savages!"

My mother sighed. "My brother Edmund was never fortunate, it seemed," she said wearily. "He was ever apt to feel sorry for himself, and to turn to drink more than he should, hindering any possibility of success as he was so weighed down by the burden of his own self-sorrow."

"Well, nothing seems to have changed there," I spat. I was furious. During the ride back home to Hever I had become angrier and angrier thinking of those children in their wasted finery and of their father drowning in wine and self-pity falling all over the floor.

"My brother, Edward, tried to help him several times," my mother continued, her face clouding with sorrow as she thought on her dead brother, killed in the last English-French war. "But somehow Edmund always ended up back where he started; in debt and desperation." She looked up at me. "I will write to my stepmother of Norfolk and ask her to take the girls into her household. My brother, Thomas, can take at least the eldest boy and there are others that I know that will take the other boys. They will be taken off of Edmund's hands and then he may be able to cope with the rest of his debts. Come now, Anne, play something for me, I have such a headache this night and this talk saddens me. We will do all we can to help Edmund, but I fear that unless he attempts to help himself, that there is little we can do."

I acquiesced and took to the virginals in the room. Playing on them soothed me and soon I was lost in the music, thinking no

more of my poor Howard cousins and hearing only the music
as my lithe fingers slipped and plucked from note to note.

Chapter Twenty

Hever Castle
1524

The days moved slowly for me at Hever. I was desperate for news of court, of new dances and new music… of anything really. My days felt long as I read, sewed and hunted. I wrote to Margaret and to Bridget, telling them of my sorrow at being so far from them and received answers which warmed my heart. I rode out every day but even the thrill of new falcons or books, sent by George, could not lift the dull sheen that had fallen over me since I was banned from the brilliance of court. I was not made for a life in the country.

In January, as harsh winds battered about the castle and snow fell in wide droves blocking the lanes and passes, Percy was married to Mary Talbot. There were reports almost immediately that the marriage was a horrible failure. The couple despised each other, it seemed, and could not keep that fact from others. They argued in public, and Percy was so obviously miserable that all who saw him noted it. In some ways, although this will not charm you, I felt better for knowing that. Percy had refused to fight for me, and now he was in a match he loved not. In some ways, I believe I thought it served him well to be unhappy. I loved Percy no more. In many ways, I believe I hated him. I felt resentful towards him. He should have fought for me! He should have stood up to his father, to the Cardinal, even to the King! But he had not had the strength to fight, and I bore a grudge against him for it. In my mind, I murdered both Percy and the Cardinal many times… I did not wish to be matched now with such a witless worm as Percy, but that did not mean that I wished him well… Oh, my temper was resentful indeed.

Tom rode over to see me at times from Allington Castle, the seat of his family; he took time away from court whenever he could during the days of my banishment. He read me his poetry and we rode out, or played at cards with my mother who always enjoyed his company when she was strong enough. Tom did not question me about Percy; perhaps he feared riling my temper, so ever near the surface in those days of my exile. Perhaps he did not want me to remember Percy at all... I was grateful, to be honest. I did not want to talk of Percy to another person. I was sick of Henry Percy. The thought of him made me almost nauseous now. Such a worm! Such a boy!

When Tom came to visit, I was reminded of my first days in England, when I came, new, fresh and furious to have been removed from my beloved France. I remembered how he had made me feel then... As though I were welcome, as though I were a part of this new land I had come to rest on. And without the rest of the court, I felt as though I were a butterfly to his flower, flying to him once more. I believed I relied a lot on Tom Wyatt in those days of my banishment from court, perhaps more so than I would have admitted at the time. I was still attracted to him; I never sought to deny that I was not. But nothing had changed in his situation, nor in mine. At such times, when I saw him, I had to remind myself over and over that the reason he excited me so now was that there was so little in my life that was exciting. I had to remind myself that I was not in love with him, that I could not love him for he had a wife already and all I could be was his mistress.

I had to talk to myself a lot in those days; reminding myself that here was a friend, a courtly admirer... and nothing more. I found myself comparing him to Percy, and finding much that was better about Tom Wyatt than there was about Henry Percy of Northumberland. But still, there was nothing for me in a match with either. I must look elsewhere if I wanted to contract a marriage, find love... have children...

My mother was recovering, but the strange illness had left her weak. She was visited by doctors that my father sent from London, who bled her regularly, saying that her illness was caused by an imbalance of the humours. But the blood-letting only seemed to make her weaker still, and I worried for her often. They left little sugar-sticks of medicine, infused with rose water, but these medicines seemed to do her little good either. A strange old woman from the nearby village was a frequent visitor at my mother's bedside too that winter. She came often, bringing baskets of dried wild herbs and instructing me in their use. I tended to mother, fed her chicken broth with powdered almonds and rice, a good food for invalids. I gave her bread soaked in wine and kept her warm, for she was often cold. At night I would sleep in her chamber, and read the Canterbury Tales to her, an old favourite of hers, as she lay in bed and I sat by the fire. In the nights she would shiver despite the good layers of woollen blankets, and I would climb into her bed from my pallet on the floor to keep her warm. It was as though she could just not hold the heat in her own body.

I was scared for her, my sweet mother. But soon and in parts, she became better. Well enough to walk in the gardens and ride a little, although we had to be careful about wearying her. Tom would come and keep her spirits merry, telling us snippets of court gossip to make her smile. I was grateful to him once again for that.

And as my mother started to recover, I longed more and more to return to court. The affair with Percy felt like a hundred years ago and I felt like a fool for having given my heart to such a weak and ineffectual boy. I wanted to return to the dances and intrigues, to the life and excitement. My blood sang for the candle-light and the sunny gardens, for the gossip and the talk… for anything other than more months or years of constant embroidery, locked away in this castle that I had once loved, but was now a prison for my soul.

After six months of languishing in the country at Hever, my father returned home to announce two things. The first was that talks of my engagement to James Butler were officially dissolved. Due to the lack of enthusiasm on my father's part, Piers Butler had walked away from the match, but my father still had hopes that the title of Ormond would be his with time. The second announcement was that the Queen had requested my mother's presence and mine at the Christmas celebrations at court, adding a kind note that we were only to come, "should we *both* have recovered from our late illnesses."

Apparently, and unbeknownst to me, my family and friends had circulated a rumour that I had left because I had contracted the same illness as my mother, and that we were both recovering from this sickness in the country. Although many knew the true reason for my banishment, this lie had been allowed to live, and grow, until most people had accepted it as a truth. Strange how a lie that is told often may come to be known as truth, but that was the way of the court…

My mother was better recovered now and I think to a certain extent she, like me, longed to be back at court. But she was not totally recovered and I feared that the Christmas celebrations may be too much for her to undertake.

"Oh, nonsense, child!" she laughed, and drank deeply of her wine as we sat at the table with our father upon his return. "Who is the child and who the parent here? If I say I am well enough to return to court, then I am well enough!"

My father looked steadily at her, trying to read her. "If it is too much, Elizabeth, then I would rather you regained your strength here."

She scowled at both of us. "Should you *order* me to stay, husband, then I shall stay at Hever as a good and obedient wife. If you do not order me, and you value my own opinion, then I shall return to court, by your side, where I wish to be."

Father looked down at the table and I saw what looked like the glimmer of tears in his eyes. But when he lifted his face there was nothing there to suggest that he had felt any such emotion. "It is settled then," he said. "You, Anne, are to return and take up a place in the Queen's chambers as maid of honour, as you were before. You, Elizabeth..." He paused, looking at her, and for a moment there passed between them a flash of what once had been so strong, of what once had been theirs alone. I wondered again on what the trouble had been between them. Neither would confide in me, so I was left much to wonder.

"You, Elizabeth," he repeated, "will return with me to court as you wish and we shall be a family together for the celebration of Christmas." He took her hand and smiled at her. "I could think of nothing I should like more," he said and clasped her hand tightly. It hurt her, but she didn't mind.

I returned to the court that winter and nothing was said about my disaster with Percy or my months of absence. In fact, it was as though the whole thing had never happened, and that was just the way that I wanted to think about it too.

The court and I had always understood each other well. I fell in line with its fabrications on the reality of life.

My circle of friends was reconvened; when I met with Bridget and Margaret again I rushed to them, embracing them with a happy laugh. There were new additions to our circle, too, Will Compton and Henry Norris were much in the company of George now. New voices and new talents; our ring of poets and courtiers was strong and vivid. We ruled the heart of the court. I was in love once again, but with no man, not even with Tom, who had, over these months, become more like a brother to me. Much as I had fallen for the Court of Margaret of Austria as a girl, I was now in love with the Court of England. I was just so pleased to be home, at the court, where I belonged! My circle moved much with that of Mary Tudor,

Duchess of Suffolk. She loved to surround herself with the youth and wit of the court, perhaps because with a husband like Charles Brandon, she saw little of wit within her own home. Mary and I often played in masques she devised, and she delighted in talk of the old days in France when she had been Queen.

Since we now moved in circles that included royalty within them, and the King's mistress also, it was not surprising that Henry himself was a frequent and active member of the group. He seemed to have all but forgotten his anger at me, and when we met, he was charming and polite. We were a lively bunch and it was with us that the themes and music for the court's dances and masques took shape. Mary of Suffolk was often given credit for ideas that came from our heads, but that mattered little; princes take what they wish of their servants. All knew that it was more often George and I, or Tom and others who came up with the entertainments. The circle was a hive of ideas and games. We were the ones to watch at court, we were the bright young things.

My sister Mary's pregnancy was advancing and her belly was swollen; no one could doubt the condition she was in now. The Queen was gentle and gracious to my sister and was interested, perhaps rather too interested, in the advancing stages of the pregnancy. When my sister came to the Queen's chambers to serve her, Katherine would hover over Mary's belly in a strange manner that often disturbed my sister. Despite the fact that Katherine must have known the child may have been fathered by her own husband, she seemed attracted to Mary, as she was to any woman with the lump of a babe in her belly... She was drawn to Mary in a fascinated, if desperate, manner.

Queen Katherine now was known all over the court to have lost her monthly courses; she could not keep something as momentous as that secret for long. It was not made known by proclamation of course, but gossip in the halls of court carries as much weight with courtiers as the Great Seal of the King, and so everyone knew. No one spoke of it around Katherine; within her chambers we had to pretend that her signs of ceasing to breed were but symptoms of other things. But Katherine had passed her days of bearing children, and we all knew it.

Katherine still prayed daily, thrice daily at least, and silently at every Mass she attended, for a child to be given to her, a son to grant the King, though we all knew that it would have to be some miracle indeed; for not only was she without monthly bleeding, but Henry had ceased visiting her bed at night. There were rumours that should she die, for in many ways she seemed quite frail and old, he would marry again and quickly, to provide an heir to the throne. There were other rumours also, more dangerous than the first, that perhaps Henry intended to annul the marriage between he and Katherine, to send her to a convent as previous kings had done with wives who could not bring them the sons they wanted. If the Queen went to a convent, then the King could marry again. There were many whispered conversations on whether a princess could be found in Spain, or even France, who could bring the long-awaited heir to the King of England. The last rumour seemed the most fantastical; that the King intended to place the bastard-born son of his mistress Bessie Blount on the throne. Henry Fitzroy was now a fine, well-grown lad of six, who seemed hale and hearty. Bastards had assumed the throne before in the absence of a legitimate male heir; would the base-born son of Bessie Blount become next in the Tudor line to the throne?

We knew not what the King's plans were, in truth, but often I saw my father regarding Mary's swollen belly with a speculative look, as though he were imagining those very things I had said to Mary in Hever; what if her child were a boy born to the King and what if he should acknowledge it as such? Henry was in need of a male heir… what if my sweet sister should provide him with another? Would the bastard born of the Boleyns be acknowledged by the King and stand the same chances as Henry Fitzroy? We knew not, but I could almost hear the hope in our father's heart beating like a drum.

All anyone could say for sure was that the Kingdom was without a male heir, and if Henry wanted a son to follow him, he would have to get one from someone other than Katherine.

Both Henry and his nobles feared what might happen to the peace of the realm if the King died. His only legitimate child was his daughter, Mary, and no woman had ever ruled England in her own stead. The one time that a woman had tried to do so, the country had been plunged into years of civil war. Without a legitimate male heir, the future of the country was in peril. There were too many possible distant claimants to the throne who might all stake a claim, if the one who inherited the throne after our King was not strong enough to hold it. There would be a war, just as there had been before the Tudors ruled, just as there had been when Matilda, granddaughter of the Conqueror, had tried to rule England.

And so Katherine prayed. She prayed on her knees until her flesh broke and her skin bled. Her knees wept and split from hours spent on the cold floor of her chapel. She prayed until her voice broke and her heart wept. As the celebrations of Christmas sounded around us that year, Katherine took herself to her personal chapel to pray to God and the Virgin over and over again. Asking them to grant her a son, as God had done to the Holy Mother of Christ.

Unless God favoured her with a miracle, there would be no more children born of this royal bed. And it seemed that God was not listening to his most despairing daughter, Katherine. It seemed that God had turned his face from her pain, and would not grant her the most frantic wish of her heart.

Chapter Twenty-One

Greenwich Palace
1524

In March, the King ordered a new piece of equipment from the workshops at Greenwich; a new harness and saddle for his horse. It was his own design, and Henry was sure it would turn out to be a wonderful modern achievement. So great was his enthusiasm for this new creation that he ordered a tournament to test the harness, and celebrations to follow in the wake of the joust. Henry could be rather boyish in his enthusiasm for new things, especially new things that he had had a part in designing; but the court needed little encouragement to enter into a new entertainment.

All the court turned out in the chill of the early morning to the brightly coloured jousting rings at Greenwich, our eyes bright with the expectation of enjoyment. The air smelt keen and clean; a heady scent of England as she withstands the last of the winter and looks to the first days of spring. Our gowns and cloaks were lined with furs and our undergarments were thick with wool to hold off against the cool air that whipped around us. It was a fine March day; cold, bright and brusque and the thrill of the coming contest was in our veins. Katherine was to preside over the entertainments as the *Queen of Hearts*, and her drawn, pale face was shining with happiness to resume her traditional role as Henry's object of desire. He rode to her side and took a token of her colours upon the edge of his lance. To see her face rekindled with happiness for this public proclamation of his loyalty to her was dually a sweet and wretched sight. This public show may have honoured her openly, but in private we all knew that the King did not seek to make love to her wasted body. She was the *Queen of Hearts* here, but he did not show that same affection to her in private.

During the entertainments I had remained, as befitted my place, mostly by Katherine's side within the stands that lined the jousting pitch. I brought heated wine and sweetmeats to my mistress as she asked for them, but as Henry and the Duke of Suffolk prepared to undertake a match, Katherine sent me to refill her supply of wine from barrels in the lower stalls. As the King and Suffolk took up their positions at either end of the jousting ring, I had moved forwards, Katherine's jug in my hands, awaiting the wine bearer to fill it from his barrel. I tapped my feet impatiently at the slowness of the man filling the leathern jug and looked up at the match preparing to begin. Each of the competitors were fine jousters. It was likely to be an exciting match and I wanted to be back in my position at the top of the stalls near Katherine, so that I could view it better.

The trumpets blasted out heavy notes which filled the stands with the ringing notes of battle. The crowds quietened their conversations and all eyes were drawn to Henry on his great horse. The huge stallion reared in anticipation and there was a cheer from the gathered crowd as the horses of the Duke and King started to ride at each other with furious speed. And it was then that I noticed something was wrong… very wrong. As the two knights thundered towards each other across the wet earth I saw that Henry had not lowered the visor on his helmet. He was in terrible danger; riding towards Suffolk's raised lance with his face bared, naked and unprotected. Suffolk had not noted the vulnerable position his master was in; from behind the steel wall of his own helmet, visibility was much limited. Henry had not seemed to notice, either, that he was riding at Suffolk with an entirely unprotected face… Should the Duke's lance hit the King, then he could be killed.

Others, apart from me, had seen this too. Shouts of alarm and fear broke out through the crowd. "*Hold! Hold!*" cried many voices, all lapping over each other, as the great horses galloped towards each other with the deafening noise of metal and hooves beating on wet earth. I shrieked in fear as I saw Suffolk's great lance pointed squarely at Henry's bare and unprotected face. Throwing Katherine's jug to the floor, I raced forwards to the edge of the stalls where I grabbed a guard and screamed into his face.

"He will *die*!" I shouted at the surprised guard, who evidently had been snoozing in his position, and turned to stare at me with dazed eyes. I pointed at Henry. "The *King*!" I shouted. "His face… his helmet! The Duke will kill him!"

Just at that moment the two men came together in a great crash. Suffolk's lance first hit Henry's chest, but its tip, splintering into a hundred pieces, crashed upwards into his unprotected face. Henry was hit hard. Time and noise seemed to stop as I saw the stretched faces of the crowds convulse in horror. The King of England flew from his new saddle, sailing backwards through the air, and he smashed with a great crash on the dirty floor of the tournament ring.

He did not move.

I screamed and before I knew what I was doing I had ducked under the barrier and found myself sprinting over the jousting pitch to Henry's side, my skirts bundled in my hands, my legs flying across the ground as though I were a wild hind. I fell to my knees at his side, looking with horror on his face. I was one of the first to reach him. I grabbed his hand, staring in fearful fascination at the thick, bright blood that covered his face, and the wealth of splinters that stuck out from his helmet's visor. The helmet was pushed so far back on his head that I gave it one touch and it came off entirely, taking many of the splinters with it.

Blood and wooden shards covered his face; his eyes were red with gore. I fought back a powerful urge to vomit as I stared in frozen horror. There was so much blood that I thought our beloved King was dead. He was not moving. I pressed my ear to the plate on his chest and tried to listen for a heart beat, but I could hear nothing through the metal. I looked again at his face and down at his unmoving body. All seemed to happen around me as though time had slowed.

From around me I heard shouts and screams of shock and terror and then, it was as though time had started again. All around me there were people. A pair of hands tried to take me from Henry's side, but I shook them off and shot a crazed, savage look at the guard who had tried to remove me. The man backed off as he looked into my demonic face and wild eyes. I did not care. I turned my attention back to Henry, to the unmoving body before me, my King, lying battered and broken on the dirty floor.

I took my sleeve of heavy green velvet, embroidered with a beautiful pattern of golden honeysuckle, and held it to the blood gushing from his handsome face. I pressed the thick fabric of my gown against wounds from which blood burbled like a stream, flowing over his face and neck, dripping to the brown earth beneath him. I thought he was dead. Tears that I had not noticed until now started to blind me as I wiped clean his face. Then, even as my heart sank in sorrow, knowing that our King, this great man, was dead, suddenly, to my relief, I saw two open blue eyes staring up at me with dazed wonder and awe.

"I knew not…" Henry whispered as he looked up at me.

"Your Majesty!" I cried out in relief. "My King!" I wept, unable to say any more in my relief at hearing his voice. Others around me seemed to sag slightly, and there were shouts from the crowd gathered about the King that he still lived… that he had spoken.

The pale face and weak body of the Duke of Suffolk collapsed on his knees at my side with a great bang and crash of metal. "Henry," he croaked in a voice that grated with despair as he groped for the King's hand. "Your Majesty… My friend… Henry… say that I have not killed you." Suffolk put his head to his King's metal-covered chest and groaned with pain and despair. As well he might, for if he had killed the King of England, he would pay for it with his own life, friend or no.

Henry was not looking at Suffolk, however; his blue eyes were fixed on my pale and weeping face. I used my sleeve to wipe more, fresh blood from the wounds on his face, and I tried to smile at him. Henry smiled up at me, his eyes dazed, unfocused, and his words slurred as they left his mouth.

"I knew not…" he repeated as he gripped my hand tighter.

"What did you not know?" I whispered back, not caring for the proper method of address as I leaned in towards his broken and swollen face.

"That angels… were so dark of hair," Henry said wonderingly, staring at my face. His eyes were flickering strangely as though he were not quite in this world. There was a dreamy quality to his words as though he were half-asleep; his words were muffled and unclear. I felt fresh fear break out in my heart for him; he seemed already half-taken to the realms of heaven in this confused state.

Suffolk laughed at Henry's words, almost hysterical in relief. "That is no *angel*, my lord, it is Mistress Anne Boleyn! You are well, Henry… you are at court… the joust… do you remember?"

Henry frowned a little, and winced, and then his eyes travelled to Suffolk. At seeing the King's eyes focus on his face, Suffolk started to stutter at him in panic. "We charged each other in a fair joust, Majesty… You were knocked from your horse… Your visor was not lowered… I knew this not when we charged. My lance hit your face. My Lord, my King, forgive me, please." Suffolk's voice cracked as he spoke his last words and I saw tears running down his face. Despite my general dislike of the Duke, I could not doubt that he loved his master well, and also feared greatly for what might happen to him should Henry die of his wounds. Suffolk grasped at

Henry's metal-covered hand, banging it against the steel of his own armour, over his heart. I shook my head at the Duke, trying to remove Henry's hand from his; bruising the King was hardly going to help him now. Suffolk seemed not to notice the fluttering of my hands at his, however, so fraught were the emotions of his heart. Henry's other hand, removed of its metal glove, still lay in my own hand.

He blinked. Blood fell like tears from his eyes. He took his hand from Suffolk's grip, shaking at it to remove the metal casings. We helped him, and he lifted his hand to his eyes, wiping at the bloody mess that covered them. He looked at the blood on his hand, then at the deep stains on my sleeve and back to the Duke's pallid face with amazement.

"The joust… yes…. I remember, Charles. I did not think until the last to wonder why I could see you so well. I remember…"

Henry looked at me; his face creased with confusion, he tried to lift himself. Suffolk and I pulled him up to the sound of armour creaking and groaning. Sitting up, Henry's face was closer to mine and I could see the piercing ice-blue of his eyes, bright against bloodstained sockets. I felt his breath on my skin, and his hand, warm and alive, was still holding my fingers. In the sudden intimacy of the position, on the dirty floor of that yard, I felt such a strange mixture of emotions. It was not desire as I had often felt for him before; this was not a moment for such an emotion. It was more like a wave of sadness, of happiness, of protectiveness, of… love. It washed over me, born from the fear that he might have been taken from me.

I choked suddenly on fresh tears, overcome by the different emotions that were fighting for space in my heart. I fought them back, staring into Henry's eyes as he stared at me. It was as though he had never seen me before; as though he were looking at me anew. He stared at me as though I were a cup of water and he a man crawling from a desert. My face flushed under his stare. I lowered my eyes and he reached out to take my chin with his hand. He stroked my cheek with his thumb, streaking blood and dirt upon my face.

"I thought you were an angel," he whispered with wonder in his voice.

"Anne was the first to your side even as you fell, Your Majesty," I heard the familiar voice of my brother say behind us, gruff with relief. "It was as though she *flew* to your side past us all."

Henry glanced at George and then looked back at me; a small smile appeared on his bloody face "The first to my side?" he asked and I nodded, gulping back tears of relief. "Ahead of all my guards? Ahead of all my lords and servants… you, my lady?"

"I feared..." I choked and could not finish the words as another deep sob rose from my chest suffocating my mouth.

"Hush, my lady," Henry consoled. The blood on his face still trickled; a light rain had started to fall that carried it in tiny streams down his face and onto his fine armour. "I am well, and with devotion such as yours, I shall live a long and happy life. I thought you an angel, Mistress Boleyn, but I am happier to find you still a woman and I still a man."

The noise of the crowd about us grew with shouts of relief. We were packed in by a huge crowd of people gathered about the fallen form of our King. There were shouts that I recognised; voices of my circle of friends, and then of the King's sister, Mary, who broke through the crowd with imperious cries. She saw the bloody sitting figure of her brother and sagged to her knees at Suffolk's side.

"Sweet *Jesu* Henry!" she exclaimed as she took in Henry's face and my blood-soaked clothes. "Sweet *Jesu*!" she said again, her face pale as she broke into tears. Suffolk took her roughly in his arms and held her as she sobbed, her face in her hands like a child.

"I am well, sister," Henry said to her. "Fear not. I am well. Come, Charles, help me to rise, the people must see that I am fine or there will be panic, there will be rumours of my death." He turned to me. "Wipe my face once more, Anne," he said. "The Queen will not face my blood as bravely as you." He smiled at me again. "But then, you are of good English stock, and your heart is like that of a lioness in the protection of your King."

I did not feel like a lioness now, trembling and shaking. I lifted my dark green sleeve to his face and wiped the wounds on his handsome face as clean as I could, feeling him wince in pain under the stroke of velvet against torn flesh. He released his hold on my hand and as he rose, whispered in my ear words that made my cheeks flame and my heart race. I still remember the feeling of his breath on my cheek, and the way that my heart pounded to feel him so close. Refusing support from Suffolk or the others crowded anxiously around him, Henry then stood and raised his hands to the skies.

"Praise be to God!" Henry cried out in a booming voice. "Praise be to God! Your sovereign is well and unharmed!"

The crowd around him roared in frenzied, hysterical cheering. There were shouts of joy and relieved laughter bursting out from all around us. I rose shakily to my feet and saw the ashen face of Katherine as she sat down heavily on her great chair in the stalls, weak with relief that her husband was not dead. The King refused to sit down, or be tended by physicians; he was fine, he insisted. He had the splinters removed from his face and took to his horse once more, riding another six matches to prove that he was well. He could not appear weak or injured before his people; this, we understood well. To do so would create fear throughout his lands, and spread panic into the hearts of the country.

The Queen looked on as her husband rode out again and again. She tried to regain her composure and stay calm during each of the following matches, but her face remained pale and her hands shook as she clapped them each time he won. But she remained in her seat, watching her husband bravely as he knocked all other combatants from their horses. Although Henry had great skill in the joust, I doubt that the other lords he was matched against that day tried hard to best him. They had almost seen their King die… none wanted to be the man who knocked him from his horse for a second time that day.

Suffolk looked green as a frog for the rest of the day; he had, after all, almost killed Henry, and had the King died, Suffolk's head would surely have rolled for it. As it was, Henry kept saying that it was no one's fault but his own; he should have made sure the visor was down. Henry had emerged bloody, but victorious. He looked like a true knight on his horse. The crowds were entirely enamoured of their apparently invincible sovereign, but I, who had seen his bloody face up close, knew how much pain he must have been in, and how much strength it must have taken to ride out again. He did it for his people, to show them that he had not been harmed in truth. Henry showed strength for them. He was truly a man to be admired.

I went to change my bloody gown with the permission of the Queen who said nothing about my, perhaps, *improper* behaviour at flying to her husband's side. When she looked at the blood on my gown her face fell another shade of white, looking almost grey. She had not seen Henry close up as yet, but she could guess at his injuries by the long streaks and stains of red-brown upon my dress. It must have taken a great deal of self-control for Katherine to sit there and continue to cheer for her husband, when all she could really have wanted was to tend to him in private.

Margaret came to me and put a hand to my shoulder as I left the Queen. "Are you alright?" she asked, her normally pale face even whiter than before.

I nodded, although I was by no means sure that I was fine. "I will be well, Margaret," I whispered, feeling a little sick as I looked on the blood on my sleeves. "I need to change."

She looked at me with worried eyes, but nodded to me.

I was still shaking with shock as I changed. I could not untie the ribbons or unclasp the pins on my gown myself. Bess had a hard time undoing my dress as I shivered and shook before her. She brought water and I shook my head at her as she went to heat the water over the fire. I wanted the blood off me. Now. I could not bear to have Henry's blood upon my hands and my clothes any longer. It only increased the shaking of my hands and the pounding of my heart to see it there.

As Bess helped me to wash, I watched the blood of a king flow from my hands and my face with silent and detached horror. There was blood everywhere, it seemed, blood floating, brown-red in the bowl of water before me and blood smeared on the floor from my gown. Blood on my hands, blood stained on the white edges of my undergarments. The blood of the King of England covered me.

As I regained my composure, as I gulped down wine and felt my maid's hands cleanse me, I thought that England had come close to another civil war on this day. We had almost lost our sovereign. *I* had almost lost him; that sudden thought brought new tears to my swollen eyes. I had to hold my chin and clench my jaw to stop my teeth from rattling against each other.

Cleansed of the blood and changed into a dress of grey and pink silks, Bess plied me with wine until the shaking of my hands had stopped. By the time I emerged at court for the evening's entertainments, I was mostly recovered.

A great feast had been laid on for the aftermath of the joust; Henry and Katherine were at its head. The King was cleaned, cleansed and changed into a fine purple and gold tunic. His wounds were still there, of course, but they were pink now, and bled no more. Rude, ruddy wounds ran over his face, marring his handsome visage, but his manner was utterly unchanged, as though nothing terrifying had occurred that day. He laughed and jested with his lords and complimented ladies. If he mentioned the accident at all, it was only to assure people that it was nothing, and that his wounds were mere scratches. He jested that Suffolk had better work on strengthening that arm for the next time they came to face each other.

But I saw Henry press his hand to his head when he thought few were watching; I knew that he was in great pain and trying to disguise it. He was trying to reassure his courtiers and his enemies alike of his strength and vigour, to reassure us all, to make it seem that he was invincible. But it was a show, it was an act. Henry felt great pain and I could see that even if others could not. In my breast, as I watched his efforts to disguise his suffering, I felt more admiration for him; he would disguise his personal pain and fear for the good of his subjects and the good of his realm. I felt my heart beat with a special kind of esteem that day, one I had never felt for a man before. It was a new feeling, not born solely from the admiration for a fine pair of eyes, or a good leg… It was for the man beneath the crown… It was for the strength I saw within him.

George came to partner me at the dance after the feast. My brother was an excellent dancer and our steps complimented each other well. He was a pleasure to dance with. "Thank God that Mary was not here today," he said as we passed each other in the dance. "Or there might have been an early arrival of the babe."

"Is that all you think on?" I whispered angrily. "You and father… thinking of nothing but the prospect of what may come from this pregnancy? Does nothing else concern you? The King could have *died* today."

"*Hush*! Anna!" he whispered reproachfully, but not denying the charge I placed. "None may speak of the death of the King, you know that. To do so is to commit treason!"

I nodded and gave my hand to him as we left the dance. He was right, no matter what my irritation with him. I should be more guarded of my tongue.

"What was it that the King said to you as he rose?" George asked as we stood at the side through the next dance, taking wine to our lips. "I was not close enough to hear."

I blushed a little, half for the thought of how close Henry had been to me in that moment, and half in chagrin, thinking of my fear. "He said, *I shall not forget this.*"

George looked at me and nodded. Then he shivered a little. "I shall not either," he mused, shaking his head. "The speed at which you flew across that field was amazing. Everything else seemed to have frozen, as though I looked at the joust through ice on a pond…. No one else could move, it seemed, but you."

"I knew not what I was doing. I just knew that I had to get to him," I said wondering at my own actions of the day. "It is strange, is it not? I cannot think why I forgot myself so."

"Can you not?" George countered and looked sideways at me with a speculative look that reminded me so much of our father that I felt a finger of ice move up my spine. "Well," he said. "It seems that the *King* will not be forgetting you, even if you forget yourself, sister."

I followed his glance to the raised dais where Henry and his queen sat overlooking the assembly. I saw the King looking in our direction. I swept to the floor in a graceful curtsy and as I rose, he held his goblet up to me. I curtsied again and a flush of blood rose across my neck and my cheeks.

George rose from his bow and whispered in my ear. "It would seem that the King has a fondness for the name *Boleyn* on a woman." My brother moved swiftly away before I could retaliate.

I looked up again, but Henry had moved his glance elsewhere.

Chapter Twenty-Two

Beaulieu, Essex
1524

In May, my grandfather, the old Duke of Norfolk, passed into the arms of God, and his son, my mother's brother, Thomas Howard, took his title. Thomas Howard was fifty-two when he became the Duke of Norfolk. An older man, although still strong, he suffered much from pains in his bones, and apparently constant indigestion. My uncle of Norfolk was always grumbling just under his breath, something that gave him a distinct, if slightly irritating, presence in any room. He was a thin, hawk-like man with a great long nose and piercing, clever eyes that missed nothing.

It was at this time, too, that my sister took to her chambers to wait for the coming of her child. Being a younger son, Carey had no estate of his own. Most of the time Will and Mary resided at court, where they had chambers together, but for Mary's confinement, they had chosen to remove to Beaulieu, near Chelmsford, where Will was the Keeper of the King's house. They had a right to lodgings there from this appointment, and it was thought that a house as beautiful as Beaulieu would serve as a good place for Mary to raise their child. It was also not too far from London, and therefore convenient for her to return to court once the child was born. The house had many family connections for us Boleyns. Once called "New Hall", it had been granted to our great-grandfather, Thomas Butler, Earl of Ormond. Our grandmother, Margaret Boleyn inherited the house from her father, and passed it to *our* father who sold it to the King. Henry lavished vast amounts on the house, restoring and rebuilding it, and it was he who renamed it Beaulieu. The front of the house was of warm red brick; there were waterfalls in the courtyards, stained glass in the chapel and even hot and cold water flowing in the royal chambers. It was a goodly place for a babe to be born and to live, and Henry had approved it as the place where his mistress could give birth.

Mary's last months of pregnancy had progressed without incident. We had told her, of course, of the jousting accident, but had played down Henry's near scrape with death so as not to panic her in the final stages of pregnancy. Only female relatives or servants were allowed to enter the darkened lying-in chambers and so mother and I went to see Mary while she awaited her baby, in the muggy, gloomy chambers that were synonymous with the last stages of pregnancy for nobility.

The fires were lit and burned happily, even though the sealed windows and candles would have made the room warm enough for comfort. The scent of sweat filled the air, unable to be washed away with the fresh bouquet of new air, for there was none. The chambers of a woman awaiting a child had to be sealed off from the air of the outside, lest it bring in disease to threaten the life of the child, or its mother. Herbs lined the floors and their smell brought some relief, but I could see only by the light of the candles and the fire. The lying-in chamber was dark and oppressive. There was no sun. There was only thick air to breathe. I shivered at the thought that someday I would face such chambers too, when having my own children, but perhaps the thought of holding a son or daughter in my arms would compensate for being shut in dull, dark quarters.

Birth was a difficult time for women, a dangerous time. Fear of dying in childbed merged with love and desire for the baby, so that the waiting for the child to come into the world became such a mix of terror and pleasure that there was nothing to compare it to. Mary was worried, of course, this being her first child, and ready to take the advice of anyone who would offer it. But she was also excited. I could see her longing to look upon the face of her child, and to know the feel of her babe in her arms. Once again, I envied my older sister. I would like to feel the weight of a child of my own in my arms. I would like a child of my own to love, to hold, to teach and to bring up. I was twenty-three now, and longed for a settled life, for a husband, and for children of my own. I still wanted to be a part of the court, of course; it was as close and precious to me as the blood within my veins, but I was starting to see that there were other things in life I wanted just as much... family, love, marriage, children. The simple wants of most women, I believe.

Some few weeks into Mary's lying-in, she felt the first pangs of birth. They came somewhat earlier than expected, and my poor sister went into a long and painful labour. My mother and I helped the midwives to do their bloody work, reassuring Mary, holding her hands, and helping her to hold or push as she panted and screamed through the final stages. We muttered and cried out words of comfort and strength, yet we spoke those words to reassure ourselves too; we feared for her life at times. The strain and trial she endured were long, and my pretty sister groaned like a horse with colic as she strove to bring her child into the world.

Eventually, two days after her first show of pains, I heard the first powerful screams of a possible Tudor bastard reverberate around the walls of the estate. Fat little arms waved in the air, and cries of distress emerged from the infant's mouth as the child wailed at being taken from such a safe, warm place as Mary's body. The birthing chamber was heavy with the sickly scent of blood and gamey afterbirth which hung in the air and stuck in the nostrils, but Mary's pained, exhausted and triumphant face as she cradled her first child in her arms will endure in my memory as one of the most beautiful things I have ever seen in my life.

"A girl..." Mary breathed with great satisfaction. "This will stop father and George from flapping those mouths," she laughed weakly. Mary was so beautiful. Her eyes were bright with exhaustion and the aftermath of the pain, her cheeks flushed with tiredness and with pleasure. Seeing her lying there with her child in her arms, I longed to be her; to hold my own child, to know its health and strength. The women took the child from my sister and washed her in herb-scented waters and wine. Cleaned pink and wrinkly, the baby started to gurgle and whimper to be returned to her mother. My little niece. I felt as though my heart would burst with happiness.

Mary's husband, Will Carey, was delighted in the child, who, like her mother, was beautiful from the first day she opened her mouth and screamed to us to acknowledge her presence. Whether the child was his or not, he seemed to care little, but took her often in his arms and swept her through the air like a grand lady to be admired by any company come calling, as the babe screamed in protest to return to the more gentle arms of her mother. Will was happy to have a wife who found favour with the King, and seemed not to mind that he may have had a bastard fostered upon him. I came to understand that my brother-in-law was much as his wife in character; he took what life gave to him, and made the best of it. He had a pretty little child now, a life of much ease and a beautiful and gentle wife. If life was not perfect, it seemed little to matter to him. He made the best of things, like my sister did, and kept joy in his heart. In the days after the birth of Mary's child, I came to know, understand and find great pleasure in the company of Will Carey. He was a good man.

As I watched Mary coo over her new daughter, I understood why she was so happy the babe was a girl; this child could be of no great importance to anyone but Mary and Will, and could not be used as a pawn, at least for a while, in the games my father played at court. Had the child been a boy, the babe may have found himself in a precarious position before he could even talk or walk, as the potentially acknowledged bastard son of a king with no legitimate male issue. As a girl, the child was deemed to be of no great importance. Henry would not acknowledge a girl, for she would be of no use to him. Mary's baby was safe to enjoy her childhood without political intrigue. Daughter of the King or daughter of William Carey, no one cared too much for a girl-child until she was old enough to be married off to the highest bidder or the suitor with the grandest title. In having a daughter, Mary had avoided having to share her baby with anyone. Once more she had proved herself the King's perfect mistress by giving birth to a politically neutral child. Our father would not be so happy, but he would have to live with a granddaughter rather than a grandson and be done with it.

"I am going to call her Catherine," Mary told us, "for the Queen." My mother's face puckered at the sweetness of her daughter and in delight at her first grandchild; the future of the family lying happily burping in my sister's arms.

Our father was, of course, rather disappointed that his first grandchild was not the boy he had hoped, and that the King was not likely to acknowledge this child as his own as he had done with Bessie Blount's boy. The reasoning was clear; Bessie had her babe whilst unmarried and since it was a fine boy and perhaps because Henry felt that the birth of the boy showed he was capable of getting sons, he had acknowledged Henry Fitzroy as his own. Mary was married; there was another man who might be the father of any children she had, and a girl was of little interest or value politically.

Mary and Will received rewards after Catherine's birth in addition to those they had been granted before, making them wealthier and more prominent at court. Henry was acknowledging my sister's contribution to the proof of his fertility, even though he made no move to acknowledge the child as his own. Our father, too, received more titles, and George was rewarded when Henry took a special interest in his coming nuptials to Mistress Jane Parker.

It seemed, soon after the birth of little Catherine Carey, that Jane Parker should at last become Jane Boleyn, accompanied by the manor of Grimston in Norfolk and a tantalising sum of 2,000 marks; a sum that her father Morley could never have had or raised by himself. It was a richer benefactor, one who held our family in great esteem, who contributed coin to see the match prevail. The King was much pleased with our family, and George was his almost constant companion. Henry wanted to honour George, for sure, by helping fund the rich dowry our father demanded, but I believe it was Mary's proof of Henry's continued fertility that was really being rewarded. The lack of children in the marriage between Katherine and Henry brought great fear to the King's heart… But in seeing children like Henry Fitzroy and Catherine Carey, Henry knew that the fault of fertility did not lie with him. Such children, though they were bastards, tended to his wounded pride in being unable to have more children with Katherine. It was at this time, once more, that further rumours were whispered about court; that the King was thinking of annulling his marriage.

Mary was not long indisposed by the birth of her first child and was soon at court again, although with lighter duties than before. Mary was not one of Katherine's regular ladies, but the Queen seemed to enjoy having her nearby. Katherine was delighted that Mary had named her babe for her, and gave Mary a great deal of lenience, allowing her to return often to Beaulieu to be with her child, who was being tended by Carey's servants and the carefully chosen wet-nurse when Mary was not there. It must have rankled Katherine, though, that this child born to her husband's mistress came at a time when her own womb was dying inside her, that her husband was choosing the fertile beds of others in which to plant his seed rather than try again in the royal bed. But Katherine said nothing. She knew that the office of a Queen is to accept the affairs of the King, and she did not want to lose his favour by reproaching him for his liaisons. Katherine was also still grateful to Mary for being a quiet and respectful mistress, when she could have been quite the opposite.

The new addition to our family settled in to her life with ease. Little Catherine Carey was one of the most welcome and best loved babes I ever knew. My sister looked as though she had come into her true element when I saw her with her child. When Mary stood holding Catherine, I felt as though I were looking on a picture of the Holy Family, no matter how incongruous that idea really was.

Chapter Twenty-Three

Richmond Palace
1524

That summer, the armies of the Emperor Charles of Spain, our now-ally, invaded Italy to fight the French for possession of that territory. François himself set out for Italy to face his enemy, Charles, but I imagine that he went with a heavy heart. Already there had been personal loss for the charming French King; his daughter, Princess Charlotte had died suddenly, and as he set out to lead his troops in Italy, it was rumoured that my old mistress, the gentle and good Queen Claude, was growing weak and ill. She had given birth once more in June, to a daughter named for my dear friend Marguerite; seven children in nine years was more than enough toll for poor slight Claude to bear. In July, I heard the news that she had died, only a few days after saying goodbye to her husband. I grieved for the loss of such a gentle soul from this world. Memories of the time I served with her swam within the streams of my thoughts all summer. I remembered the fresh air of Blois where Claude's household had often been, and the warm scent of the wild roses. I thought of Claude's temperate smile, and her plain, but virtuous face. I remembered of the manner in which she approached all people, with her calm and steady ways. One ambassador said of Claude that she was "the very pearl of ladies, and a clear mirror of goodness, without stain." Another said, "If she is not in paradise, then very few people will go there." All of the things they said of her were true. I was only one of many thousands whose hearts cried out to lose such a good lady from this wicked world. Claude's body was left to rest for some time in the chapel at Blois, and it was said that many of those who came to view her body experienced a healing power upon their various wounds and aches. It was hailed as a miracle.

The care of the royal nursery was given over to a young lady I had served with briefly in France, a *dame d'honneur*, named Diane de Poitiers. Now the wife of Louis de Breze, Grand Senechal of Normandy, the golden-haired beauty, Diane, was appointed to care for the Royal Nursery and the children therein.

François was not told of Claude's death until the autumn, for he made for Italy over the Alps, and although he had never been a faithful husband, he wrote of Claude with grief. "Could I buy her life with mine," he wrote to Marguerite, "I would do it with all my heart. I never thought that the bonds of marriage, ordained by God, could be so hard to break." Claude left her beloved homeland of Brittany to François, something that had never been done before by any Duchess of Brittany, and I believe it showed her trust and love in his abilities to rule her people justly and well.

I found myself heavy with grief that summer, not only for the loss of Claude, but for what I saw happening to France, the country I still thought of with great affection. In some ways I felt as though I had in fact been born in France, and brought to England. I did not resent England now, and I loved my position at court, my friends, my family... But still within me there was a great affection for France and her people. It was dear to me.

In August, the Duke of Suffolk led twelve thousand English men into Calais on Henry's command, set to march upon Paris. It was rumoured in England that the French people themselves were calling out for the English King to invade; the high taxes that François had imposed upon his people to finance his invasion of Italy were not popular, it was true. But I doubted whether it was true that the people of France called out "*Long live the King of England,*" as we were told they did. It was a truth not often acknowledged that our King was a master of rumour and myth... Often what he wanted to believe became as a truth told to his people. Knowing the great pride of the French, I could not see that they would welcome an invading force landing on their shores to take their own country from them. But I, like all others, marvelled at the news when it was relayed to me; for a good servant of the King of England must at least appear to believe all that he wished us to believe.

As autumn turned to winter, the newly elected Pope, once Giulio de Medici, now Clement VII, sent secret messages to François, saying that he wished to give his support to the French invasion of Italy, and free the papacy from the domination of the Holy Roman Emperor, Charles of Spain. Wolsey was most upset to learn that he had not been considered for the Papal Throne... it was of some satisfaction to me to see the dark face of the Cardinal as he wandered the halls of court. And, as the frosts of early autumn sparkled white on the banks and knolls of England, the French moved into Italy, seeking to take Naples and Pavia.

Although war was raging about us, we seemed most removed from all of this in England. Only the information whispered about court and that our father gleaned through his many contacts in the courts of Europe allowed us to know all that was going on. But despite my fears for France, for Marguerite and for François, there were other things to occupy my thoughts that autumn, such as the marriage of my brother, George.

Chapter Twenty-Four

Great Hallingbury, Essex
1524

George married Jane Parker in November, at the church of St Giles at Great Hallingbury in Essex. The church was near to the estates of Jane's father where we celebrated afterwards. And a great bargain George made of the marriage bed too! Jane brought her husband fabulous riches, partly supplemented by the King himself. In addition to Jane's dowry, George was granted the manor of Grimston in Norfolk, a healthy increase on the income he already received from the King, and a position as one of Henry's cupbearers. George had made a fine match with Jane, although he always seemed to be in debt. My brother was a great spender; clothes, hunting hawks, dogs, horses, and losses from the many wagers he made all meant he regularly overstretched his income.

George had a good position at court, although about a year later, he was to lose his position in the King's Privy Chamber, as one of the King's many chosen companions, due to what became known as the Eltham Ordinances; a series of reductions in court placements put forward by Cardinal Wolsey. Their aim, officially, was to reduce the cost on the King's purse... but we all knew the true aim of the slippery Cardinal was to reduce the influence of others on the King. Wolsey wanted Henry for himself, and did not want others to influence his decisions.

At the time of George's wedding however, we did not know this was to come. George seemed pleased with the match. He had known for some time that Jane was intended for him; she was beautiful, came with great estates and was from a fertile family. He could settle into breeding with her to get his heirs, and continue on with the mistresses he had at court; such is the married life of men.

But as Mary and I sat near each other at the wedding feast, it seemed that my sister had seen something of Jane that she found off-putting. As I was spooning flaked carp in white sauce onto my plate, Mary leaned close to me and whispered that she thought Jane looked like a snake.

"With those hooded eyes…" Mary said, a succulent strip of rabbit meat and purple carrot balanced on her jewelled knife. She looked at Jane and our brother at the head of the feast, laughing with the King. Henry had not only paid for some of Jane's dowry, but had come to the wedding feast. We were most honoured by our sovereign.

"Yes," I agreed. "I have little found ways to know her spirit in truth. She is not unpleasant company but I feel a little uneasy with her. I think her the type of woman who prefers the company of men over women."

Mary snorted in amused agreement, and turned the indelicate noise into a short cough, as people looked around. "She is the type of woman who sees competition everywhere," she whispered. "George will have to watch out."

"What do you mean?"

"That woman is too… heated for him," Mary said. "You can almost see the vapours coming off of her… She wants him so much, too much. She might think it is love, but it is not. It is possession. It is obsession… not love. He will never want her as she wants him and she is a jealous woman. She will not be pleased if George does not remain faithful. She will give him hell when she finds he loves her not. You mark my words. If he strays from her bed…" she popped the flesh of the rabbit into her mouth and chewed thoughtfully, her pretty lips moving up and down.

"Which he will, of course," chimed in Will Carey, who had evidently been listening from Mary's side. Mary lightly chafed him with her knife for eavesdropping, but it was playful. She smiled at him and he grinned wickedly at her.

"A marriage is better made when both parties accept the realities of life and are content with what each may offer the other. Whether it be love, wealth, titles or company in dotage," Will said in a low voice which did not carry past our ears. "But pure fantasy will never make a happy marriage, as George and his new lady are sure to find out soon enough, no doubt to their great unhappiness. She will love him to *death*. She will suffocate him, and he will flee from her as a man from a burning building."

Will looked at Mary and smiled; there was not a hint of rancour in it. Both she and I knew that he was talking of himself and Mary when he spoke of finding happiness in what each may offer the other in marriage. It amazed me that a couple such as they could still find happiness and satisfaction in each other, although he knew, accepted and profited by her unfaithfulness to their marriage bed. Mary and Will were fond of each other, but they accepted their match for what it was. It was a bizarre arrangement, in many ways, but it worked for them. I smiled at Will, thinking that my brother-in-law was a man of great and hidden depths.

I raised my cup of good wine and around the table others did the same. "To happiness in marriage!" I cried. The others about the table echoed my words and we drank to the newly married pair. In my heart, I drank also to the marriage of my sister; such a marriage was not for me, I knew, but it was a pretty thing none the less, when two people are able to understand each other so well.

A cheer rose around the table and George and Jane raised their silver goblets. On Jane's face, however, there was a flicker of slight annoyance that her new and handsome husband's attention should have been diverted suddenly. Her expression turned easily back to a smile as George looked at her with somewhat wine-soaked affection, and I mused on what Mary and Will had said, wondering if my brother would find anything like the happiness they had in their marriage, in his own.

As I mused, I became aware that Henry, the King, was watching me. As I caught his eye, I saw such an expression of pain on his face that I almost started to my feet to help him, thinking that somehow, he must be hurt. But then, I realised that the pain was one that *I* had caused him, in the contemplation of what would have made his own marriage to Katherine a happier one. There was an empty space where his wife should have sat, for she was apparently unwell and had not joined the Boleyn celebrations. But as I saw that expression pass over his face, I knew that Henry was thinking of his own marriage… and perhaps on the sorrow of not having a male heir. This lack marred all other pleasures and joys he had in Katherine as a wife.

Later there was dancing. I loved to dance and had drunk deep of the ready wine, which only encouraged me to dance all the more. I was partnered by Tom, Henry Norris, Nicolas Carew, the ever-naughty Francis Bryan, *and* my brother George. It seemed everyone wanted to dance with me that night! Then Henry, who had danced first with Jane as the honoured bride and then with my sister, came to my side. He bowed to me and took my hand for the *pavanne*. There was no resisting the King's will when he wished to dance. It was an honour, but I was suitably taken aback. I had never been chosen as his partner before, perhaps because he tended to dance with my sister. Henry's dancing was polished and elegant and as we danced I watched others fall back to watch us, both in sycophantic admiration and in real awe. He was a gifted and beautiful dancer and although his frame was larger now than when I had first seen him, when I was a child, he was still slim and powerful. He was graceful in the dance despite his great height and size. Such a king was our Henry of England. There were no other princes like he.

As the dance continued, Henry spoke softly to me. "I have long waited to partner you, Mistress Boleyn," he said gently.

"Your Majesty did not have to wait to ask," I replied raising my lashes playfully at him and smiling, feeling a little heated with the wine and the closeness of his company. "I am your subject and must obey."

"In all things... Anne?" he asked; there were little lights of desire in his eyes. I started to breathe quickly and not because of the exertion of the dance. The way he was looking at me... I had seen that look before, when first I was presented to him at court. But there seemed to be something else within his gaze now, something of a determination, something of a challenge.

"In all things... Saving the preservation of my own soul and honour, Your Majesty," I said carefully, feeling his interest in me keen, and his eyes roam upon my body. I could feel, too, the eyes of the wedding party upon us, my sister's and father's eyes included. I suddenly regretted the flirtatious manner in which I had spoken to him before. I little wanted to look like I was seeking to draw the King's attention away from my own sister.

He smiled at me. "I would not want you to dance with me only because I ordered you to, as your King," he murmured softly. "I would wish that you, perhaps, *wanted* to dance with me."

"Your Majesty is a fine dancer," I smiled cagily. "Any woman should wish to dance with you."

"But you are not just any woman, Anne..." He gripped my hand tightly as he turned my body smoothly into his waiting arms in the dance. "You are not like other women at all." His voice was soft, breathing upon my cheek closely as he turned me once more to dance from his embrace.

I flushed. "I hope I have not displeased Your Majesty," I said haltingly. I slid free from his arms and clapped my hands, then moved once more close to him, for the moves of the dance dictated such. His blue eyes were soft as they looked on my face, and he smiled at me.

"I do not think that would be possible." He took my hand as we bowed to the last notes of the dance.

Henry returned me to my seat and left with a bow. I felt all in the room watching me, and I turned my eyes to the floor as I sipped my wine, but I could feel them still. Margaret and Bridget were smiling at me, noting how I was favoured by the King. There was my sister's surprise and slight hurt, my brother's admiration, speculation from my father and other courtiers, and from behind me, there was an icy chill. It was as though a ghost were standing right behind me. I shivered and turned to see my new sister looking at me; her hooded green eyes were frozen on me and carried all the warmth of a hard frost. Suddenly, she smiled as she saw my face turn to her; a stretched and false smile that spread over her face with the greatest of ease, as though she had been practising it for so long that it was all she knew of happiness.

She raised her goblet to me and I did the same to her, but in my heart I knew, that Jane Boleyn meant me no good that day. She did not like anyone else given attention. She did not like to see me honoured by the King. I shivered. Jane was a strange creature indeed, I thought, and now, she was a part of our family.

Chapter Twenty-Five

The English Court
1524 -1525

After George's wedding we returned to court. The court was always on the move, and the constant stream of packing, moving and preparing chambers in each new palace was something that I was used to by this time. It had been much the same in Burgundy and France, although the French palaces had seemed to withstand a volume of courtiers and court hangers-on that the smaller English palaces could not. The huge numbers of people at court made huge amounts of mess, and after a while, even those who were not fastidious in their personal ablutions were forced to admit that the palaces of the court *stunk*. As the court moved from one palace to another, the previous palace underwent a thorough cleansing, readying it for another assault later in the year.

This perpetual need for cleansing, along with Henry's need for continual amusement, meant that we were always on the move. This was especially so during the summer months when the hunting was good and the heat made the palaces smell even more pungent. The King would usually go on a progress through his country, to visit with honoured courtiers and to allow his people to see him. It was important that the people see their King, and to remember his greatness and generosity. But before the days of the summer progress, the court was generally to be found in one or other of the many palaces near London, along the River Thames. In the winter we moved less regularly, mainly because the weather was cooler and the various smells the court created and maintained were lessened. But still, some movement between palaces was always required, no matter the season.

Sorrow came to Bridget that year, when her husband, Richard died, leaving her with seven living children to tend to alone. She returned to court to her duties to Katherine not long after Richard was laid to rest, and I consoled her as best I could.

"Think on your children now," I said to her; Bridget would not be able to support them alone, her dower was not enough. "You must marry again, to ensure their future," I pulled her to me and embraced her. "Choose a man of the court, so that you might stay near to those who love you, we will support you through this."

She nodded to me. "I believe you are right, Anne," she sighed. "Although I do not have a care to marry again in truth. Richard was a good husband, and a good father. It makes my heart ache to think of lying with another man. But my children need a father, and I need the protection of a husband… I cannot support them on the meagre allowance of my dower."

She married later that year, with Sir Harvey of Ickworth. He was a good man, and he treated her well. My dear fertile Bridget went on to have another six children with her second husband over the years. She seemed made to be a mother!

I had returned to my duties at Queen Katherine's side, and returned to my friends at court. I was feeling quite comfortable within the court, and finding in the routine of my days, some comfort in knowing that I was now, perhaps, a part of the court in truth. But even as I felt more at home in England, there was news that came from France that brought sorrow to me. The war between the alliance of Spain and England against France brought me little joy. I thought of my beloved France with a heavy heart when I heard news and dispatches. I could not show my sorrow to anyone, of course… It was hardly done for one to feel sorrow for the enemies of one's country, after all. But within a secret chamber of my heart, there was much sorrow for the troubles that my countrymen brought to a place and a people that I still considered my own.

Late that winter, the English troops marched on Paris, aiming to take the capital as their own, but they were let down by the Duc de Bourbon, who had turned traitor to his master, François. Bourbon had promised reinforcements for the English, but he was forced to flee, and could not fulfil his promises. The English, facing a terrible and hard winter, retreated to Flanders, their spirit much broken. It was a terrible embarrassment for Henry. The Duke of Suffolk, who led Henry's armies, sent many dispatches pleading with the King that it was Bourbon's failure, rather than his own that had led to this military disgrace. Fortunately for Suffolk, Henry held his brother-in-law in such high regard that he accepted his pleas and did not hold the Duke responsible for England's exclusion from military glory.

In February of 1525, the French were holding the city of Pavia in Italy when the Emperor's army moved in. Under the cover of a stormy, dark night, the Imperial troops wore white shirts over their armour to distinguish themselves from the French forces. The white-shirted Imperial army burst into the Chateau of Mirabello, set on taking the French King himself prisoner, but François was that night stationed away from the castle. François went out to meet the Emperor's forces with his English ally, and Henry's foe, Richard de la Pole. Some saw de la Pole, "The Last White Rose", as a contender for the English throne for his Yorkist blood.

Although the French had, at first, been caught unawares by the invasion of the Imperialist troops, they fought back with great strength, and at first it seemed as though the battle would be won by François... But as he and his men-at-arms charged again and again at the Spanish troops, they were shot at through the cover of the forests by *arquebusiers*, carrying new-style weapons with a great range. The French were bewildered by these new tactics, and more and more of them fell. They did not have time to reconsider their strategy at the height of this battle. They simply kept coming, and wave after wave of men were blasted back by the new weapons of the Spanish. Many drowned in the River Ticino. Their numbers diminished. In the resulting slaughter, the flower of French nobility was cut down. Many couriers and military heroes were killed. Amongst the dead was Richard de la Pole. François' horse was shot from beneath him, yet he rose to fight on, on foot, a figure resplendent in a surcoat of silver… But he could not last. First his face was wounded, then his arm and hand, and at last he was struck to the ground, falling beneath the swords of his enemies. Not realizing that this was the King of France, the Imperial soldiers were about to kill him, until one of François' own men called out "mercy for the King!" François was taken as a captive; his sword taken as a trophy, his forces destroyed and his pride in ruins. I, who knew him well, could imagine his humiliation and shame.

The Battle of Pavia was over in less than two hours. In those two hours, more than eight thousand French troops fell to the guns, swords and pikes of the Holy Roman Emperor. Only seven hundred Imperialist troops were killed. The French were now in the hands of Charles of Spain and his allies.

I mourned for the destruction of the French troops, and worried for the sake of François, whom I had admired and been charmed by in my time at the French Court. He was a man of great pride, and no doubt he felt the stain of his disgrace and defeat keenly. I worried, too, for his sister, Marguerite, and for Françoise. I knew how precious François was to them, and how sorely they would fear for him now. How I wanted to write to them! To offer the solace of friendship at such a time! But I could not. To write to the Princess of France, or the mistress of the King of France when our countries were at war was a thing impossible, for I would be held as a traitor if it were ever discovered. How I wished that they could feel the strain of my heart in wishing to comfort them! I prayed often for my friends of France in those cold days… and hoped that they would feel the love I had for them, even as I hoped God would listen to my prayers for their comfort and safety.

When Charles heard of the Battle of Pavia, and of François' capture, he apparently little rejoiced, but went instead to pray in his chambers. When Henry heard of it, he leapt from his bed, praising God and all the saints, and called for wine and celebration. He was overjoyed to hear that Richard de la Pole had been cut down in battle, for it removed another potential rival for the Tudor line on the English throne. But Henry had other reasons to celebrate. He now hoped that the lands that had been promised to him in the original treaty between Spain and England would finally be granted. With the removal of English troops, however, from France to Flanders the year before, after the failed invasion of Paris, many wondered if the Emperor would indeed keep his word and honour the original treaty... In time, we would see that the slippery Emperor would not keep his promises to England.

France passed into the hands of Louise of Savoy, François' mother, as Madame Regent. She negotiated with Charles, and with the Pope, for her son's safe release. Attempts were made to release François both through negotiation and duplicity, but he remained in the Emperor's hands, and was taken to the tower of the Alcazar, in Madrid. François was given but one small room, with space for a bed, a table and a chair, but no more. Poor noble François, who had spent most of his life in the most opulent of chambers in the most opulent of palaces! Who had delighted in building and architecture! He was now imprisoned in a tower that was over one hundred feet tall, with but one small window to look from. Later, François would write of his captivity, saying "*Le corps vaincu, le Coeur reste vainqueur*" or "The body is conquered, the heart remains the victor." He fell ill within that dismal tower, and ran a fever that many thought would bring him death. Marguerite herself travelled to Spain, and was allowed to tend upon her brother. Such was the love between them that she could not allow him to languish in that awful tower alone. They heard Mass together, and François' fever broke. It was viewed as a miracle, and proclaimed about France.

Marguerite could not stay with François for the whole time of his captivity, but she left him a small dog, who leapt into his bed every morning, which seemed to bring him some happiness. All through that year, the French King, captured and held prisoner, but still refusing to give in to the demands of the Emperor, refused to sign the treaties put before him, and refused to abdicate his throne. François was a man of iron under the charming light of his character… He would not give in to Charles, even though he was his prisoner.

How I admired such mettle within the French King's spirit! Here was a man who, even in defeat, would not be defeated. I was cheered to hear that Marguerite had gone to François, and touched by the strength of their sibling love. I knew that if such a situation had ever happened to my own brother that I too would have flown to his side. And my heart was happy to hear of François' unbroken spirit. Silently, I cursed at the Spanish, for in their victory they had seen the humiliation of the French, the country I adored. But at least all the world could see what a man the King of France was, and even in the height of their humiliation, the French could lift their chins at the spirit of their ruler, and say "Such a man, such a king as this, is *ours*."

The wars that had raged about Europe seemed, with the capture of François, to be on the decline, and Henry of England waited for the Holy Roman Emperor, Charles of Spain to grant him the lands and titles that had been promised. Henry wanted to rule France as well as England. He wanted to take back that hereditary title, so beloved to the English since the heady days of Agincourt…. But he would wait that summer in vain for Charles' promises to become truth. The Holy Roman Emperor, it seemed, had no intention of holding to the terms of his treaty with England. Henry grew suspicious of Charles' intentions, and started to send dispatches to his prior enemy, France, in the hopes of a new treaty with them. It seemed strange to think so soon after engaging in war against the French, that we could become their friends again, but the French were willing and happy to enter into talks, hoping to gain support against Charles. Henry did not break with Spain, as yet, but he was happy to play both sides of the conflict, to see what came of it for his own gain. Wolsey was *most* busy that summer, trying to bring about the promises made by the Emperor, whilst also dancing attendance upon France when the Spanish were not looking… The slippery eel was gifted at such delicate proceedings, and the King trusted Wolsey without question to always work for his gain.

And so, as the wars of Europe closed for another chapter, we at court put aside military thoughts and started to think on the pleasures of the coming summer. Spring days melted away, and a fresh scent could be smelt on the wind. As though something was coming, something new, something interesting…

Chapter Twenty-Six

Richmond Palace
1525

The court was a lively place to be that year; entertainments were frequent, as were tournaments, and on good days we often went out to watch Henry playing his men at tennis in the courts. The King was a truly gifted tennis player, and could ricochet the hard ball like no other about the walls of the courts, usually catching his opponent entirely off-guard. We placed wagers on the matches, but you were a fool if you did not bet on the King when he was playing. I won many wagers due to Henry's swift stroke and keen eye. When we were not about the court, the Queen's ladies were kept increasingly busy with the good works that Katherine wanted us to undertake. It was of some relief when I found that I could take an hour's rest, one afternoon, and leave the dismal space of Katherine's chambers, to escape into the gardens.

It was an early summer's afternoon when I stepped from the confines of the palace and out, into the glorious gardens. I lifted my head and caught the keen scent of rosemary stalks being plucked from their hard centre by the able hands of a kitchen maid in the near distance. Winged stalks of flowing fennel danced merrily in the light breeze, and bright yellow flowers of water-flag shone happily in the sunshine. I breathed in a sigh of relief, and of pleasure, to have the sun on my skin, and feel the clean air in my chest.

Lately, it seemed, Katherine had us so busy sewing altar cloths and clothes for the poor that I had hardly a moment to myself between morn and dusk. It seemed that we were to dance in her chambers no more, nor were we to play on the virginals or clavichord, or sing to pass the hours.

Katherine's vigour for charity seemed to be a cloak for her sadness. We all knew now that the King no longer came to her bed; she was past childbearing age and was no longer desirable enough to tempt him to bed on her own merits. In her rooms there hung a portrait of the pretty, delicate-featured princess that Katherine had been when she came first to our shores to marry Prince Arthur, Henry's older brother. Then, she had been a happy young bride, with her all life in front of her. There was little left of that girl now in amongst the figure ruined by unproductive child bearing, there was no rose tint in her pale cheeks. The happiness and sense of hope that radiated from that portrait was absent now from the desperate, sad woman before us. Day after day, hour after hour, she spent in prayer. Her knees were raw and scabbed from kneeling on cold and rough floors begging God to bring a miracle to her empty womb and give her a prince to present to the King. I believe also that in each altar cloth and each rough tunic for the poor that we sewed, there was a desolate prayer for God to remember her, his servant, and to grant her the child she desperately craved. I found Katherine's constant sadness oppressive. Think badly of me if you will for that, but I was young and bright. To me, the court was a place of enjoyment and entertainments. I wanted little to spend all my days wrapped in the misery of Katherine's troubles.

I walked to sit on a large oaken bench by the side of one of the ornamental ponds in the grounds of Richmond. Early dog-roses bloomed pink and pretty by the pond and the slight shade, afforded by a happily placed tree, kept my pale complexion from being burned by the sun. I had a book that I was most interested in that George had brought back from a recent diplomatic mission to France. Peace was being talked of between England and France once again, and my brother and father had been amongst those chosen to enter such talks. George was really accompanying our father to be tutored in the skills an ambassador required, but it was still a high honour. It looked as though we might turn once again to our nearest neighbours for alliance. I was pleased, obviously, for I had rather England be friends with France. George had managed to meet with friends of Marguerite, who had passed on a volume of her work that she had apparently wished to send to me for some time. It was a section from a book of short stories that she was working on. I was most pleased that Marguerite would remember me with enough affection to send me a part of her as yet unfinished work. I personally could not show my poetry or other works to anyone until I was sure they were of a standard I could bear to hear in public without wincing. But then, Marguerite was a braver and more talented woman than I.

Her book was as yet untitled, but was very much in the style of Boccaccio's *Decameron*, or Chaucer's *Canterbury Tales* in that it was a collection of stories told by various members of a party. Marguerite's was, however, somewhat different, as each story was in some way about the relationship between men and women and the various tricks each employ in the game of love… or lust. I had not the whole collection, as it was by no means finished, but I had enough tales to read with pleasure and sometimes with distress.

Marguerite was a beautiful story-teller and a powerful one. As I sat by that small pond and the fish lapped the top of the waters, I read one tale that brought tears to my eyes. After finishing it, I was sobbing into my hands. It was the fourth tale of the book and it was so familiar as I read it that I could hear Marguerite's voice ringing out from the past. I felt as though I sat once more before her, dishevelled and disgraced after that whore's bastard had tried to force himself upon me. In my mind's eye, I saw Marguerite's dark eyes glisten with pain as I read the tale before me. It was a story about attempted rape, you see, on a princess who is told by her waiting woman that she cannot pursue revenge for the assault for fear of staining her own reputation.

Marguerite had drawn from her own experiences and laid her soul bare on the pages spread before me.

After my own experience in France with a man who would not take *no* as an answer from a woman, the story cut deep with old memories of sorrow and pain. I felt that night's fear return to my heart. I heard my own cries as he forced his hand over my mouth, and I felt the terror that only those who have ever been in such a situation can know; the awful feeling of having your own personal power taken from you by another. The humiliation… the abject terror… the pain of feeling someone rip your soul as they seek to take their disgusting satisfaction. Even though he had not succeeded in raping me, that man had taken much from me that night.

I read the story, but could not continue to read the volume afterwards. I wept with the parchment in my hands, held so softly to prevent it from crumpling. My tears came thick and fast, falling against my cheeks and raining on the ground at my feet. I noted nothing about me, until I heard a footfall directly behind me. Someone had come near whilst I had been occupied in my sorrow, and was standing right behind me. I folded the papers hastily and tucked them into the pockets of my dress folds. I wiped furiously at my eyes. I had not wanted anyone to see me in such a condition. As I stood, turned and curtseyed, I could see nothing before me but the blindness of my tears. The form before me wavered in and out of focus, distorted by the water flowing in my eyes. I made a curtsey, and mumbled something as I tried to leave quickly to recover myself away from the eyes of others.

"Mistress Boleyn?" It was a man's voice, soft, gruff with gentleness and concern. I recognised the voice, as all members of his court must. I blinked back heavy tears that flooded my face with their salt water and stumbled to curtsey again to the tall figure of the King standing before me. My cheeks flushed red with chagrin. I did not want to be found, in such a personal moment of sorrow and anguish, by anyone, but certainly not by the King! I swiped at my eyes once more and smiled, lowering them from his worried gaze.

Unusually, Henry was not escorted by a whole group of men, but by one; Thomas More stood in his habitual dark robes by the King's looking, as I could see now through my clearing vision, both amused and slightly disapproving of me. Ladies of the court should not be found so; alone and in a state of dishevelment.

But in Henry's face there was none of the sanctimonious disapproval of his servant. He nodded to More who noted the gesture and quietly left with a short bow towards me.

"Mistress Boleyn, are you well?" he asked gently, taking a step towards me and gesturing at the bench from which I had risen as a place to sit again.

"I…" I began to stutter, but was stopped by his leading me to the bench and sitting me down next to him. His hands were gentle and his expression held nothing but concern for me. I sat next to Henry and felt comfort radiating from him. I could not entirely stem the flow of tears from my eyes now that it had begun, and found my King silently passing a piece of gold-trimmed cloth towards me, with which to wipe my eyes. I was glad suddenly that I was not made a fright to look on by the act of crying as some women are. My pale cheeks picked up colour when I cried and my black eyes shone wildly bright. I blinked back the remaining tears and smiled at the fine-looking man who sat at my side.

I shall always remember him on that day; his golden hair shone in the sun and the blue waters of the pond were reflected in his piercing eyes. There was such gentleness in his manner that I felt entirely safe, something that was all too rare after the experience I had undergone in France. Although I had trusted other men, such as Tom and Percy, there still had been moments when I had felt wary of them. But with the King, with Henry, as I sat there in the sunshine, I felt as though he would allow nothing to harm me. I had never felt so assured of anything in my life before. He wanted nothing from me at this moment but for me to be happy again. I knew that as well as I knew the skies were above me and the earth was below.

I passed his cloth back to him and took a deep breath. "I am grateful, Your Majesty," I muttered. "I am sorry to have inconvenienced you."

He looked directly into my eyes, and I felt my heart quicken. "You have not inconvenienced me, Mistress Boleyn." He tucked the little cloth into his sleeve of purple and silver. "But I will discover what knave has made you weep so, and I will make them aware of our displeasure." He looked at me again and I was amazed to see a faint blush across his cheekbones; whether it was through anger or embarrassment I knew not.

I smiled at his words, and a little laugh escaped my lips. He lifted his eyebrows and I pulled the sheets of paper from my dress, handing them to him. "I fear that making the person who caused me to cry aware of your displeasure may incur an international incident, Your Majesty." I showed him the seal of Marguerite on the bundle of papers. "The culprit is the sister of the King of France, the Princess Marguerite, whom I served in France when I served in the household of the late Queen Claude. Since our countries are so lately in talks of peace, the Princess sent me this through mutual friends. It is of little importance to international affairs, but of personal interest to me. It is some stories from her new collection of tales and there was one that chilled my heart and brought forth such tears from me that I knew not that the King of England stood before me." I showed him the papers, slightly worried that despite my diplomatic words I might be called to account for receiving papers from France. He said nothing on that matter, however. He glanced at them and then at me.

"It was naught but a tale that made you cry so?" he asked with a little amusement, possibly thinking that my femininity was a little dramatic.

"It was a tale that shows the dangers a woman must face in this world," I replied heatedly, anger rising in me as I somewhat forgot I was talking to the King. "It tells of the unfairness of the world where a virtuous woman may be set upon by a man and yet gain no retribution. It is the injustice of the world and the pain I felt for the woman in the tale that made me cry so." I looked away from him, staring ahead, not meeting his eye and keeping my face, flushed with anger, fixed ahead of me. I saw his eyes narrow from the corner of my eye, but he did not reproach me for my anger.

"May I read the tale?" Henry asked me, and there was still that tone of gentleness in his voice, despite my anger vented towards him. I hesitated. The papers had been sent to me as a friend, to read in confidence, but I could hardly refuse the King of England in such a request, especially after I had hissed my last words at him. He saw my hesitation. "I shall tell none of what I may read there, my lady." He placed a finger to his lips with a smile. "I shall keep your secret as though it were my own, I promise."

I handed the pages to him and was silent as he read the tale. I saw him wince from the story more than once; it was not happy reading after all. When he finished, he returned the papers to my hand gently. "I understand why you were distraught, Mistress Boleyn," he shook his head slightly. "Although this is not the type of tale I would have expected a young lady such as you to be reading on such a lovely day." He paused. "It has interesting points to it that are valuable, even if they are not so easy to read."

I nodded. "I would not wish you to think me foolish, sire," I blurted out, and he snorted with quick, easy laughter, smiling widely at me.

"I think there are few who would *dare* call you a fool, Anna Boleyn," he smiled at me again. "I have heard your tongue spoken of in fear by more than a few lords who had been lashed with it. There is fire in you that many would fear to come close to. And yet, I do not fear you. I find you most... interesting." He looked at me again and there was hunger in his eyes.

I held his gaze for a moment and then dropped my eyes to the pages in my lap. There was such intensity in that gaze that I dared not hold it. I knew not what might happen if I did. My breathing was quickening as was the feeling that the space between us was growing smaller. I could feel him starting to lean towards me, as though he intended for us to grow closer still. I suddenly felt most uncomfortable, awkward, excited, and perhaps a little scared. My fear, though, was not of him, it was of the feelings he brought to my heart. This was not only my King, he was my sister's lover! It was hardly appropriate that I was drawn to him, or he to me. I rose suddenly and stepped forward, standing by the pond, tucking the pages into my pocket in a distracted manner. I turned to him. "Tell me, sire, have you read the tales of Giovanni Boccaccio? They are similar in style to tales that Princess Marguerite is writing."

Raised eyebrows greeted my question and my stance as I stood like a hind ready to flee. He must have been surprised that I leapt from him; there can have been few who would dare to jump away from the King as though he were made of fire. But he did not seek to redress this lack of decorum; indeed, he looked somewhat amused and confused by me. "Indeed, I have read those tales and others such. You are interested in books, Mistress Boleyn?"

I nodded, smiled and began to talk at length and in a slightly rapid manner to cover my confusion and embarrassment. I spoke about many works I had read that I loved. Henry joined in; speaking with passion and enjoyment on works we had both read. Immersed in conversation, I forgot he was the King, forgot my embarrassment and talked with zeal about the literature I loved. We talked of the tales of Arthur and the works of Polydore Vergil. We talked of the verse of the French Court and the histories of Monmouth. My tongue ran away with me and I shone, talking of the books and poetry that I loved so. I felt as though I were conversing with an old friend, for it seemed that we had much in common with our taste in books and poetry, and with our enjoyment of history and philosophy.

"But I prefer the French translation," I interrupted the King hastily and rather rudely. Henry blinked at me. He had been talking of Erasmus' new translations of the New Testament in Latin and Greek which he had enjoyed. He looked taken aback with my boldness. I had indeed quite forgotten that I was required to be humble and demure in the King's company. I laughed and reached out my hand to his arm, touching it with some affection as I smiled at him.

"Forgive me, Your Majesty," I looked with genuine warmth into his startled eyes; as much startled I think at being interrupted and contested in an opinion as he was startled at the touch of my hand on his arm. "Forgive me," I said again, and took my hand from his arm quickly, as though I had just noticed it was there. "I feel as though you and I understand each other so well that I quite forgot you are my King and I your subject. It was as though I was talking with an old and beloved friend. I have over-reached myself. I am sorry."

I stood and swept to the floor with a curtsey. I looked up at him through hooded eyes with a saucy smile playing on my lips. I was not sorry at all that we had talked thus, it had been of the utmost enjoyment to me and I am sure he could read that in my smile. He expelled his breath, widened his eyes at me, and then laughed suddenly. There was both interest and puzzlement on his face, mingled with hunger in his eyes as he looked on my naughty smiling lips and at the curve of my breasts. I knew there was no harm now in the words that I had said.

"Did I go too far, Your Majesty?" I asked with a laugh. "Would you forgive me?"

His eyes narrowed, but there was a smile of desire on his mouth. I was safe, despite my outrageous outburst. "I would forgive you, Mistress Boleyn," he said and stood, reaching for a twist of my hair that had come loose from my pearled hood. It seemed for a moment that he would draw me to him, that he would kiss me, and the beating of my heart quickened as I realised I longed for him to do so. It felt as though the birds had ceased to sing in the skies and the wind had ceased to blow. There was no movement, there was nothing but him, his closeness, the scent of his skin... Just then, there was no one in the world but us.

Then a shout came from close-by; his servants were looking for him. No king could be alone for long without his servants finding him. We both started as we heard the noise, but as I went to step backwards from him, he reached a hand around my waist and swiftly, strongly, drew me to him. Pushing my head back gently with his hand against my cheek, he pushed his lips to mine. I felt my mouth respond keenly, happily, to the softness of his lips and the roughness of the short beard against my skin. My blood raced in my veins and my head felt light. I pushed my body against his, feeling the touch of desire pulse through me like wild-fire. My hands reached around his head and his broad shoulders and entwined in his hair and on his back. My body moulded itself to him and my lips moved on his. It was a totally unplanned reaction to his kiss; I was as wanton as any bath-house whore.

There was another shout, someone calling the King's name, which seemed to startle me from the kiss. I leapt backwards from his embrace and stared at Henry. I stood touching my lips with amazement. My face was on fire; however much I had thought that he might kiss me, I had no idea that he actually would, or how deeply it would affect my body. My every response seemed tailored to his touch. I flushed deeper, crimson red bled through my pale cheeks. He was panting slightly, staring at me with equally amazed eyes.

He reached for me again, but I drew back.

"I can't be found like this, Your Majesty, please…" I pleaded, and stepped back as we heard his servants drawing near. I looked wildly about me. My gown and hood were rumpled and from the blush on my face it would be easy for his approaching servants to guess what we had been doing. I flushed again in shame, and looked around for a suitable place to hide myself from the approach of these men. Henry understood me and nodded to an almost hidden arbour to one side of the court garden; it was a shadowed place hidden in a cloak of honeysuckle. I fled, my thick skirts billowing behind me as I flew into the arbour and pushed my back against the wall of entwined vines and leaves. Hiding in the shadowed arbour I saw his servants, my brother, Henry Norris and the Duke of Suffolk amongst them, discover the King standing alone in the gardens, his face flushed and a strange look on his handsome face.

"Your Majesty!" my brother cried merrily as they came about the corner of a large hedge. "We were seeking you to settle a dispute between his Grace of Suffolk and myself on the particular virtues of a pretty new girl at court!"

George swept in with a bow and then went to make a little dance before Henry, like a court fool. Suffolk quietly cuffed him from behind making him trip forward. Suffolk, Norris and the King all laughed to see George try to right his balance like a tumbler. To his credit, my brother also laughed once he had regained his balance and made another bow to Henry.

He laughed at George's stumble. "We are glad you are lighter with your tongue than with your feet, George," Henry said, taking their arms in his and leading them deftly away from the courtyard where I was hidden, my flaming face cooling in the shadow of the arbour.

"Are pretty girls all that the two of you can think on?" Henry asked as he led them out of the garden. Then, almost imperceptibly, he looked back at my shadowed figure, hiding in the alcove.

I watched them leave and then fled in the other direction for the Queen's quarters. My heart was in my mouth, and my soul in a riot of confusion.

Chapter Twenty-Seven

Richmond Palace
1525

A few days later, Mary returned to court from another of her trips home to Beaulieu to watch over the progress of her daughter. I could hardly confide my encounter with the King to my sister, and yet there was a part of me that longed to ask her of it and hear her frank words on what it may mean. I wished I could talk to her of it, for I had no one else I felt I could speak to. Perhaps I could have spoken to George, but there was a part of me that felt strange in confiding such an intimate moment to my brother. I could have confided in Margaret, but knowing her brother's love for me, I hesitated. Bridget was absent from court with her new husband. I felt a little alone…

I thought over what had happened in the gardens, sometimes with chagrin, and sometimes with excitement. Perhaps to Henry, it was but a light fancy with another maid who was all too willing, apparently, to succumb to him. I blushed to remember the effect he had had on me. I imagined he thought now that I should be easy prey, as easy as my sister? The thought of him comparing us made me want to curl up and disappear, like a frail leaf crumbling in the autumn wind.

And what of my own feelings? In truth I knew not what they were. I had long known that I carried something for Henry Tudor in my heart, and yet I had also long thought it was but a youthful fancy, a feeling that came from a child's heart. The feelings that had arisen when I first saw him at his coronation and in Burgundy had left echoes of love upon my heart. And yet… I had to admit to myself that I had admired him since that time. I had been jealous of my sister. I had wanted to be noticed by this King, wanted him to touch me, to want me…

But my resolutions were unchanged. I did not want to become mistress to any man. Did not want to be a plaything to be used and cast aside. To become mistress to the King… The King, who was my sister's present lover? Never! I swore to myself that it would never happen. And God only knew what my father and mother would say if they heard aught of this! But I could not help myself in questioning Mary on her relationship with Henry, could not help wanting to hear of him… wanting to know if he was well and what he was doing. I was a mass of confusion and feeling. I knew not what I wanted, for all my feelings took me in different directions. Mary noticed nothing of this confusion, however, and confided in me that she was somewhat confused by Henry's behaviour of late.

"Tell not our father," she said as we walked together in the beautiful knot gardens at Richmond. "But I fear His Majesty's affections towards me are somewhat weaning, although I know not why. Two nights ago he sent for me in such a passion; it was as it was in the first days of our relationship when he could not keep his hands off me. And yet afterwards… He seemed un-sated, as though I could not satisfy him, although I did nothing different from all the other times we have encountered each other."

She looked ahead, her face puckered and thoughtful. "I think there may be another," she mused. "He is distracted; he talks to me less…" she sighed a little sadly. "But I have had a long reign with him; perhaps it is now the time for another to take my place. I would not be sorry to return to Will and be his wife in truth rather than being shared. But I wonder at what our father shall say; he will not be happy that I have lost such favour for the family."

I knew not what to say. Was it possible, after all, that I was the "other" she spoke of? I knew not what to do or say, an event unusual in my life, where words had always come so readily to me.

Two days later, a parcel wrapped in velvet arrived at my chamber door, carried by a discreet servant. A bundle of precious, costly jewels sent to me, from the King. I opened the velvet bundle and gasped. Sitting in a row were a large diamond set with pearls, a stunning emerald in a bed of gold and a dazzling, huge pearl set on a rope of smaller pearls that glistened in the light of the sun as I held it in my hands.

There was also a polite note, asking me to attend on Henry at his pleasure. I stared at the jewels and at the note in my hand. It was a bribe. I was being bought with shiny trinkets.

I looked at the jewels again and felt a shiver, both of excitement and fear, pass through my blood. For I knew, as sure as I knew my own name, that these fabulous jewels were payment for my virginity; Henry intended to buy me into his bed. I heard Marguerite's voice in my head as an echo of the past floated back to me. "*Virtue is our most precious gift and cannot ever be returned.*" For a moment, I thought I could hear also a deep, throaty laugh from a sensual mouth. In my mind's eye, I could see Françoise shaking her head at me, her hands on her hips. *"Men… they are hunters. They want to chase and capture. But the quick and easy chase will not satisfy them… They will tire, they will wander, they will stray, and then what are we women left with but an empty bed and a name all speak whilst laughing?"*

"I cannot accept them," I blurted out at the man whose face fell from a gloating and rather unpleasant grin to a look of pure shock. In a rush of panic, I asked the bearer to send the jewels back to the King with a message; I was not worthy to receive such gifts of His Majesty and, as an honest maid, could only take such gifts from the man who would be my husband. These gifts were to be sent back with humble thanks. The man looked amazed, and, rather terrified, at bringing such an unwelcome message to the King, but he turned and left, leaving me shaking and feeling faint. I went over and over my words thinking on them, wondering if they could bring me into disgrace. Would I be sent from the court?

Would Henry inform my father? Would he simply accept my refusal and be done with me? Whatever I said, I had just refused and possibly insulted the King of England. I rather expected to be sent from court immediately, but nothing happened.

There was silence from Henry.

At the next entertainment I was not chosen to sing or perform. I felt Henry's glowering temper before he even appeared, and, sure enough, when he did, there was such an expression of irritation cast my way that I felt afraid that rather than be sent from court, I should be sent to the Tower.

He ignored me and did not come to socialise with my circle at court. It was noted and remarked upon that the King was in a foul mood, although none knew why. Courtiers started to keep their heads down to avoid trouble. Henry's temper was frayed. He spent time out hunting from first to last light, and when he was about the court his servants were in no rush to be the one to serve the King that night.

Could all this anger be because I had refused him? It seemed too incredible to believe. I could not be so important to him, could I? No, there must be another reason.

Mary, however, was happy again. She confided in me after the entertainment that her fears of His Majesty's waning affections had been perhaps premature. He was once again affectionate with her, had presented her with many presents and given a generous grant to Carey for another year. Her place as royal mistress was, it seemed, still assured.

I was somewhat relieved for Mary and our family, yet somewhat grieved at the apparent ease with which Henry replaced one woman with another, one desire with another. But it seemed that his offer to me had just been a passing fancy. There must have been another reason that he was so angry for those days about court where it seemed that his temper could affect the very skies and stars over England. My fears had been unwarranted. He had forgotten me, perhaps. All that had been between us was simply a moment's desire, nothing more. I had refused him and he had replaced me with another, with his existing mistress. That was the way he was. I was no more important to him than was any other girl at court.

Or so I thought then.

Chapter Twenty-Eight

Windsor Palace
1525

When a simple accident occurred, a flame seemed to be lit within Henry of England, causing him to take action we hardly imagined, and placed the question of the royal succession at the forefront of everyone's minds.

Henry had been out hunting with his gallants. It was a normal enough start to a hunting trip. The King and his men, my brother included, were hunting with the hawk in Hertfordshire. Food and servants had accompanied them on the trip; hunting was now Henry's favourite pastime. After the joust at which he had been in peril of his life, such tournaments were held less frequently at court. Perhaps it was his unspoken fear; that if he died now, without a male heir, then his country would be in great peril. Henry knew that his duty as King was to provide an heir for prosperity and security of his realm. His father had done such a duty; even after he lost his elder son, his second son was there, able to take the throne. Perhaps, in the most secret places of his soul, Henry feared to undertake the joust too often, for fear of endangering his life once more.

No one spoke of this to him, of course; to question the vigour of the King in any way would incur his immediate displeasure, and dismissal from court. But the accident *had* caused physical problems for the King. He had been slow to recover from his various injuries. George told us that Henry had headaches that caused him such pain that he would chew on his pillows and cry out through gritted teeth. At such a time his temper was like that of a demon, and none wished to serve him if they had any other choice.

But the headaches and the other health issues caused by the fall did seem now to be on the wane. In the meantime, hunting was enough to sate the King's appetites for exercise and adventure. And so, on this one of many hunting trips, Henry's life, and the safety of our nation were called into question by the slightest and silliest of accidents. George related the tale to the family, one night as we gathered in our father's apartments at Windsor Castle.

"We were riding through the country when we approached a ditch, wide enough that the horses might risk their necks trying to jump it, and with steep muddy sides. The ditch was filled with pungent mud that smelt... although not reeking with illness, it still had a musty and not pleasant smell to it. I suggested that we ride around, but His Majesty was taken with a grand impulse to vault the ditch using one of the long hunting spears that a servant carried. The Duke of Suffolk then wagered a bag of coin against me that His Majesty could complete the vault with ease."

George broke off to give us a cynical look that spoke volumes as to Suffolk's sycophantic nature and continued. "The King was then determined. Although none of us wished to bet against him, the King insisted that Norris and I take up the wager. He took the spear and took several runs to the side of the ditch, measuring up the distance. All this time, I was thinking that the ditch really looked a lot wider than I had previously thought, but there is no saying no to His Majesty when he decides on something. Henry squared up, ruffled his shoulders, and ran towards the ditch. He leapt, thrusting the pole into its very centre. He flew across the expanse and for a moment I thought that he would make it. But suddenly, as he was almost over the ditch, the pole, under the weight of his body, broke, and Henry fell headlong into the filth!" George gave a strange, strained grin to our father who was watching him with narrowed eyes.

"We could not help but laugh," said George, shaking his head and not looking as amused now as he had been then, apparently. "Everyone was wiping the mud and filth, that had been thrown at us as the King hit the water, from their eyes and faces. But when my vision cleared, I saw that rather than sitting in the ditch, as I supposed he would be, all I could see of Henry were two great legs flailing in the air. Our king was buried, head-first, in the muck with no way to breathe or draw air."

George grimaced at our father's darkening face. "There was sudden panic, although not amongst all of us, it seemed; Suffolk, Compton and Norris were still doubled up with laughter and had not seen the danger that Henry was in. Bryan called out in horror, seeing that the flailing of the King's legs was growing more urgent and that His Majesty was perhaps in danger of his life. One of the guards leapt into the water and hauled Henry from the grasp of the sticky mud. They all stopped laughing when they saw His Majesty, purple and red in the face, spitting out morass and mire, and choking. The King retched and vomited on the grass as they heaved him out. He was clasping his hands to his head in pain. He couldn't even speak, lying on the grass, still vomiting…. Poyntz got him on a horse and we rode for the lodge. He was in terrible pain with his head, and we finally found a physician." George shook his head glumly. "The King would not speak of what happened," he said. "And he had to take to his bed for two days before the headaches ceased."

Our father lifted his eyebrows. "The King is a proud man." He shook his head and glared at his son. "I think that we should step more carefully with the life of our liege lord, George," he warned. "Although I realise that convincing His Majesty to *not* do something that he has set his mind on is an onerous and dangerous task, perhaps there are some times when we should consider that this country has no male heirs to its throne, none that could come to the throne easily or without unrest. Perhaps the life of our King should be more of a concern than it appears to have been to you."

George bristled with anger, but our father, nonplussed and calm, continued, ignoring him. "I mean that *you* should have been the one to drag him from that mire," he said staring into the fire and talking quietly as he thought. "Then, perhaps, you would be amongst his more favoured servants now." Henry had recently promoted our father to the post of Lord Treasurer, but as ever, our father was on the look-out for further advancement. I watched him and felt like sighing, although it would not do to show him my true feelings. I had felt fear for George's tale; fear for Henry, and the welfare of the King. Our father had seen what could have been a terrible accident as a chance for advancement... But then, our father had not been kissing the King in secret in the gardens of Richmond, so his feelings towards the sovereign were likely to be different to mine...

George exhaled and sat back in his chair. There was no use in arguing with our father. It was he who led our family, and he who would always have the last say on how we did things. That was how it was... then.

"Perhaps the King will begin to realise that he is not invincible," our mother said quietly, pulling a stitch through her embroidery and watching it as she fed it through the cloth. We spoke softly when we talked of such matters; such talk was dangerous for servants to overhear.

Our father nodded at her. "The succession is as yet unsure," he agreed. "The King is still young enough to have many children, but Katherine is not, and now I am told by our daughters and you that she has lost her courses and can no longer bear children. There is the Princess Mary, but no woman has ruled this country. I doubt that any woman would be strong enough to unite the factions growing at court or hold off the Scots or the French for long. We are a small island and there are many who would take our country from us were there no king to unite the people. Henry knows this as well as any of us. There must be a male succession to the throne of England."

He broke off and pondered into the fire. "I think change is on its way," he said portentously as we all stared into the glowing ashes of the dying fire. It was late, the darkness outside was growing and the evening was cold.

"Change is on its way," he said again; our father was rarely wrong.

It was not long after this time that the King indeed made steps to assure the succession; although he did not express such sentiments in word or proclamation, we all knew that the matter was on his mind. It started with the bastard boy of Bessie Blount, Henry Fitzroy, who was taken from the life he had been living in relative, although richly lavish, obscurity, and brought to London.

The child was six years old when he was voted into the Order of the Garter, the highest order of knights in England, headed by Henry himself. He was installed on the 7th of June in St George's Chapel in Windsor and took the place of precedence next to his father in the following ceremony. Then, on the 18th of June, there was a ceremony to create multiple peerages amongst the nobles of court. It was the first such occasion since 1514, and Henry Fitzroy was created Duke of Richmond and Somerset and Earl of Nottingham. These titles had previously belonged only to members of the royal family; to the Beauforts, to Henry VII and to a younger brother of Henry VIII who had died in infancy.

To anyone who could read the signs, there was a message in the titles given to that infant lord dressed up in all his finery; Henry was placing his bastard son higher than any lord in the realm. The King had lost faith with the Emperor Charles who had not made any move to fulfil the promises of the treaty. Perhaps Henry believed that Charles would not wait for Princess Mary to grow old enough to marry either. Henry was making new plans... In Henry Fitzroy he was crafting a possible solution to the problem of the succession

I was present on the day Henry Fitzroy became a Duke. I watched the little lord as he made his way through the presence chamber at Bridewell Palace up to the throne where Henry stood under the cloth of estate, attended on by the premier nobles of the country. Suffolk, my uncle Norfolk, Cardinal Wolsey and the earls of Arundel and Oxford were all in attendance. Henry Fitzroy was dressed in a crimson and blue mantle with the giant sword of estate by his side. He carried the sword very well, I thought, considering he was only six years old. He knelt before the King and the other lords as the patents of estate were read and then, to great applause, the diminutive Duke took his place by the side of his father, taking precedence over all in the room, save the King himself.

The six year old bastard son of Bessie Blount was now next in rank only to Henry himself. He was, in essence, made a prince of the realm… ranked in the same estate as the Princess Mary, the King's legitimate daughter. Not long after, perhaps in deference to his queen who was not pleased with the elevation of this bastard to the same rank as her daughter, Henry sent Princess Mary to Ludlow Castle, in Wales, to undertake the first steps in leaning how to rule. The same procedure had been used for Henry's brother, Arthur, when he was heir to the throne; it was traditional for the heir to take up their own council, and to rule over some of the King's lands, in order to gain experience and authority.

Although Katherine was, I believe, pleased that her daughter was being put forth as the official heir to the throne, and this appointment showed such, she was not happy about Mary being sent to Ludlow. Ludlow Castle was the place where Katherine's first husband, Prince Arthur, had died in the early months of their marriage, and Katherine herself had come close to death at that time too. It was rumoured that some type of plague had taken hold of the young couple, but Katherine had recovered where her husband had not. Ludlow was, for Katherine, a place of sadness and danger. It was not a well-kept castle either, as she remembered it, but a place with many damp and ill airs. She could not refute the honour done to her daughter, but to be parted from her beloved daughter, to have Mary go to a place she feared and detested, added greatly to her sorrows. It was a mixed honour for the Queen.

There was another reason that I was in that chamber watching the promotion of a six year old to the premier estates of the land; my father was amongst those honoured at that day. Sir Thomas Boleyn was given the title of Lord Rochford. After the ceremony, however, when we were called to his chambers, I learnt that he was far from being entirely pleased, despite the new lands, grants and chambers he had been given. For in receiving the title of Lord Rochford, our father had been stripped of the office of Lord Treasurer, without any form of financial compensation. Whilst the title of Lord Rochford brought our father wealth, the loss of his position as Lord Treasurer cost him more.

"Son of a *butcher's whore*!" our father hissed through gritted teeth, trying to keep his voice down, whilst anger radiated from him like lightning from a storm cloud. He was formidable in his rage, and since it was not directed at me this time, I marvelled at it, feeling slightly detached as I stood by the fire in our father's chambers, watching him seethe and bluster. His face was that of a demon and I wondered idly whether I might look somewhat like him when my anger was raised; my temper, it seemed, had not come from our mother.

"That dirty, *cow-herd's piss*! That *bastard-born son of the devil*! That inn-keeper's cur!" Our father, his face red and his eyes bulging, cursed the Cardinal Wolsey, who had taken the Treasury office from him. Our mother sat, calmly sewing by the fire and looking up now and then to check where the progress of her husband's anger had taken him. It is better at times when people are suffused with anger to let them get it all out before attempting to talk to them. George stood by too, idly playing with a book in his hands and waiting for our father to calm down.

"I *worked* for that position," our father spat, ending the stream of curses that had come from his mouth by throwing himself into a chair by the fire.

"As did I," Mary said quietly from the window seat.

Our father ignored her. "One day, I swear I shall return the favour that that Butcher's whoreson has done me today." His eyes narrowed with the thought of what he should do to Wolsey. "He has the King's love and his ear for now, but one day…" he trailed off.

"I think we can be clear," I said calmly, smoothing my gown, "that the Cardinal has no love for the Boleyns. He has taken your office, father, and he prevented the advantageous match I could have made with Henry Percy. He tried to remove George from the Privy Chamber, although my charming brother found a way to the King's heart to get back in." I smiled at George who grinned at me. "Perhaps he does not wish the Boleyns to grow in favour much more than we have already." I nodded at Mary. "I believe that he sees us as a threat, which means he fears us. That is a good thing. He should fear us. We are many and he is one… and we are strong."

My father looked at me and grunted, nodding. "You are perhaps right there," he said. "With Mary in the King's bed and George and myself growing in favour at court, perhaps there is enough there to worry the Cardinal." He paused and smiled, looking most pleased suddenly. "Good!" he laughed and my mother cast me a grateful look for managing to divert father's anger towards planning for advancement once more. "Good," our father said again. "I long now to do nothing *but* worry the Cardinal," he grinned with glee on his face. "Come, family, let us make a pact… from now on, we shall do our utmost to worry Cardinal Wolsey."

We all agreed, although at that time, I remember thinking that the great Cardinal would still have little to worry over from the Boleyns.

Just after that time, perhaps even as we made our pact, the Cardinal made the grand gesture of presenting the King with his most fabulous possession; Hampton Court in Surrey, a palace Wolsey had built up and re-designed from a mere manor into a grand house which outshone even the palaces of the King. Henry was delighted and Wolsey was regarded in higher favour than ever.

It seemed that the Cardinal was here to stay.

Chapter Twenty-Nine

Greenwich Palace
1525

At the height of the summer, on a misty afternoon as we sat sewing in Will Carey's apartments at court, Mary confided in me that she was once again with child.

"How far are you gone?" I asked, and she told me she thought not more than a month or so.

"Do you know the father this time?" I asked with a mischievous smile.

Mary blushed, rosy and pretty. "This time I believe it is more likely to be Carey's child than the King's…. Will and I have grown closer these few months and the King has sent for me less and less often. Truly, these last few months I have rarely been in his bed and he seems less interested in me than ever before. I said to you some time ago that I thought his affections were waning, and now I am sure. I think there is another he wants, and soon I believe I shall be replaced as mistress." She looked a little sad.

"You will miss being the King's lover?" I asked. "I thought you were eager to be a true wife, and not be shared."

She smiled. "Yes, but I will perhaps miss him a little; he is kind and gentle and has been good to me. There has been no scandal and there have been no hard words against me; my family and my husband have done well from the arrangement and it has been pleasant in many ways." She paused. "But perhaps it would be nice to live with my children and see them grow up. To visit court, of course, but retire enough to enjoy Will and the children as a wife should be able to," she touched my arm. "To own the truth, Anne, I am a little tired of all the politics and scheming at court, and in being the King's mistress. I was gladder than any woman when Catherine turned out to be a girl so that she could not be thrust by our father and George into the King's face as a possible candidate for the throne. Imagine the danger in which they would have placed my child! And all for ambition! All for power! I would wish a quieter life for my daughter and this new child than that which I have lived. Although, you, it would seem, are made for this world."

She smiled again at me, and suddenly I really did feel like the younger sister and she the elder. So often I had thought of Mary as unsophisticated, seemingly younger than I. But every now and then, I understood that her experiences of the world were not as sunny as the shine she tried to place on everything. There was wisdom under the surface of her merriment, and gravity under the cover of her lightness. She understood a great deal of patience and of giving up her own wishes for the wants and demands of her family. She was not the elder in years alone.

As the summer wore on, the King announced that his progress would soon embark from the court in London. He would travel down through Kent, and then upwards along the River Thames, visiting noble houses in Essex, before stopping to embark on a long hunting trip at Woodstock. A royal progress was almost the only time when the monarch was seen outside of London, and when the King would favour his courtiers by visiting with them, and staying at their houses. It was something that also caused great concern; housing the court, and its expenses, could be ruinous for a lord, but there were none who would deny the honour of such a visit. There came a great honour to our family when Henry announced that his progress would include a stay at Penshurst Place, his own grand residence that was but a few miles from Hever Castle. Whilst the bulk of his courtiers would lodge at Penshurst, Henry would spend a few nights with us at Hever. Mary and Will were at Beaulieu and he intended to visit them there also.

Queen Katherine was to accompany him. Our mother flew home in a frantic frenzy to make Hever suitable for royal guests and I went with her to help.

Hever had never been so busy! The kitchens were in a roar, making enough food for the King and the select group he would bring to the castle, for Hever was simply not big enough to contain the whole court. An encampment was constructed within Hever's park which all but the King's closest servants would occupy whilst Henry stayed within the castle. The King's chamber had to be perfect, the bed he was to use stuffed with the best eiderdown our father could afford, and covered with the finest linen and blankets we owned. Laundering began on a scale, the like of which I had never seen; our gardens looked like a ghostly masque with all the white bedding dancing in the breeze.

Every day I was out hunting with our master of game to gather enough of the local beasts and birds to sate the King's great appetite. The fish ponds were stocked with living fish and my mother was busy ordering in Henry's favourites; lamprey and trout were shipped to the stock ponds, and many fish of the seas were brought from the oceans still flapping and swimming in huge barrels of salted water, ready for the pot or pie.

The whole manor was cleansed; walls washed down with vinegar water and then wiped with fresh-smelling herbs and rose petals. Servants polished and cleaned like the hand of the devil was driving them and everywhere there was a feeling of expectation and excitement. The smell of cooking emanated from the kitchens through the day and through the night as bricks of sugar were worked into subtleties, beasts were roasted, pies were baked, and fruits stewed. Whole flocks of geese and chickens were herded squawking into pens so they were ready to catch the moment they were needed. Fresh game I brought to the kitchens was hung to gain flavour, and vast, round cheeses were prodded daily by anxious hands to check if they were ripe. The castle was heavy with noise, and the air thick with excitement.

The servants were most excited to catch a glimpse of the King and to serve upon him. Although some who served as maids or footmen to our family had visited the court, to many others, it was a far-off place of mythic romance and chivalry. Bluff King Hal was a figure of legend. They all wanted to be able to boast to their children or grandchildren that they had waited on the King. They wanted to make the best of this visit, as we did; everyone was anxious that the Boleyn family home should not disappoint Henry and his party.

I was nervous... Nothing had happened between Henry and me since I had returned the jewels he had sent to me and I had told no one of it; I wondered now if he had forgotten our kiss in the gardens and if his attentions and affections had waned in the face of my refusal to bed him. It must have been an unusual experience for him, after all; he was surely not used to being refused by the ladies of the court. I had said nothing of it to my friends or family. I suspect that my father may have had me boiled alive for threatening our family's position at court through refusing to bed the King of England. And he might have insisted that I take up the place my sister was about to leave in order to continue our family's fortunes. Since I did not want to take the still-warm place of my sister, I was not about to let my wily father know such a thing was a possibility. To give Thomas Boleyn information was to give him opportunity. I wanted no such opportunity as the one the King had offered me.

The rush of the travelling court arrived at the end of a frantic week of activity. Queen Katherine remained at Penshurst with most of the courtiers, but the King and a select group, "his riding household", came to Hever. Penshurst was the King's own house, one of many lesser houses he kept in the country; George was steward there, and so he too had been nearby over the past week, preparing the house for his master. I had seen him little, despite the spare miles between us. We had all had much to do before the King arrived.

My mother was in a great panic before the crowds arrived, lest the tireless work she had done to provide Henry with adequate splendour should be unsatisfactory. I felt the household's rising excitement as we waited and watched; from early morning, when we all knew he would not be arriving anyway, to the afternoon when every small noise caused us to rush to the windows to look for the King's arrival.

The servants were in their best, and my mother and I clothed in our richest attire. I wore a dark green gown with a crimson kirtle and my customary hanging sleeves, embroidered with tiny yellow and pink honeysuckle flowers and swirling vine leaves, my own work. My hair was caught in my French hood with pearls over the crest and a great chain of gold hung at my waist. I wore, too, my pendant with the letters *AB* wrought in gold, around my pale, long neck. All women at court were now imitating the style of jewellery that I wore. It was pleasing in some ways to find myself aped so, but in order to remain ahead of the others at court, I had to keep changing parts of my dress or jewels. Sometimes I wondered… if I should paint myself with saffron should I find tomorrow that all the women of court had also turned yellow? Was there anything I could do that they would not follow me in, or had they ceased to think for themselves and learnt only to ape me? How dull if they could not think of a new idea themselves!

My mother and I had washed in water of lavender and rosemary in anticipation of Henry's arrival. The King was most fastidious in his cleanliness. My maid, Bess, grinned at my shining eyes, noting the colour in my often pale cheeks. She giggled as she brushed my thick dark hair that morning, sending me looks that said she understood my excitement at the richest and most accomplished King in Christendom visiting our home; this was something that our servants would talk of to their children and grandchildren. The day that they were close enough to touch the King himself.

The colour in my cheeks was not all excitement, however, but some trepidation also. I wondered if he was angry at me for refusing to become his mistress. A part of me hoped that he had forgotten it, and another part hoped just as much that he had not.

Finally, and just before we were all set to explode with excitement, they arrived. I was called to the great hall where my mother stood, hastily dusting her gown free of imaginary dirt. My father and George went out to greet the King and his riding party as they clattered into our courtyard. There was great shouting and laughing as the party dismounted and Henry and his men greeted my father and brother; he was fond of both, I knew well. This visit was an honour; a sign to others at court that the Boleyns were in his favour. I hoped that I should not be called on to do anything that would alter the growing love that Henry had for my family... such as having to refuse him once more...

They entered, and I felt my heart pound in my breast as Henry looked around the hall and stopped, his eyes on me. With my mother, I swept to the floor in a curtsey, and rose only when I saw his shoes before me, and saw his hand indicate that we rise. I brought my eyes to his face as I rose and behind him saw my father watching every move that mother and I made. I looked into Henry's eyes. He was staring at my face with an unreadable expression. I knew not if he was pleased or grieved to see me again.

"You are pleased to see us here in your hall then, Elizabeth?" Henry said informally to my mother, smiling at her.

"We are greatly honoured, Your Majesty," she said, dropping gracefully again to curtsey, but Henry held out his hand to her. "Away with so much ceremony!" he cried gaily. "I am here as a *friend* to your family; how am I to visit well with you if all I see of you are the tops of your heads?"

The party around him laughed and then there was applause at the grand gesture of doing away with ceremony, although we all knew it to be a fantasy.

"And you, Mistress Boleyn?" he addressed me directly. Instinctively, I went again to curtsey, and was stopped by his hand touching my shoulder lightly. There was a mischief in his eyes as he looked at me, and a softness too. "No more of this bowing," he said gently. "From such a pretty lady as you, Anne, I would rather have a kiss to welcome me to your hall."

I could hardly refuse. The King and his whole party were there before me, as were the watchful eyes of my most critical father. I was glad that Mary was not here as yet. I lifted my face as he lowered his lips to mine. There was a brief and courtly kiss as his hand remained on my shoulder and then we parted. Again, the party broke into applause. Henry looked at me with softness; there was a spark in those blue eyes, and I knew then that he was not finished with me. He thought he should have me yet, I thought… Perhaps here! Perhaps *I* was part of the reason for the visit! But I knew not for sure. Perhaps I was just an added bonus to the trip; a chance to bed the haughty daughter at last whilst he made friends with the covetous, greedy father!

I blushed; it would not be so! I would not be sold off as my sister had been!

The party dispersed as they went to wash and dress for the evening's entertainments, as did my family. I craved a moment to myself and left the house and the grappling, busy servants for the peace of the gardens. Summer was in full bloom, and the gardens of Hever were always so beautiful just now. The grasses were still lush; the roses were a mass of reds and whites and the shady honeysuckle that I so loved was sweet with perfume, lending a touch of beauty to the darker areas of the garden.

I was pausing to touch the sweet, budding young blooms of the honeysuckle when I saw Henry approaching. He had, it appeared, not seen me, and was once again unaccompanied by his people as he had been in the gardens at court when we had met, and kissed, earlier in the year. I straightened myself and pushed back the hair that had fallen loose of my silk hood. He saw me and paused, his blue eyes narrowing as he came nearer. I bowed to him and impatiently he motioned for me to stand.

"It seems we often meet in gardens, Mistress Boleyn," he said. "Do you have a love for them?"

"Yes, Your Majesty," I replied. "I relish the peace of my mother's gardens when I am able to visit my family home."

He grunted slightly. "Yes, when one is surrounded by people all the time it is pleasant to find solitude in at least one place," he sounded annoyed.

I faltered. "I am sorry, Your Majesty," I said hurriedly. "Would you have me leave?"

He looked up at me, puzzled for a moment, and then he smiled ruefully at me. "I was not, in fact, talking of you, Mistress Boleyn," he said. "Your company is one that I desire, and yet am forbidden, it would seem, whereas all others' company I am given without question... and yet I seem to desire none of such."

I said nothing, for I knew not what to say.

He looked at the flowers and around at the gardens as though thinking of what to say, and then, in rather a rush, said, "You returned the jewels I sent to you."

"Yes, Your Majesty," I dropped my eyes and curtseyed, for he looked annoyed once more and I wanted to appease him. It would not do to irritate the King when he was honouring our family. He clicked his tongue impatiently at me, bidding me to rise. I looked into his blue eyes. He was frowning, but he did not seem exactly angry with me.

"Not many would have done as you did," he admonished. "Most women would be grateful for the honour done to them when their prince sends them a gift."

"I was most grateful for the honour, Sire," I replied, "but unable to accept such a gift … if I were too to keep my own honour."

He sighed. "What mean you, my lady?" he asked with colour rising to his cheeks, shaking his head. "Anne, I understand you *least* of any person I have *ever* met. You kiss me in the gardens of my own palace and you dance with me as though we were lovers already abed, and yet when I offer you the chance to become my mistress you refuse me *and* my love for you *and* send back the jewels that I chose for you from my own inheritance." He shook his head at me. "You rush to aid me when I am fallen, faster even than my soldiers and yet you ignore me for the company of prattling, prancing *boys* at court. You are a mixture of virtues and vices, Anna, and I know not how you think of me nor what you desire of me. All you do seems to frustrate me, to anger me… And yet, I cannot seem to be free of you. Not in the arms of others… Not in my waking days, nor in my dreams… You *haunt* me. You are all I seem able to think about." He stopped and sighed, running his hands through his blond-red hair and making it unruly. "I am most confused," he said looking at me, as though I had an answer. "I am most confused, by you."

I stood amazed; not only by what he was saying, but by how he was saying it to me. We had talked informally before, but he had never expressed himself so honestly, nor so openly before. And the things he said… *I* was all he could think about?

"Your Majesty," I started falteringly, and he stopped me by putting his hand on mine.

"We are not now Majesty and servant, Anne." His voice was earnest, pleading. "Tell me truly… as you would tell another man, king or no king, what is there between us?" His blue eyes bored into mine with fire in them. His hand was strong and forceful upon mine. "I swear that… that I *love* you, Anne. I have loved no other as I love you and I would know what there is in your heart towards me. Tell me truly of your feelings."

I hesitated. "Your Majesty," I said, my heart beating loud within me, half in fear and half in wonderment at Henry's words… the King *loved* me? He loved *me*? I had been in his thoughts all this time… in his dreams? I was half dazed by the revelation and my heart sang out to tell him that I loved him too, that I always had loved him… But my mind spoke harshly to my heart, dampening its spirits. *Men say many things, to get what they want of a maid*, it warned. D*on't be a fool! He is done with Mary, and would have another Boleyn girl in his bed as a conquest… Don't be a fool…* My mind, too, spoke to me of my resolution to not become mistress to any man, even if he be a king…
I drew myself up, knowing that I had to refuse the King of England once more.

"I was raised to be an honest maid and I ask that what I say now should not be taken as an insult to Your Majesty, but as a compliment to your sensibility. You must see that a maid such as I has little in the way of a great dowry to bring to the estates of a husband. As such, the greatest dowry I could offer is my own self, untouched by the hands of other men, and given in lawful marriage, and love, to one man only."

I looked up at him. He was a towering man and I felt diminutive before him. "As a knight and a great lord, Your Majesty must understand that I hold my virginity and my honour in great carefulness against the dangers that court may present to it. And whilst the office of Your Majesty's mistress is one that I know many would occupy happily and with great prestige to their family, it is not one that I seek or wish for. *I will be no man's mistress.* I will come to the bed of my husband as a true maid. I hope that to the man I marry, this will be a greater prize than lands or gold, for I shall bear the sons of *his* seed and no other. I would wish no husband of mine to be a cuckold, no matter how high their station or personal values of knighthood or other titles, or…"

I paused and looked in his eyes, and my words faltered as I gazed on his handsome face, that face I had seen so often in my dreams, that face I had worshipped as a child. "Or how… attractive that person may be to my person… How dear he may be, to my eyes or to my heart."

I had spoken carefully, but with strength, and in his eyes I could see anger, desire and also… perhaps respect? I knew not. He looked at me in silence; there was such a mixture of emotions in his face. He faltered as he returned my words. "Then I *am* dear to your heart?" His voice was pleading. I felt my heart wrench for him.

"Yes," I said, and then held him back with a trembling hand as he sought to embrace me. "But it cannot be; *this* cannot be… I cannot be yours in truth, for you have a wife already… It is an impossible situation." I pulled away from him and folded my arms before my chest, as though that would protect me.

"You would that I should leave you alone, then?" he asked with anger colouring his face now that I had removed myself from his grasp and refused him again.

"Your Majesty, your wife I cannot be, for you have a wife already and I am unworthy to hold such a title in any case. *Your mistress I will not be.* I cannot be mistress to any man, not even to you. I prize my honour, and myself, too highly to allow such."

The colour in his cheeks rose and I trembled despite the heat of the sun in the gardens. I was afraid. I had spoken boldly, perhaps too boldly to a prince so used to getting his own way.

But I could not, I would not, occupy the warm space in the bed that Mary would leave when she ceased to be his royal mistress. I would not squander all my hopes for marriage and for virtue on this fancy of the King's. In no time he would move on to another, and I would be left with a screaming bastard or two; a broken hearted and discarded whore. I could not give him what he wanted of me, no matter how tempting the offer was to those secret parts of me that called out for him.

God help me… I did desire him just as he desired me, but I could not allow that to vanquish all of my beliefs, all that I had held dear in my life.

"And this… is your answer?" he asked, not looking at me but at the roses. His face was petulant, like a child denied his favourite toy.

"It is, Your Majesty," I nodded, feeling most unhappy and worried. "But I beg you that your displeasure should fall not on my family who are very guiltless of anything but love towards Your Majesty, and if your displeasure should fall on anyone, then let it be only on me."

Henry sighed and laughed shortly. There was little humour in it. "I know not what stories you have heard, Mistress Boleyn," he said. "But I am no satyr or tyrant who would punish you or your family for what you have said to me here. I asked you to speak with honesty and you have; not many would have spoken to me thus. I respect you for it, even if I like it not." He sighed again. "My life is ever-surrounded by people who would only tell me that which they think will please me. You are very different to them."

I knew not whether this was a good thing or no.

"But I shall not give up," he said raising his blue eyes to my dark ones. "I *cannot* give up. You *are* the mistress of my heart if not the mistress of my body." I went to speak again, but he stopped my words, holding up his hand. "It is not your choice,

Anne," he said. "I cannot help this desire I have for you, this love I hold for you. I am yours, if you would have me and perhaps, when I am worthy of your love, then your heart will open to mine. Before that time, if I needs must, I shall be your knight and you my mistress without the touch of pleasure to accompany that office. If you would have me as your knight of courtly love, then I am yours."

I stepped back from him. "I do not think that you are unworthy of me, sire, and if you were to take the place of my admirer in the offices of courtly love, I should be most honoured." I said gently, smiling, feeling a little relieved. It would be an honour to have the King as my knight. As long as he did not want anything more from me, then I would remain safe. "Perhaps, if I explain something to you, then you will understand my heart better… When I was a girl," I said carefully, "I was in service to the Archduchess Margaret at the Court of Burgundy. I was sent there to learn my lessons most carefully and I feared each day that I should be sent away from such a brilliant court for my own ignorance and gracelessness."

I smiled and Henry and I stepped into walking the paths together. It was far easier to distract him in conversation as we walked; to steer him from the intimate gestures that he made towards me if I was still.

"There came a day when there was a visit from a foreign prince." I smiled at him, teasing him with my words. "The Prince was handsome and young, his clothes shone with rich jewels and his hair was the colour of the sun itself." I watched him as some anger crossed his face at the idea of this prince I had so admired. Henry did not realize I was talking of him. "He came to stay with the Archduchess as he was *winning* wars in France…?" I continued with a light and teasing note to my voice that he picked up on. Suddenly he realised I was talking of him. Henry beamed at me, happy again now that he understood he was being flattered.

Henry was ever a little childlike. I think that was one of the things I came to love him for, and later, to fear. He had an innocence about him, much like that of Henry Percy, which I found appealing, and a petulance which came from ever and always having his own way. Somehow it blended admirably, in those early days, with his masculine appeal; it made him fell less of a threat to me. The fears which I carried with me from France never truly abated, but with a handsome man who seemed in many ways to be a young child at heart, I found some balm for those worries. Of course later, it was that petulance, that insistence in having his own way that would cause many trials and troubles… but that was how he was. That is how he has always been. Then, I loved him for it.

"On the day you arrived, I and the other maids were watching secretly from a window. I had never heard anything as wonderful as your great laugh, and seen nothing so wonderful as you with your arm around the shoulders of a friend. You were so easy in your friendship, so charming in your power. There was never anyone so handsome or admirable. But then! Ah! We were heard as we chattered and giggled at that window and away we flew with our hearts pounding." I laughed. "We were all so afraid to be caught by the Archduchess spying on your arrival and that we should be sent away… We flew like falcons to her chambers, where we should have been sewing all along like good maids!"

I laughed again, remembering my great fear. Henry let out his great laugh and clapped his thigh; he loved to be amused. I looked at him with great gentleness in my eyes, for these moments of privacy with him were precious. I felt like I was with the friend I had always longed for, this great man whom I so desired and who desired me. The gardens were sweet with the sun and the flowers' scents and his company by my side was the best that I had known.

He was looking at me now with a strange, fogged expression in his eyes, as though he was trying to remember something.

He shook his head in wonder. "You… you were Margaret's little songbird," he said quietly, and I nodded.

"Your Majesty," I went on, "I was that day assured that there was no other king or prince in all the world as great as you. I have met other kings and princes since and not found anything or anyone to alter that opinion formed when I was but a girl. If there were any temptation that God could put before me to challenge my vow of chastity until marriage, if there were any temptation stronger than you… then I know not what it could be."

I bowed again, trembling both with desire and fear. "It is not, then, that my heart is *not* yours, or that you are not worthy of my love, that holds me back from you." I explained. "It is that I can enter into no honourable state with you. That is the reason I refuse your offer. That is the only reason why I cannot be, as you wish me to be, with you…"

He looked at me with narrowed eyes and then reached out for me. His eyes smouldered and his lips vaguely murmured my name as he reached to take me into his embrace. He grabbed at my arm, but I pulled it free. I stepped back again, and curtseyed to him, then I turned and almost ran to the house before he could say aught. I knew that if I stayed then he would have tried to kiss me again, and more. My words of refusal, containing as they did, words of love, seemed only to encourage him to try and hold me. If I stayed, then there was no knowing what might happen. What I said was true; he was the greatest temptation I had ever faced in my life.

I looked back as I reached the house and saw him standing, staring after me with the mixture of emotions on his face that I was getting used to seeing when he looked at me; anger, desire, softness and irritation… all bound up with confusion. I felt my heart go to him for I felt much the same way about him. This mixture of ambiguous feelings was forever in my heart when I saw or talked with him and I almost choked on the pity that rose in my chest for Henry. I understood his confusion and pain better than anyone. I longed to be with him, too, but could not be.

As I walked into the house, and up to my chamber, I could hear my heart pounding in my ears. Oh yes, I knew I had long held feelings within my heart for the King of England. I knew that I had admired Henry, long and often. Known that I was attracted to him, and that I also held other, deeper feelings for him… But I had never admitted such out loud. In speaking of my feeling for him, to him, I felt as though something I had carried for a long time had been released within me. I felt as though a hawk soared in my heart, its wings beating to its pounding pulse. At the same time, I felt scared, scared to have revealed such emotion to him. What could possibly come of this? He wanted more from me than I was prepared to give, and even though he said he would be but my courtly admirer, I knew not if such a state would remain pleasing to him.

When I looked into my polished mirror that evening, I saw the same expression on my face that I had seen on Henry's; a mixture of excitement, pain and confusion that I could not reconcile any more than he could. One phrase kept echoing over and over in my mind…

The King loves you, Anne Boleyn… Henry loves you…

Chapter Thirty

Penshurst Place
1525

That night, as the dusky skies turned from orange-pink to cobalt blue, we rode with Henry's riding party to Penshurst to take part in a grand celebration. Our horses clattered up the cobbles towards the grand house and in that great hall, overwhelmed by the magnificently carved high timber ceiling, we feasted and drank merrily.

My body and mind were on fire with the events of the afternoon and my skin felt heated where Henry had touched me. There was a small bruise appearing on my wrist where he had grasped at me; although it hurt, I was glad of it, for it proved to me that I had not imagined the whole thing. The King of England had professed his love for me that day and sworn to be my knight even if I would not have him as a lover! I was a giddy girl that night; suffused with the excitement of his passion and the overwhelming feeling thronging in my blood that I too loved him. God's Blood! I did love him! I loved his handsome face, his short beard and his knightly form. I loved the sharp blue of his eyes, and the way my skin tingled when he looked on me. I loved the small crease of a frown in between his eyebrows, and the way he spoke of books with such warmth and love. He was intelligent, kind, and somewhat childlike in his enthusiasm and his feelings. His boyishness endeared him to me, much as it had done with Percy, but here was no witless worm pretending to be a man… here was a *man*! A knight, a king… the most glorious jouster and ruler in living memory… the most powerful man in England… And he was in love with me! He wanted me, desired me, *longed* for me. It was almost too much to imagine.

I had never felt like this before and I was both enamoured of the feeling, and scared by the force of it on my body and mind. It was as though all these years I had held this feeling back within my heart, never allowing it to be free… but now, it was. Like a lion let loose of a cage, it roamed through my blood and through my bone. I was flighty. I felt quite unlike myself. I felt wild. I felt *free*.

At the dance I could not go near him. I could not stay away. I was trapped near him by my station, by my honour and my feelings. I drank deeply of the wine, thinking it might free my mind of the questions that beset me, but it only fired my passion for him.

We danced together that evening, me with my heart in my mouth as I stepped the delicate steps of the *bear dance* feeling his hot hands on mine and seeing the grace with which he moved before me. As we came together in the dance he whispered to me. "Lady, you torment me..."

We swept apart and came together for another pass, and he again whispered, "I still know not where we stand, Anne." But I kept silent. I knew not what to say. The Queen had joined her husband for the evening's entertainments and we were dancing in front of her. Also Mary and Will were amongst the newly arrived party that evening. I had never felt more sinful than I did now!

The air was heavy with the fresh sweat of the dancers, with the deep sound of the tabor and the silky smoothness of the lute, with the scents of the feast now done and eaten and with the crushed herbs that he and I danced upon, our feet releasing sweet perfumes each time we turned and trampled them beneath our feet. All I could hear was the sound of his breathing. All I could feel were his hands on mine, and the heat and desire of his body. It felt as though all others in the room must be able to see and hear each of these intense sensations too, so keen and sharp were they to me. I did not answer him because I did not trust myself to. I cautioned myself to dance, just *dance*, Anne, as though you are naught but a lady of the court, favoured for a brief moment by the King. But I was haunted by the idea that everyone could read on my face the revelations I had found within myself that day…. That I loved him… I *loved* him… Oh, dearest God in heaven! I knew not what to do with this realisation that had come to me! How was I to control it, now that it had been let loose?

He returned me to my brother who was standing in the throng laughing with others and watching me. I drank deeply from a goblet of wine and felt George tug at my sleeve to follow him out into the cool air of the courtyard. It felt wonderful on my hot skin, and we wandered with cups of wine to the courtyard's edge which looked down on the stylish gardens. George was Penshurst's warden, so he knew it well. The gardens and grand house were well kept and bountiful; the gardens pretty and modern. Henry was well-pleased with George's work here and at court and sought his company often. My brother was doing well.

As we stood watching the gardens, beautifully bathed in the light of an almost-full moon, George took a long drink of wine and spoke thoughtfully. "Did you know that this was where I first came, when we three were sent from home?"

"I did not," I muttered. My mind was elsewhere, lingering on the memory of Henry's hand on my waist.

"Yes," George turned to me. "This was the house of the Duke of Buckingham… that same man whose head I showed you when we first rode into London together, do you remember?" His voice was low, for to speak the name of a man executed for treason at the King's entertainment was not wise. There was something in his tone which made me pay attention; suddenly all the excitement drained from me and I felt cold in the moonlight.

"I was in his house until a couple of years before they executed him," George continued, his voice measured, low and cool. "He was a fair master. Proud, oh yes... But fair to those in his household. The other pages and I used to play and ride in these grounds when we were in residence here, and the Duke would allow me to visit Hever often to see our mother." He turned to me. "The King would visit often, too... That was how I came to know him and how I moved into the royal household. He and the Duke, it seemed then, were great friends; they would visit often and hunt together. I saw Henry walking in the gardens here with the Duke once, when the royal household visited after I had joined Henry's service. The King had his arm around Buckingham like a brother." George looked at me, our eyes meeting, as he continued. "That was but two days before the Duke was arrested for treason."

I shivered. "Why do you say this to me?"

"It is just..." George tailed off a little. "You seem, perhaps... *fond* of the King and he of you. Sometimes, you see, the King is like King Arthur or St George of old. There is in him such valour and spirit, he would be the greatest knight of all, he would be the shining hero, but there are times..." he trailed off again.

"When he is the dragon" I said, completing the sentence that George could not quite say. George looked at me and nodded.

"He wants to be the knight with all his heart," he said to me, looking once again out at those gardens where I knew he could see the ghostly forms of his past master Buckingham, and his now-master King Henry, walking arm in arm amongst the flowers.

"I understand, brother," I said. All gaiety was suddenly gone from my heart. The warning of my brother's words rung in their place; beware the disappointed knight, for he may have the temper of a dragon. I shivered and George took me inside from the cold. I left the gathering early with some servants and rode back to Hever, claiming a headache. As I got into bed and slept, my dreams swirled with ghosts of headless men, the shrill laughter of children and the terrifying vision of Henry, dressed as St George and piercing me through the mouth with his spear as though I were the vanquished dragon. I awoke early, in the darkness of the morn before the light and sat by the embers of the fire in my room, lost in thought of the feelings that Henry had stirred in me, and of my fears of what this may mean for me. Could I continue to hold his favour whilst refusing him the office of a true lover? Would he be satisfied to remain no more than a *courtly* admirer? I knew not.

The royal party left Penshurst the next day. As Henry and his riding party departed from Hever to join them, we were all gathered in the courtyard to see them off. There, he came to me before my assembled family and servants and took his leave in the same way that he had greeted me, with a kiss. His hot hands burned through my scarlet gown as he touched my shoulders. As he was saying a cheery goodbye to the household, he turned to me once again.

"I was sorry to hear that you left last night's revelries early for a headache, Mistress Boleyn," he said. "I trust that the pain is now healed?" I nodded and kept my eyes as downcast as I dared. He looked confused and a little angered; I had danced with him in great passion and then fled without explanation. He was right when he said I was the most confusing of women. I would have been confused by the way I behaved, but in all honesty, I knew not what to do with the situation I had been granted.

"I would have of you, Mistress Boleyn, some token to remind me of this visit. For amongst the halls of your house, Thomas," he indicated to my father who bowed, "and the pleasures of your gardens, Elizabeth," my mother bowed too, "I have found such delight that I would carry it with me on my journey. It is from *you*, Mistress Anne, that I would take a token of true friendship to solace me on the dusty road."

There was applause from the crowd. It was a pretty piece of play-acting made to show favour to the Boleyns, but it had another, more secret, meaning for me; he was asking to carry a token of my acceptance of his position as my courtly suitor. It was a well-honoured tradition, and before all these people, I could hardly refuse. Nor did I *want* to refuse, even if it might cause problems for me later... I wanted him to be my courtly knight. I understood George's warning, but I could not ignore the feelings within me. I made my choice. I took a ring from my finger and gave it to him. It was a large ring on my delicate hands, but would fit only on his smallest finger. The ring held my family's crest in gold, over a tiny ruby.

I held it out to him with a shaking hand and as he took it from me I whispered very quietly to him. "You are *my* knight, Your Majesty." His eyes shone with pleasure as he looked into mine. There, on his face, was that boyish look of happiness that I loved so. I smiled at him and then curtseyed again.

There was more applause and another cheer as the King kissed my cheek. He and his party then mounted their horses to ride off and join the court again. Mary stared at me a little as she saw me watching the King's party. He had asked me for a favour, not her. I looked up at her with wary, worried eyes but she smiled a little sadly, but gently at me and squeezed my arm before walking in to the house, arm in arm with Will. It seemed that she did not mind her lover giving his attention to me, although she could little guess at all else that had passed between us in these short days. My father nodded curtly to me, happy enough that the King's approval had been won, and left me to watch the last traces of the riding party as they galloped away from Hever.

As I watched him ride away I felt my heart sink, thinking that I should now not see him until I returned to the service of the Queen, the wife of the man I loved.

And I did love him. Yes, I loved him. I wanted him. I longed for him... but I knew myself to be separated from him by more than just the ties of his marriage. When I came back to court, when Henry's progress was done for the summer, I wondered and feared on what was going to happen… Could a man like Henry be satisfied with but the trappings of love, or would he insist that I give up my honour and my body to him in order to keep my family in favour?

Chapter Thirty-One

Greenwich Palace
1525-1526

In the soft snows of winter, Mary gave birth to a fine boy. She named him Henry, for the King, and all, our father more than anyone, wondered whether or not the child was Henry's son. It had become clear that the King's passion, ever discreet at the best of times, had cooled for my sister; he had not sent for her for some time before the birth. Many put that down to the pregnancy, but even after she was churched and purified in the eyes of all Christendom, he still did not send for her. He paid her no special addresses and there were no extraordinary gifts at the birth of her second child… which, of course, was possibly was his son.

There was a look of some small regret in Mary over those days following her return to court, although she seemed to find ample consolation in her children. She would ride out to see as often as she could. The King, it seemed, was done with my sister, and was not going to acknowledge the child as his even though it was a boy.

Our father went around court with an expression like a dog left out in the rain.

My mother and I had returned to court and had wintered with the Queen's household, enjoying the entertainments and pageants laid on for the court at Christmas and New Year. I was reunited with Margaret and Bridget once more. I found myself at the centre of attention, for I was chosen to play the lead role in all of the entertainments. Suddenly, it seemed, we were to have more dances and masques than we had ever had before. Tom and George were often writing for the King's pleasure, and Henry would pick me to play the title roles above all the other women at court. George was excited, thinking that this showed the King's favour for our family, but I saw him eyeing me with a speculative look that was more at home on our father's face. I hid all I could from them. I hid my secrets from everyone, even my closest friends… although I trusted Margaret and Bridget I knew well enough how whispers grow at court. I did not want my family to know the secrets of my heart. I did not want my secrets to become tools for my father, or for George. Perhaps as the sister of the King's mistress, I suggested, I was shown special favour. I do not think they were totally convinced, but I cared little. As long as they did not question me openly on the matter, then I did not have to lie.

Tom, too, seemed curious about Henry's new interest in me. Since the affair with Percy, Tom had taken a step back from my company at court, perhaps licking wounds that I had inflicted on him. But now, with Percy gone from the court, perhaps for good, and Henry singling me out above all others, it was almost as though Tom sensed his interest in me… As though he smelt the arrival of another wolf on the fringes of the pack. Tom seemed drawn to me once more, like the honey-bee to the flower. I was cautious with him. I wanted little to hurt him again, and I knew that I had done, however unintentionally, before. Many of Tom's poems were circulated at court that winter, and all were on the subject of a love that was strong within him, and yet was rejected by the object of his affection… I did not have to take many guesses to know that I was the object for which he yearned.

Unable, as I was, to deter Henry from pursuing me as a mistress, I could not help but feel pleasure when all the court's eyes were on me as I danced and sang before them. I could not deny either the pleasure that came from having the King's attention on me. I could feel admiration and jealousy emanating from the crowd, and at first, these sweet and sour tastes mingled wonderfully. I had ever been a fan of complex sauces. Every woman knows that it is pleasurable to feel a little envy from others at times.

In the nights in the great palaces of London, I wore light velvet gowns and silk slippers. I donned the elaborate costumes of the principal dancer in all the entertainments. I was the centre of the court and in those dark rooms, dancing in dappled candlelight, I became each and every character that George and Tom wrote for me.

I danced as *Fortune*, my feet tripping lightly around the wheel I carried that showed all men's fates. I felt the heat of the open fires behind me as my blood warmed with every move of my slim body. I felt the beat of the drums rock through me and the sound of the pipes send shivers through my veins. I danced as *Victory* with her sword; the other women of the court prancing around me with flaming torches as my dark hair whirled in the smoke-ridden air. I felt the silk slide on my legs as I danced; flashes of bare flesh causing the men of the court to suck in their breath sharply. Trickles of giggles wanted to run through me as I saw their pained expressions. I felt power as I whirled in front of them; masked and dressed as images of a story.

I was not Anne Boleyn, the courtier's daughter, when I danced. I was every desire they had ever imagined and more. I knew the power that I had when I was in those costumes, when I stepped to those dances. And I knew just as well that I had to be more careful than any other woman at court to not become caught by any of them, lest the balance of power should escape from my hands and into theirs. I danced with danger each night, and something in me found it thrilling. And all the time, every night, I felt the hot eyes of the King on me as I danced. I knew that he wanted me more than ever and although I did not want to be his whore, I wanted him to want me. To want me as I wanted him. Each dance, I danced for him. I danced so that he should not learn to forget me. I danced so that he would remember all that he had said to me. Although I could not have him, I wanted him to want no other than me. I did not want his gaze to fall from mine. I did not want to be forgotten by the man I loved. I held him at bay, even as I wanted to beckon him closer.

George, Margaret, Tom and I would write together often. I found those sessions, writing with those talented poets, wonderful, and my head and my heart were active in the creation, criticism and praise of their work. They were kind about my offerings, although I was profoundly less talented than my brother or than Tom, who was becoming a consummate poet. I do not flatter myself when I say that many of Tom's poems were written for me; he told me as much himself. Tom was still in love with me, and saw me as his torture and his muse. Some of the works were very fine, and when he read them at court, there was no doubt to anyone that he was talking of me. Margaret was sad when she heard such poetry, but assured me that she understood my feelings and principles. Although she was sorrowed to see her brother hurt by his love for me, she knew as I did that it could come to nothing.

That a great poet should be pursuing me as his mistress in the game of courtly love for the whole court to see was a heady experience. No less exhilarating than the King speaking of his desire for me. I was rather swept away by my own self in those early days of 1526. I exhilarated in the vain feelings that swept over me, and although that does little to recommend my character to anyone, I had never felt more desired, or more fragile than I did at that time. Although I had the love of my friends, I felt the dislike and jealousy that other women felt towards me as I walked the halls of court, just as I felt the desire of the men. Whilst this was enjoyable at first, eventually it left me feeling as though I might shatter if I were but touched; so brittle, so fragile had this person I had created, this centrepiece of the court, become. The Anne Boleyn of those days was as much a creation as were any of the personas as which she danced …

"You are a true beauty when you dance, Anna," Tom said to me one evening as I returned to the rest of the court after changing my gown. I nodded to him and smiled.

"Thank you, Master Wyatt," I smiled, "but I believe my sister Jane to be the greater beauty of those who danced this night." Jane looked at me with a rather surprised smile, but I meant the compliment. Jane was far more of a beauty than was I, or perhaps even Mary.

"But when the lover's heart looks on the one he admires," said Tom, "there can be no comparison with others."

"I know of none who could claim to be my lover, Tom," I reprimanded.

"But you know of many who love you, and are bound to you, in spite of your disdain for their feelings."

I sighed a little. "I disdain none, but nor would I admit to something I know to be untrue, Master Wyatt."

"Perhaps one day, your heart will be reached beyond the coldness of the maiden pride that covers it," he sipped at his wine, a bitter twist on his mouth.

"The man I would give my heart to would not view a maiden's wish for honour with bitterness," I said lightly, although feeling anger in my heart at him. "Nor see my offers of friendship to be cold comfort."

"Then he is a more patient man than I."

"Apparently so, Tom."

I turned to Jane, who was listening to this exchange with slightly flushed cheeks, and asked her to walk with me to my chambers. At such times, I had to escape Tom. Much of the time, he could still be merry and well with me; at others, he was saturated with the sourness of rejection. But I had always been honest with him, and he kept coming back to me knowing that my heart was not his. I offered him my friendship, and accepted him as a courtly admirer, but he always wanted more of me. I was frustrated a little that winter as I thought on the offers that had been made to me by the men in my life. Was I never to be offered a place as a wife? Was I only ever looked on by the men at court as a potential mistress?

But such conversations, even ones as sour as the one I had with Tom, did not seem to put him off. I enjoyed his witty company when he was given to more light humour. I maintained that I wished to be his friend, and although he did not accept this, he did not shy from my companionship.

As Tom's attention towards me became more public, the attentions of other men increased, too. I walked the halls with gallant and handsome men, such as Francis Bryan and Henry Norris, the new Groom of the Stool, at my side, jesting in the games of courtly love. I do not flatter myself that it was because I was the most attractive woman at court, for I was not; but I was unobtainable where other women of the court were not. Other women were granted as wives, and gave themselves up to be mistresses, but not I, and all knew it. Delay is always the most potent ingredient of desire. Some men, Tom included, called me cold and cruel, but what should I have done? Given myself to all who asked for me? For then they would call me a whore. A woman's life at court must be carefully balanced between the thin lines of flirtation and respectability in the games of courtly love, but the truth is that she can never really win against the contradictions of the male heart. She will either be called a whore for accepting them, or a cold, cruel mistress for her refusal. I would rather be known as a cruel mistress than an idle play-thing, but either title was hardly complimentary. There is no way for a woman to ever truly win, you see? Unless she dons a habit, and shuts herself away in a hermit's cave.

Tom wrote poetry, with his love for me as his muse,

> *But I see now that your high distain*
> *Will nowise grant that I shall that attain*
> *Yet ye must grant at the least*

This my poor and small request
Rejoice not at my pain.

I did not rejoice at causing anyone pain, but I was not going to alter my own spirit and give in to Tom, nor to Henry either, for that way there lay pain only for myself. I had made up my mind long ago. I refused to whore myself even for a man I truly loved. I was determined. I was resolved. Henry was not a man who had much experience in being refused by maidens, but I had learnt my lessons well in seeing how my sister was treated in France... And, early that year, another lesson was granted to me by God, to teach me of the changing nature of men's affections to the women they profess to love.

Chapter Thirty-Two

Hampton Court
1526

In January of 1526, François of France had capitulated to the Holy Roman Emperor, Charles of Spain and signed the Treaty of Milan. The treaty allowed François' release, but it came with a heavy price. The French King was to give up his claims on Milan and Naples, and hand over the territories of Flanders and Artois, amongst other lands, to the Emperor Charles. François was also to take Eleanor, the Emperor's sister, as his new queen. Worst of all, in exchange for the person of the King, the Emperor had demanded that François' sons, the eight year-old Dauphin, and his seven year-old brother the Duc d'Orleans, be sent as hostages, exchanging their freedom for their father's place in captivity. François had agreed to all the terms, and in March, on the River Bidassoa, his boat crossed paths with that of the one bringing his two eldest sons into the prison he had just left. François called out to them to take good care of each other, to eat well, and that he would see them soon. All those who witnessed the event said that the King was inconsolable as he watched his sons delivered to his own prison; tears flowed down his cheeks as he watched their boat sail away.

But when the French King returned to his court, it seemed that he was in a more joyous mood. Assured that his sons would be released soon, he sunk into relentless rounds of hunting, hawking and dancing as the French Court celebrated the return of their sovereign. And it was perhaps a month or so later that I received a message from my old friend Françoise, who had for many years been the official mistress of the French King. The note held little comfort.

Upon François' return to France, it seemed that his sister Marguerite and his mother, Louise of Savoy, had decided he should have a new mistress; one who was perhaps more reserved than the fiery Françoise. The lady they put forward to entice François from Françoise was named Anna de Pisseleu d'Heilly, daughter of the Seigneur d'Heilly of Picardy. François was captivated by Anna; she was bright, young, beautiful and charming… and he replaced Françoise with Anna. Françoise was in Normandy when she heard of her beloved's return, and went to the French Court, only to find that the King's heart had been taken from her. She abused Anna in public, calling her a "fuzzy chit." At this, François banished his former mistress and beloved from court and wrote to her, telling her that he loved her no longer. François also called Françoise a "rabid beast" for abusing his new love in such a fashion. Anna asked the King to take back all of the jewels that he had given Françoise, because they were engraved with messages of his undying love to her. Françoise wrote to me that she had returned the jewels, but had had the items made of gold melted down into ingots before she sent them back.

"Since our love is destroyed, then so shall be the words he spoke to me in deceit," Françoise wrote to me. In places on the letter, she had pressed so hard with her quill that I could see the rage of her heart imprinted on the page.

François sent the ingots back to Françoise, saying that he had wanted them for the inscriptions, not for the value of their worldly worth. "Give them all back to her…" he said. "She has shown more courage and generosity than I would have expected from a woman."

I was sad for Françoise, and her letter rang within my head in warning. I had thought that her officially recognised position as François' mistress was untouchable. And yet, as another woman had danced before his eyes, he had turned from Françoise, banishing her from court and from his heart. For me, as Henry was hotly pursuing me, it seemed like a timely warning on the frailty of the promises of men. If Françoise, with all her allure, all her power and spirit, could fall from the favour of the King of France, then why should the same not be true for me if I allowed Henry of England to become my lover in truth? Would he not, one day, lose the love he had for me and cast me off for another? If I became his mistress, as I knew he wanted, would he not one day simply abandon me for another... as he had done with Mary? As the French King had done with Françoise? I wanted to believe Henry's love was true, but how could I know? Françoise had believed that François loved her... and I had believed this also. I had no way of knowing if Henry's love was true and lasting, or if it would dissolve with time. There was no security in the position of a mistress, I had known this before, and I knew it all the better now. Poor Françoise! I knew that her temper and fire had been the reason for her banishment, but what woman of any spirit would do otherwise, when they saw their love stolen by another? And yet, I still could not reconcile my feelings for Henry. It was a situation without an answer, as far as I could see; for I feared to be used and cast off, and yet he would not leave me alone... And I did not want him to. And so, our games went on; me refusing any post other than that of the courtly mistress of his heart, and Henry pleading with me to give him everything.

Not long after writing her letter to me, Françoise' husband Jean all-but imprisoned her in their home at Chateaubriant. Since she was not welcome at court, Françoise had nowhere to go and no longer had a powerful lover and friend to protect her from her husband. There were dark rumours that Jean de Laval was a brutal man, and exacted a heavy price from his wife for her years as the lover of the King of France. I wrote to her often, but I do not know if she ever received my letters. I worried for her, I feared for her, but I could do nothing. She was the property of her husband now that François had abandoned her. There was nothing anyone could do to intervene. I never heard from her again.

In March, we received news at court that the Emperor Charles had married an Infanta of Portugal, Isabella. The eldest daughter of Manuel I of Portugal and Maria of Aragon, Isabella had been named after her maternal grandmother, Isabella I of Castile, Katherine's own mother. Charles and Isabella were first cousins, but received dispensation for the match from the Pope. It was an arranged marriage, but apparently turned out to be a love-match also. She brought a huge dowry to the Spanish King and was noted for her beauty but also her intelligence. Charles was immediately taken with his new bride, and it was said that even when they were surrounded by others, they had eyes and ears for no one but each other.

However charmed Charles was with his marriage, Henry of England was not. The King was furious that Charles had gone against the terms of their supposedly secret treaty; the Emperor had been promised to his daughter Mary! The insult was vast, but it seemed the Emperor had not wished to wait for the young princess to grow into a woman; and the dowry, and person, of Isabella was a great deal more tempting to him than our English Princess. Adding further insult to the pride of the King of England, Isabella fell pregnant almost immediately, and later the next year, bore a healthy, handsome son for her Emperor. They named him Phillip.

Henry cursed Charles of Spain, saying that he had refused to honour his promises in many ways, and he would not deal with Spain again. Katherine kept quiet on the matter, but all of her servants could see her disappointment. She had thought of her nephew almost as her own son, and had longed to see him joined with her daughter. To have her beloved Mary cast aside for the Portuguese Princess was almost unbearable for her, and to lose the Emperor as a surrogate son, was perhaps just as painful. Katherine's slight but ever-present frown deepened that year, and she looked older and more harried than ever. She ceased to come to many of the court entertainments, and it was rumoured that a great rift had opened between the King and her, as a result of his annoyance at the Emperor, and all things Spanish.

That year a young page came to the court. At just fifteen, he was almost an infant to me then, but he resolutely made his way into our circle. His name was Francis Weston, and Bridget in particular found him sweet company.

"He is such a child," she giggled to me, "he reminds me of my own boy Henry... but one day I am sure Francis will be a handsome gallant. Look how he tries to ape Tom and your brother so, and he admires you greatly, Anne, you should hear how he talks of you... as though you are Diana of the forests!"

I smiled. It was pleasing to have more admirers, even if this one was little more than a child in truth.

That spring, a servant came to my chambers with another gift from Henry. This time there was no written message. The servant handed me the bundle, wrapped in beautiful yellow silks. "The King sends you these and requests that you keep them, without prejudice and without fear," he said. "He asks that you keep them, as nothing is desired in return for them."

I nodded. "Tell His Majesty, if that is indeed the case, then I will accept them gladly." I gestured for the man to go.

Inside my rooms, I opened the parcel to find four beautiful gold brooches of the most delicate workmanship. The gold winked at me in the sunlight of my chamber. There were four separate designs engraved on them; Henry's message, it seemed, was upon the brooches themselves. One of the brooches was intricately carved with an image of Venus and Cupid embracing; one depicted a lady with a heart in her hands; one showed a man laying in a woman's lap, and the last was of a lady holding a crown. The symbolism was not hard to read. I was the mistress of his heart and the power rested with me.

I looked at the gifts; they had clearly been fashioned for me alone, and with such amazing delicacy and talent. I could not but be impressed and excited. My resolve to refuse any advance that Henry made towards me had not weakened, but

I could not but feel exhilaration at the prospect of having such a man, and such a king, chasing me in this way. I felt the strong attraction of power, of *my* power over the King, and it thrilled me. That sense became a part of my love for him, in those early days. It is a heady thing, to have a king declare love for you; to send you gifts and ask for nothing in return... yes, it pleased me, but it worried me too... for how long was this power to be mine? Could I control Henry? Could I control the ardour of his passion for me, keep him at bay, and retain my honour? I felt a little dizzy with all that had gone on in the last few months.

I picked up the brooch that was engraved with a lady holding a crown, and fastened it to my dress. I took it off again... Then put it on again. I took it off again, and put it on the bed, staring at it. I took it up and pinned it to my breast. I felt like a child. What was I doing?

What if he were to offer me a position of an official mistress? I thought. Perhaps secure me a fine husband first, and then offer me the same place that Françoise had once occupied in France? But no, I thought next, my head swimming. Henry of England is not François of France. Henry of England does not have acknowledged mistresses, only covert ones that hide under the covers when the Queen arrives. *And even if he were to offer you that, Anne Boleyn,* I said sternly to myself, *you would take it after all your resolutions on the high price of your honour? You know there would come a day when his eyes would stray elsewhere and you would be cast off! You could be imprisoned in a castle, like Françoise! You would give in, because he sends you pretty trinkets? You would give up everything so easily?*

So distracted was I that I left my chambers with the brooch still attached. I walked straight into my brother George, who did not miss the shining bauble pinned to my dress.

"What's this?" he asked and then his eyes widened as he saw the imagery of the crown in the woman's hands. I snatched it back away from him and blushed.

"Tis' nothing," I blustered, "a mere trifle that an admirer sent."

George raised his eyebrows at me. "A trifle?" he asked, smiling. "It is interesting to me what you consider to be a trifle, sister. You must have become fabulously wealthy through some private enterprise to consider such a thing a trifle. Come…" he looked seriously at me as he drew me to a window seat. "Tell me."

I sighed. "There has been for some time, discussion as to who it is that has replaced our sister in the affections of the King," I said. "I believe that I know who it is."

"Yes?" said George.

I pointed at myself and George whistled. "I had suspected," he admitted. "Does father know?"

"Not as yet, and I beg you, George, to say nothing to him."

"Are you his mistress then?" he asked, his eyes narrowing at me. I shook my head.

"No?" George said with incredulity.

I shook my head again. "He asked me… and I refused."

George laughed, but his expression quickly changed from grin to grimace. "You refused the King?"

"Yes."

"You refused the King?"

"*Yes!*" I cried with some exasperation. "I said to him that I could not become his wife as he had one already… and that I should not ever play the part of mistress to him, or to any man."

George whistled backwards, drawing in air through his mouth and letting out an off-key note at the same time. He stared at me and blew out a lungful of air. His face was pale. "What said the King to that?"

"Well… I think he was surprised," I said and then laughed. George laughed with me, his face a peculiar mixture of panic and admiration. I was nervous to tell George to own the truth. I worried that his ambition, much like our father's, might over-run his loyalty to me as a sister. But I was also glad to tell someone… to tell someone finally! I hoped that I could prevail upon him, for the love he had for me, to protect my secret.

"Sister, you should have been born a man for all the courage in you!" he exclaimed.

"Had I been born a man, I should not be in this trouble now," I countered dryly.

George became serious again. "What do you mean to do?"

"I know not," I sighed. "But I will not succumb to him. Think you that I wish to take the place that Mary has just left warm in his bed? No, soon enough this will pass and he will find another to dally with. It is nothing in truth, I am sure."

I was *not* sure. Not sure at all. Not sure of anything. I wanted to believe that Henry loved me, but I did not know if it was love in truth, or if he merely wanted to convince me of such so that he could bed me. It was difficult, and my feelings ran up and down and hot and cold… When I was with Henry, I believed he loved me in truth. When we were apart, I doubted.

I tried to dismiss Henry's interest in me as nothing to my brother; in truth, I felt awkward discussing it with my brother. Even though I trusted George, there was still much of our father in him. I did not want this to become a tool they could use to further their end... *I* did not want to become a tool... I remembered when Mary and I had talked about my engagement to Henry Percy, and father's order to me to pursue him as a husband... '*Whatever it takes*,' father had said. He had said those words to Mary, too, when Henry first noted her. I did not want to hear those words spoken to me now. I did not want to be ordered to give up what I had long held dear.

There was conviction in my voice, but George looked unsure. "How long has it been?"

I breathed in. I could not lie, but I also could not quite meet George's gaze as I told him what I had been keeping from him, from everyone, for so long. "Since first he sent me jewels, I think it is a little less than a year."

"Since *first* he sent you jewels?" George gaped at me. "What happened to those jewels?"

"I sent them back," I admitted.

George's eyes bulged.

"Do not tell me that I should have taken them when he was still bedding our sister!" I cried, my voice and body rising. George hushed me and pulled me back to the seat.

"It is just... no one has ever done such as you," he whispered. "Most women come gladly when the King beckons them. And to own the truth, he is hardly prolific in his affairs. He tends to favour women who are like gentle does... like our sister. To return jewels and refuse his attentions is... unprecedented." George looked wonderingly at me. "But then," he said, "I have never heard of the King retaining interest in *anyone* without gratification for so long. A year since first he expressed interest?" I nodded. "That *is* interesting."

"George, promise me, for the love you bear me that you will speak none of this to our father," I pleaded, my words rushing over themselves. How I wanted to trust George! He was my brother and my friend, but would he keep my confidences in the face of our father? "I believe he will crucify me."

George laughed, but agreed to remain silent. "As long as you do not keep secrets from me," he said, "for I want to know all about this affair with the King As long as you promise that, I shall remain your secret keeper."

I agreed. It was a relief to be able to talk to someone of it, after all.

Chapter Thirty-Three

Greenwich Palace
1526

It was at Shrovetide when the first indication came publicly that the King had a new love. Henry had arranged the usual tournament in celebration of Easter, and the court was housed at Greenwich. My brother and father were to ride in the joust amongst other members of the court. All courtiers were excited as we thronged together, standing in the early Easter chill, watching the arrival of the knights on their great horses.

The grand procession into the tourney grounds began; the marshals of the joust entered first, followed by the footmen, then the drummers pounding out the slow beat of the march, and the trumpeters ringing out the glorious progression as though it were a battlefield. Tudor colours of green and white sang in the sunshine, fluttering from the stalls and stands. Then came the lords and knights, following on two by two in their rich and glittering costumes. The metal of their armour glittered and their great horses snorted clouds of mist into the cold air. Then the pages appeared, then the jousters themselves, mounted on their war-like chargers. It seemed as though the Knights of the Round Table had risen from their earthly graves to seek glory once more. I heard the ladies around me gasp in admiration; for nothing and no man looked as well as one of these knights as they guided their horses through the cheering crowds.

Finally, and to the most applause, the King himself appeared in the procession. There was a great ringing on the trumpets and the drummers pounded the triumphant beat that echoed through the ground and through our bodies as we watched him arrive. The Queen stood in her royal stand to watch the arrival of her *Coyer Loyal*, her Sir Loyal Heart who had ridden for her favours so often and so gallantly. Her tired face was shining with love as she watched his arrival. I could see her chest rising and falling rapidly with all the excitement of a maiden waiting for her lover.

How disappointed she was to become.

A great murmuring started as the King arrived in the lists. On his jousting costume of gold and silver cloth, there was emblazoned on his chest a motto: *Declare je nos*, or, in English, 'Declare I dare not'. The picture above the motto was of a man's heart engulfed in flames made of red silk and gold cloth. It was evident that the King was proclaiming that he had a new mistress, a new love, and all the court were wondering… Who could it be?

There was great muttering in the stalls as people looked around as if thinking that they should be able to tell who the woman was merely by glancing. I kept my face a mask of astonishment like everyone else, but I could see Margaret and Bridget looking at me. I had told them nothing, but perhaps they had guessed at something. When I glanced at the Queen I saw that she had sat down again, her face impassive. Although few would have been able to tell that she was in any way disturbed by this public display of probable infidelity on her husband's part, I could see a small twitch of grief enter her face. Its bright happiness had fallen away, and she looked so tired and old in the dismal light of her disappointment. Gone was the shining face that had re-lived memories of her early life with Henry as he rode for her alone in the joust. Gone was the excitement, the pleasure of the day, and instead, there was the face of the consummate Queen she was. No one but those who knew her well would have been able to tell that she was grievously hurt. She was the master of her emotions and of her public face. I felt a twinge of guilt, for I knew well enough who her husband's new love was. Katherine clapped her hands with everyone else as Henry, his athletic and muscular body ever at home on the hoof, rode into the grounds for the commencement of the tournament.

My father was lately returned from a diplomatic mission to France. I could see his fox-like eyes surveying the crowds for some sign about the identity of this new mistress that he had somehow missed. He looked at me directly, and although he made no outward sign, I knew there would be a meeting of our family later, to discuss this news. I gathered myself for the storm that was to follow. I could perhaps conceal some things from him, but if I were asked directly, I should have to answer truthfully; he was my father and I owed him my obedience and duty. For now, as I had no husband and no other titles but those which were due from him, I was as much in my father's possession as any of the jewels he wore, or the clothes on his back. I feared what he might ask of me when he heard that I was the woman the King desired.

It was during that tournament that Francis Bryan, our cousin, suffered a near-fatal accident as his opponent's lance shattered on his helmet, earning the opponent high points in the joust and granting Bryan the loss of an eye. I saw and shuddered for Bryan's bloody face, as he gritted his teeth to stop from screaming in pain. As he was carried from the field, I remembered well the accident that had seen Henry thrown from his horse with a face-full of splinters and blood.

I shivered to remember that day, for Henry's nearly-averted disaster, and the disaster his country would have faced as a result. Although I had never seen civil war in these lands, I had often enough heard the stories of those who had lived through them. The King had nearly died that day without a male heir to take his throne. We could have been plunged back into battle with our neighbours, as had happened in the conflict between York and Lancaster; brother fighting brother, son fighting father, as different claims to the throne came from all those with a scrap of royal blood... But nothing had changed since that day. The King had promoted his bastard to the position of a prince, but there was still no legitimate male heir to the throne, and not likely to be one in the future either. What good could poor Katherine's dead womb offer to

England now? What good could a girl-child offer to the country but more years of desperation and death? As Henry rode in the joust, I could see that such thoughts were not only on my mind, but on the minds of many others around me. I could see the same fears that gnawed at my own heart on the faces of the White Sticks, the nobles who acted as the leaders of Henry's Council. If the King were to die in a tournament such as this, then our country would fall into war and ruin.

But Henry would not be stopped from riding in the tournaments, no matter the danger to his country. He saw it as a test of his military and kingly skills, and made sure that his exploits on the jousting field were relayed to all visiting ambassadors, so that all the courts of Europe would hear of them too. He was proud of his skills in the joust, and would not hear of remaining a mere spectator. His father, Henry VII, had not allowed him to compete in the lists as a young prince, fearing for the life of his son. Perhaps this was what spurred Henry on to ride so bold, and take part in so many competitions once he was free of his father's yoke. Henry was driven by his pride: he did not have a list as long as man's arm of battles he had fought; he did not have the greatest army in Europe; but he was a valiant knight still. If he could not be the greatest military king in Europe, he would still show his many talents to the world. If he could not get a son on his lawful wife, he would still outshine other men in other ways. Henry wanted his people to see him as the knight and the King he wanted to be… Jousting, tennis, archery, hunting, dancing; all these feats of the physical served to show his people just how glorious their King was. I played many a part at court; I believe Henry did the same.

In truth, when Henry started to ride, it was difficult to imagine that he was *not* invincible. When you saw his thighs grip the horse's flanks and heard the grinding cry of metal as his lance struck true and deep against his opponent's body… When you heard the cries of the men who fell before him and the heavy grunt of satisfaction that emanated from beneath his splendid armour as he surveyed the damage he had wrought on each opponent… Henry was truly skilled and he looked stunning on his horse.

With each pass, there came a gasp of fear and admiration from the gathered crowds that filled the stands. The glittering eyes of the court ladies, the admiring silence of the men, the excited chattering of the common people when they were allowed entrance to an entertainment… all these would have showed you, even if you knew nothing of the sport, that Henry Tudor was but another name for brilliance on the field.

I felt rushes of passion for him as I watched his horse thunder before me. I felt the pounding beat of my heart in my ears as I watched him clash and throw men from their mounts. I sat squirming for the desire I had for him. God's blood! I felt such desire course through me. As I sat so near to his lawful wife, I felt already as though I had betrayed her, and my own honour, for the rampant thoughts spinning in my head for the King of England.

There was such fire in him on that day; he looked like Saint George in person, a knight of truth and beauty and justice amongst us mere mortals. But somewhere still, warnings rang in my mind… my brother's voice, *Beware the dragon inside the knight.*

I was sent for after the day's entertainments. A discreet messenger bade me to come to an apartment where Henry waited for me, his face flushed by his successes in the day's tournament.

"Anne," he exclaimed warmly as I entered and curtseyed. There was no one else in that chamber but him. I felt immediately nervous; it was as though I could hear Marguerite speaking to me… *"If you feel something is dangerous, then it is. Trust your instincts."*

"What thought you of the entertainments?" he asked, his eyes searching for my approval of his endeavours.

"Your Majesty rode well and struck truly," I said, diplomatically. His face fell.

"What thought you of my costume?" he asked, walking to me and taking my hand.

I moved backwards, a little away from him. My heart started beating hard with fear. I did not like the enclosed nature of this meeting. I felt afraid of the look on his face. He was flushed with excitement and his eyes looked somewhat wild around the edges. I had seen a look like that before and my heart froze suddenly in my chest. I loved Henry, I loved him truly, but I did not know if I could trust him. Both these conflicting ideas were true within me at the same time. I wanted to believe in his love for me, but I had experienced the animal nature of men before, and I feared it.

"Your Majesty was most splendid, both in costume and in feats of arms," I said, removing my hand from his and moving towards a window. I know not what I thought that would avail me... Was I intending to jump if his advances became too amorous?

"Come, Anne," he said, advancing on me, his face flushed. "I shall show you how it is between us; you *are* my mistress."

He grasped at me with strong arms and forced a kiss on my lips. As I tried to move away he pulled me closer to him and pushed his mouth down harder on mine. This was not like our encounter in the gardens. He wanted more of me now. Suddenly all before me was gone. I was in France once more with the foul mouth of the lecherous beast, Charles of Navarre, upon me. I felt the cold night air on my hot cheeks. I heard the distant noise of people who were too far away to save me, and I felt the panic and fear of that night surge through me like wildfire. Vomit shot into my throat and my heart seemed as though it should explode from inside my chest. I stiffened in the King of England's arms as though I were frozen, as he kissed me. Then, the heat of panic threw me into action. I cried out in fear, my voice muffled and strange as I tried to scream whilst his mouth was on mine. I shook myself wildly like a hare caught in a trap, my hands flailing at his face, my body shaking in terror and confusion. I shook my head as hard as I could, trying to throw him off with all the strength I had.

He dropped me as though I were made of fire and looked upon me with the utmost astonishment. I leapt away from him the moment his hands let up their hurtful pressure on my flesh. I backed away from him, looking about me for an escape. He was standing between me and the door. I held my hands before me, shaking slightly, as though they alone could hold him off me.

Henry was staring at me, his face aghast. I am sure that he was expecting nothing of the sort of reaction I had shown to his kisses. I am sure that no woman had ever before reacted like that to his kisses. *I* had certainly not reacted thus the last time he had held me in his arms. But for me, this was an entirely different situation. He had called me here, alone, to meet with him. I felt trapped. I felt afraid.

I backed away from him towards the window, with my hands still up. My face was bloodless, my skin was pale and I was shaking. He looked amazed, confused, and somewhat helpless as he stood before me. His arms dropped, and hung by his sides, his face was dumbfounded and the excitement he had worn before had vanished. He looked entirely miserable and stunned.

There he stood, this great King, brought so low by a mere woman. He stood staring at me from the centre of the room. For a moment, neither of us moved. And then, as though all memory of my life came washing back to the shores of my mind, I remembered suddenly that he was my king and had the power to destroy my family as well as myself. I fell to my knees before him, still shaking and terrified by the thought that once again I had come so close to the danger that I most feared. I knew my words must count and I looked up into his handsome blue eyes with tears in my own. I took hold of the end of his cloak. When my words came from my throat, they croaked with fear.

"Most gracious King," I said, feeling tears gather in my eyes. "Most noble knight, please, for the sake of my honour, and your own, do not seek to take from me by force that which I will not offer to you freely. You are my king, and I your subject, and I am in your power as much through bonds of duty as through my own weakness as a woman. But I beg of you, to consider the offices of a knight to a lady, and to refrain from taking any action which would so impeach your good name and character, especially in the eyes of this lady, who loves you."

Henry looked down on me and shook his head. His face was bloodless, ashen and grey. He looked entirely bemused and horrified by the suggestion that he might try to take me by force. "Anne," he said softly, "I love you. I would *never* take you by force... This I swear to you. I want you to become my mistress. I thought that if we were alone, I could show you the force of my love... but I want you to return my love. I want you to be mine. I promise you that I would not force you. I would never do such a thing to you. I love you."

He looked so hopeless, so destroyed by my dark suspicion of him. I felt my heart surge out to him, but I could not relent. To do so now would be to make all I had said before into a lie. I had to make him understand that I was in deadly earnest about my beliefs, and about my honour. I believed him now when he said he would not have taken me by force. He looked so entirely appalled by the idea that it would have been hard not to believe him. But still, I could not relent.

I swallowed. "I think, Your Majesty, that my most noble and worthy king, speaks such words in mirth to test me. Without intent of defiling your princely self, you think nothing of such wickedness, which would justly procure the wrath of God and of your good queen against us… I have already given my maidenhead into my husband's hands." I paused and looked up at him, holding the edge of his cloak in my hands. "I seek not to anger or to offend you, Great King, when I say that your wife I cannot be, and your mistress I shall never be. There is no office left for me to take in your life. Please hear the pleas of an honest maiden. Seek not to remove from me that which is the greatest prize I shall offer to my husband, and which is my greatest honour."

I dropped my head and my hands from his cloak and remained at his feet with my eyes downcast, trembling. There was silence in the chamber. I saw his feet walk away from my body. I shuddered in relief.

"This is then, your final answer?" he asked, his voice gruff from the other side of the room."

"It is, Your Majesty,"

"You can go, Mistress Boleyn,"

I rose and hurried to the door; my hands trembled on the lock. I was no confident temptress of the dance now. I was a scared girl ready to burst into tears. I had accepted him as my courtly admirer. I had been honest with him in all ways about my feelings. But he wanted more than I was willing to give. If the love that I held for him, the love that was between us, ended here and now because of my refusal, then that was how it would have to be… but the thought made me sadder than I can tell. At the same time as I thought these things though, I shuddered to think how close I had possibly come to rape once again. Would he have forced me? I wanted to think that he was, in his own estimation, too much of a knight to actually go through with such an act, but I had not been certain until now. I had appealed to his conscience, and his offices as a king and a knight and this had reached him.

But it was more than that, I thought… there was true horror on his face when he had seen my fear. Unlike the lecherous beast in France, my fear had not been pleasurable to Henry. Charles of Navarre had enjoyed my fear, enjoyed the power he had over me. Henry was made of a different mettle; he wanted me to want him, to love him, and he knew now that he could never achieve that by forcing me into something I did not want. The King of England was not like the man I had fought in France, I knew that. Although the encounter had scared me, although I was shaking, there was still a part of my heart which cried out to Henry's. I knew that he was different to many other men.

"Anne?" he said as I reached the door. His tone was gentle, sad… and I turned feeling as though my own heart might break for the sadness I felt emanating from his.

"I *am* a true knight." He looked up at me; his face was crestfallen and puckered as though he might cry at any minute. He looked like a small boy and I felt my heart break to see him brought so low. In that moment, I knew that I loved him as I had loved no other in my life.

"You are the best of all knights." I meant it truly, for he could have disgraced me in that chamber and never been held accountable for it. Who would have stood for my honour? My father? I doubted it greatly. "And the best of men," I added.

His face lightened with that, and then fell to confusion again. "If I were to promise that there would be no others but you," he said desperately, "would you say yes, then?"

I opened the door and spoke quietly. "There will always be others," I said. "You are married. *There* is another. And you are a king… Henry; there will always be other women ready and willing to give you all you want because of your title. But I am not made of such stock. I have made a promise unto myself, to God and to my husband; there shall be no one's touch upon me but his. That is my promise. There is no offer that I can accept from you however much I may wish to. For you are not only dear to my heart because you are my king; you are dear to my heart because of the man that you are."

I turned and fled, leaving the King of England looking like a little boy who has been told he can have no more sweet custard that night.

That afternoon, I was called to my father's chambers.

Chapter Thirty-Four

Greenwich Palace
1526

My father was standing at his fireside when I came in on the heels of his servant. "Good," he said, barely looking up at me. "Now that we are all here, there are matters to discuss."

My mother was sat near the fire with George, who smiled at me as I came in. Mary and Will were not at court, for the King had sent Carey on some task, and Mary was still in the country with her babe Henry and her daughter Catherine. I breathed a little sigh of relief thinking that should I have to divulge the identity of Henry's newest love, I would not have to do it before my sister.

"The King has a new object of affection," said our father, rubbing at his head a little and looking at George and me. "Who is it?"

George looked uncomfortable. He had sworn not to reveal my secret, and yet a direct question from our father was as good as a royal command. Would he lie for me? I knew not, for the same worry was in my own heart.

"The lady's identity is a mystery," George lied smoothly, looking up at our father. "The King's own motto at the tournament showed this... *Declare, I dare not*? Even the King cannot reveal her."

"You must have some idea, George," our father leaned against the fireplace, staring at his son. "You spend so much time with the King... Is there not a lady of whom he talks? Spends time with more so than others?" Our father looked at me and narrowed his eyes. "You, too, Anne," he continued.

"You spend time in the King's circle… I did wonder at times whether…" he trailed off and looked at me piercingly with those dark eyes.

I breathed in deeply, bracing myself for what was to come. "The King is enamoured… of me," I said. All the faces in the room turned to stare at me with wide eyes.

"How long have you been his mistress?" asked my father, his eyebrow twitched a little, showing perhaps the slight surprise which lay beneath the surface of his ever-controlled expression. He did not look displeased, exactly, but I was more than aware that my father did not like surprises.

"I am *not* his mistress," I said. "At least, not in the physical sense. He has asked to be my courtly knight, my admirer in the games of courtly love… It has gone no further than that."

"But he wishes to be your lover?" asked my mother, her face a little pale.

I nodded. "He has asked me to give myself to him." I blushed a little. Revealing such to my own parents was embarrassing.

"But you have not," said our father. He did not sound either angry or amazed at the news; his mind was pondering over what to do with this knowledge, how he might best use it to his advantage.

I coughed uncomfortably, for I knew that what I was about to say could land me in the net of trouble. "He asked me… and I refused him," I said.

"You refused the King of England." It was a statement, not a question and it came in that dangerously calm tone of voice that I knew so well. I felt my heart beat faster; I, who knew my father so well, could sense the ominous clouds gathering in his temper. But I would not be subdued in this matter, not as

Mary had been, not as I had almost been so long ago in France... I would not be forced.

"As I would refuse any man who asked me to become his whore," I ruffled my shoulders backwards, gathering my courage to me. "I am not my sister, father. I hold no ill thoughts towards her for becoming the King's mistress, but I am not made of the same mettle as she. I wish to one day become a wife, an honest wife, not to be a play-thing for the changing whims of man... even if he be a king."

"Don't be such a child, Anne," spat our father, glaring at me. "The office of the King's mistress is one that can open many doors at court. Your scruples, such as they are, are nothing to the advancement of our family's interests. We, all of us, have to do things at times that are difficult for us to do... But if they advance our family..."

"So I should take up the space in the King's bed so recently vacated by my own sister?"

My father did not answer, and I was surprised to see a faint blush creep over his cheekbones. My mother was still staring steadily at me. "Do you *want* to be the King's mistress, Anna?" she asked.

I shook my head and then shrugged. "I... admire the King a great deal," I said, a blush creeping slowly across my neck and to my breast. "But I cannot be what he wishes of me. I refused him, but he said that he would not give up until he had won my heart in truth. That was when he offered to be my knight."

"At Hever?" she asked, and I nodded. My mother nodded softly. In the manner that mothers often have, to know the hearts of their children without having to ask, she seemed to have known that something was going on. My father tapped his finger against the stone fireplace.

"You refused him... but he said he would not give up?" he asked, and I nodded again. An expression of hopeful scheming waxed darkly over my father's face. "That is good... It shows that he is perhaps in earnest about caring for you, daughter. If he merely wanted a conquest, then he would have given up when you refused...." He glared at me. "You should have come to us with this news when it occurred," he growled, "but as it is, it seems I have less to worry on than I had thought. When I saw the new motto, I feared that another family had a daughter in the King's bed. Now I find that the King turns once more to our family, and has my daughter in his heart..." He nodded at me. "You will continue to hold the King's attention," he ordered.

"I will not become his mistress," I insisted, staring at my father with glittering eyes as though daring him to order me to.

"It matters not to me if you hold his attention by being in his bed, or being without it," said my father gruffly. "Even though you refused him, he has continued to court you. And sometimes, that which is unobtainable is more... *desirable*... than that which we can have easily."

"Thomas," reprimanded my mother, her voice strained and her face looking vaguely ill. "I would that you would cease to talk of our daughter in such a fashion before me."

My father ignored her, and nodded to me. "You have your task, Anne. Retain Henry's interest, in whatever way you see fit. If Mary has lost the love of the King, then it is fitting that her younger sister should rise to take it. That way we have not lost anything, and we still have a place within the King's most intimate circle."

I nodded, feeling a little ill myself. This strange man who was my father... Did he consider anything that was not power and advancement? These things had been drummed into us from an early age, and yet for me, there were scruples, there was honour… And what might my sister say to all of this? Did he care for none of these things? It would seem not.

As though he had read my mind, my father shook his head at me. "You think me grasping, unfeeling," he snarled softly, "but in truth, we must use all the advantages that God has given us to make a mark on this world. When I am gone, when your mother is gone, we want our children to have a step up in the world of nobility which we could not have had ourselves. Sometimes this means that we must do things that others would never consider. Sometimes this means that we have to reconcile our consciences with the ways of the world. You think me cruel to tell you to retain the interest of the man who only recently courted your sister's love… But I do not ask you to go against your own conscience. Mary was *willing* to bed the King, and so I asked her to. You are not, so I ask you to keep his interest in your own manner. Is it such an onerous task… to spend time with a cultured and powerful man who desires you?"

I shook my head. A small, unsure note entered my voice. "He has… been insistent at times," I stammered.

"Has he tried to force you?" asked my mother, looking shocked.

"I have thought that he might…"

"Then we shall make sure you are protected," said George boldly. "I will be with you whenever possible. We will ensure that you are not alone, or isolated with the King."

I nodded, feeling a deep wave of love for my brother break over my heart. I felt regret too, for above all things, I did want to be with Henry. "I do not think he would harm me," I said softly, "but I would feel heartened to know you were watching for me, brother."

My father nodded. "That is well then," he said, turning to stare at the fire thoughtfully. "You may go, but you know your tasks."

As I turned to leave, our father called out once more. "Anne?" he asked. I turned back to him; he was looking at the fire, not at me. "I told you once before that you would never keep anything from me again. That you have once more done so is not pleasing to me. Do not seek to keep anything of this affair with the King from me. I can only help you if you are honest with me."

"By loyalty and love, father, I am honour-bound to speak the truth to you when you ask it of me," I said stiffly, feeling a stab of bitterness in my heart. I was bound to obey my father, but I was starting to feel as though I was nothing but a tool to him, a pawn. I resented it. I resented the way he talked of Mary, and me. I liked not that his ambition was dearer to him than his children, no matter how he protested that this was all done to advance us. "But my heart is my own, as is my body. I need no counsel from any other to decide what to do with them."

My father started, and turned towards me from the fireside. I took George's hand and we left abruptly, almost running through the halls of court to the other side of the palace.

"I thought I might die when you said that!" George gasped for breath, laughing and gazing at me, his eyes warm with affection and admiration. "You are my spirited sister in truth… Why, Anne, you are bolder than a buck!"

"Not so bold as to stay and face our father after claiming my heart and body as my own," I laughed, leaning against the wall and panting. "But at least he knows my will."

"And you will do as he asks? Attract the King and hold his attention?"

"I will… it is indeed not arduous to me… I… I *love* Henry, George, I will admit it to you even if I will not say it to father… and as long as I am not in danger from his passion…"

"I will ensure that you are not," George said stoutly. "You should have told me if Henry was growing insistent with you. I would have made sure that he could not press his attentions on you."

"It only just happened…" I said, putting a hand to my hot cheeks. "I suspect that one of his gallants told him that my resistance was only an act, and that he should press me with the force of his affections." I made a sour face. "Men often think that way of women; that they wish to be forced, that it is all some game with them. It may be so for others, but not for me. If anything such as that happens again, I shall remove myself from court. I will play our father's game, and try to hold Henry as a mistress without giving myself to him, but I will not be beset by force."

"You will not," assured George, "I will make sure of that."

I smiled at him and took his hand again, squeezing it. "You would protect me, brother?" I asked. "One day, I wonder if you will have to protect me from our own father, if I fail to capture the King."

"What of Mary? Will you tell her?"

I wrinkled up my nose. "That is not something I look forward to doing, even if I am commanded in this task by our father… I will wait a while. It may well be that Henry's affection for me is already failing in the light of my constant refusal. After all, how many men would pursue a woman and get nothing in return? It cannot last, George. I will try to do as father wishes, but I fear Henry will tire of me eventually and go on to a woman who gives him what he wants…"

George shrugged. "We shall see, sister-spirit," he said, taking my hand and leading me into the fresh air of the gardens. "We shall see."

Chapter Thirty-Five

Hampton Court
1526

But Henry did not give up. At court I was the one that he sought each and every day. When he visited to his wife's apartments, I was the one he would call to play cards with them; when he walked in the gardens I was the one commanded there with my brother to entertain him; when he went to the hunt there was rarely a time when all the ladies of the court were not invited and that I was not seen to be by his side. He invited me to bowling matches and tennis games. He was respectful and gentle towards me. When I walked into a room, his blue eyes would rest on no other; they shone for me alone. He gave me thoughtful presents; a beautiful new falcon; cloth to be made into gowns and strings of pearls, for he knew I loved them. We talked of philosophy and poetry. He sang songs with me and we made a fine coupling in the art of music. I even began to talk to him of my passion for reform, something that he was interested in, but I never went as far as to tell him of *all* the books I had read… Many of these were banned in England, and such a disclosure could have got me into a great deal of trouble, no matter what his affections were for me.

Margaret and Bridget came to me as though they were one person, and questioned me on the matter.

"The King admires me," I admitted.

"And how do you feel for him?" asked Bridget.

I shook my head. "I admire him… and more," I said, "but you two above all others know my resolve. I have allowed him to become my courtly knight, but I will not allow anything further."

Margaret whistled slightly in admiration. "You are a bold chit, Anne," she marvelled.

"You know my mind as well as anyone," I replied. "I wish to be a wife one day, not a mistress, even to a king."

They listened to me, but I did not reveal all to them. I could not. Some things in this affair were still secrets for my heart alone.

Henry had become my courtly admirer in truth, and everyone could see it. Although he seemed to accept thus far that I would not offer him the place of a lover, I was worried about how long I should be able to keep this up. I wanted to be with him, but I still did not wish to be his mistress, for I knew that he would tire of me as he had done of Mary and would leave. And there was nothing that I wanted more now than to have him stay with me for as long as I could. I told him of this, and he was charmed. But he said my fears were groundless. If I should let him into my bed then I should see how things truly were between us.

"And if you truly loved me, Your Majesty," I said, "then you would know that I cannot give up my virtue, even for the one I love."

And so it went on; I refused and he cajoled. I stepped back and he caught my arm. I shied away and he kept chasing. He professed love… and I said that I loved him too, but with no honourable estate to take in his life, I also said I could offer him no more than my heart.

I would not allow us to be alone together again, so George had become our almost constant companion. As long as I could hold Henry at bay, holding his own image of knighthood and chivalry before me like a shield, all would be well for now, but I did not see how any of this could end well. Either I must give in to him, or he should tire of me anyway and find a woman who would open not only her heart to him but her legs as well. I wanted to believe in his love for me, but I was still unsure. And the pressure was mounting on me to decide one way or the other.

I was running out of ideas. I did not want to lose him, but I did not want to lose all I held dear either. Perhaps, I said to myself, you should just try to enjoy the time that you do have with him. This time, this *now*… This may be all that you have with the one you truly love. If he loves you, then he will not leave you, and if he loves you not, then he will. Only time could test the truth; did Henry truly love me, or was this all just a game to him? A challenge? A hunt? I wanted to believe in his love… All fools do, when they fall in love.

I was in my shared quarters at Hampton Court one afternoon, when George came racing in to see me. There was a bang as the outside doors reverberated with his coming and through the oak doors my brother flung himself in great panic, his face flushed red. I stood in amazement at his sudden entry and held out my hands in question at his sudden appearance.

"The King!" George gasped at me.

"What of the King?" I asked, thinking for a moment that something dreadful must have happened to Henry, for George was in such a fluster.

"He sent me to fetch you," he panted. "He is angry with you and he wants to see you."

"Why?" I snapped. "What cause has he to be angry with me?"

George told his story quickly, in between gasps for breath. "The King and some of his men, Tom Wyatt amongst them, were playing bowls in the gardens. There came a pass when the King's bowl and Tom's had both fallen close to the marker with very little between them. There was a genial dispute about it and the King said to Tom, 'Wyatt, I tell thee it is mine.'

As he spoke so, he pointed with his little finger, on which he wears that ring you gave him." George gasped again, struggling to speak through his laboured breathing.

"Tom recognised the ring. How could he not, after all? It has our crest upon it. And the fool took out a gold pendant with a long red ribbon on it. I knew it was a jewel of yours, as did the King; I could tell by the face he made as he saw it. Tom straightened up, and bold as anything, answered, 'If it may like Your Majesty to give me leave to measure it; I hope it may yet still be mine.' We all saw the look in the King's eyes… He was furious! Wyatt used the ribbon to measure the distance of the bowls to the marker. Tom was defiant, standing there before the King, with your jewel in his hands, and twiddling the ribbon with his fingers.

"The King flushed and frowned; he replied 'it may be so, but then I am deceived!' And he stalked off, calling for me as he went. As he walked off with me running behind him, he shouted at me to go and get you and bring you to the privy gardens immediately." George gasped in air again.

The inference was clear; Henry was showing Tom, an admirer of mine, that I was his, and was won. And Tom was showing that I was perhaps *his* instead. What was I to these men? I felt suddenly like a coin wagered at cards. I could barely contain the anger I felt. "What a *fool* Tom is!" I snarled between my gritted teeth. "And how dare Henry believe such of me!"

George put his hand on my shoulder. "That is hardly the problem now, sister," he warned. "There is a very upset king waiting for you in the gardens who needs calming."

"There is a very upset lady here who needs calming!" I shouted at him. "What am I to these men but some trinket? To be used to rile each other with tales of imagined conquest. *Oh!*" I shouted, for fury was upon me. "They play not with bowls but with my honour and reputation, before the whole court no less! Take me to the King," I growled, turning on

George with my eyes ablaze, "and I shall smother his temper with this fire of mine!"

George stared at me aghast as I stormed past him and strode to Henry's apartments; courtiers dodged out of my way when they saw the look on my face. I arrived with my anger simmering, threatening to boil over. I asked a servant to announce me to his privy gardens. There were, as usual, a number of courtiers in the presence chamber who seemed most interested in what I was doing there. I cared not for any of their stares or their looks; there was but one upon whom I wished to vent my anger at this moment. Everyone was staring at me with astonishment, and some amusement. They had never seen a lady march so openly to the King's apartments before and demand to see His Majesty!

I cared not for any of them. I was fury itself.

A servant let me into the privy gardens. I could see Henry at the other end, pacing amongst the beautiful knots and fountains. I walked through the first section where unicorns and lions were mounted on white and green striped poles. I strode with measured steps. A voice in my head warned of caution, but that voice could not stand up to the wall of anger that blocked my head. My footfall behind him caused Henry to turn; his face was black with anger and his blue eyes were full of hurt and ice. His eyes narrowed as I swept to the floor in a curtsey.

"My brother told me that you wished to see me, Your Majesty," I said coolly from my position on the floor.

"Rise," he ordered. He was magnificent in his anger, as I was. He was all majesty; there was little of the lass and his lover between us now.

"Wyatt is your lover," he accused, his voice harsh. There was jealousy and hurt in his words. Beyond the anger I could see the small boy inside him begging me to make it not true. But I was not going to let him off that easily.

"*Is* he, Your Majesty?" I asked, equally coldly, and with a measured voice that was betrayed by the wildness and anger of my black eyes. If I had been in any way in control of myself, I would have thought of the possible repercussions of talking to my king in such a manner; but here and now, I cared not. I cared nothing for his titles, nor the harm he could do my family. I was furious, at *him*. To me now, he was not even a king… he was Henry and I was Anne. He was the man who had professed to love me, and yet he had stained my reputation before his gallants, and played for possession of me. My temper was wild within me. I was ready to reach out my hands and lash out at the face of my king.

I drew myself up, my anger bubbling at the edges of my words. "Wyatt is my lover, Your Majesty? You would have thought I should have noticed something like that occurring." I paused and laughed a mirthless laugh that sounded somewhat unhinged and eerie. "Perhaps Master Wyatt is not as accomplished a lover as I have heard tell, for if I noticed him not in the office of my lover, then there must be something desperately wanting in him."

Although it was an entirely outrageous thing to do, I turned and walked down a passageway as though the conversation was over. Suddenly I felt Henry's heavy hand on my arm. He whirled me around so fast that I almost lost my footing and fell, but his grip was like steel and his face was suddenly next to mine. He was almost crimson with anger.

"*Do not walk away from me!*" he uttered through clenched teeth. "I am your King! And I would have the answer to my question, lady."

I shook him off; my own anger matched his. "Let *go* of me!" I screamed into his face and flung his arm from me. He was strong but unprepared for my reaction and I managed to wrestle free from his grasp. I stood a little away from him. "I heard no question, *Your Majesty,*" I said, hissing at him in wrath. "I heard only an *accusation* and one that I should not have to answer from you. *You*! You, who claim to know my heart so well, are so easily caught up in some court gossip, some wild fancy that takes you to suppose that I am any man's for the taking! You claim to be my true love and yet you believe such of me?"

Henry was staring at me in the utmost amazement. I doubt that anyone had ever spoken to him in the manner I did now. That anyone would *dare* to speak to him in such a fashion was inconceivable, and yet here I was, shrieking at my King. There was, too, something else on his face mingled with his fury. There was passion, there was desire. He was attracted to me even as he was furious at me. To own the truth, I had to admit that Henry looked rather handsome when fired by anger to my eyes as well… but I was not going to let him know that now.

"No friend and no *true* love of mine would believe such slander!" I went on, flinging my hands in his face and glaring at him. "I am betrayed by the one who claimed to love me! You leap to believe slander about me, you leap to believe I am a liar, *and* a whore! You dare to be angry at me? *I* am the one betrayed by *you* in this matter. The right to anger here is mine alone!"

Henry looked at me; his gaze held deep desire for me and I could see his anger was cooling. "Then you deny it?" he asked, his voice still cold and harsh, but there was softness creeping into his eyes. He wanted desperately to believe me.

"There is *nothing* to deny!" I cried loudly. I could see the courtiers in the upper hallways looking out of windows at the sound of us shouting and I cared not. "There is nothing to deny, when a lie is told."

"Wyatt had a jewel of yours," Henry said. "There was your family crest on it. He made it appear as though… as though… perhaps, you were considering him as a lover."

I drew myself up coolly. "I am no man's whore," I said and was then caught off-guard as tears of fury and hurt came to my eyes. "I have *been* no man's lover and I shall *be* no man's lover. Do you think that I should deny you with one arm and with the other beckon Thomas Wyatt into my bed? Do you think so little of me? If so, then *I* am the one who has been deceived in *you*, for you are no true knight to believe such wickedness of me, with no other reason than the prattling of some lowly lord who once took a jewel of mine and claimed it for his own. On such evidence, then, I must be guilty of anything!"

I walked away from him and laughed without mirth. Tears in my eyes stood out even as I boiled with fury. I was angry. I was hurt. I was wounded. Wild laughter rose in me, as though my soul wanted to laugh at the foolishness of the situation, even as my heart was pained by his lack of trust or belief in me. I turned back to him. "Hold out that ring on *your* hand, Henry of England, and tell me whether I have given you aught more than that? Tell me, does that ring mean I am your jade just as a pendant is evidence I am Wyatt's? I am wronged by those I thought to be my friends, by Tom and by you. How dare you play for my honour in public, the two of you? It is my choice whom I should love, and here and now I can say that Anna Boleyn loves *no* man! For the man I thought I could love, the man I who thought would always protect me and love me, believes falsehoods of me, believes the worst of me…" I drew breath, shaking, "for but the show of a pendant…" I shook my head and drew myself up, pushing back my shoulders. "I ask Your Majesty's permission to remove myself to the lands of my family," I said coldly. "For I feel I am not wanted or desired at court."

Henry stepped towards me. "Anna…" he said softly, reaching for me, but I stepped back again and observed him with cold eyes. His face that had been waning in anger started to blacken again. He was not used to being treated in such a fashion. I think it caught him off-guard and although he was angry still, he was also bemused by my reactions to him. Perhaps he had expected supplication, submission… but if so, he had clearly picked the wrong lady. "I was angry," he said, looking rather angry now. "But if you say it is not so, then I shall believe you."

"I should have to say nothing," I barked. "I should have to say nothing, for if your love were indeed true for me, then you would never dream of believing such slander of me, nor of allowing it to be said in your hearing."

"Then it is not so?" he pressed.

"I have not been, nor shall I ever be, any man's whore," I said, "just as it seems I have never been, and shall never be, truly loved by those I admire." And, not waiting for an answer I walked out of those gardens, turning my back once more on the most powerful man in the country. As I walked, however, I heard his footfall racing up behind mine, and he grasped me before I reached the doors.

"Anne, I was a fool," he pleaded and pulled me to him. I did not resist this time but I was stiff in his arms. "Anne, say it is as it ever has been between us, and do not seek to leave court. Do not leave me. I am sorry."

My temper was cooling, and turning to ice within me. I was wounded that he would be so quick to believe such of me, and my honour had been tainted by the actions of Tom and himself. But I too, felt powerful in my anger. I knew that he would not punish me for this. I knew that he was about to submit to me. It was a giddy feeling, and it washed about with my anger and my hurt until I knew not what I felt.

"It is as it ever has been between us, Your Majesty," I said coldly. "I am your humble servant, of course."

He let go of me slowly, seeing the coolness in my eyes and my body towards him. "I will hear from you soon?" he begged. "We will go riding on the morrow, or take a turn at the archery butts, perhaps?" I shrugged and exited the gardens. I had to leave court for a while, this I knew. I was too angry to stay near him. As I walked away, the King of England pleaded like a child.

"What more must I do, Anne? What more *can* I do? *Anne!*"

I did not reply. I was furious; furious with Henry, with Tom, with all those men who had no doubt stood about and laughed at their competition for my favours. How many at court were now whispering into their sleeves about me? How many comparing my position to that of my sister? Oh, I was angry enough to have flown in the skies on that day, to have run from one end of England to the next, so great was the energy within me from my anger!

I went straight to Katherine. As my mistress, she was the one person, apart from the King from whom I could request a leave of absence from court. I was hardly likely to petition Henry in this matter again. I needed to be away from court. I could not continue to see him when I was in such a temper; I would say something that may lead to my father locking me away for the rest of my life.

I came to her presence chambers, and, as usual, there sat the Queen amongst her ladies, one reading aloud from a book of devotions. I bowed before her. Katherine's calm gaze rested on me as I was announced. There, before her, was the woman that her husband was pursuing most resolutely and increasingly publicly. Yet in her expression there was nothing to tell of hatred or disapproval towards me.

"You asked to see me, Mistress Boleyn," she said calmly.

"Your Majesty," I said, leaning to the floor in a bow. The ladies looked on me speculatively. Some, like Margaret and Bridget looked worried for me, noting my anger simmering beneath the surface; some, including the Lady Margaret Pole, looked on me with disapproval. Katherine was a mistress most beloved to her servants and there were none who could not see Henry chasing me. They did not like to see Katherine humiliated in such a manner. Perhaps they thought I should be more like my sister, to be the King's mistress and yet fade into the shadows with ease. And yet, I had given him nothing other than my heart. But still, they despised me for the attentions he paid to me.

"What is it that you wish to ask of me?" she asked, smoothing her glorious dark purple dress and feeding a scrap of meat to the rocking ape at her side. The beast snatched the morsel from her fingers and chewed on it with its few remaining teeth, staring at me with those hollow eyes and drooling.

"I wish to ask permission for a leave of absence from court, Your Majesty," I rose at her signal. "I wish to return to my father's house for a while."

Her calm face registered a little interest. "When do you plan to return?" she asked.

"I know not at the moment, Your Majesty," I said truthfully. "I feel... unwell at court, and I believe that the airs of the countryside would better suit my sprit at present."

Katherine raised her eyebrows briefly. "You will take your dog and maid with you," she commanded, "so that they will not be a financial burden to my husband." I inclined my head in assent. "I give you permission to leave court, Mistress Boleyn. And I hope that in time you will feel recovered from the... ill airs that presently assault you."

I curtseyed before her again. "You are most kind, Your Majesty."

"Time brings change to us all, Mistress Boleyn." Her voice was warm with approval. Perhaps she thought that I was leaving to deter her husband from chasing me. "And I hope that you shall find the peace that you deserve, in the actions you presently undertake."

I nodded, curtseyed and left her chamber. She had approved my removal from her husband's side, and perhaps, she approved of my actions as an honest maid in leaving as the King was pursuing me so vigorously. No doubt she thought that I was leaving to preserve my honour from him. She was right in some ways.

I left for Hever, looking for sanctuary. Henry knew nothing of my leaving until the next day when he looked for me in his wife's rooms and found nothing but a gap in the place where Anne Boleyn had recently served.

Soon after I left for Hever, Tom left for his family estates, and there he remained. That winter, he was visiting London, and on the banks of the Thames he fell into conversation with a diplomat he knew named John Russell. Tom asked Russell where he was going. "To Italy, for the King," was Russell's reply, whereupon Tom turned to him and said, "and *I*, if you please, I will ask leave and get money to go with you."

Russell was surprised, but nodded. "No man more welcome," he said warmly. Tom obtained coin from his father, and together he and Russell left for Italy a day later via Paris and Savoy. Russell was gong to Italy to meet with the Pope, in hopes of convincing him to remain in league with England, united with France, against the Emperor. Henry and Wolsey believed that Charles had grown too powerful, and clearly did not mean to keep his promises to make Henry King of France. They wanted François and the Pope to be England's allies against Charles. Pope Clement VII was under pressure from the Emperor's troops menacing his state from the north.

Russell carried 25,000 crowns to entice him to remain in the anti-imperial league of France and England.

I did not see Tom before he sailed and he did not request to see me. His role as suitor in the game of courtly love had become dangerous. I knew that he loved me, of course I did. But I could not be his wife or his mistress, just as I could not be the same to Henry. Whilst Tom was not willing to let me go, he *was* willing, it seemed, to play with my reputation, to publicly stake a claim to me. At that time, I could not think of Tom without anger; he was no friend to me, not any more. He had acted like a fool and he knew it. It was not just I who was angry at him however, for Henry was furious with his former friend. I believe Tom skipped out of the palace just before Henry could lose his temper with him entirely. Margaret wrote to me, telling me the story of Tom's exit from the isle of England. Although she was sorrowed to find her brother leaving, she assured me that she bore me no ill will for being, at least partly, the cause. I smiled and found comfort in her words. At least one of the Wyatts understood me.

Later I came to miss Tom, to miss his friendship and companionship, but it took me a long while to calm down.

Chapter Thirty-Six

Hever Castle
1527

There were no other family in residence at Hever and so I was alone, apart from my servants. I found the clean airs of Hever and the quiet of the country peaceful after my time at court by Henry's side. I had been in such a mass of confused thought and worry that just leaving to another place seemed to give me space to breathe, to think. There was a peace in riding out each day, hunting, or reading the books that my brother sent me that was unmatched by the glamour of the court. In sharp contrast to the time I had spent in exile at Hever after the affair with Percy, I did not feel trapped by life in the countryside now, but freed by it. The situation at court, with Henry, had been pressing on my spirits in a way I had hardly recognised until I was freed from it. The little games and the battles between us, the love that I felt for him, the fear that I might lose him… all these things had weighed upon me. To be released from such was a relief.

I had begun to feel more at peace than I had ever done, to find time to muse on my thoughts… And then the letters started to arrive.

One afternoon, I returned from hunting with a beautiful falcon that Henry had recently given to me, and I found a letter, and a messenger, waiting for me. The Royal Seal was upon the parchment and I recognised the writer's hand as I opened it.

Although, my mistress, it has not pleased you to remember the promise you made me when I was last with you- that is, to hear good news from you, and have an answer to my last letter; yet it seems to me that it belongs to a true servant (seeing that otherwise he can know nothing) to inquire the health of his mistress and to acquit myself of the duty of a true servant, I send you this letter, beseeching you to appraise me of your welfare, which I pray to God may continue as long as I desire mine own. And to cause you yet oftener to remember me.

I send you, by the bearer of this, a buck killed late last night by my own hand, hoping that when you eat of it you may think of the hunter; and thus, for want of room, I must end my letter, written by the hand of your servant, who very often wishes for you instead of your brother.

HR

I smiled as I read the letter, feeling my anger subside as I heard his pleading voice through the dark, bold strokes of the missive. In the few weeks I had been here, I had had time to think on Henry, and in the space afforded by the distance between Hever and London, I came to think on him with affection once more. Had it really ever left me? No. But in loving someone, in knowing that I loved him, it seemed anger towards him came more readily than before. Strange, is it not, that the one we love the most in this life, can also be the one who moves our heart and blood to stir with the most furious anger? I had resented the manner in which he and Tom had played for me, but perhaps I had been too harsh on Henry. He had only feared to lose me, after all; a fear most common to all who dare to love, even kings.

And he wished my brother George was me instead? I grinned at the thought… Did Henry want me to help him change vestments in the mornings then? Or help him wash? Perhaps that was just what he wanted of me; the kind of constant companionship that came between servant and master…

I sighed, suddenly feeling a little lonely. I missed Henry, I had to admit it. Although I was peaceful at Hever away from his relentless pursuit, I missed the sound of his voice and the eager way he looked for me in the crowds. I had forgiven him,

I think, for his unfounded accusations born of jealousy and fear, although I was not willing to allow him to insult me in such a way again, or to let him off lightly for the hurt he had caused me. It would not do to be too sweet to him in my reply, but at the same time, I did not want him to start looking elsewhere for another heart to grow fond of in my place.

The messenger stood waiting for my reply and I wrote a quick letter to Henry.

Sire,

I give great thanks to you, for thinking of me as I reside apart from court. I find that the goodly airs of my family's home have brought restful peace to my spirits, but I promise you that I intend to return to court, and to you, in time. Although I was most wounded by our late conversation in the gardens of Greenwich, I am assured by your words that you no longer believe ill of me, and will continue to be the knight of my affections. I swear to you that I am well and hale, and am finding the lands of my family most pleasant at this time.

I thank you for the gift of the buck; a fine beast who I will order to be prepared for the house this night so that I might taste his sweet flesh. I will think of the hunter as I dine, with love.

Your servant,

Anna Boleyn, Hever.

Once the silence was broken between us, more letters came; a veritable flood of them. Messengers seemed to be carving new depths to the roads between Hever and London; riding up and down to place letters from Henry in my hand almost daily. He was, it seemed, most happy that I had responded to his first letter, and could not stop writing to me in his excitement. Perhaps he had believed that I was so angry with him that I would not respond at all… Perhaps he thought he had lost me for good. George had always told me that the King despised writing, even though he was a prolific reader. Henry usually dictated to others, but now he wrote to me in his own hand, and not only that, but many of the letters he wrote to me were in French, the language in which I felt most at home. He sent me poetry of his own composition; gifts of food, such as the buck; and fine cloth, French hoods and jewels. Every gift came with a message that he expected nothing in return for such things, and yet almost every letter asked that I take him as my lover. There were protestations of love, affection, and of how greatly he missed me; they were intoxicating letters to receive. The most powerful man in England, one of the most powerful men in the world, was on his knees before me... And he was a man whom I loved truly. The peace that Hever had brought to me dissipated under the barrage of Henry's affection, unstopped and unquenched by the miles between us. He had not lost his love for me in the face of my anger, nor in my disappearance from court... He was more mine than at any time before.

Such thoughts are likely to turn a young woman's head. In truth, I knew not what to do. My family were unlikely to disapprove if I did give in to Henry and become his mistress, but would he simply tire of me in time, no matter what he said now? There was a part of me that wanted to give in, of course there was! What woman can hear a man she adores, a man she loves, talk and write so to her, and be unaffected? Not I... But still, I had held off so long from this... Was I willing to give up everything I believed in, had believed in so strongly, for the temptation of love?

Perhaps Henry read my indecision, for one of his letters said as much.

On turning over in my mind the contents of your last letters, I have put myself into great agony, not knowing how to interpret them, whether to my disadvantage, as you show in some places, or to my advantage, as I understand them in some others, beseeching you earnestly to let me know expressly your whole mind as to the love between us two. It is absolutely necessary for me to obtain this answer, having been for above a whole year stricken with the dart of love, and not yet sure whether I shall fail of finding a place in your heart and affection, which last point has prevented me for some time past in calling you my mistress; because, if you only love me with an ordinary love, that name is not suitable for you, because it denotes a singular love, which is far more common. But if you please to do the office of a true loyal mistress and friend, and to give up yourself heart and body to me, who will be, and have been, your most loyal servant (if your rigour does not forbid me) I promise you that not only the name shall be given you, but also that I will take you for my only mistress, casting off all others besides you out of my thoughts and affections, and serve you only. I beseech you to give an entire answer to this my rude letter, that I may know on what and how far I may depend. And if it does not please you to answer me in writing, appoint some place where I may have it by word of mouth, and I will go thither with all my heart. No more, for fear of tiring you.

Written by the hand of him who would willingly remain yours,

H.R.

Late that May I was formally requested to return to court to serve the Queen once again; she wrote, however, that it was her *husband's* ardent wish that I return and I wondered whether, in that letter, Katherine was offering me a warning. She perhaps believed that I was indeed as I said I was; a maid who valued her honour. But my heart was as ever divided, and more so than my mistress could possibly know.

If I chose to return, I should still have Henry chasing me; if I stayed away, his passion may cool. Being honest, I knew not which of the two I wanted. I did not want him to stop turning his affections on me but I did not wish to have to fend him off for the rest of my life. I was torn, but I missed him. I missed Henry and I missed the court. If I kept my head about me then

I should be able to keep the role of his mistress of courtly love and yet retain my virginity… I just had to play carefully.

Chapter Thirty-Seven

Greenwich Palace
1527

I returned to court in May, and was riding into the great city of London when I heard the news. There was great tension in the air and there were everywhere shouts and conversation in heated and high voices; something of importance had happened. I sent my men to find out what.

The news that came back to my covered litter was almost unbelievable. The Emperor Charles V and his armies had sacked Rome; the Holy City was undone. Pope Clement VII had signed a treaty with France; and Charles, the Emperor, had taken the Holy City in retribution for this. But Charles' armies had raged wildly, out of his control. Mercenaries in the Emperor's pay had overturned the city, churches were on fire, their riches robbed; monks were struck down by the swords of the soldiers on the city streets and blood ran in rivulets, turning the canals and the river red. Men said that the brides of Christ were raped in their habits, across the holy altars of the City of God. I crossed myself with horror as my guard told me what had occurred. The pictures in my head of the atrocities were overwhelming. I felt the screams of those nuns reverberate through my body. I felt the fear and the pain of people watching their city burn. I mourned, hidden within my litter, as we approached the court in residence at Greenwich. I could not stop weeping for the fate of the Holy City. I was not alone; all of England, and indeed the rest of Christendom were in shock that day.

I believed there were problems within the Church, I had long believed so, but that belief did not stop me from feeling horror and disgust at the actions of the Emperor's troops. How could Charles have allowed such atrocities to take place? Why had he not stopped those mercenaries raping and pillaging through the City of God? He was the Holy Roman Emperor, supposedly the protector of the Pope and the Holy City!

We heard more news as time went on; that the Pope had fled to his citadel and was safe, that the Emperor had sought to control his troops, which still rioted in the Holy City, looting, burning and defiling. Katherine had all of us pray daily with her for the deliverance of Rome and the Pope. It was an event that shook us all. For war made upon man is one thing, but war made upon the servants of God is another.

There was more news, almost as distressing to me as the last. Before the sack of Rome, Tom and John Russell had made it to Italy, and met with the Pope. The Medici Pope took the money offered by Henry to remain in the anti-imperial league, but had offered no firm promises to the King. As they were travelling back, Russell's horse stumbled, throwing him from his saddle and breaking his leg. With such an injury, Russell could not go on and was forced to stay behind as Tom went on to continue negotiations on his behalf. Just outside Bologna, Tom was captured by mutinous imperial troops, much like those who came later to sack Rome. They ransomed him to the Duke of Ferrara for 3,000 ducats, a princely sum. It was usual in such circumstances for the liege lord of a captive to pay the ransom, but it was also usual for the captive to re-pay his lord once returned. Perhaps because Henry now believed that I had never been Tom's lover, he agreed to repay Ferrara and urged Tom home to England. Henry seemed to have forgotten his anger at Tom in the face of so much occurring in Europe, and was keen to have him report back to him, seeing as Russell could not.

I felt quite sick to hear that Tom had been taken a captive, and relieved to know that he had been freed. In many ways, this, rather than anything else allayed my anger towards him. I began to hope that I would see him soon, and let him know that I was no longer angry at him. I prayed for his safe return. Margaret was distraught to think of her brother in such danger, but I consoled her with soft words and gentle lies until the time we heard he was safe and on his way home. Poor Margaret, she loved her brother a great deal. I understood, for it was the same for me, with George.

As time went on, we heard that Henry had sworn to join with France to best the Emperor and remove him from the Holy City. I was proud to see Henry stand in front of his court and announce the union of France and England against the Spanish King's tyranny. Katherine, sitting quietly beside him, said nothing. After all, the sacker of Rome was her nephew, her own blood; a man she once told me she considered as much her own son as her nephew. Whilst we knew that she deplored his actions from the bottom of her soul, we also suspected that she remained more loyal to her old country than she let anyone know, especially Henry.

When I returned to court, I felt as though my position had changed subtly, especially within the chambers of the Queen. Although Katherine was as polite as ever, she was distant, and her ladies, at least those loyal to her, acted in the same way as their mistress. I am sure that most of them thought I was now Henry's mistress. I still had my friends, of course, those who did not think ill of me… and others at court began to seek out my company, thinking that as I carried favour with Henry, I would be able to speak for them. I was unsure where I stood, for on the one hand, I had Henry's love and devotion, I had his attention held upon me, and yet, I still held him at arm's length. I was his mistress and I was not his mistress. I had power; I had no power. I felt most precarious and at the same time, wildly excited.

My father called another family meeting to examine what Henry's favour could do for the Boleyns. This time, I was surprised to find my uncle of Norfolk standing amongst the rest of the family, with his little habitual moans and groans punctuating the conversation. My mother, Mary, George, and his wife Jane were also in the chamber.

"Are you the King's mistress?" our father asked me bluntly almost before I had entered the room.

I curtseyed. "Good afternoon to you also, father," I said, and went to kiss my mother who stood near the window. She smiled at me. Mother still looked pale. Each winter, her mysterious sickness returned and she seemed to grow frailer every year. There was fear in my heart for her.

"None of your sauce, Anna," our father said sternly. "I would know now, are the rumours that the King is much in love with you and that you have become his mistress true?"

I shrugged. "It may be that one of those rumours is true."

My uncle's face blackened and his cheeks fired with red blotches. "Impudent girl!" he cried and strode across the room. "Answer those better than you in age and wealth and sex! Have you no respect for your father?"

I stared into his angry face and then I laughed. My reaction surprised me as much as it did anyone. I seemed to laugh at entirely inappropriate moments, often when I was under pressure. But this time, perhaps I knew the reason. I knew suddenly, you see, that they could not touch me or hurt me. I knew that for once I was not just the lowly pawn in their games. I was the one moving the pieces on the board, not just one of the pieces to be moved.

I turned pointedly to my father who was looking extremely annoyed; a sight that would previously have lowered me to fear. But now I stood confident and strong before him. After all, I had faced the wrath of a king and survived... I did not fear my father's anger now, nor that of anyone. "I am not the King's mistress," I said. "But he wants me to be such more than anything else in this world." I looked at my father's speculative face and smiled. "You asked me to hold his interest, and I have, but without giving my body to him. The King writes messages of love to me, asks that I be present in every party, near him, and asks me daily to allow him into my bed. I have not allowed him any such favour and I do not intend to. I have told him this, repeatedly, and it has not cooled his passion for me in the slightest. He calls me his sweetheart and the mistress of his heart. He has told me he loves me and will forsake all others for my company. Does that answer your question, father?"

There was surprise in his face. He went to speak, and nothing came out. It was satisfying to see, for once, my father speechless. My mother turned to me and beamed. "You have kept true to your own heart, Anne," she said. "I am proud of you."

"The King asked that you become his mistress, his sole mistress… and you *refused* him?" asked my uncle with incredulity.

"I did." I stuck my chin into the air in defiance of what they should say next.

My uncle had stepped back and was viewing me as though I were a cow at market, and he was working out how much milk I should yield. "The King was not deterred by your refusal?" he mused. "Interesting…"

"Men always want what they cannot have," Mary said quietly from her space in the corner. I searched her face, but it held no rancour. Perhaps enough time had passed since she left the office of the King's mistress for her to accept my situation without resentment. I wanted to talk to her on the matter, but now was not the time. "It makes it more worthwhile to gain that which is more difficult to hunt."

"And the King is a prolific and enthusiastic hunter," nodded our father, regaining his power of speech.

"Have you considered what you are to do next, niece?" Norfolk asked me, a growing note of respect in his voice.

I faltered. "I know not," I said and sunk down on a chair. "I do not wish to be his mistress," I said quietly. I wanted to have Henry's love more than anything else, but never as his mistress. I was afraid that I would be ordered to take such a position, and that perhaps Norfolk had been brought in to harass me into this choice. But it seemed that there were other possibilities emerging in the mind of my wily uncle.

"Perhaps... you do not have to be his *mistress...*?" our uncle suggested quietly. His eyes narrowed and there was a far-off look on his face.

"What are you thinking, Your Grace?" our father asked sharply.

Norfolk smiled. "I do not believe that the thought has not passed through your mind, Thomas," he said. "It is not as though you are a dullard, or my father and I would never have allowed you to marry my sister," he nodded his head towards my mother who was suddenly looking paler than before. The thought was there, hovering in the air like the English morning mist, but no one had had the courage to voice it out loud, except my uncle.

"Some years past, Wolsey was asked to look into the King's marriage..." our uncle Norfolk continued, smiling darkly at me with his hawk-like grin, "... to check its validity. Many fear what will happen if the Princess Mary continues as the only heir to the throne, and our King is still young enough to sire a male heir, in a lawful marriage to a woman still young enough to breed. There are precedents; infertile queens have been relieved of their position and entered holy orders allowing a king to marry again and produce an heir. There have been questions on the validity of Henry and Katherine's marriage since even before it took place in light of the Queen's previous union with Henry's own brother. Multiple objections were raised, and dispensations were drafted out. But even when the dispensation from the Pope was granted, there were many who still questioned the legality of a man marrying his brother's widow. Henry and Katherine married in private, for that same reason. At the time, Henry was much enamoured of Katherine and wished to push the wedding through without further opportunity for any to raise opposition… but that was long ago. He loves her no more. Many times in the last few years, Henry himself has voiced scruples on the matter, to Wolsey and to me. The Holy Bible states that a man may not marry with his brother's widow, or else the marriage will be seen as sinful in the eyes of God… and will remain childless."

George nodded. "Leviticus," he murmured. "But there are conflicting passages… in Deuteronomy it is written that a man *should* marry with his brother's widow."

"Canon law instructs that Leviticus holds precedence over Deuteronomy," replied Norfolk, groaning a little and rubbing at his stomach thoughtfully.

"But the Queen is not childless," my mother said, staring at her brother.

Norfolk shrugged. "She may as well be, for all the good a girl can do this country." He shook his head. "For a noble man to have but daughters is poor fortune… for a king, it is a disaster. This country cannot be held together by a woman. To have only the Princess as heir to the throne will destroy this country. We all know that, and so does the King. Such things as these have come to trouble his conscience. Even more so of late, since Katherine has long passed the time when she might give him another child." Norfolk looked directly at me. "There was a rumour amongst the highest of the land, that Henry could put Katherine aside, and take a new wife to allow a fruitful marriage, one that could provide sons for England. Katherine would be persuaded to enter into a holy order. Many princesses of Europe were suggested. But what if an English noblewoman could perform the same task, and take Katherine's place on the throne beside our King?"

My mother gasped and went white. Mary was looking much amazed. But my father and brother were clearly intrigued. Everyone's voices dropped to whispers.

"What of the Queen?" asked Jane.

"What of her?" my uncle snapped coldly.

Jane looked at George, as though unsure of herself without his approval. He nodded to her to speak, but did not smile as he would have done perhaps to Mary or me. I wondered on the state of their marriage. It did not seem unhappy, exactly, but it was hardly merry either. They were still childless, something that concerned my mother greatly. "The Queen has great pride," Jane warned, "and she loves the King with all her heart..." Here, she glanced again at George. Although no blush or paleness on her cheek gave reason to think that she was speaking of her own emotions as well as the Queen's, I believed that she was. "Katherine will not leave the man she loves so dearly," she whispered, her voice hot with passion.

"The Queen is old, and there is no life left in her womb," our father said bluntly and calmly. "She cannot give England an heir. If Henry wants a legitimate son, he must look elsewhere for a legitimate wife."

"And what of the Princess?" asked Mary.

"A girl cannot rule this country," said our uncle Norfolk. "We would again be plunged into civil war, and all we have built would be ruined. I am no stranger to battle, but I would not wish to fight through to the end of my life and lose all that I have worked to achieve."

"Besides..." mused George, thoughtfully. "There are precedents, are there not, that a child born in good faith to a union that is annulled may yet remain legitimate in the eyes of the law and land? The Princess could keep her title, and her place in the succession, even if her mother went to a convent."

"If the Queen could be prevailed upon to take the right choice for her husband and her country," said our uncle, "then it could be done."

"So what say you?" I asked, almost laughing, for the idea seemed too huge, too impossible… too perfect. Had my uncle and my father lost their wits, or was it possible? It seemed too lovely to be true… Too perfect to believe that Katherine would submit and leave the post of Henry's wife vacant for me… but how I wished it could be so! "You think that I should become the *wife* of the King? That I become the *Queen*? I am not a princess!"

"You are born of noble blood; you are descended from *royal* blood on one side of your family," our uncle reminded me "And it is not unheard of for a king to marry where his heart leads him rather than merely for duty… think on the King's grandfather, Edward IV. He married Elizabeth Woodville did he not? And she was but a lowly knight's widow… But, more importantly, the King is pursuing you as he has never done with another woman, even with your sister and that Blount woman. He was never as public in his desire as he is now. Why could you not hold out for the prize? Would you not wish to become Henry's wife? To become the Queen of England? It would be an honour above all others… the best match you could ever dream to make. Your sons would be kings of England, your daughters would be princesses… You would bring greater glory to our family than any other has done."

I smiled at him. "That is all I should wish for," I said, watching Norfolk nod at me with approval. "But how can all this come about? I am unsure."

"You will have to *become* sure," our father counselled, with a respectful note I had rarely heard in his voice. With this idea flowing through the minds of the family, it seemed I was suddenly much more than a mere pawn… if this came about, one day, I could be their Queen. "This is down to you, daughter. If we choose this path, it will not be without danger. Katherine is popular in England, and has many friends in Europe, not least her nephew the Emperor. We may make powerful enemies if any perceive this as a slight on her. The only thing we have is the King's love for you. It must be you who holds the King's heart in your hands; it must be *you* whom he desires more than anything put in the way. It will be up to you to steer him, to make sure that he does not falter. If you can do this then we can succeed; this would be the greatest step for our family that we could have never imagined."

I nodded. I stood up; my family were staring at me; some with awe, like Mary, and some with fear, like my mother. My uncle looked like an expectant weasel eyeing a hen house.

I breathed in. This was a solution to all my fears, and all my wishes. If I could, indeed, *marry* Henry, then I could give myself to him freely and without restraint. He would not leave me... we could have a life together, as man and wife. I kept my face straight, and calm, but within me my heart was hammering at my bones as though it would break them apart. My uncle and father wanted me to marry with Henry for their own advancement, this I knew well enough, but if I agreed to this, to persuade Henry to view me as a possible wife, rather than a possible mistress, then I could have everything I wanted. I nodded to them.

"I will continue to hold the King's attention without allowing him into my bed," I said. "I would wish more than anything to become his wife, for my own sake and that of my family; if you will help me then I will do all I can to make this happen."

My uncle's smile was the very edge of the darkest side of the moon.

Chapter Thirty-Eight

Greenwich Palace
1527

More than ever, I was the centre of all attention both at court and in my family. My uncle of Norfolk suddenly became a most enthusiastic host; giving many great entertainments. Henry was invited to join the Boleyns and Howards at hunting lodges, and at picnics in the gardens of Norfolk's London houses. My father showered me with new clothing, to make the best of all my natural graces, and my mother became my almost constant companion, acting as a chaperone, ensuring that Henry did not overstep any boundaries in his exuberance for me. Mary and George were busy singing my praises at court and finding new ways to show me off to Henry. Despite her former position in the King's bed, my sister seemed entirely calm about the situation. She worked as hard as any to see me wedded to her former lover. A strange time, a heady time… I was excited and flattered by the attentions of my family. One and all, we had come together with a common purpose; to ensure that I was the King's sole desire; to see me made Queen of England. I did not tell Bridget or Margaret of these plans… to do so would be premature. I told them that I was beloved of the King, but still had not given myself to him. They admired me for my fortitude and offered to be my escorts in Henry's company, for my own safety. It was heartening to have such friends.

My family wanted me to become Queen for their advancement. I wanted it so that I could be Henry's wife… but I will admit that the prospect of becoming a queen was a dazzling one too. The lure of power was intoxicating, and I was not immune to it. But to me, that attraction was secondary to my feelings for Henry, and my wish that I could marry the man I loved. For how long had I wished that such a fate might be my own? To marry for love, and to please those I loved in return? If only Henry could see me as a wife, rather than just a mistress…

Even Jane, my brother's wife, who had seemed to be less than fond of me in the past, took her instruction in this matter to heart. Perhaps my brother had demanded that she play her part as a member of our family, or perhaps, with that steady green-eyed gaze of hers, she had seen for herself the advantages of having a queen as a sister-in-law, but for whatever reason, I found that she often accompanied me at court now. She laughed at my jests, and often took the place of my brother or mother at my side when I required a chaperone. I found myself actually enjoying her company.

Jane was *made* for intrigue. A life growing up at court had moulded her well for it. She was clever, and could read people well; valuable skills in a royal court. Although I had ever thought that Jane liked Katherine, for she had shown such as we both served the Queen, she seemed more than able now to put aside such reservations and work for our family. As Jane continued to demonstrate her loyalty to the Boleyns, I came to admire her more and more. A kind of wary friendship grew between us at that time. And with the general disapproval of many of Katherine's women ever glancing off my back, it was pleasing to have another friend within the Queen's household. I was pained when I thought of what Katherine's thoughts and feelings would be when and if this plan were to come to fruition. She had been a gentle, if dull, mistress to me, and I was not keen to cause her harm. But with the ability so strong in those who are in love and believe the world should move only for them, I set aside such feelings. Henry and I were *born* for each other, we were tailored for each other… It must come to pass that we become husband and wife. Why had God granted such love to me, if He did not wish to see it prevail? No, Katherine would be convinced to enter a holy order; she was devout enough to *run* a holy order… She would be happier within the confines of such a place than she was at court. She was growing old, and could do no more for England. I convinced myself that Katherine, like so many other queens who came before her in other realms, would retire with grace and dignity to a life of prayer… and Henry and I would be together.

The task was challenging, but in the early summer's sunshine that year I felt that anything was possible. Henry wanted me at his side at all times and as we wandered the galleries of the palace, as we walked the paths of his beautiful gardens and as he watched me sing or dance for him, I felt more in love with this man than anyone I had met or known in my life. Perhaps my confusion on the matter of the love between us had been lifted somewhat, now that there was a hope for its outcome… And an outcome that would not only allow me to retain and hold my own beliefs, but one that would bring greater glory to my family than I could have ever imagined possible. To be the wife of the man I loved… to be the Queen! Such a thing seemed impossible, and yet the idea of it brought me hope. If only Henry could be prevailed upon to think of me not as a mistress, but as a potential wife, then perhaps my dreams, as well as his, could come true.

My love for him flowered greatly, nurtured by the sunshine of hope and the soft rain of possibility. I felt myself turn to him as a flower turns to the rays of the sun. I loved him more each day. And I told him of my love for him.

But it was not all happiness; there was fire in Henry's temper as there was in mine. We were a heated couple, able to converse and laugh one moment and then scream and shout the next. His frustration at my constant refusal to give my body to him caused jealousy and heat between us. He was more than able to invite my temper to rage, and I was apparently both the most irritating and desirable person he had ever met; a sure recipe for explosions. We always came back to each other, though, and he would always come to me first. It had to be that way, no matter if I felt sorry for him, no matter if the fault had in truth been mine in our latest argument. I could not be the one to run to him, not now. I had to hold him in the power that I had. I had to be the one in control. Many of the court were amazed to see the King not only allow such behaviour from a subject, but seem to bow to me as well. It was unheard of... but Henry barely sought to control me. When we were together, it was not as King and subject, but as two hearts brought together, beating as one.

I was now truly in a position of power at court. Most people thought I was Henry's mistress and I was certainly receiving many honours, as though I were such. It was not just my father who heaped cloth and jewels on me, but also Henry; I was becoming a rich woman in my own right. But none truly knew that my purpose was to become united honourably with the man I loved, other than my own family. We were united in intent, and that gave me strength. It all seemed wildly impossible, but Henry's constancy gave me reason to hope. Perhaps, in time, if his affections were indeed true, then he would think on me as something more than just the mistress of his heart.

When we came together, I found ways to put off the question of a physical relationship; we talked of books and of clothes, about which I was as passionate as he. We talked of philosophy and of the architecture we had both seen in France, and of palaces and monuments which he wished to create here in his own kingdom. We talked on religion and reform. I was still cautious and careful on such matters, as Henry was a most conservative Catholic; my leanings towards reform and interest in the teachings of the Lutherans and similar thinkers were not likely to win me his favour. We had much in common, and we spoke in earnest with each other, swapping books, underlining passages that we thought would interest each other, and coming together to discuss many and varied topics. We argued about religious theory, often ending in one or both of us storming off... only to be reconciled the next day with kisses and smiles. It was not only that there was desire between us, there was friendship growing amongst the feelings of want and passion. But all the time, there hung over us the question that he asked of me over and over; when would I give myself to him and become his 'true' mistress?

Whenever the pressure grew too great, I would return to Hever. My father was on a knife edge, waiting to see what the King might do, what I would do next... Many of my actions caused my father to look as though he might faint away, especially when I argued with Henry. But Norfolk's hooded eyes watched on with approval. He did not like me, I knew that well enough, but my uncle Norfolk could see that Henry was only becoming more enamoured of me every day, and the possibilities that this introduced pleased him.

Chapter Thirty-Nine

Hever Castle
1527

That summer I took retreat at Hever from the pressures of the King and court. It was necessary at times to absolutely remove myself from Henry, for my own sake perhaps more than for his. But the summer's peace at Hever was short-lived. Soon the steward came to announce that Henry had taken up residence at nearby Penshurst. He requested that I, in the absence of my parents, who were still at court, receive him and his party the next day. What could I say? I could not refuse him. I was eager to see him, but here, I had no chaperone, nobody aside from Hever's servants, to protect me from him. I wanted to believe that now, after all that had passed between us, he would not take from me by force that which he desired. He wanted me to love him in return, and knew that forcing me into something would not achieve this. But still, I worried. I asked Bess to remain at my side at all times, no matter if Henry gave a direct order to leave. She looked at me with wild and frightened eyes at this command… How could she, a mere servant, refuse to obey the King?

"Please, Bess," I implored. "For the sake of all the years you have served me and my house, you must do this for me. The King will not punish you for remaining loyal to your mistress; I will make sure of that."

"Yes, Mistress," she said in a small voice, looking at me with some admiration. To be able to command a king! What power I must have! To own the truth, I was nervous. Although my family were sure that I could entrance Henry into offering me a place at his side in lawful marriage, I tripped with ease from desperate hope and elation, to misery and doubt. As ever, when it came to Henry of England, my emotions were in constant turmoil.

He arrived the next day with a small riding party of servants. He was escorted through Hever's courtyard and halls to the great hall, where I stood arrayed in my finest, awaiting his arrival. As he entered, the many servants I had asked to gather about us bowed deeply to him, but he saw none of them as he rushed towards me and took my hands before I could bow to him.

"Nay, my Anna!" he cried buoyantly, his face flushed and his blue eyes bright. "This is not the time for reverence to your sovereign, but the happiness of a man reunited with his true love."

I laughed and looked at him happily. "I am most pleased to see your face again, Your Majesty," I smiled. "But you find me unprepared for this honour. My family's house is only equipped to offer you but humble fare," I said, quite untruthfully, as the kitchens had been in a roar of preparation since we had heard of his impending visit the day before.

"I came not for any great feast, Anne." He kissed my hands. "I came for you. I understand your purpose in leaving court. I know that much has happened between us, and the frustrations of the love that we feel for one another grow great upon us both. But I have a solution to all our woes. Nothing can take you from me, nothing will take you from me ever again, and that is what I have come to talk to you of. Show me a chamber where we may talk undisturbed, for I have much to share with you, Anne. Much that will amaze you."

I acquiesced, and took Henry and his few servants to my father's study. Poor Bess stood at my side looking as though she wished she were anywhere but there. Although it was summer outside, the fire was burning brightly and the wine was already decanted into a jug for us. Henry stood before the fire with one great arm over the stone fireplace. He indicated that I sit on one of the chairs before him. There was such an air of expectation about him that I could not help but feel excited… Were my family's plans coming to fruition?

"Anne, when I first came to this throne I was young, I was romantic. The last charge that my father laid upon me was to take a wife, one worthy to be a queen as my own mother was, and to produce the heirs that this country needs in order to be saved from ruin. My father was a careful man in all that he did. You know that my elder brother, Arthur, was to succeed to the throne and for a long time that seemed as though it should happen. But when Arthur died, my father was left only one son, me. He knew that he had to preserve me for the good of his country and from the age of ten I was protected like I was a girl-child, kept always close to my father, cosseted, prevented from taking part in the sports and martial acts at which, now, I excel."

He smiled at me with pride and I could not help but smile back at the boyish look on his face. He took my smile as agreement and continued. "When my father died he charged me to marry the bride that my brother had left widowed on his death; Katherine, the Princess of Aragon and Castile. We had been engaged before, whilst my father lived… but my father had refused to allow the marriage to come about as he feared I was too young, much as Arthur had been, and that early marriage might exhaust the strength of my body. There were objections raised against the match, too, because Katherine had been my brother's wife, although she swore they had never lain together. My father hesitated on both counts. He was always careful with me, you see? Careful to the last to ensure that he could hand his throne to a son, an adult son, whom he knew could lead and protect the country he loved so."

Henry breathed in and sighed a little. "You must understand, Anne," he said. "When I was young and first come to the throne, I was overtaken with my new freedom and my new power. I threw off the shackles of my father's constant protection with relief. I looked on Katherine, then, with the eyes of a youthful boy who knew nothing of love really but what is writ in books of romance. I saw Katherine as a great princess fallen low. I felt as though I were a knight of old who, in promising to marry her, had rescued a maiden from a terrible life of destitution and despair. Although she had been a wife to my brother for many months before he died, Katherine swore to me that she was a maid, untouched by the hand of my brother or of any other man. A dispensation was required in order to allow us to marry due to our consanguinity. The Pope decreed that since Katherine swore she was a virgin, then the normal laws of canon and scripture that would prevent our marriage were not applicable and we could marry as intended. But still, he issued the dispensation, wording that a union between Katherine and my brother had 'perhaps' taken place, as it seemed that there was confusion on this point in the court of Spain where her royal mother and father reigned."

He breathed in again and shook his head. "When I told you that my father protected me from all things, Anne," he said softly, "it was true in more ways than one. When I first came to Katherine's bed, I was a boy. I would not have known then whether she was a virgin in truth or not, for my father kept me all but locked up in his palaces. I was… untried, as a man, when I came to her bed as her husband."

He looked at me with a little fear in his eyes, he was, after all, admitting quite something to me; it was certainly not something that he should wish repeated.
"That is more for your honour than against it," I said quietly. "None who see you now, or saw you then, would think you were anything less than a great man."

He smiled at me and touched my shoulder. "None looks to my comfort as well as you…" He turned his head and glanced wryly at me. "And none my discomfort!" I smiled at him, laughing a tiny bark of a laugh at his words. "But I still have more to tell you," he continued, pouring wine for me and then for himself from the leathern jug at the table. I relished the stiff jolt it gave my senses as I drank. Henry continued.

"Over the years we have been married, Katherine has borne me children, but some did not survive more than a few days; most were born already dead. There were so many disappointments, so much grief. I had a son once, Anne, a handsome little boy who slipped from life after barely two months. Only Mary, only a daughter, was left to survive the years of disenchantment and sorrow that our wedding bed produced. I asked myself time and time again over the years, after every new and fresh sorrow, my conscience troubling me so; why would God punish a couple such as Katherine and me? I am pious, I attend the Church and I give much to it in riches and lands as well as prayer and thought. The Pope himself named me 'Defender of the Faith'! Katherine, too, was surely above reproach on that score... Her duties to the Church are legion. So why, why after all this time should God only give me a sole daughter as my heir?"

He looked grieved. "Do you know the history of the Empress Matilda?" he asked, and I nodded. "When once before a woman was heir to the throne she plunged the country into civil and bloody war... Only when the succession was restored once more unto a man, her son, did peace return. I cannot leave my country to such ruin. I cannot! A woman cannot hold this country together. A woman has not the strength to make war, to lead men into battle, to treaty for peace... to do the things that a king must do. I *must* have a son to follow me."

I sat there, amazed, that Henry was confiding such intimate, personal thoughts to me. Although I had known that he had confided such thoughts and doubts to his friends, it was quite something else to hear them straight from his mouth. I felt as though, truly, we had crossed over some barrier together. I was his confidante. He was trusting me with his most private fears and concerns. My heart was fluttering within me. I could not help but hope that what I desired more than anything, was be about to be said.

He sighed again and drank from his goblet. "For years I have wondered in earnest why God, in all his mercy and righteousness, should punish so virtuous a country as England. Why He should choose to punish myself and Katherine? The question of the succession, of my painful lack of sons, of God's purpose in all of this, has consumed me, vexing my conscience sorely. When I come to think on the problem rationally, disregarding the respect that I bear still for Katherine as my wife, the only thing that I can muster is that God disapproves of something that we have done. God is withholding a male heir from me to show me my own fault in His eyes! God is showing me His displeasure for some sin, committed either by Katherine or myself. Until this sin is atoned for, I will have no male heir granted to me!" He reached up and ran a hand through his hair. "At first, Anne, I looked to my own sins, such as they were. I had taken life in battle, and I will admit to you that there had been times when I had strayed from the marriage bed and into the arms of others."

He looked at me as though this might be news to me, but I nodded to him, keeping my face impassive. My sister had been his mistress, and he had been petitioning me to become the same for over a year now. It was not as though I were unaware of his dalliances outside of marriage! Henry flushed slightly. "But for all my own sins, whether the killing of men in battle, or the natural straying of a man from the bed of his wife after so many years, for all these sins I had confessed and my sins had been forgiven… So if I was absolved of the sins I had committed, then the fault could not be mine for this failure of our marriage. Other men have committed worse than I, in any case, and still have sons to follow them. The fault then, had to lie elsewhere."

He paused. "I have ever been interested in theology and I took to studying the Bible with renewed attention, looking for an answer to my worries. After much searching, I *found* the answer. In the book of Leviticus, God has told us that should a man take his brother's widow to wife, then they shall be cursed… they shall bear no living heirs. For in God's eyes, such is an *unclean* union."

I suddenly became painfully aware of the servants around us. Henry, who was used to being so surrounded, shook his head at me, ignoring the others. "These are *my* men," he said. His servants kept their faces stoic and unreadable, although I wondered at what they thought in their secret hearts. Bess was staring at the floor as though it were about to say something of the utmost importance.

"The answer is, Anna," he continued. "That there was a mistake in the Pope's judgement on the matter of my marriage to Katherine. I cannot say whether I was deceived by Katherine in her vow that she was not touched by my brother when she was his wife, but I believe the sanction of the Pope in this matter was wrong. He was at fault to allow our marriage because she *was* my brother's wife in the eyes of God, making her my sister. If Katherine lied to me, and she was not a virgin when I came to her bed, then the sin is doubly made. I have suffered for the ill-judgement of the Pope and possibly for the lies of a woman I would not have thought capable of such sin. Katherine can give me no heir, for the displeasure of God is upon our marriage. Both of our souls are at risk for this sin, and we cannot be released of it until we are separated and the sin is confessed and forgiven. The answer to this problem is to annul the marriage between Katherine and me as no true marriage, and for me to take a true wife. Then I shall know the blessing of God, and the blessing of male heirs that shall save this country from destruction. "

I looked at him with wonder in my eyes. Not at what he was saying he would do with Katherine; many kings had left their wives and married another under the blessing of the Church. No, my own wonder was the dawning realisation of what this may mean to me. Even though I had thought on it, even though my family had plotted for it… It still seemed incredible to hear the King himself speak of it. This could *really* become my destiny? It was too much to be believed even as I heard it.

"Wolsey knows my mind well on this matter," said Henry, "and is in agreement with me. He thinks that I should make a match with a princess of France." There was a teasing light in his eyes. "What think you of that?"

"France is a fine country, Your Majesty," I said smoothly, not rising to his mischief, "and it breeds fine women."

"It does indeed," he smiled good-naturedly at me. "Come, Anne, can you not guess my meaning? Do you seek at every turn to plague and confound me? I had not known you a week before I saw the proud mark of a Queen on you."

Although I had been expecting it, I was unprepared for his question and sat with an open mouth looking at him. He laughed.

"You are astounded?" he chuckled, well pleased at my wide-eyed expression. "Anne, I have never loved anyone as I love you. I had never known what it *was* to love before I met you. Would God in all His wisdom send me such a woman; a woman of both allure and virtue at this time when I had realised God's truth, unless He had a plan for us? You were *sent* to me, here, and now, as a sign…. You were brought to me by God Himself, to provide an answer to the questions that have so vexed my soul and rent my conscience. You were brought to me to show me the way, the true way! And your refusal of me as a lover, your insistence on maintaining your honour… all these things were brought about *by* God, do you not see that? We are meant for each other, you and I! We are *destined* for one another."

He sat down before me, his eyes grave now, as they travelled over my face. He put his hands about mine and leaned forward. "Say, my lady, that you will become my true wife, the Queen of this country and the mother of my sons. Say that you will be mine, and I will raise you from noble seat to the throne of England. Say that you will become my wife, under the eyes of God and the law of this country. We will have a great life together, Anne, you will be gloried and raised up, honoured and respected by all the world. And we will have children... Our princes, Anne! Can you not see them now? With our spirits conjoined, they will be the greatest kings that ever walked this earth! This is what we are called to do! Say *yes*, Anne, and become the greatest Queen that this country has ever known!"

He kissed me then, his hands on my face and in my hair and his arms seeking to ensnare me with great force and passion. I struggled free and stood, "Wait, Your Majesty... Henry..." I breathed in and looked down on him with a mind that was racing with all he had said.

He stood and looked at me with a suddenly worried expression. "I have turned your head around with all this talk..." he mused. I nodded.

"I am not worthy of such a position as that which you offer to me," I murmured, my heart pounding in my chest like a drum.

He snorted at me. "Not worthy?" he laughed. "Anne, think you that I missed your virtue, your goodness, in all your refusals of my offers to become my mistress? No, *that* was the position unworthy of you; the position of Queen was what you were born for and by God's Blood!" he swore, his face flushing with passion and excitement. "It is the one that you shall have!"

"What of Katherine?" I asked, my head swimming, my heart racing and my blood rushing through my body.

He gestured impatiently. "I have already told her that I am concerned about the validity of our marriage and that my men are set to investigate it. She will accept the truth of this when it is put before her by me and other learned men. Katherine will concede readily once the situation is made clear to her. She is a virtuous woman and once put right in this, she will go quietly to seek the forgiveness of God. You and I will be married in a matter of months, as soon as the proclamation of the Pope is heard in this matter, and soon we shall have our sons… Many of them! And they will father the dynasties that shall rule this country, and others, for the greater good of the world, for all time! Come, Anna, say that you are mine. Say that you will be my wife… my Queen, and we shall live as we were intended, as the rulers of this land and as the rulers of each other's hearts. Say that you love me and that you are mine. None shall ever surpass you. You will be the Queen of this realm and you will have my never-ending love. Say that you will have me as your husband and that you will bear me the sons of England. *Say it*."

I was shaking; it was a brilliant proposal. I could have everything I ever wanted. I could have Henry and have him as husband. I could be Queen and have the country at my feet. I could live in honour and still take all I wanted of this world with the blessing of God. I looked at him with shining eyes, but warded him off when he sought to kiss me again. I took a jewelled ring from my thumb, one that I had worn since I was young, and gave it to him. The little gem flashed in the dim light from the window panes as he pushed it onto his finger. He took a ring from his finger and pushed it onto my thumb, for my slim, long fingers were all too small to fit his ring upon.

"I am betrothed," I whispered with my head reeling.

"I am the most happy man in this world!" He reached around my waist, pulling me to him in a great kiss. His body encompassed mine and I felt the stiff heat of his manhood through his clothing. I pushed him away and whispered to him. "Not until our wedding night, Henry."

Although he was clearly disappointed, thinking perhaps that the promise of marriage might be enough to undo me to succumb to him, he nodded with a prudish look on his face. "Our heirs will be legitimate, without question," he said and stroked my face. "Besides," he said, leading me from the chamber towards the great hall where a feast had been put on in his honour, "it will not be long before we are married, and you are mine in truth."

I laughed and squeezed his hands. I had never felt so excited. I was dazzled by the offer he had made to me. Even when my family had put the idea forward, I had thought of it perhaps more of a lovely dream, than something that could become reality. But here it was... the promise of the King of England... Henry's heart, granted to me, and to me alone. He loved me; he wanted me to be his Queen! It must become so, I thought. I could not have such a wonderful dream handed to me, for it not to come true.

That night was a roar of dancing and feasting. Henry and I sat next to each other and he fed me dainties from his plate with great gentleness and respect.

When he left the next morning, riding for court in a flurry of excitement to see what could be done on "our matter", as he called it, I wandered alone into the gardens.

For a moment, I stood still, and looked about me. The early morning's sun was shining on the petals of the roses and glimmering from their leaves. There was a scent still of the cool of the night on the air. Light rain was falling, stroking my heated skin. A little breeze bobbed merrily through the trees, making them sigh and whisper, like the sound of far-off waves.

There was no one around. I turned and I ran through the paths as I had done when I was a child, playing with my brother and sister, or with my mother. I ran, letting the wind flow through my unbound hair, and, feeling the light rain upon my heated skin, I ran and I ran, laughing, as my feet flew over the wet earth. I stopped at the edge of the marshland forests, set my arms back, and let out a strange and wild cry, of happiness, of elation. It echoed through the trees, bouncing from limb and branch. My cry seemed to resonate through the earth below me and the skies above, as though I had become a part of the wonders of the Almighty.

As I stood there, flushed and panting, a fierce cry came from above me; in the skies I saw a falcon sailing over me, as free as my heart felt at that moment. It let out another shriek, as though answering my call and I threw my head back and laughed. I felt as though I was being sent a sign, perhaps from God.

Henry was mine, would be mine in lawful marriage, and I would let nothing stand in the way of my future with him… or of my future on the throne, as Queen of England.

Epilogue

The Tower of London
The early hours of the 18th May, 1536

The fire burns low, and my candle flickers with the last of its life. Outside the window, the stars are retreating against the coming of the sun. Night has turned to morn, and still I sit here, lost in my memories of the past. But they have brought me comfort, and I find strength in them. All those memories, all those times… the first flush of the love between Henry and me. They bring back the strength I thought I had lost, as I saw my brother die.

The morning comes… soon Master Kingston will come to me, to tell me if I am to die this day or no. Will Henry's promises that I might retire into a religious order become the truth? I think not, and yet I am left some hope to believe still in the love of my husband. There was a time, a time when I was all there was that could bring comfort to his heart and life to his soul. Perhaps, even now, he has not forgotten that, as I have not. Perhaps there will be something that echoes still within him, of the powerful love that lived and breathed between us.

The dawn comes, bringing red and gold fingers to stroke the heavens. The women are stirring about me and soon enough I will be no longer alone with my thoughts. What will come of this day? Will they tell me of my fate now, or will I be left to languish more, in this place between reality and dreams… sorrowing for the loss of my brother and the other men falsely accused with me of treason and adultery? I must gather the strength that my memories have brought to me, and hold them as a shield before me… I must be strong. I must have courage. I must stand and face whatever Fate has in store for me. Once, I was as a lioness in the face of the censure of the court and Katherine's supporters… But that was later… that will be the next part of my story to remember, if I am left to wait longer to know what my fate will be.

There is noise outside in the corridor. I believe they will come and tell me what the King has decided... The present calls me from the past, and I must turn to face it, no matter what may come.

This is the end of *The Lady Anne. Book Two of Above all Others; The Lady Anne.* In Book Three, *Above All Others,* Anne faces the censure of the world as she and Henry seek to annul the marriage of the King to Katherine, and marches towards her goal, to become Henry's wife, and the Queen of England.

About the Author

I find people talking about themselves in the third person to be entirely unsettling, so, since this section is written by me, I will use my own voice rather than try to make you believe that another person is writing about me to make me sound terribly important.

I am an independent author, publishing my books by myself, with the help of my lovely editor. I write in all the spare time I have. I briefly tried entering into the realm of 'traditional' publishing but, to be honest, found the process so time consuming and convoluted that I quickly decided to go it alone and self-publish.

My passion for history, in particular perhaps the era of the Tudors, began early in life. As a child I lived in Croydon, near London, and my schools were lucky enough to be close to such glorious places as Hampton Court and the Tower of London to mean that field trips often took us to those castles. I think it's hard not to find the Tudors infectious when you hear their stories, especially when surrounded by the bricks and mortar they built their reigns within. There is heroism and scandal, betrayal and belief, politics and passion and a seemingly never-ending cast list of truly fascinating people. So when I sat down to start writing, I could think of no better place to start than somewhere and sometime I loved and was slightly obsessed with.

Expect *many* books from me, but do not necessarily expect them all to be of the Tudor era. I write as many of you read, I suspect; in many genres. My own bookshelves are weighted down with historical volumes and biographies, but they also contain dystopias, sci-fi, horror, humour, children's books, fairy tales, romance and adventure. I can't promise I'll manage to write in *all* the areas I've mentioned there, but I'd love to give it a go. If anything I've published isn't your thing, that's fine, I just hope you like the ones I write which *are* your thing!

The majority of my books *are* historical fiction however, so I hope that if you liked this volume you will give the others in this series (and perhaps not in this series), a look. I want to divert you as readers, to please you with my writing and to have you join me on these adventures.

A book is nothing without a reader.

As to the rest of me; I am in my thirties and live in Cornwall with a rescued dog, a rescued cat and my partner (who wasn't rescued, but may well have rescued me). I studied Literature at University after I fell in love with books as a small child. When I was little I could often be found nestled half-way up the stairs with a pile of books and my head lost in another world between the pages. There is nothing more satisfying to me than finding a new book I adore, to place next to the multitudes I own and love... and nothing more disappointing to me to find a book I am willing to never open again. I do hope that this book was not a disappointment to you; I loved writing it and I hope that showed through the pages.

This is only one of a large selection of titles coming to you on Amazon. I hope you will try the others.

If you would like to contact me, please do so.

On twitter, I am @TudorTweep and am more than happy to follow back and reply to any and all messages. I may avoid you if you decide to say anything worrying or anything abusive, but I figure that's acceptable.

Via email, I am tudortweep@gmail.com a dedicated email account for my readers to reach me on. I'll try and reply within a few days.

I publish some first drafts and short stories on Wattpad where I can be found at www.wattpad.com/user/GemmaLawrence31 . Wattpad was the first place I ever showed my stories, *to anyone*, and in many ways its readers and their response to my works were the influence which pushed me into self-publishing. If you have never been on the site I recommend you try it out. Its free, its fun and its chock-full of real emerging talent. I love Wattpad because its members and their encouragement gave me the boost I needed as a fearful waif to get some confidence in myself and make a go of a life as a real, published writer.

Thank you for taking a risk with an unknown author and reading my book. I do hope now that you've read one you'll want to read more. If you'd like to leave me a review, that would be very much appreciated also!

Gemma Lawrence
Cornwall
2016

Thank You

...to so many people for helping me make this book possible... to my editor Brooke who entered into this with me and gave me her time, her guidance and also her encouragement. To my partner Matthew, who will be the first to admit that history is not his thing, and yet is willing to listen to me extol the virtues and vices of the Tudors and every other time period, repeatedly, to him and pushed me to publish even when I feared to. To my family for their ongoing love and support; this includes not only my own blood in my mother and father, sister and brother, but also their families, their partners and all my nieces who I am sure are set to take the world by storm as they grow. To Matthew's family, for their support, and for the extended family I have found myself welcomed to within them. To my friend Petra who took a tour of Tudor palaces and places with me back in 2010 which helped me to prepare for this book; her enthusiasm for that strange but amazing holiday brought an ally to the idea I could actually write a book... And lastly, to the people who wrote all the books I read in order to write this book... all the historical biographers and masters of their craft who brought Anne, and her times, to life in my head.

Thank you to all of you; you'll never know how much you've helped me, but I know what I owe to you.

Gemma
Cornwall
2016

Printed in Great Britain
by Amazon